Musk Rain

by

Terri Branson

Paranormal Romance by
Dragonfly Publishing, Inc.

MUSK RAIN

Paranormal Romance

Paperback Edition
EAN 978-1-949187-02-1
ISBN 1-949187-02-0

Hardback Edition
EAN 978-1-949187-03-8
ISBN 1-949187-03-9

Published in the United States of America by
Dragonfly Publishing, Inc.
Website: www.dragonflypubs.com

* * * * *

Dedication

For Barbara, who said I would.

* * * * *

CHAPTER 1
Musk Rain

TAKE care of the land, and the land will take care of you.

Grandma's voice echoed in the back of Phoebe Henderson's mind, just as thunder rattled across the prairie and collided with northwest Oklahoma City. She had ventured into this stormy afternoon, seeking to solve the riddle that had haunted her for nearly seven years.

Rain battled thin windshield wipers, and stiff wind herded the red pickup across a half-empty parking lot. Phoebe eased into a slot in front of a cozy corner bookstore. After shifting into Park, she turned the key and yanked it from the ignition. The engine growled once in protest. Then fell silent, leaving the windshield wipers stuck in mid-assault.

Deciding the downpour would last longer than her patience, she tucked the keys in her front jeans pocket and jumped out of the pickup. Ankle-deep water soaked her old sneakers, and warm rain stung her face. In breathless disarray, Phoebe dashed into the Twylight Bookstore.

"On the rug, Phoebe!" a stern voice warned.

"I know. I know." Phoebe shook off what rain had not soaked into her flannel shirt, faded jeans, and sneakers. She caught her reflection in the plate glass front window. Long auburn hair was pulled into a high ponytail. Gray-green eyes sparkled in the odd light of tired fluorescent panels. At thirty, she was in the prime of life. Just the right mix of Cherokee with a sprinkling of Scottish and Delaware gave her an exotic none-of-the-above quality that turned heads. However, it was advice Phoebe needed, not attention.

Twyla Jones, owner of the bookstore and self-proclaimed personal councilor, eased from behind the counter. A bright barrette secured a braided coil of silver hair to the back of her head. Colorful beaded earrings dangled from pierced ears. Warm gold eyes held a strange twinkle. Old enough to be Phoebe's mother, she treated Phoebe like a niece, perhaps even a daughter.

"This is a lot of rain for a little dragonfly," Twyla said.

A smile tugged at Phoebe's cheeks. Dragonfly was the Cherokee name her grandmother gave her when she was only seven. Few people knew it.

Even fewer used it. It was nice to hear again after all these years.

She remembered the reason for this rainy-day visit and allowed the smile to fade. "I just had to get out of the house for a while."

"Jack acting up again? I know a man who knows a man in Muskogee who'll take care of things for fifty dollars. No questions asked. Hell, I'll do it for twenty."

Phoebe knew Twyla was kidding, but the point of the joke was abundantly clear. "It's not that bad."

"Yet." Twyla's voice sliced through the air like an assassin's blade. Snorting in disapproval, she tucked a bundle of used books under one arm and slipped around the end of the central aisle. Her voice echoed through the store. "What did he do this time?"

"He's just being Jack." Phoebe followed Twyla down the aisle. Her gaze drifted from shelf to shelf, noting the changes in height and color from one dusty book to the next.

Twyla did not look up from her sorting and shelving work. "A widow and brother-in-law living alone together in a big house out in the middle of nowhere. That must be uncomfortable."

"To say the least." Phoebe's tone of voice had turned as sour as her frame of mind.

"Are you afraid of Jack?"

"Not the way you mean." Phoebe understood the reason for the question. Jack had learned karate during his stint in the army and had taught it for years in the metropolitan area. He was not only a bully, but a well-trained one.

"He's not going to scare me out of my own house," Phoebe added after a noticeable pause. That response gave more information than she intended. She tore away from Twyla's probing gaze and ran a long finger down a worn book whose spine no longer bore author and title.

Using a rolled-up magazine, Twyla swatted the bookcase. The vibration traveled down the wooden shelf. "How bad is it?"

Phoebe's eyes again met Twyla's. "Nothing I can't handle."

"Have you tried negotiating with him?"

"A hundred times," Phoebe snapped. Then took a deep breath to get her emotions under control. "I offered to split the 160-acres with him. I'd take the north eighty and the house. He'd get the south eighty."

"Sounds reasonable."

"That's what I thought, but he won't budge." Phoebe stared at the line of books in front of her, but saw only the house and the land shimmering in the back of her mind. "I don't want to deal with Jack, but I don't have a choice. I made a promise. A promise I can't break."

"One of those, huh?" Twyla said in a knowing tone. "Okay, spill it."

Phoebe tapped a finger on a dusty bookshelf while her mind whirred. Widowed barely six months. Caught up in a stupid property fight with her brother-in-law. No close living relatives. No distant relatives she cared to acknowledge. An uncertain future. And nagging visions of the past.

Come November it would be seven years since her grandmother's death. She had never told anyone about her last conversation with the elder medicine woman. It was time to break that silence, time to solicit a little help.

Phoebe choose her words carefully. "The night Grandma died, she said: *Take care of the land, and the land will take care of you.* It's sort of a riddle. She made me promise not to leave the property until I understood what it meant."

"And you think I can decipher it for you?" Twyla shrugged. "Sorry. I don't know what it means, either."

Phoebe dropped her forehead against the front of a dusty book. "I've asked Grandma for the answer a hundred times over the last few months. I can see her, but I can't hear her."

"You've seen your grandmother's ghost?"

Phoebe straightened and gave a casual nod, as if to infer that ghosts were common occurrences. "She showed up the night Jack moved in and has been there ever since. Grandma really disliked Jack. He used to tell her he didn't believe in her *Indian hocus-pocus.* He talks a big game, but I think he was afraid of her. And still is. Jack has seen her, too."

"Your grandmother was too evolved for petty haunting." Twyla's face remained as intense as the tone of her voice. "If she's making her presence known, there's a good reason."

"Like what? The riddle? Jack? Losing Danny? I don't have a clue."

"Maybe she's just worried about you. And so am I. I don't like you living out there alone with Jack. I don't trust him any farther than I can throw him. And neither should you." The echo of that last comment faded, just as Twyla disappeared around the end of the aisle.

Phoebe found comfort in the squeak of Twyla's sneakers on polished wood. They let her know without a glance where her friend was in the quaint corner bookstore. Grandma had loved and respected Twyla. So did Phoebe. Twyla was solid and steady and ready with an acid wit that would make the devil proud.

The rhythm of the rain filled Phoebe's ears and calmed her nerves. She picked up a wrinkled paperback that had been stuffed in with the hard-bounds. Disappointment churned in her stomach. Eventually she would solve Grandma's riddle, but now she needed help dealing with Jack. She did not want Twyla to know the truth. Did not want to admit she was afraid of Jack.

A sensual aroma warmed Phoebe's nostrils.

She looked over her shoulder and found a man watching her from the other end of the aisle.

Dressed in black, from denim shirt to jeans to dusty sneakers, he made a striking appearance. Long limbs complimented a solid six-foot frame. Shoulder-length coal-black hair was woven into a sturdy single braid. A tan complexion and handsome features denoted Native American ancestry mixed with something else. Thick lashes framed intense gold eyes. His aroma was primal and exotic, as if nature had poured musk into the rain clouds and sprinkled in a few pheromones just for good measure.

Offering a smooth smile, he broke eye contact and ambled forward, like a panther stalking prey through the rain forest, his movements powerful yet agile. In fluid motion, he brushed her with a shoulder. Then a hip. And did not apologize for either.

Usually Phoebe objected to men intruding into her personal space, but this implied panther's kiss was nothing short of orgasmic. She took a deep breath to shake off a silly schoolgirl flush, and then turned. To her surprise, he was gone. Only the scent of him remained to coat the store. That black-haired panther was not like anything she had ever seen on the edge of the Oklahoma prairie.

After stuffing the old paperback into the nearest slot, Phoebe walked to the front of the store. The tiny brass bell hanging over the door had not rung. He should still be in the store somewhere. Forgoing any pretense of nonchalance, she stalked the length of the store and peered down straight aisles. In the far corner she found only Twyla.

"Where is he?" Phoebe demanded with an odd mixture of confusion and annoyance.

Setting down an armful of books, Twyla headed to the front and slipped behind the counter. "Where's who?"

"You didn't see him?" Phoebe followed, sliding up to the old counter and dropping her arms on its scuffed surface.

"What did you see? Another ghost?"

Phoebe shook her head in absolute certainty. That was no ghost. "A man, dressed all in black."

A small perfume bottle sitting on the countertop caught Twyla's eye. "Did you put that there?"

"No." Phoebe picked up the amber bottle and noticed it was from the small display box in the window. The label read: *Musk Rain*. "That's what I was just thinking, musk and rain. Are you sure you didn't leave it there?"

"Not me."

Curious, Phoebe unscrewed the bottle's cap and took a strategic sniff. It smelled like the panther, whoever or whatever he was. She dabbed a drop on the inside of both wrists. Then rubbed a little behind each ear.

"I'll take three bottles," Phoebe announced.

* * *

A rain-soaked figure waited in a darkened corner of the covered sidewalk a few paces from the Twylight Bookstore.

Lightning flickered. A second later, thunder reverberated. A strong wind bent vicious rain to an acute angle. Like low-velocity shotgun pellets, small hail jingled on the sidewalk's metal awning and pinged against the glossy red paint of the old pickup.

From the shadows, a tall, black-clad figure watched Phoebe hurry into her truck. The engine roared to life and the headlights flashed, forcing the man to sink deeper into the shadows. He did not want her to know he was watching, at least not yet.

With the metallic sound of old gears shifting in protest, the pickup backed up and then plowed forward through the inches-deep lake that moments ago had been a parking lot. Soon the truck pulled onto the deserted street and headed out of the city.

Shivering in a sudden blast of chilly air, the man made his way down the waterlogged sidewalk and stopped, keys in hand, at the second storefront from the end. At first, the lock refused to cooperate, but a jiggle here and jerk there freed the deadbolt. It popped back, offering a muffled metallic thud.

With the agility of a wary cat, the man slipped inside and re-locked the door. He scanned the dark and empty building. The ceiling was high, which was good for his purposes, and the small studio apartment above was more than adequate shelter for the time being. Barring any delays, the equipment and the rest of his things should arrive in the rental truck tomorrow morning. With a little hard work, the place should be ready to open by Monday.

The wisdom of this plan demanded some re-evaluation. He had wanted to come to Oklahoma City, but not under these circumstances.

What have I gotten myself into?

CHAPTER 2

Treading Water

"IT'S raining cats and dogs," Phoebe thought out loud.

Lightning laced through layered storm clouds. Thunder followed like a cosmic temper tantrum, and fat raindrops pounded the windshield. Rain mixed with pea-sized hail would not hurt anything, but large hail could ruin a vehicle in minutes. It was not an expensive pickup, but it had been Danny's favorite weekend wheels. She would hate to bring it home damaged.

Relentless rain made the drive home slow. Northwest of Oklahoma City, slick four-lane streets faded to two-way country roads and stop signs replaced colorful traffic lights. Water collected at the bottoms of rolling hills, but Phoebe eased the pickup through each dip without any problem. The windshield wipers slapped furiously at sheets of rain. Condensation formed on the inside of the glass and ran along the dashboard. The more humid the air got inside the cab the stronger that perfume smelled. Sensual and intoxicating, the fragrance stroked her skin and pulled at deep desires.

At the last mile section before the county line, she turned left onto a blacktop driveway. Phoebe held her foot on the brake and hesitated in front of a security gate. Headlights reflected off the brass "H" in the center of wrought iron. What she wanted to do was turn the truck around and return to the bookstore in hopes the *panther* would wander back for another sniff and shoulder rub.

Instead, she scolded herself, her breath fogging the windshield. "What's the matter with you, Dragonfly? Haven't you had enough trouble with men?"

Headlights pulled up behind the truck. Then blinked twice from high beams to low. The gate rolled out of the way, which meant only one thing: Jack was home.

With nowhere to go but forward, Phoebe stepped on the gas and headed up the long, twisting driveway. By the time she reached the four-car garage, the right double door was already open, thanks to Jack and his ever-handy remote control. *What is it with men and gadgets, anyway?* Phoebe eased the red pickup into the only clean garage in the county and killed the engine.

The burgundy sedan screeched up on the left side of the truck. With the car engine left purring, a tall and lanky brown-haired man in tight jeans and a denim blazer piled out. He stomped to the pickup and rapped his knuckles on the driver's window.

After securing the tiny perfume bottles in her purse, Phoebe opened the pickup door.

Just as her feet hit the concrete, Jack closed in on her. His voice found a particularly nasty edge this afternoon. "What are you doing with that truck out in this storm?"

A sharp reply rolled off Phoebe's tongue before she stopped to think of the consequences. "My car's too low for the rain and you know it."

Surprise widened Jack's stark gray eyes. He took a step back and let her get out of the pickup. "Who put the burr under your saddle?"

That worn-out Oklahoma cliché did not deserve the breath of a reply. Jack liked big houses and shiny cars and all the remote-control gadgets money could buy. It was a shame such a handsome man had such a mean heart.

Offering a contemptuous sneer, Phoebe tried to back out of Jack's long reach. It did not work.

Long fingers wrapped around her arms and shoved her hard against the wet side of the pickup. "What's gotten into you?" Jack demanded through clenched teeth. "You know that old truck stalls out in wet weather. Haven't we had enough cars in the creek for one year?"

That remark hit too close for comfort. Phoebe did not know which made her shiver more: Jack's manhandling, the cooling air, or the reminder that Danny died under similar conditions. "It's just a little rain, Jack. I had the truck fixed last month, remember?"

Some semblance of sanity returned to those icy gray eyes, but his hands remained clamped around her arms. "Oh, yeah. I forgot. What were you doing out in this weather, anyway?"

"I thought it was only supposed to rain. The storm caught me by surprise. I just went shopping. That's all."

Jack loosened his fingers and began to massage her tense arms. "Find anything fun?"

Yeah, a gorgeous six-foot panther I'd like to trip and beat to the ground. Phoebe fought back a smile. "Nothing I could afford."

"You're just cheap, girl."

"Frugal," she amended and tried to squirm out of his grip. A thread of panic tugged at the knot in her stomach and reminded her of last night's fight. It had not been much of a fight, really. A little shouting. A little screaming. Then one loud crack, as Jack slapped her. He had retreated to the den. She had gone to bed, locking her bedroom door and reminding herself she was doing this to honor her promise to Grandma.

"Whatever," Jack retorted. Like greedy tendrils, his fingers roved up her arms, brushed her collarbone, caressed her shoulders, and tugged at stray strands of auburn hair. "Will you miss me while I'm gone?"

Like Europe misses the plague! Phoebe's voice found new strength. "Where're you going?"

"Sam and I have to go to Tulsa tonight. We'll be back sometime Sunday."

Yes! Two whole days of peace and quiet! Despite the joyful ruckus in her mind, Phoebe kept a cool exterior. "When are you leaving?"

"Right now. I've already packed the car. Sam's waiting for me at the office. And, by the way, next time you take off, leave a note." With an evil chuckle, he stepped back and slid his hands down the front of her shirt. "Take care of my property while I'm gone."

"I'm not your property," she seethed through gritted teeth.

Jack's words rolled out in crisp threat. "Sure you are. I inherited you with the house. If you don't like it, be out of here by the time I get back. It's that simple."

Looking quite pleased with himself, Jack climbed into the burgundy sedan and threw it in reverse. He backed out into steady, steamy rain and disappeared down the long driveway.

After the garage door closed, Phoebe wiped away Jack's unwanted touch and shivered in disgust. She remembered what came to mind a few minutes ago: *It's raining cats and dogs.* If the mystery man was the cat, then Jack was definitely the dog.

* * *

AH, peace and quiet. The first thing Phoebe did inside the house was reload the kitchen CD player with good old rock-and-roll. No crying country music tonight.

The driving drums of blues-rock tested the crystal in the china cabinet, while she heated a quick dinner in the microwave. Carrying a hot bowl of cornbread crumbled over a typical western hash of hamburger, potatoes, and onions, she walked to the corner of the breakfast nook and peeked through bright window blinds. The storm had moved east. She envisioned nasty clouds following Jack and Sam all the way to Tulsa, like schoolyard bullies chasing a couple of nerds. The analogy brought a smile.

Phoebe tried to enjoy the food, the rock and roll, and her privacy, but her mind kept spiraling back to Jack. She needed to find some way to appease him. A way that would not cause her to break her promise to Grandma.

What does Jack really want?

In the eleven years she had known her brother-in-law, he had never shown any sign of interest in the family farm. Yet, he now claimed the land was important to him because it had been his grandfather's and vowed not to part with even one acre.

Phoebe's life took a harsh turn six months before when her husband of ten years, Danny Henderson, lost control of his car on an icy February road, going over a bridge and crashing upside down in the shallow Cimarron River. He had died on impact. At that same instant back home, Phoebe dropped her coffee mug and shivered in psychic realization. Danny's brother, Jack, called that next morning to make it official. Three days later, they had buried Danny in a quiet cemetery on the edge of the prairie.

As if losing a husband had not been traumatic enough, the next week Jack moved in with Phoebe and staked jealous claim to both the house and the 160-acre tract on which it was built. At the reading of the will, Phoebe learned Danny and Jack had inherited a fifty-fifty share of the land from their grandfather. Not half of the land, but half-interest in the whole acreage. Because Danny built the house without the burden of a loan, there had been no paperwork to indicate Jack's claim on the property. Danny never told Phoebe there was a problem with the deed. According to current Oklahoma law, all permanent structures had to be sold with the land. They could not be owned separately. Therefore, Jack co-owned not only the land but Phoebe's home, as well.

For the last six months, Phoebe and Jack had stumbled over each other in that big house. Jack said he wanted the property because it belonged to his grandfather. For Phoebe, it had been her home of ten years. Danny built the house for her. She had watched the foundation laid and the walls erected. She had picked out the bricks and paint, carpet and wallpaper, furniture and drapes. Her grandmother had died in the house. Her husband had loved the house.

To further complicate an already difficult situation, Jack also inherited Danny's share of the family business, leaving Phoebe without an income. The life insurance settlement on Danny was a sizable sum, but that and what money remained in the bank were all Phoebe had. It would pay the bills for a while, but not forever. She needed a new plan for her life. Maybe finishing college. Perhaps investing in a business. Something to provide for her future.

For the moment, she lived in a house without a mortgage. All she had to do was keep up monthly bills and yearly taxes. Selling the house to Jack would make her life much more difficult. It would put her on the street looking for a place to stay. It would force her to take whatever job she could find. It was neither fair nor right. She deserved the chance to build a good life. She would not accede to Jack's demands.

Phoebe's mind drifted back eleven years. After the death of her parents, she dropped out of college to care for her aging grandmother. Then Danny had come along. Handsome and slick, he made her an offer just too good to turn down. "Marry me, and I'll see to all of your grandmother's needs," he had said. She did, and he did. She respected Danny and had been a faithful wife. As far as marriages went, theirs probably had not been so bad.

Almost seven years ago Grandma died peacefully in her own bed. Danny took care of the arrangements and did not even fuss about a proper, albeit hushed, Cherokee funeral for the old medicine woman. Jack kicked up quite a lot of verbal dust over the matter, but Danny came to Phoebe's defense. Actually, it was the first and last time she saw Danny stand up to his older brother.

Phoebe's mind returned to the present. If not for Grandma's riddle, she would pack her bags and disappear this night. Apart from everything else, honor kept Phoebe from running.

* * *

WITH dinner out of the way and the kitchen back to squeaky clean, Phoebe made a methodical security check of the huge house and then headed up the back stairs. As she reached the landing, the image of the man she had seen in the bookstore coalesced in her mind.

What a delicious dessert. What a nice diversion from an unpleasant here and now.

Her feet navigated the upstairs hallway, as if on auto-pilot, and took her to the master bedroom she used to share with Danny. The connecting bathroom was luxurious, to say the least. She ran water in the tiled bathtub and added a generous splash of the new perfume oil. Like foam at the bottom of a waterfall, it bubbled up and rode the rising steam.

Phoebe smelled the shoulder of her shirt where the panther had brushed against her. Musk and rain. It was hard to believe something so evocative could actually be bottled. Drunk on nothing at the moment but good old-fashioned desire, she shed her clothing and stepped into a sinfully scented bath.

Closing her eyes, she sank to the bottom of the tub. When she emerged, her long hair molded across firm breasts. Feeling like some mythical mermaid, she laid her head on cool tile and let her mind drift. It had been a long time since anyone stirred her as much as the scent and touch of that unnamed panther. His image solidified in the back of her mind, coaxing her to follow him across the boundaries of imagination, beyond the precepts of time....

* * *

IN one of those in-between worlds of astral essence and personal design, Phoebe found herself walking the shore of a lily-covered pond. Delicate trees clung to grassy banks. Tiny, soft green leaves shimmered in the breeze like thousands of mute bells struggling to announce her arrival.

She brushed a hand across her chest and looked down. A red silk, oriental-style dress molded to her curvy figure. Black frog closures ran from her neck to her knees. She wore nothing but the dress, no underwear, no shoes. Silk caressed every part of her body.

Pausing near the water's edge, she dropped to her knees and reached out to pick a soft-pink lily. Just as her fingers touched the delicate flower, a black panther surfaced in front of her, his movements sending undulating waves across the pond. He sprang out of the water and knocked her backward to the grass. She thrust out her hands. Instead of burying in fur, however, her fingers found wet silk outlining a taut waist. The panther had transformed into a man. The air was thick with the smell of him.

His liquid gold eyes blinked in slow motion and water dripped from his long black hair. A wide palm stroked the dress, counting her ribs, cupping a firm breast. Nimble fingers twisted the frog closures, unfastening them one by one until the dress fell open. A muscled form covered her. Strong legs forced open her knees and settled nicely between her thighs. Hot breath washed her cheek. A growl rumbled from the back of his throat. His mouth dropped over hers, and the tip of his tongue pushed between her teeth.

The dress still caressed her arms and provided a pallet on which to lie, but in an instant the man's wet, naked body pressed to hers. His skin was hot and surprisingly soft. The feel of his arousal jutting against her crotch created a mild electric shock that warmed her thighs and traveled up her spine. It felt so real, so complete as he joined his body to hers, slipping inside, adding warmth and completion. Her face molded to his neck. Strands of wet hair fell into her open mouth and left a spicy taste on her tongue. Her long fingers explored the curve of his back and made a slow run across firm buttocks. As if by royal command, he began to stroke, rising and falling in bits of broken rhythm that kept her guessing.

In the absence of earthly air, energy became the environment, weaving in and around like currents in the water. Then he found it, that one position that inflamed both of them. Repetition and sheer tenacity ground together to bring a heady sexual climax. She felt his body go still and rigid, before relaxing on top of her. Then a golden flash of light seemed to nullify gravity. The sensation of sailing above the Earth brought a forgotten state of freedom. She exhaled and let her body go limp....

* * *

GRABBING the sides of the tub, Phoebe rose from beneath scented foam and sputtered for air.

Maybe mermaids could breathe underwater, but she could not. She told herself there was one rule to dreaming in the bathtub: *keep your head above the water.*

* * * * *

CHAPTER 3
Jacks Are Wild

JACK chewed on an improbable curse and slowed the car.

Windshield wipers slapped furiously at sheets of rain, and headlights parted only enough of the darkness to keep pace with the long line of brightly lit diesel trucks in front of him. He hated the turnpike, but it was the fastest route between Oklahoma City and Tulsa.

"Don't fight it, Jack. We have plenty of time." Sam yawned and raked his fingers through short-cut sandy hair. Dressed in new blue jeans, snakeskin cowboy boots, and a denim shirt, he looked more like a rancher than Jack's office manager and long-time friend.

In Oklahoma, appearances could be deceiving. An old man in greasy overalls might be a millionaire, while a young man in a three-piece-suit was probably a used car salesman from down the street. Without a recognized dress code, it was impossible to know who had the power or the money. It made doing business a little dangerous, just the way Jack liked it.

"All you sure about this? I didn't think Chief Hayes was interested in leasing those minerals." Jack's voice could barely be heard over the hum of the windshield wipers and the whine of the car's tires on wet pavement.

Sam flashed an evil grin. Stark blue eyes twinkled with implied mischief. "Trust me, Jack. I have it all set up. The way to get that lease is through his daughter, Erin. She fell head over heels for you at the Fourth-of-July party."

"I don't remember her," Jack admitted with a frown.

"Well, she remembers you. Just smile and show her a good time. She'll get you the inside track on that lease. Piece of cake."

"As long as it's a nice piece of ass, who cares about the lease." Jack laughed and pulled the car into the fast lane.

* * *

UPSCALE hotel bars always had two things in common: they were loud and stuffy.

Jack leaned on the polished bar, snapped his fingers at the smug bartender, and screamed over the incessant blare of so-called music. "Four margaritas on the rocks. Salt and lime. And don't short me on tequila."

"Yes, sir," the bartender piped back with a crisp nod.

Jack gave an arrogant snort before heading across the crowded, darkened bar. He eased his long, lean frame into a corner booth near the back, joining Sam and two gorgeous Native American girls he hoped were at least 21. The last thing Jack needed was a scandal with a teenager, but Sam swore these tender young things were old enough to be legal.

"Drinks are coming," Jack half-yelled across the table. Loud music was bad enough, but lousy loud music really grated on his nerves. Without warning, warm long fingers glided across the top of his leg and brushed close to his crotch. He arched an eyebrow toward the lovely creature who dared to touch him under the table. "Be careful, Erin. You're about to get my undivided attention."

Erin Hayes grinned, flashing perfect white teeth. Her enormous brown eyes caught the sparkle of the dance floor lights. Long, soft, black hair played in the valley of half-exposed breasts. She crossed her legs, slipping a silken ankle behind his leg. Leaning toward him, she offered an even better view of that spilling cleavage. "That was the plan."

Jack casually dipped a finger just inside the front of her red knit dress. "Well, it's working, little girl."

A sultry expression eased onto Erin's sculpted face. "I've thought about you since the Fourth of July party."

"And just what were you thinking?"

"How to get those tight jeans off those long legs."

Have mercy! Erin was the hottest little number Jack had run across in quite some time. If he was not careful, she might wind up in his lap right here in this smoky bar. He had better get the girl upstairs before things got out of hand.

The drinks arrived with more ceremony than was necessary. Throwing a wad of cash at the bartender, Jack gestured for him to go away. Sam appeared to be getting along well enough with the other girl, keeping her occupied as agreed. That left Jack free to work on that saucy piece in the red dress.

Jack tucked Erin neatly under one long arm and whispered in her ear. "Why don't we go upstairs and talk a little business?"

"Business?" she echoed, sipping on her margarita.

"I thought we could discuss that mineral lease in private. You did bring it?"

"I brought it." Erin rolled her tongue around the edge of the wide-mouthed margarita glass, lapping up the salt before taking another sip of the stout tequila concoction. "But I'm going to make you work for it."

Jack allowed a grin. "Promises, promises."

* * *

THE next morning found Jack searching the hotel room for his jeans and socks.

A rough moan escaped from clenched teeth. He sat on the end of the rumpled bed and tried to assimilate the time of day. Glancing over his shoulder, he smiled at tangled sheets. The girl was gone, but he could still taste her on his tongue.

A knock on the door pulled him back to the present. "It's open!" he yelled, stepping into his jeans.

The door flew inward to reveal Sam's smiling face. "Good morning, sunshine. And how did we sleep last night?"

Offering a snarl, Jack meticulously donned the rest of his clothing. Maybe his 42-year-old face showed some wear and tear this morning, but he wanted his attire to be as spotless as possible.

Sam pointed at a document folder on the corner of the dresser. "Is that it?"

"See for yourself," Jack replied nonchalantly.

The plain manila folder gave up its contents with one expert shake. Sam sifted through a small stack of papers. "She must really like you."

"Are we still on for lunch at the club?"

"Yeah, eleven-thirty. And golf afterwards. How's your swing today?"

"Limber and oiled up." Jack offered a broad grin. The situation reminded him of an old joke: *What do girls and oil wells have in common? They both need a good pumpjack.*

* * *

A late-summer thunderstorm urged Jack and his golf partner, Fred Kaufman, off the course and into the country club.

Too much lunch today and too little time on the courses in the last few weeks had put a rough edge on Jack's usually clean game. Instead of par golf, the best he could manage was bogie after bogie. It did not matter. He had come to broker a contract, not qualify for a tournament.

With a whiskey on the rocks in one hand and the tee he broke on the last drive in the other, Jack ambled to a corner of the covered patio and watched lightning lace through curdled clouds. Thunder followed almost immediately. Before the echo died, rain pattered on the wood-shingled roof.

"Unpredictable, isn't it?" Kaufman's tone was serious. He shook his drink, rattling the ice cubes.

Jack arched his eyebrows and tried not to smirk.

Of course, the weather is unpredictable. This is Oklahoma, for crying out loud.

The weekend was becoming quite profitable. Things had worked out to perfection with the Hayes girl. He got laid and secured his mineral lease at almost the same time. Now if Fred Kaufman and Mother Nature would just cooperate, he should have this sneaky little bit of business wrapped up before dinner.

He glanced at his partner and wondered how such a polished man could play such sloppy golf. As long as he looked good, maybe it did not matter if he played like shit. However, it probably would be a mistake to underestimate a man of Kaufman's reputation. For all Jack knew, a poor showing on the course could be strategic bait for the coming negotiations. Jack's grandfather used to call that *playing 'possum*. The California tan and ponytail made Kaufman look more like a movie star than a corporate executive, but Jack never let appearances fool him. Kaufman was obviously shrewd and understandably cautious.

As far as anyone else knew, Northwest Properties was helping Kaufman Enterprises secure development property in the Tulsa area. The rest of what Jack and Fred plotted was not illegal, just politically unpopular. Even Sam did not know the real reason behind this innocent-looking golf match.

When Jack was sure no one else was within hearing range, he sidled up to Fred. His focus remained on the vibrant green of the rain-peppered golf course. "I acquired a nice piece of rights just last night."

Fred's thick eyebrows raised but his voice maintained a steady, uninteresting monotone. "Burning the midnight oil, Jack?"

"Something like that." Jack chuckled and rolled the broken tee in his right hand. "It's in southwest Oklahoma. Near Anadarko."

"Just the minerals or the land rights, too?"

"Just the minerals at this point. I'll check it out and get back with you in a couple of weeks."

Nodding, Fred shook the whiskey glass again, making the ice cubes clink. So far, he had only held it in his hand. "That's great, Jack. Our other contract doesn't run out for six months. Take your time and find us a good location. A nice quiet site."

"Agreed." Jack grinned and glanced at his unlikely golf partner. "Is that just a prop or are you going to drink the damned thing?"

"Is our business concluded?"

"Yes. You can drink now." Jack upended his glass and dumped fiery whiskey in his mouth. One loud swallow preceded a contented moan.

"Cowboys," Fred muttered and took a careful sip of the stout drink.

Jack raised his empty glass in mock salute. "Welcome to the wild west, Fred."

* * * * *

CHAPTER 4

Forces of Nature

FRIDAY afternoon, Phoebe walked a quiet meadow on the southwest corner of the 160-acre property.

A red flannel shirt made her visible to any uninvited hunters, and faded blue jeans provided a buffer against stickers and insects. Worn moccasins shuffled through knee-deep prairie grass. Grasshoppers fussed at her feet, and bees zoomed past in zigzag chaos.

At the base of the meadow she climbed a weathered wooden dock and looked across a tear-shaped pond. Sunshine warmed her face, and the smell of sweet prairie grass filled her nostrils. Warm wind came in little puffs that turned her auburn ponytail into flaming fire bouncing above the meadow. Like feline whiskers, cattails poked up on either side of the old dock. Small concentric circles appeared and disappeared across muddy water as crappie and bass fed. Dragonflies drifted by in cordial silence. Above, a red-tail hawk rode the high thermals of a powder-blue sky and gave one long cry in salute.

Phoebe walked to the edge of the dock and sat with her feet folded in front of her. Away from the noise and hustle of the city, she basked in a moment of peace and belonging.

Reaching into her shirt pocket, she retrieved a small leather bundle tied with a strip of red cloth. Inside the soft leather wrap was her grandmother's tobacco pipe. It was just a small one, not like the large pipes used for tribal ceremonies. She had not used it since Grandma had given it to her the night before she died. For all those years Phoebe had been afraid to use the pipe, afraid Danny or Jack would see it or smell the tobacco on her breath. Yet, she had felt guilty for not continuing her grandmother's spiritual work. That pipe was more than a family heirloom. It was a tradition to be carried forward.

Holding the leather bundle in one hand, Phoebe looked down at the rippling water. The smell of gingersnaps and coffee wrapped around her like a warm blanket. For a fraction of a second, she caught the reflection of an old woman with long silver braids and gray eyes. But the image vanished before it arrived, serving as only a tickle in the back of her mind.

In the distance, the redtail hawk called once more and then floated out of sight. Her fingers closed around the leather bundle, and emptiness tied a knot in her stomach.

For the moment, Phoebe's physical needs were being met. She had a little bit of money, a place to live, adequate food and clothing. There was, however, no love or joy, no safety or belonging, all those intangible things that cannot be measured in a cup or cured by a pill. She had come to an important crossroad. Perhaps she had been standing in the middle of that intersection for years and did not know it. Perhaps it took the scent and smile of an enigmatic stranger to point it out to her.

She scanned the horizon. The future lay somewhere beyond a fuzzy haze of liquid prairie grass. If only brother hawk could fly over the hill and return with a glimpse of tomorrow. If only he could bring back a hint as to what she was supposed to do next.

That morning Phoebe had awakened with one thought: *get Grandma's pipe*. Now in the warm light of a late-summer afternoon she sat on the dock of a muddy pond and looked at the leather bundle. All she had to do was untie the red binding, put the cedar stem in the green pipe bowl, add a generous pinch of tobacco, light it and offer prayers. She remembered the rest of the ceremony, but hesitated. It had been so long. Was she prepared to reenter her grandmother's realm?

Self-doubt made her feel unworthy of such a powerful pipe. She tucked the small leather bundle into her shirt pocket and got to her feet. Stepping off the dock, she waded through acres of tall, dry grass.

At the top of a small hill, she paused, staring at an odd clump of western red cedars. Like some ill-tempered companion, poison ivy carpeted the ground beneath low prickly branches. Within that irregular ring of trees lay the remains of the original Henderson homestead cabin. It was a mute reminder that Jack did have a reasonable claim to this land. Phoebe's senses, however, told her the land did not want Jack.

She put a hand over her shirt pocket and felt the outline of the pipe. Like faint stars seen only out of the corner of an eye, silver voices hovered at the edge of hearing. She held her breath and tried to pull in elusive vibrations. Riding across time on spider-web strands of reality, the voices shied away without being fully heard.

Too many years had passed since Phoebe first listened to those distant sounds. Her skills were rusty. She was not sure she remembered how to pull in the voices. At the moment, she was afraid to try.

* * *

THIRTY minutes later, back in the house, Phoebe stashed the pipe in the back of the walk-in closet of the master bedroom. Depressed, she lay on the bed and grabbed the telephone. Long fingers flew across numbered buttons.

After two tinny rings, a familiar voice answered. "Hello?"

"Rachel?"

"Hey, stranger. What's up?"

Phoebe rolled onto her side and stared out the glass balcony doors. "What are you doing tomorrow?"

"Nothing much. The kids are going to their dad's for the day. So it's just me. What do you propose?"

"Lunch, for starters." Phoebe could not help but smile at the cheerful force in her best friend's voice. "You want to meet me at the cafe about eleven?"

"You bet. Eleven o'clock," Rachel said. "Where's that hound dog, Jack?"

"Tulsa. He's due back sometime Sunday."

"There's something else going on here. Spill it, Dragonfly."

Phoebe carefully chose her words. "I saw this man in Twyla's last night."

"What kind of man?"

"I'm not sure. My first impression was a panther on the prowl."

Rachel offered a flirtatious purr. "Oh, I like this already. Tell me more."

Rolling onto her back, Phoebe stared at the textured ceiling. "Last night I dreamed the panther jumped out of a lily pond and turned into a man. It was a very vivid experience."

"Was this a dream or a dream-walk?" Rachel's tone was almost clinical.

"I'm not sure. I haven't dream-walked in so long," Phoebe admitted. "I took Grandma's pipe to the pond this afternoon. I was going to smoke it. But when I got there, I couldn't do it."

"Why not?"

"I don't know. It just didn't feel right. You know how things are with Jack around here." Phoebe let out a long sigh. "I've got to get him out of the house and off the property."

Rachel's fingernails drummed sharply on the telephone receiver. "What made you get out that pipe in the first place?"

"I think it was the man in the bookstore. He was unusual, kind of spooky, but in a nice way. Something about him reminded me of the things I used to do with Grandma. I don't know. I can't really explain it."

"It's okay. We'll talk about it tomorrow. Eleven o'clock. Don't be late."

The telephone clicked on the other end and Phoebe hung up. Still staring at the ceiling, she wondered if tonight would bring more dreams of the panther.

* * *

THE next day, just before noon, Rachel Gray glided into the restaurant. Immediately, all male heads turned, and Phoebe could not help but chuckle.

"What?" Rachel squawked but retained a sensuous smile. She slipped into the booth and looked across the table.

"You," Phoebe said, shaking her head. It had been at least a month since she had seen her best friend.

A full-blood Apache and proud of it, Rachel never apologized for her culture or her ethnicity. Thick black hair tucked around full cheekbones, and dark eyes sparkled with special mischief. Rachel was as competent as she was beautiful, and Phoebe admired every facet of this no-nonsense Native American.

The waiter brought a bucket of fresh tortilla chips and hot salsa. Without asking, he added a generous side order of jalapeños and a pitcher of beer. He obviously knew their routine. "Beef or chicken tacos?"

Phoebe and Rachel looked at each other. "A little of both," they replied in unison. Then laughed together.

"Got it," the waiter mumbled and returned to the kitchen.

Rachel poured them both a beer and attacked the tortilla chips. "Tell me about the panther."

"I told you everything on the phone."

"Look me in the eyes, Dragonfly." Rachel raised a trim eyebrow. "What do your instincts tell you? Dig deep."

"Dig deep," Phoebe echoed and absorbed a psychic shudder. "At this point I don't know what I saw."

"Were you afraid?"

"In the bookstore?" Phoebe shook her head. "No. Intrigued. A little uncomfortable, maybe. But he didn't frighten me. He was—I don't know how to put it. Magnetic? Is that too trite?"

"No. Do you think he's a medicine man? Is he dangerous?"

"Medicine man? Maybe." Phoebe thought for a second. "Dangerous? Yes. But a nice kind of dangerous."

The waiter interrupted the awkward moment by delivering a platter full of tacos. "A little of both, girls. Enjoy. Yell if you need me." Quick and polite, he moved to the next table.

Rachel offered an incisive observation. "If you bring a medicine man into Jack's house, he's going to blow a gasket. You know how Jack feels about *Indians*."

"Are you suggesting I back off because of Jack?"

"No. I'm reminding you to be careful because of Jack. As long as you live in that house with him, you're going to have to deal with his bigotry, his drinking, and his violence. Honestly, I don't know why you stay there and put up with him. Why don't you just sell him the house and be done with it?"

"I have my reasons," Phoebe hedged. She would like to tell her friend about the riddle and the ghost, but felt the time was not quite right.

Rachel raised a hand in gestured peace. "All right. When you're ready, you'll tell me. So what do you think you'll find with the panther?"

"I don't know, but I have to look. There's this voice way down inside, Grandma's voice, telling me I have to look."

"Then that's the voice to follow, Dragonfly."

***

LIKE cosmic clockwork, dark clouds gathered and rain soaked another lazy Saturday afternoon. Phoebe wandered the back section of the last tribal store still in business on south Portland Street. Somewhere up front, Rachel grilled a store clerk about the designs on the ready-made dance shawls. Pow-wow music bounced through the overhead speakers.

The store smelled of sweetgrass and cedar and leather and tobacco. It was a tiny island of native harmony surrounded by a sea of foreign chaos. From the moment she stepped through the doors, she was assaulted by the sound of flutes playing from the overhead speakers. The heady mixed scent of cedar and tobacco and leather filled her sinuses. Her fingers tested the cool smoothness of glass seed beads on finished earrings and key chains. And she could not resist running the back of a hand across the silky flow of fringe on ready-to-wear dance shawls.

Phoebe wandered down the back aisle and stopped in the far corner. On the bottom shelf, hunks of red pipestone waited to be carved into tobacco bowls. Above that, a nice selection of cedar pipe stems, some decorated with beads and feathers, rested patiently on a strip of what Phoebe guessed was buffalo fur. On the top shelf was a glass case containing several nicely carved pipe bowls.

She remembered Grandma huffing at the idea of buying a pipe instead of making it. All materials had to be gathered in a correct manner and then smoked off in a proper blessing. Everything was to be handmade with love and respect. It did not matter that it looked homemade or was not as fancy as something fashioned by a master craftsman or mass-produced. In fact, that "handmade look" made each piece precious and unique. Grandma's belongings had character, as well as power.

Phoebe stared at the case with the pipe bowls. Her favorite photograph of Grandma had been taken by a family friend, who had pointed a camera at the old woman one day and pushed the button. Grandma had quickly tucked her hand beneath the ruffle of her flour-dusted apron, hiding the small pipe clutched in her fingers. It was not that Grandma cared for people to know about the pipe, but a pipe in use should was not to be photographed. The family friend never understood why the old woman had hidden her hand from the camera.

Something prickled at Phoebe's sense of the here and now. Her eyes changed focus from the pipe bowls inside the case out to the reflective surface of the glass. There he was, the panther. Standing so close his aroma warmed her neck and burrowed into her hair. His eyes offered the same sparkle and color of *gold-stone* that was once popular on string-tie bolas. His handsome face sported unusual lines, suggesting a mixture of races.

With his hands clasped behind his back, he leaned forward to get a closer look at the pipe bowls. In sensual mischief, he brushed a shoulder against her back. His deep voice bounced off smooth glass and carried a hint of elusive accent. "You know about pipes?"

Phoebe was afraid to move, afraid the panther would eat her, afraid the panther would leave. She managed a jerky nod. "A little."

The crook of his arm settled against her ribs while his knee warmed her lower thigh. "Medicine woman?"

"Who, me?" she stammered and offered a wide-eyed stare. "No. But my grandmother was a medicine woman."

"Which tribe?"

"Cherokee."

"You didn't learn from your grandmother?"

Surprised by such a point-blank question from a stranger, Phoebe thought a moment before answering. "My grandmother taught me many things, including the pipe ceremony."

"You don't have your own pipe?"

Her posture stiffened. The man was as audacious as he was sexy. "I have my grandmother's pipe."

"But you don't use it?"

Phoebe was stunned by the question and a little miffed. "I don't think that's any of your business."

"I meant no offense. Please, forgive me." Flirtatious eyes blinked in slow motion, while an easy smile settled across his tanned face.

A sharp voice interrupted from across the store. "Phoebe! Give me your opinion on this shawl."

Phoebe glanced back at Rachel for just a second. When her focus returned to the glass case, she found only her own reflection on the smooth surface. The panther had vanished, leaving behind that marvelous aroma.

With a stunned expression Rachel crossed the store and stopped in front of Phoebe. "Where'd he go? I was looking right at him. Then he just wasn't there. What kind of booger have you attracted?"

"He's not a booger. I'd be afraid of a booger."

Rachel looked over the tops of merchandise-crowded aisles. "Well, he scares the hell out of me. Don't tell me that was your panther."

Leaning in, Phoebe teased, "Here, kitty, kitty."

"I don't think so." Rachel gave a disapproving glare. "You're crazy. You know that? Mother always said Cherokees were crazy. Now here you go and prove it. I'm telling you that panther is dangerous."

"More dangerous than Jack?"

"Definitely. That cat eats dogs for lunch and picks his teeth with the bones."

"All he did was ask me about pipes."

"He's stalking you." Rachel pointed a long fingernail in her friend's face. "Be careful, Dragonfly, or he's going to have you for lunch."

For some reason, Phoebe just could not manufacture any fear of the mysterious man. Yet, Rachel's concern could have merit. Maybe he was a medicine man. If so, was he working medicine against her? Or was he working medicine to protect her?

She waved a hand through the space he had occupied only a moment before. Residual energy tickled her fingers. His touch had been so warm and gentle, like a hint of breeze preceding a storm. Some internal force compelled her to seek him out, no matter how unwise or dangerous that might be. Phoebe had to learn who and what he was.

* * *

ALTHOUGH it was only six o'clock, heavy clouds covered a drowsy sun. The line between afternoon and evening remained a bit blurry, as Phoebe stepped into the Twylight Bookstore. The brass bell over the door announced her with its usual off-key voice.

"Oh, for me you're noisy," Phoebe complained.

Twyla emerged from the back room, coat and purse in hand. "Who are you talking to now?"

I've returned to the scene of the crime," Phoebe declared.

"I know what you're looking for," Twyla said, turning the sign to read Closed. "The man you saw in here Thursday."

Phoebe noticed that Twyla said *saw*, not *thought you saw*. She shook back her ponytail, still wet from a recent round of rain, and leaned one arm on the counter. "Rachel and I saw him at the Trading Post. He asked me about pipes."

Twyla pointed out the window. "He's in the next store from the end. The one with the second story apartment. Martial arts teacher."

"A Native American martial artist? That's interesting."

Digging in her purse for her keys, Twyla nodded. "He was in here this morning. Bought a couple of books on herbs and a package of incense."

"Which flavor?"

"Musk Rain, of course." Twyla gave an enigmatic expression.

So, that was what Phoebe had seen, a martial artist. That explained why his movements had been so fluid and silent. "Come on, Twyla. Let's go check it out."

"You mean, check *him* out." Twyla raised an eyebrow and jingled the keys in her hand. "What will Jack say? You know how he feels about Indians. Haven't you had enough trouble with him lately?"

There was an edge to Phoebe's voice, one that had been absent for many years, like someone had honed the rust off an old knife. "I wasn't thinking about Jack."

* * *

THE sidewalk was still wet from the afternoon rain. Steam rose where cool air skated across hot concrete. Somewhere behind resting storm clouds, the sun raced toward the western horizon. The parking lot was almost empty. Even Twyla had bailed out and gone home.

Phoebe paused in front of the supposed martial artist's storefront and rethought this bold action. Large golden shades covered the windows, and a smaller shade was mounted on the glass door. The lights were on, but there was no sign saying *Open* or *Closed.* No lettering on the storefront. Maybe Twyla has been mistaken.

Just as Phoebe considered turning and running for the truck, the door swung outward. With quick reflexes she caught the handle and put a foot to the metal base of the door. A black-clad form filled the half-open entrance. His hand was on the inside handle. Hers was on the outside one.

There they were, just staring at each other. Stalemate.

"Please. Come in," that deep voice coaxed. He applied just enough pressure to rock Phoebe off balance, causing her to turn loose of the door handle. A strong hand cupped over her elbow and eased her inside the building.

The door closed behind her, rattling the narrow shade and giving her a quick pat on the butt. She took a couple of nervous steps forward. Twyla had been right. It was a martial arts class or one in the making, at least. There was an altar on the east wall with a pencil drawing of this teacher's master. Below that, incense burned atop a square wooden table. Paintings hung on either side of the altar. Weapons were stacked against the wall, while shelves and racks remained under construction. Lumber lay across two sawhorses and dust mingled with curling plumes of incense.

Phoebe's attention shifted as the teacher skimmed by her. Since Thursday, that panther metaphor had resurfaced several times, and there it was again. She marveled at the silence and grace of such a solid man. He was lean and limber. Something besides Native American flowed in his veins, she again thought perhaps a trace of the Orient. She tried to estimate his age but could only determine that he was somewhere between thirty-five and forty. Then again, he could have been much older.

He disappeared into a back room, his old sneakers making not a hint of sound on dusty carpet. In a moment good old rock-and-roll echoed through the store. With a couple of cans of soda in hand, he padded back to the center of the room.

"Sit," he said in a sexy purr. "I needed a break."

Since there were no chairs or benches, she dropped to the carpeted floor and folded her feet in one polished motion.

He was not what Phoebe had expected. Sitting in front of her, his gold eyes sparkled with what appeared to be approval. The toes of his sneakers tucked rather flirtatiously under her knees. He handed her a can of soda. Then he opened his can and took a long drink.

Phoebe simply stared at the can in her hand.

Wearing an elusive expression, he reached out and popped the metal tab on her can. "I promised I didn't shake it. You're not very trusting, are you?"

"I'm sorry. It isn't you."

"Trust me enough to tell me your name?"

She ducked her head to pull away from those alluring eyes. "Phoebe. Phoebe Henderson."

"Phoebe. I'm Master Lin."

The sound of that surname tumbled through her mind. *Is that Lin, as in Asian? Or Lynn, as in European?* It bothered her, but not enough to make her ask. Instead she made a different inquiry. "Do you offer classes? Or is this a private training facility?"

"Yes, I give lessons. What can I teach *you*, Phoebe Henderson?"

Several things raced through her mind. She hoped he could not read any of them. "I'm not sure. I came because I was curious."

"Or because you have a need to fill?" When she hesitated, he continued. "Phoebe Henderson, you're out of balance. And very frightened."

Phoebe nodded in silent admission and let the conversation lapse into a short pause. Then she asked a simple question that was sure to cause complex results. "Will you teach me?"

"What do you wish to learn?"

A deep breath cleared her mind. "Teach me what you think I need."

His face warmed with a smile. Nodding, he offered a salute: wrist bent, palm up. "I will teach you."

She returned the salute and wondered what kind of pact she had just made.

* * * * *

CHAPTER 5
Oil & Water

MONDAY came with sunshine and a warm wind.

Phoebe rattled around the big kitchen, cleaning up Jack's breakfast mess for the one-thousandth time. He had returned yesterday evening about nine o'clock, said he was tired, ate a little, and went straight to his bedroom down the hall from hers. That was the normal pattern when he had been mixing business with pleasure, which was most of the time from what Phoebe could tell.

She dropped the last glass in the dishwasher and closed the door with her foot. Instead of smelling dish soap in the air, a strong male aroma tickled her nose. Master Lin's enigmatic smile glowed in the back of her mind.

The telephone rang on the wall beside her. Startled, she jumped back from the sink. Just before the third ring she collected her wits and lifted the receiver. "Hello?"

"Phoebe? This is Master Lin."

That sinfully sensual voice reached right out of the telephone to caress her pink cheek. Phoebe's tone softened to a noticeable purr. "Yes, Master Lin. Good morning."

"Is it?"

"It is now," she answered without pondering the implication.

He offered a low chuckle. "Can you come to class tonight?"

"Tonight?" Her heart pounded from a sudden rush of adrenaline. She could not tell whether it was fear or anticipation or a little of both. "You're ready to open so soon?"

"Sure. I have several students coming. Just beginners. Can you be here a little before seven?"

Phoebe hesitated. An evening class was just what she needed to get her away from the house while Jack was in it. But Twyla could be right. When Jack discovered Master Lin was Native American, he would probably try to spoil any chance Phoebe might have for friendship or more with her new teacher. Lately, Jack used anything and everything to springboard into full-scale battle. Should she take the risk or play it safe?

From the back yard came the distinctive song of a cardinal. A stiff breeze rustled fat cedars and looming pecan trees. Through the kitchen window, she noticed a translucent image pacing back and forth in the manicured yard.

Grandma.

The ghostly form paused and nodded. In conjunction with the call from an unseen cardinal, the old woman's image burst apart like a dandelion spreading its seeds to the wind.

There was her answer.

"What do I need to wear?" Phoebe asked Master Lin with newfound boldness.

"Don't worry. Just be here."

"I will. And thanks for calling."

The tone and cadence of his voice made a dramatic change. "Phoebe, I'll see you tonight."

She opened her mouth to reply, but the line clicked. The disconnection left a strange emptiness in the pit of her stomach. Frowning, she eased the receiver back on its base. Rachel's warning from Saturday afternoon rang in the back of her mind: *That panther is stalking you. Be careful, Dragonfly.*

* * *

AROUND six-thirty she rushed down the back stairs and into the kitchen.

With her purse tucked in a small black gym bag, she reached for the door leading to the breezeway. Before she could get a grip on it, the brass handle turned and the door swung inward.

Jack stopped on the threshold, blocking the exit. His eyes raked her up and down. An oversized T-shirt hung almost to her knees and black leggings proved there was nothing wrong with her figure. The tone of his voice inferred a dare. "Where are you off to?"

Like a child hanging onto a teddy bear, Phoebe clutched the gym bag. "I'm going to work out. I told you yesterday, remember?"

He dropped his briefcase on the snack bar and scratched his head. The dark circles under his eyes betrayed last weekend's debauchery. Fatigue dulled the edge of his demeanor just enough to be noticeable. "Oh, yeah. You said you joined an exercise class of some kind. Why are you going at night?"

Bouncing on her heels spent just enough nervous energy to keep her calm. She didn't want Jack to spoil this for her. "That's when the class is."

Jack offered a glassy, evil glare. "What kind of class and where is it?"

"Self-defense."

"What's the name of the school and where is it?" he repeated in a monotone don't-give-me-any-shit tone of voice.

She considered telling him it was none of his business, but knew it would be better just to answer the questions and get out of this argument as gracefully as possible. And, hopefully, without a fight. "Lin Martial Arts. It's a new place in Red Cedars."

"Martial arts? In a stall near Twyla?" Jack backed against the snack bar. "How many times have I told you to stay away from that old Indian witch?"

Phoebe cringed at the remark. "Twyla was Grandma's best friend. And it's none of your business who I see."

Before Phoebe could react, Jack backhanded her. The crack of the slap echoed through the kitchen. When the sound died, the house fell into eerie silence. "As long as you live in my house, you'll do as I say."

A strong breeze found its way down the long central hallway. It rolled into the kitchen, past Phoebe, and hit Jack in the eyes, bringing a round of salty tears. The smell of coffee and gingersnaps permeated the air. *Grandma.*

Jack blinked and gritted his teeth. He stood straight, glaring down at Phoebe. "Indians. I'm so goddamned tired of Indians. The next time that old ghost messes with me, I'll do worse than slap you. You think about that tonight while you're sleeping alone in Danny's big bed. I can kick in your little door anytime I want. You make sure that ghost leaves me alone. And stay away from Twyla Jones."

Try as she may, Phoebe could not keep her lower lip from quivering in rage. "Are we done?"

"For now." Jack grabbed his briefcase and pushed Phoebe out of his way. Long strides took him down the darkened hallway.

It took her only a minute to navigate the curved breezeway, enter the huge garage, and climb into her little black car. She started the car, shoved it into reverse, and backed out just as the creaking garage door reached the ceiling.

New tires squealed on the clean pavement. With the visor pulled around on the passenger's side to shield the setting sun, she navigated the long driveway and maneuvered through the entrance gate. Her shaking fingers rammed a CD in the stereo. Rock-and-roll thundered through the car. She shifted into second gear, popped the clutch, and blasted onto a two-lane country road.

* * *

PHOEBE eased the car into a space in front of the Twylight Bookstore. On weekdays, most strip-malls got a good stream of business just after standard office hours. Tonight the parking lot was busy. Through the bookstore window, she saw Twyla at the cash register. Phoebe offered a terse wave and then glanced toward Master Lin's storefront. Sure enough, the lights were on, offering silhouettes of several people milling around inside the kwoon.

It took Phoebe a moment to talk her fingers into releasing the steering wheel. Part of her wanted to go home and avoid more scenes with Jack. The other part wanted to go to the class and find out more about Master Lin. After a mental coin toss, the latter won. Grabbing the gym bag, Phoebe opened the door and planted her feet on dirty pavement. Her eyes focused on the glow of golden shades. Without looking back, she nudged the door closed and activated the car alarm.

She loved that little 5-speed V-6. What she could not outrun, she just plain out-maneuvered. Phoebe had grown up on a farm and could drive anything. Tractors, pickups, hay trucks, and every type of car imaginable. Ten years ago she had considered herself a decent shade-tree mechanic. Walking toward the class, she wondered what happened to that no-nonsense girl who used to shake out air filters, tighten belts, and change the oil.

Just as Phoebe reached the door, it swung open and Master Lin's tall form came into view. She took a quick perusal of his black silk uniform, noting the gold sash tied around his waist and suede boots on his huge feet. But those gold eyes drew her the most. Something about him felt familiar. Something just beyond the boundary of recognition tickled at conscious thought but would not come into focus.

"Come," Master Lin insisted with visible annoyance and ushered her inside. "You need to dress."

Phoebe looked down at her T-shirt, knit pants, and old moccasins. *I thought I was dressed.*

A mischievous grin contorted Master Lin's handsome face. "I have something better. Come to the back."

Phoebe raised a brow in surprise. It had been a long time since anyone was able to read her mind. Once in a while Rachel managed to pluck a thought or two. But Grandma used to rummage through the attic of Phoebe's mind at will, pushing past cobwebs and digging through dusty trunks. Phoebe realized she had better reinforce her mental perimeters. If Master Lin got inside her head and found that panther metaphor, she was not sure she could face him.

His expression changed to reflect mild annoyance. "Come on. Hurry."

Swallowing last minute doubts, Phoebe avoided eye contact with the odd collection of the dozen or so students. She followed him across the practice area and into the back room. In the far corner on the right an open door revealed a darkened stairway that presumably led to an upstairs apartment. In the left corner, there was a door with a restroom sign. A black silk tunic and matching pants lay across a cluttered desk.

Master Lin tapped the uniform. "Put this on. The bathroom is over there. No shoes for now. Hurry. The others are waiting."

With smooth motion he pivoted on the toe of a suede boot and returned to the practice area.

"What have I gotten myself into?" escaped Phoebe's open mouth.

She ran her fingers across the frog closures on the tunic and remembered the exquisite red silk dress from her bathtub dream. Burying that scene as deep in her mind as possible, she grabbed the uniform and headed toward the restroom.

* * *

EMBARRASSED for being late, Phoebe tried to sneak past Master Lin with hopes of hiding in the back of the class. A large hand, however, snatched her silk-covered arm and used her momentum to swing her around to the front row. It reminded her of an old carnival ride.

Master Lin's deep voice reverberated through the building. "Pay respects to the Grandmaster." He bowed to the picture hanging over smoking incense.

The class repeated his gesture.

"Pay respects to your master." Facing his students, he bowed in unison with them. "Always pay respects coming in and going out. Even going in and out of the back room. Understand?"

"Yes, Master Lin," Phoebe said. When she realized she was the only one who had answered, she ducked her head, embarrassed.

Master Lin's face remained the epitome of stoicism, but those eyes sparkled. "Good. We begin."

His feet glided out to shoulder-width with toes turned slightly inward and knees bent just a little. Huge fists curled up at his sides while his shoulders remained square and his back stayed straight. With a stern voice, he gave the order to get into stance.

Phoebe strained to understand what he said and had absolutely no idea how to spell it. To her ears it was *chah-ma* and that was good enough. As best she could, she mimicked the stance. From the front row it was difficult to see what the other students were doing, which was no doubt what Master Lin had intended.

For a few minutes the master circled the room, making adjustments here and there to shoulders and knees and fists and feet. When he reached Phoebe, he put a large hand on her shoulder and forced her to sink deeper into the stance.

Then he moved to the front of the class and offered that wonderful smile. "Very good. Learn to stand. Then I'll teach you to walk and chew gum."

Laughter filled the room, and Phoebe began to relax.

She looked around, familiarizing herself with the new faces bobbing above a sea of black silk. Meeting people had never been easy for her. Once she finally became acquainted, however, friendships usually were long-lasting. Grandma used to say, "Take people as they are, flow with the day, and do not borrow trouble." Remembering advice and being able to put it into good use were two different things, of course, but Phoebe tried.

Moving past the adjustment to new people, she focused on the flavor of the room. It had an oriental quality and yet did not. Then again, so did Master Lin. Weapons glistened in a long rack along the right wall. A red silk fan with lethal metal spines was displayed above the swords. A silver chain whip with a dagger-like end hung on the other side of two bamboo poles. A tall trident stood between two wicked-looking pikes. A well-worn wooden practice dummy sat at the far end of the rack near the back room.

The left wall, however, carried a very different feel, one much more familiar to Phoebe. One painting depicted the typical oriental crane, while another showed a leopard. Between those hung a Native American mandala, replete with what looked like real eagle feathers arranged around a black panther painted on soft leather. On a shelf above, the mandala sat a red pipe bowl with a decorated cedar stem.

Her gaze drifted back to the painted panther. Coincidence? She thought not, which meant either Master Lin had put that image in her mind at the bookstore? Or had she pulled it from his? Either way, it was startling.

A shoulder brushed hers and a deep voice echoed. "Horse stance."

Phoebe shook off a shiver and focused ahead, curling her fists at her sides and sinking into the proper stance. The truth was, she had learned some of the basics years ago from Danny. She always thought the horse stance was one of the easier ones.

Large hands settled on Phoebe's shoulders and pushed down until her knees were even with her bottom. Master Lin snorted in derision. "It's not so easy when done correctly, is it?"

Frowning, Phoebe watched him walk toward the front. She struggled to maintain such a low position, but did not give up. Maybe it was childish competitiveness. Maybe it was stubbornness. Either way, she managed to hold that low stance longer than anyone else in the class. It was a small personal victory.

* * *

SOMEWHERE around eight-thirty Phoebe dragged herself to the car, deactivated the alarm, and opened the door. Chatter filled the dark parking lot as the other students sifted toward their respective vehicles. The cool night air felt good against her wet skin. How could standing and throwing punches at incense-filled air make everyone so hot and sweaty? She tugged at her damp tunic and trousers. Wet silk clung sensuously to her breasts and thighs.

Trying not to think about the uniform's wicked caress, Phoebe tossed the gym bag onto the passenger seat. She slid into the car and, without looking, pulled at the door. It did not move. Out of the corner of her eye she saw Master Lin's hand on the blunt edge of the door's curved window.

Wet black hair stuck to his neck. Even after a workout he still smelled good. Sinking to a squat, he leveled serious eyes on Phoebe. His rich voice filled the small car. "Be here tomorrow night."

"I don't know if I can."

A long finger came up in warning. "You must come tomorrow. Be here before seven. And, Phoebe, be careful." Backing up, he depressed the lock and eased the door shut.

With her hands on the steering wheel, Phoebe stared through the windshield and watched him return to the kwoon. Fluid movement made those black-and-gold silks rhythmically ride his solid frame. If he turned and motioned for her to follow him, she would. After only two chance meetings and one class, she wanted him.

The lights dimmed inside the kwoon. A few seconds later a flickering amber glow filled a small window of the second-story apartment. Maybe she was focusing on a man who was neither interested nor available. Maybe he followed her Saturday only because he sensed she needed help. Or maybe Rachel was right and this panther really was stalking her.

Annoyed by a rush of lust, Phoebe shoved the key in the ignition and started the car. The time display on the stereo offered a mute reminder. She could not sit in the parking lot all night. Wishing she were headed anywhere but to a house with Jack in it, she turned on the lights and put the car in gear.

* * *

BY the time Phoebe got home, Jack was drunk. Not falling down and slobbering, but glassy-eyed and calculating. The kind of drunk that turned gray eyes into ice and rolled large hands into fists.

They met halfway up the back stairs, each blocking the other's path. The same rule applied to encountering Jack drunk or meeting a grizzly bear in the woods. If you ran, he would pursue you. Phoebe had learned that the hard way over the last few months. With her gym bag slung over one shoulder she waited for him to make the first move.

"You look like a drowned rat," he growled and took another drink. Ice cubes clinked against the glass, and amber whiskey swirled like some chemistry experiment gone horribly bad. An old T-shirt molded to his shoulders, and faded blue jeans hugged an iron erection. "Nice silks. The master dresses you well. I approve."

This time Phoebe refused to be intimidated. "Get out of the way. You're drunk, and I don't want to spar with you anymore tonight."

Jack coughed up a nasty laugh. "One self-defense class and Phoebe finds her nerve. You're going to have to take me before you take on the world."

"Either let me pass, or I'll bathe downstairs. Make a decision, 'cause I'm catching a chill in these wet clothes."

Without spilling the drink in his other hand, Jack slapped her for the second time that evening. It was not hard enough to leave a bruise, but forceful enough to make a point. "Got another smart remark, Missy?"

"No."

"Then go to bed," Jack ordered, stepping to one side. "And remember to lock your door. Don't push your luck tonight."

Phoebe appeared much more calm and composed than she really was. Soft-soled moccasins allowed her slender feet to get a good hold on carpeted steps. Focused on the decorative vase at the top of the stairs, she moved past Jack and did not look back. Her heart raced.

If he were going to attack, it would be while her back was turned and the stairs were his ally. But the moment passed.

She reached the landing without incident and then walked into the bedroom, locking the door behind her.

* * *

ENTERING the bathroom, she locked that door, too, and dropped the gym bag on cold tile. Safe for a fleeting moment, Phoebe stepped up to the wide mirror. That long ponytail drooped down her back and auburn strands stuck to black silk. Her sex drive had been in high gear since Master Lin had brushed by her in the bookstore last Thursday. But she wanted the panther, not the dog.

He's just trying to scare you out of your own house, Dragonfly. Ignore the insufferable bastard.

Brave thoughts did little to calm her fears, however. Each evening Jack's sexual threats grew more and more intense. At some point all that whiskey might make him forget this was just a game.

Twyla's voice echoed in the back of Phoebe's mind: *Don't trust Jack any farther than you can throw him.*

Phoebe feared some night Jack would kick in that door and make good on all those lascivious threats. She hoped it would not be this night.

Digging deep inside, she found a spot in her soul completely disassociated from fear, a place that held speculative sanity. A fuzzy sensation warmed her from the inside out. She ran a hand down the front of her tunic, noting the feel of the frog closures, listening to the brush of flesh against silk. The lily pond formed in her mind. Drop by drop, leaf by leaf, the astral jigsaw puzzle assembled. Phoebe took a deep breath, drinking in the scent of musk and rain, ingesting its restorative power, shivering from its sensual caress.

Her eyes closed and her imagination plunged full-force into another time, another place....

* * *

RAIN peppered the pond, tumbling tiny frogs off their precarious lily pad perches. Small fish jumped, feeding on unlucky insects driven by the rain to the surface of the water.

Phoebe found herself standing beneath a smooth tree trunk, watching the lily pond rejoice in the cool shower.

Large hands slid around her waist, and a naked body molded to her silk-covered back and bottom. Familiar lips parted on her neck, and the warm tip of a tongue licked away droplets of rain. Laying her head back on a waiting shoulder, she eyed the lines of her lover's masculine face. Large hands pulled at her long silk dress, bunching it up until smooth thighs were exposed. His arousal, so hot and stiff, slipped between her legs. He put one hand firmly against the lower flat of her stomach. His hips rolled, joining him to her, taking her with her feet firmly planted on soft grass. She hung on as best she could and tried to keep her balance as he stroked.

Rain filtered through the leafy canopy, tickling the lovers here and there. Then the tantra hit. Her knees buckled, but her lover held her close, shivering in concert with her….

* * *

WITH a gasp Phoebe opened her eyes and looked in the mirror. Her heart raced and hard nipples pushed at thin black silk.

For a fraction of a second she thought she saw a man standing behind her, just like the lover in her daydream, naked and rain-kissed, his long black hair covering tawny shoulders, golden eyes heavy with lust. Startled, Phoebe blinked three times as quickly as she could and then found a sharp focus. But he was gone. Perhaps he had never been there.

If it had been her imagination, why did her body throb as though it had participated in the delicious drama played out beneath that sheltering tree?

* * * * *

CHAPTER 6

Predator & Prey

JACK looked south out of a filmy window from the top floor of one of northwest Oklahoma City's few high-rise buildings.

It was an ordinary Tuesday morning, except for a strange, thick fog. Radio stations reported at least a dozen accidents due to poor visibility and sleepy speeders. Oklahomans were not bad drivers, but they were impatient ones. Most people made long commutes from nearby suburbs and small towns that were mere dots on the map. Some drove to the city from as far as Tulsa, at least an hour's journey down the turnpike. Jack thought anything more than fifteen minutes was insane, which, as far as he was concerned, explained most of the traffic snarls.

He heard the door open in his private office and saw Sam's distorted reflection in the glass. "Eerie out there, isn't it?"

Sam dropped a fat stack of papers on the desk. "You're awfully moody today. Are you sick? Did your dog die? Somebody dent your car?"

"I'm not sick, and you know I don't own a dog."

With his hands in his trouser pockets Sam walked to the window and strained to see through the odd fog. "You and I are the only men in Oklahoma who don't own dogs. Okay. If it's not a disaster, it must be a distraction. What's wrong in Jack's world this morning?"

Jack leaned a shoulder against cool glass. "Phoebe started some kind of martial arts class last night."

"Are you serious?"

"She came home wearing black silks. You know, real silks. Something about this class worries me."

Sam shrugged. "Why? It sounds harmless enough. Relax. It's probably just another Americanized yoga joint."

"Maybe. But it's Red Cedars, of all places."

"What do you have against that little strip mall, anyway? You've always hated that place."

"It just bothers me. That's all." Turning from the window, Jack sat in the high-backed chair and rolled it up to his cluttered desk. "Do you have those documents back from Arizona?"

"No, but he's always prompt. I wouldn't worry." Sam balled his fists in his pockets and bounced on his heels. "Are you ever going to tell me about A. L. Jones?"

"Why?"

Sam gave an exasperated huff. "Hell, Jack. I've only run this office for twelve years. You'd think I would've earned the right to know by now. Every month I send contracts and reports to some mysterious partner in Sedona, Arizona. The only thing I know about the man is that Martin left him a fourth of the business."

Rocking back in his chair, Jack offered a blank stare. "We have this conversation twice a year and it always ends the same. Why can't you just leave it alone?"

"Let me be honest, Jack. What if something happened to you like it happened to Danny? I know it's horrid, but it's a reasonable *what if.* You may own this business, but I depend on it to pay the bills."

"And it pays those bills quite nicely," Jack interjected.

"And I'd like to keep it that way."

Jack drummed his fingers on the arms of the chair. He guessed after all these years of friendship and loyalty Sam deserved at least a piece of an answer. "A. L. Jones is...a relative. I've never met the man and hope I never do. If anything happens to me, you'll just have to deal with him. That's what worries you, isn't it? Well, if you're looking for reassurances, I can't give you any. And I'd appreciate it if you didn't repeat this conversation."

"After all these years I'd like to believe you trust me."

"It isn't a matter of trust. I just don't like to talk about family. You ought to know that."

"I do, and I apologize." Sam flashed a smile and made an abrupt change of subject. "Invite me to dinner."

"Tonight?"

"Sure. We'll get Phoebe to rustle up some good old Okie chow and cruise the satellite for a few hours. Kill a whiskey bottle and watch some dirty movies."

Jack looked at his best friend's grinning face and could not help but say *yes.*

* * *

AROUND six o'clock Phoebe paused at the kitchen sink and listened.

Two cars raced up the long driveway. A couple of minutes later uneven footsteps echoed through the breezeway. She backed into the laundry room beneath the rear stairs just as the door was kicked open. Whiskey bottles in hand, Sam and Jack stumbled into the kitchen.

"Phoebe! Oh, Phoebe!" Jack's slurred voice echoed through the big house, calling his sister-in-law like he would a dog—if he owned one.

In a moment, Sam added his own off-key entreaty, complete with wolf whistles, and followed Jack toward the living room.

Phoebe knew she had better get out right now. Was this why Master Lin warned her to be careful? Why he insisted she make plans to be at class tonight? He had picked up a few thoughts last night, but could he also predict the future? How powerful was this panther?

Deciding a mysterious martial artist was safer than two drunks with mischief on their tiny minds, she stuffed her uniform in the gym bag.

Her old moccasins made no noise on the expensive carpet. She tiptoed through the kitchen and grabbed her purse off the snack bar. The kitchen door was wide open. She took a quick look down the long hallway to be sure no one saw her.

Without warning, something or someone nudged her across the threshold and applied steady pressure until she was through the breezeway. Like an echo from the past, Grandma's voice floated on the evening breeze. "*Run!*"

Once inside the garage Phoebe made a dash for the car.

* * *

A little before seven, she walked into class. This time she was the first student to arrive, not the last. With the gym bag in her lap she sat on a narrow red bench and watched an extraordinary show.

Master Lin was running through one of his forms. Soft-soled suede boots skimmed across padded carpet, and a single braid of black hair slapped at his shoulder blades. His stance stayed low and wide. Long fingers changed back and forth from granite fists to implied claws. When the form was complete, he stepped into a cat stance and gave a traditional salute to the Grandmaster. It took only a moment for him to get his breathing under control.

"Get dressed, Phoebe," he ordered over his shoulder.

With the gym bag clutched to her chest, she gave a quick bow and tried to slip past him. It did not work.

A large hand cupped around her upper arm, pulling her to an immediate stop. His deep voice caressed her ear. "Clear your mind. Focus on the here and now. Don't think of anything else. Not yesterday. Not tomorrow. Shut out all the voices, all the chaos. Think with your heart, not your head. Okay?"

"Okay." Phoebe kept her gaze on the Grandmaster's picture. She was afraid to meet Master Lin's stare, afraid her emotions would be read too easily.

Long fingers uncurled from around Phoebe's arm. She strode through the office and maneuvered into the small restroom. Locking the door behind her, she breathed deeply and tried to think only of the class. It took her a few minutes to change into the black silks. With her street clothes and moccasins wadded in the bag, she emerged from the small lavatory.

Soft laughter and mingled conversation drifted through the building. Deciding it was time to introduce herself to the others, she dropped the bag just inside the backroom door, bowed to the Grandmaster, and ambled to the middle of the practice area.

It was a varied collection of students. There were half a dozen lean young men in their twenties. A pair of exuberant college-age girls. Three burly men in their thirties sporting short haircuts and military manners. And Sara, a middle-aged woman with short silver hair and the grace of someone who had practiced yoga for decades.

Phoebe struck up a quiet conversation with Sara. "Master Lin was practicing forms when I got here."

"Which one?" Sara asked, continuing to do yoga stretches.

"I don't know."

"Leopard. My favorite," Master Lin whispered, walking past them.

Phoebe glanced at the leopard painting on the wall. Again, she wondered if clairvoyance had pulled the panther image last Thursday or if Master Lin had been pumped information into her head. Did he know about the astral lily pond? Had some kernel of his essence stood behind her in the bathroom last night?

It had been a long time since she opened up enough to see with more than her five physical senses. She had almost forgotten what it was like to work in her grandmother's realm. Every syllable Master Lin uttered seemed to coax her back to the old Phoebe who walked with her head up and her ears perked, the Phoebe who did not back down from anybody or anything. The spiritual fire had not yet rekindled, but sparks were flying.

Out of the corner of her eye, she noticed Sara's closed smile. "What?"

Be careful how you look at him. He might look back."

The only response Phoebe could think of was a mute shrug.

Smiling, Sara ran her fingers down Phoebe's auburn ponytail. "Sit and I'll braid that mane for you."

It had been years since anyone had volunteered to braid her hair. Warmed by the offer, Phoebe sank to the padded floor. Sara slipped off the elastic holder and shook out long, silky strands. Nimble fingers started the braid at the crown and worked stroke-by-stroke down to the long tail. Relaxation came over Phoebe in small waves. Sensing someone's gaze, she glanced across the room.

Master Lin stood near the front door, arms folded across his chest, his attention focused on the braiding of Phoebe's hair.

* * *

IT was almost eight-thirty before the class ended. Everyone, except the two bouncy college girls, sank to the floor and wiped sweat in breathless commiseration. Master Lin, however, had disappeared into the back room.

"Food," one of the boys droned. "I need food."

Several voices agreed, and a cacophonous discussion ensued. Finally, it was agreed pizza was the best remedy for what ailed them.

Phoebe got to her feet and politely declined.

"We're not taking no for an answer," one of college girls insisted. "Come on. It'll be fun."

"I don't know. Let me get my bag." Phoebe slipped through the office door and noticed Master Lin sitting on a corner of the cluttered desk. She grabbed her gym bag and tried to interpret his mood. For some reason Master Lin conveyed a dark anger.

Reining in re-emerging spiritual skills, Phoebe managed to look mildly aloof. "The class is going for pizza."

"You should go with them."

"I'd better not," she said after a moment's hesitation. "It's getting late."

"Go eat with the class. Trust me."

"Aren't you coming?"

Master Lin shook his head. "Not this time. Be here Thursday?"

"I'll try. Goodnight."

"Goodnight, Phoebe. Have a good time and don't worry."

She took one more visual drink from those golden eyes and exited the office.

The shade on the front door rattled as the other students filed outside. Several voices urged in unison, "Come on, Phoebe!"

* * *

THE door to the breezeway eased open and a dark-clad figure slipped into the kitchen. Whiskey bottles and potato chip sacks cluttered the snack bar. Music blasted through the large house, and murky light bled out of the downstairs den. Master Lin paused on the threshold that separated the kitchen from the downstairs hallway.

A misty figure rose from plush carpet, blocking his path. Beaded moccasins poked out from a floor-length two-piece calico dress. Two long silver braids hung over a generous bosom. Gray eyes glowed like twin suns suspended in ebony space.

"Ah-ho, Grandmother," Lin offered in a husky whisper.

The ghostly mouth formed a silent "Ah-ho" in response. One crooked, semi-transparent finger raised in warning, and diamond eyes flashed.

"Understood," he replied and offered a firm nod.

In a silver explosion, the ghost vanished, leaving behind the smell of gingersnaps and coffee.

Smiling, Lin moved down the hallway and right through the spirit's residual energy. Masked by darkness and music, he approached the den. Soft-soled boots turned the corner and paused at the entrance.

An X-rated movie filled the large television. Two wingback chairs faced the screen. Jack was sprawled in the chair on the left, while Sam lounged in one on the right. Earthy remarks and ribald laughter followed their occasional moans.

Lin's outward calm did not change. Every move was cold and calculated. Easing up behind Jack, Lin frowned at the filth on the television. Like a strike of lightning, he dropped a fist over the chair. His hard knuckles connected with the soft flesh of a nose, making a quick snapping sound. Jack's eyes closed and he slumped over, blood running down his face.

A silent step put Lin beside Sam's chair. Drunken blue eyes drifted upward and, for a few seconds, the two men just stared at each other. Then the back of a hand hit Sam's diaphragm, knocking both breath and consciousness from him.

Circling Sam's chair, Lin made his way to the television. He shook his head in disgust and hit the power switch.

* * *

IT was nearly eleven o'clock when Phoebe, still wearing her black silks, sneaked through the kitchen door.

Both Sam's sports car and Jack's sedan were parked in the driveway. Instead of being met at the threshold by drunks, however, she found the house dark and quiet.

Just enough moonlight fell through the windows to illuminate the kitchen counter and give the cabinets a fuzzy outline. To Phoebe's amazement, everything was squeaky clean, just the way she had left it.

A modicum of light drifted across the carpet at the other end of the hallway. After dropping her purse and gym bag on the snack bar, she headed toward the den. Soft footsteps masked her cautious approach.

She peeked around the corner of what she called the devil's den. From her where she stood it appeared that Sam and Jack had simply passed out in their chairs. She could not see faces, but Jack had one arm hanging on the floor and both long legs sprawled over a footstool. Sam's head lay on the arm of the chair, his short-cut sandy hair contrasting the darker upholstery. It was unlike them to shut off their usual pornographic material, but she was grateful not to have to walk that gauntlet.

Phoebe backed down the hallway and circled through the kitchen. Breathless from too much pizza and a good dose of fear, she raced upstairs.

Once inside the bedroom she locked the door.

* * *

AROUND midnight Phoebe climbed into bed. Cotton sheets felt cool against her legs, while the old T-shirt molded to her shoulders and thighs. Lying face up, she stared at the featureless ceiling.

It had been a long day but, all in all, a good one. The *Musk Rain* oil she had put in the bath water left a delicate aroma on her skin.

A peaceful feeling rippled through her. Eyelids fluttered a few times then slipped closed. Her breathing slowed, and long fingers relaxed on top of her grandmother's handmade quilt. She floated in a place that was nowhere and everywhere at the same time, a place of calm belonging.

When the bed frame squeaked and the mattress shook, Phoebe told herself it was only a dream.

From atop the handmade quilt, long legs positioned between her knees and a heavy torso settled across her. Heat radiated through the covers, warming her nightshirt. Strands of silken hair tickled her neck. Breath laced with sweet jasmine tea steamed her face, and a familiar scent coated her cheeks like a gauzy veil. It was her lover from the astral lily pond, the panther of so many dreams, the man she dared not touch in the real world.

Reaching up, she buried her hands in soft, thick hair. Feeling a rush of passion, she initiated an impatient kiss, offering the tip of her tongue in exchange for his.

What began as a sweet embrace quickly augmented into something primal. A huge hand slithered beneath the sheets, following the curve of her lower back, finding its way under the cotton shirt to cup her bare bottom. His mouth slipped off hers and molded against her neck. Muscled legs tightened and wedged a hard erection into just the right place. Bed sheets, her nightgown, and his clothing prevented a physical joining, but in spirit they were already one, entwined in the unique ecstasy of the astral playground.

Moaning a foreign phrase, he pulled up on his hands and knees, hovering over her like a warm cloud. "Forgive me, Dragonfly. Go back to sleep."

Her eyes half-opened, but the idea of the dream remained. So did the desire. "I want you," Phoebe breathed.

"You cannot have me."

"Why not?"

"Because I am not here." That resonant voice burrowed inside her ear.

Rejection brought a surge of emotion. She gasped and began to entertain the notion that maybe this was not a dream. Before that thought could solidify into conscious action, a hand clamped around the back of her neck. She felt her body go limp. Then her spiritual essence floated off to find the astral lily pond....

* * * * *

CHAPTER 7

Indiscretions

JACK opened his eyes and raised his head.

His neck was stiff from sleeping in the chair, but he could not figure out why his face hurt. The digital wall clock displayed: *7:30 a.m.* Groaning, he pulled himself to the edge of the chair and fought a surge of nausea. Then he discovered blood caked on his face and splattered down his shirt.

How did I get this bloody nose? Who turned off the television?

He sensed he should be mad at somebody, but could not quite figure out who or why. It just did not make sense.

After grabbing a pillow, Jack threw it at the rumpled mound snoring in the next chair. "Sam, get up. Get up!"

"What? What?" Sam opened his eyes, lost his balance, and promptly slipped to the floor in an ungraceful heap. He rubbed sandy hair and grimaced at the foul taste in his mouth. "What's the matter? What time is it?"

"Seven-thirty. Wake up and look at me. Look at me! How'd this happen?"

Sam rolled the stiffness out of one shoulder and pulled himself to his feet. Stepping over the footstool, he inspected Jack's bloody face. "How'd you do that?"

"That's what I'm asking you."

"Last thing I remember was a stripper hugging a pole." Sam rubbed his aching stomach. "I think I'm going to be sick."

"Not in here you aren't," Jack warned, then winced at his throbbing nose. Gingerly, he got to his feet and tried to wipe dried blood from his face. "Go clean up. I've got a nine o'clock meeting. Get a move on."

Sam stumbled across the hallway and paused just inside the downstairs guest bathroom. "You gonna be all right?"

"Yeah. I guess I passed out and hit something. I'll meet you out front in ten minutes."

"Ten minutes," Sam echoed, massaging his stomach. "That gives me just enough time to puke and shower. Peachy."

Jack went up the front stairs and headed straight for Phoebe's bedroom door. He rattled the brass knob but found it locked. "Phoebe! Open the damned door. I need to talk to you. Phoebe! I don't have time for this shit." Frustrated and half-sick, he gave the door a swift kick.

Out of the corner of his eye, he noticed a ghostly figure hovering just to his right. The hair stood up on the back of his neck, but he was too mad and in too much pain to find any fear. "Go away, old woman. This is my house now."

Cursing under his breath, he walked right through the shimmering ghost. At the other end of the hallway he entered his own bedroom and slammed the door.

* * *

STILL wearing the old T-shirt, Phoebe sat curled in a chair. Behind her, heavy curtains covered the sliding glass doors that led to a small balcony. If she had to, she could escape through there. She had heard Jack at the bedroom door a few minutes before, but could not bring herself to open it. From that perch she was aware of all activity in and around the house.

The back door slammed. Boots slapped the concrete. Car doors squeaked. First Sam's sports car roared to life. Then Jack's sedan awakened with its usual purr. Engines raced and tires squealed. A moment later all was quiet, and Phoebe was alone.

She closed her eyes and remembered dreaming Master Lin came to her bed last night. It had been so real. Even now, the smell of his breath lingered on her face. The taste of his tongue coated her mouth. The warmth of his body radiated over her breasts and thighs. The texture of his hair clung to her fingers. The sound of his voice vibrated inside her head. Hot tears streamed from her unblinking eyes, rolled over soft cheeks, and smeared telltale musk down her long neck.

The telephone beside the bed rang once, twice, three times, before Phoebe got up and answered it. "Hello," she managed in a faltering voice.

It was Rachel. "Are you all right?"

"I don't know."

"Are you hurt?"

"No, just confused." Phoebe's voice found a stronger tone. "What's up?"

"Your face just superimposed on my computer screen. I needed to check on you."

Phoebe sat on the edge of the bed. "What time is it?"

"A little after eight. I have an idea. Meet me at the bank tower for lunch. I'll make reservations for eleven o'clock. What do you say?"

Phoebe's mind filled with Master Lin's rich voice whispering one word over and over: *dragonfly...dragonfly*. She still could not decide if it had been a dream or something she had actually heard.

"Hello?" Rachel sounded a little panicked. "Phoebe, are you still there?"

"Yeah."

"Is that a yes on lunch?"

"Yes," Phoebe answered. "I'll meet you at eleven."

"Paint your face and wear something tight. Let's drive the men crazy for a couple of hours. It'll be fun. See you later."

"Later." Phoebe set the receiver back on the telephone base and stared across the bedroom.

The restaurant sounded fun. Men were easy enough to attract. The problem was finding a good one.

Rachel took a carefree look at love, despite having one divorce tucked under her proverbial belt and two small children to raise. However, Phoebe viewed life through more serious eyes. Perhaps too serious.

She took one look at the open closet and allowed a smile. Most of the business in the tower restaurant came from male executives doing the power-lunch thing. Maybe it would be fun to turn a few heads.

* * *

JACK rocked back in his chair and looked at the clock: 9:50 a.m. A mound of papers covered one side of his desk, but his face hurt too much to lean over and do any real work.

A quick trip to the doctor's office told him what he already knew. His nose was bruised but not broken. It was going to be swollen for a few days and it would hurt like hell. By evening dark circles would spread under his eyes. Come morning he would look like a raccoon. The nurse gave him painkillers and put one of those idiotic tape-things across the bridge of his nose. Everyone kept asking what happened, but passing out drunk in his den was not the tale he wanted spread around the office. No, he needed a better story.

The title over Jack's door read: *Consultant*. It was a trendy catchall for people who had their greedy fingers in everybody's business. From real estate sales to bank foreclosures, mineral leases to basic document handling, Jack did not miss an opportunity to make a buck. When the legislature was in spring session at the State Capitol just east of downtown, he really cleaned up.

November's slate of elections could dramatically shuffle Oklahoma's political landscape. A polished back-room bureaucrat, Jack knew how to embrace the newly elected and how to insinuate himself into their little political empires. It was because this year promised so many political turnovers that Jack really needed to hold his usual Election Day party at the Henderson house. He needed it to go well. It was the first one he would be giving without Danny, and hopefully the last one for which Phoebe would play hostess.

The telephone buzzed. He slapped the intercom button. "What?"

Genny's squeaky-clean voice echoed across the desk. "Erin Hayes is here to see you."

Jack moaned in approval. "Send her in."

The speaker disconnected just as the door opened. His eyes fixed on long legs and a very short skirt. It was the girl from Tulsa. A smile strained the tape over Jack's bruised nose. "I wasn't expecting you."

Big brown eyes fluttered as she waved a manila envelope. Her sultry voice begged for attention. "Does that mean I'm not welcome?"

"You're always welcome. Come in."

Erin closed and locked the door behind her. "I have the rest of those papers you wanted. All signed and copied."

"What would I do without you?"

She dropped the folder on a table and walked around the desk. "Let's not find out, okay?"

Interpreting the look in her eye, Jack raised a finger in warning. "Erin, this is neither the time nor the place. I have lunch reservations for eleven-fifteen. Besides, I'm a wounded warrior."

She leaned down to inspect his battered face. "So I heard. What happened?"

Jack's gaze drifted past soft eyes and down to the cleavage spilling from her scoop-neck sweater. She was just the incentive he needed to invent a good tale. "Some drunken idiot at the bar last night."

"How bad does he look this morning?"

"Worse than I do," Jack added to the lie. Despite what society said about women eschewing violence, a good bar fight was the best turn-on he had ever found. Not that Erin needed a push in that direction this morning.

"Does it hurt?" she asked in a coy voice.

"Yes. So don't get any ideas about kissing it and making it better."

"Okay. I won't touch your nose." With one knee, she spun his chair around to face her.

"I don't think this is such a good idea."

"Sure it is. I told the secretary we had a lot to discuss. And I locked the door." Smiling, she reached for his trousers. In a flash she unbuckled his belt, unfastened his trousers, and pulled down the zipper. Without further conversation, she climbed into his lap and proved she wore neither underwear nor panty hose.

Taking a deep breath of sweet perfume, Jack gave a long sigh and let the leggy wildcat mount him. He threw back his head and allowed a moan. "Lunch can wait."

* * *

THE interior of the top floor of the old octagonal bank tower maintained a slow and steady rotation. Patrons of the revolving restaurant enjoyed a panoramic view of sleepy northwest Oklahoma City.

Rachel and Phoebe sat at a small table near the glass. By 11:20 a.m. all they had managed to do was down half a glass of wine each, garner a dozen leers, twice that many winks, and two serious, if not insulting, propositions. The skirt to Rachel's business suit was much too short for a linen-covered table, but the other patrons did not seem to mind. Phoebe was less formal in black leggings, a long tunic, and fringed black moccasins. Like teasing bulls with a red cape, she allowed her auburn hair to cascade over the back of the chair.

Phoebe ran a fingernail across the condensation on her wineglass. "Are we going to eat something? Or just sit here and tease the boys?"

"Tease the boys." Rachel flashed perfect teeth. "Now, tell me more about this new dream."

Dropping her elbows on the table, Phoebe leaned forward and lowered her voice. "It wasn't a dream."

"Then what was it? You don't think the panther was really there? In your bedroom?"

"No. Well, maybe. I'm not sure." Phoebe's grandmother used to tell her the only reality was what the spirit knew, and the physical world was just a reflection of what the spirit did. Sometimes it was hard to differentiate dreams from reality. She had experienced dream-walks before. They could feel very real. "He was there in spirit, at least."

Rachel nodded. "I was right. The panther *is* stalking you."

"Maybe. I'm not sure. It was more than a dream. It was interactive somehow. Maybe the flesh participated. It was very real. This morning I could still taste his tongue in my mouth. Everything smelled like him. Well, here." She rolled that long tail of auburn hair around one hand and offered it across the table.

Leaning in, Rachel took a deep sniff. "You're right. It's like the perfume, but there's something else. Jasmine maybe?"

Phoebe shook her hair back into place, and then shrugged dramatically. "I don't know what kind of medicine he works or at what level he walks. To be honest, I'm a little afraid to go back to class. I'm not sure what he's capable of."

"Afraid he can read your mind? Afraid he will know about the dreams?"

"Exactly." Phoebe emptied the wineglass and set it back in the same spot. "If the image is just in my head, that will be embarrassing. If it's really him, astral or physical or some mixture of both—" She paused, considering what it might be like to pursue someone so mysterious. "No, I can't do this. It's too soon. I'm not ready for another relationship."

Rachel's dark eyes fixed on a point behind Phoebe. Her voice sharpened. "Would you look at that."

Glancing over her shoulder, Phoebe let her mouth drop open in shock.

Just to the left of the elevator stood Jack. White tape covered a swollen nose, and dark bruises rimmed his eyes. Hanging on his arm was a stunning Native American woman with long legs and raven hair.

The waiter led Jack and his companion to a small table halfway across that section of the restaurant. Jack's hands seemed to find every nice curve as he helped the woman into her chair. Smiling as much as the tape on his nose would allow, he sat down and scooted his chair close to hers. His hand slipped under the open table and slid over a tan knee.

Rachel's reaction sounded like a cat's hiss. "What happened to Jack's dictate on not socializing with Indians?"

"Apparently, that rule only applies to me."

"And what happened to his face?"

"I have no idea," Phoebe replied in a hushed tone.

"Did he look like that last night?"

Phoebe gave her normal nonchalant shrug. "I don't know. I heard Jack and Sam come in. Then I went out the back. When I got home, they were passed out in the den. It was dark, and I didn't get any closer than the hallway." She pushed aside the wineglass. Jack's blatant hypocrisy made Phoebe furious. She had been slapped and threatened for just going to see Twyla Jones, yet Jack got to fondle that leggy tart in public.

"Come on, Rachel," Phoebe said. "If we're going to drink, I know a better place."

* * *

IN a dark booth toward the back of a sports grill on busy 63rd Street, Phoebe and Rachel settled in for a little drinking and a lot of plotting. Instead of dining on fine wine and pasta Alfredo, they ordered burgers, fries, and light beer.

With the pitcher of sudsy beer came an unexpected guest, Sam Tillman.

"I've died and gone to heaven," Sam said with a wicked grin. Scooting into the booth, he dropped an arm on the curved back and sidled up to Rachel. "The two most beautiful women in OKC sitting together. What are the odds?"

Rachel gave him her infamous touch-me-and-you-die stare. "Where's your partner in crime?"

"Jack? Lunch with a client. So, it's just the three of us. Got any ideas?"

"You said something about dying and going away." Rachel batted feathery lashes and offered a cheesy grin.

With a hand over his heart, Sam feigned chest pains. "Unrequited love."

"Ain't it a shame," Phoebe sniped.

Sam laughed and poured a glass of frothy beer. "What's this I hear about you joining a martial arts class?"

"You heard right," Phoebe replied. She had never found a reason to distrust Sam and, in some ways, found him quite likable.

The conversation paused while the waiter delivered burgers and fries and took Sam's order. In a moment, the three of them were as alone as they could be in the back of a crowded, smoky restaurant.

Sam plunged right into the hard questions. "Who is this martial arts teacher? Did you have him checked out?"

Uncomfortable with Sam's interest in the subject, Phoebe tried to sound indifferent. "No, I didn't. But he seems like a nice man to me."

"Woman's intuition?" A haughty sneer spread across Sam's lightly-freckled face.

"Best barometer I know."

"Sometimes people aren't what they seem, Phoebe," Sam said. "Especially martial artists. Just because he knows a few moves doesn't mean he's a master."

Phoebe began to grow annoyed. "And I suppose you'd know a real master from a fake?"

"Maybe. I have more experience with these guys than you do. A thorough background check sure wouldn't hurt." Sam stole a couple of crisp fries from Phoebe's plate. That grin returned and mischief slurred his speech. "So, ladies, what kind of trouble do you have planned for this afternoon?"

"Shopping," Rachel announced with underlying menace.

Sam nodded in approval. "Beautiful women trying on beautiful clothes. Sounds like a good plan to me."

The only plan in Phoebe's mind was how to get closer to the panther. What could Jack say after that scene in the restaurant?

* * *

ABOUT mid-afternoon, SAM sauntered into Jack's office and nudged the door closed behind him. "Hey, slugger. How's the face?"

Jack continued to shuffle through accumulated paperwork. "It hurts. Where have you been?"

"With Phoebe."

"Yeah, right."

Sam sat on the corner of the desk and folded his arms. "No, really. I had lunch with Phoebe and Rachel."

Gray eyes shifted from the paperwork to Sam. "Phoebe was with Apache Rachel?"

"Uh-huh." Sam struggled against the residual effect of the whiskey to which he had switched after the beer ran out. "Lighten up, Jack. Rachel's smart and absolutely adores Phoebe. Personally, I'd like to hire her."

"That's not all you'd like to do to her."

"Rachel is a beauty. But, seriously. She's a computer programmer and a damned good one. Think about it. She'd be a valuable asset. And it would make Phoebe happy."

Jack just stared coldly, as if Phoebe's happiness did not warrant consideration.

"Well, it was just a thought." Sam got up and headed for the door. With his hand on the knob, he paused. "How long is Erin going to be in town?"

"A couple of days."

Sam nodded in understanding. "So if anybody asks, you're going to be working late."

"Right."

"I love this city," Sam declared with a grin and headed into the hallway.

* * *

THURSDAY night Phoebe slipped into class at seven o'clock sharp and dropped her gym bag just inside the door. It had been a rough week.

Last night Jack had stumbled into the house at four a.m. He had rattled around in the kitchen before climbing the back stairs and heading to his own bedroom. This morning he had left for work late, bitching and moaning all the way to the garage. Phoebe had not seen him since and had no idea what to expect later this evening. He might be mad and/or drunk when she arrived home, or he might not drag in until sunrise. There was no way to know.

Phoebe's focus shifted to the here and now. Clad in shimmering black silk to match his students, Master Lin lit incense at the altar. The other students were already halfway through the stretching routine. Phoebe took a deep breath, bowed to the Grandmaster, and stepped into the practice area. The second she did, Master Lin looked over one shoulder and gave an almost imperceptible nod. Those gold eyes had an inviting puppy-dog charm. Tearing away from his gaze, Phoebe got in as many stretching moves as possible and tried not to think about those luscious dreams.

Master Lin's voice bounced through the building. Everyone lined up and fell into primary stance. The master circled the class once and then stopped in front of Phoebe, getting right in her line of sight. "Everything begins with solid stances. Root to the ground. Use your energy. Use your chi to find balance. Now follow me. Fists at your side. Crane. Right knee up. Turn in your foot for protection. Stay there."

Phoebe found the crane stance comfortable but hard to maintain. It took more strength and balance than she had expected. And, of course, Master Lin made everything look so easy.

"It's magic," he whispered. After moving to the front of the class, he demonstrated the stance. "Switch."

On cue Phoebe dropped her tired right foot and picked up the left. The switch was smooth and fluid. Closing her eyes, she could still smell his breath on her face. Traces of jasmine tea and musk. The class continued through the stances, from crane to long horse, meridian to unicorn. With her eyes still closed Phoebe found herself floating in a semi-detached state. Vague awareness of her body's movements kept her from falling.

She forgot about the other students, ignored the passage of time, lost her inhibitions, and stepped into another world...*the lily-covered pond came into sharp focus. Thick grass felt cool and soft on her back and shoulders. Rain fell in delicate droplets, a few here, a few there, coating that ethereal realm with the stimulating scent of primal musk. Her lover's naked form settled on top of her. Hot breath parted her hair. Long fingers cupped around her breasts, and human teeth tested the soft part of her neck. Her eyes opened just enough to see gold orbs staring back in drunken satisfaction....*

Startled, Phoebe opened her eyes for real and found herself soaking wet with sweat. The rest of the class milled around, taking the usual five-minute break. She stepped out of the last stance and shook off a little stiffness.

"Welcome back." Master Lin lit another stick of incense at the altar and looked over his shoulder. A knowing smile clung to his face.

Heat rose up Phoebe's neck and across her cheeks. Her first thought was to run.

"No." Lin raised a finger in warning. "Breathe. Get focused. It'll be all right."

Deep inside Phoebe knew she had not manufactured this latest astral walk. He had.

Rachel had been right. The panther *was* stalking her. But why? She had never met the man before running into him exactly one week ago in the bookstore. Yet, he seemed to know her well, perhaps too well. Caution might be advisable, but the hint of danger only tickled her imagination.

The panther had called her Dragonfly in Tuesday night's dream. A dragonfly was but a demure version of a winged dragon, and a panther was cousin to the tiger. The tiger and the dragon, forever in pursuit, ready to devour each other with sharp fangs and claws. The yin and the yang of it.

"Line up!" Master Lin ordered. The mischievous bounce in his walk matched the sparkle in his eyes.

Phoebe got into the primary stance and decided not to run. At least, not for the moment.

* * *

AFTER class she sat on one of the small benches near the front door and changed into dry socks and moccasins. Suddenly aware her thoughts had been elsewhere, she noticed she was the last student to leave. With the gym bag tossed over one shoulder she bolted to her feet and grabbed the door handle.

Master Lin appeared out of nowhere. His hand wrapped around the edge of the door and held it half-open, trapping her inside the building. "Are you all right?"

"I'm fine." Phoebe looked down at her feet. It did not take much psychic ability for her to feel that golden gaze burning a trail down her sweat-soaked clothing. He had already proven he could see into her mind at times, but Phoebe wondered if he could also see beneath her clothing.

His voice showered her with welcomed warmth and understanding. "Don't fight so hard, Phoebe. The answers are inside. Quit thinking so much and just let them come."

She looked up at that sensual mouth and wondered if his tongue was as talented in the real world as it seemed to be in the astral. For a moment she was tempted to pull down his face and see if he tasted like the man in her dreams. But the urge fizzled for lack of confidence.

"Goodnight," Phoebe offered in a strained whisper.

Shaking a little, she darted through the partially opened door and found refuge in the cooling night.

*****

CHAPTER 8

Pumpjacks & Apple Pie

THE next morning Phoebe stumbled downstairs and found Jack waiting in the kitchen, coffee cup in hand, the early edition of the city newspaper strewn across the snack bar. He had taken that silly tape thing off his nose. His face still sported bruises, but appeared to be healing.

"Are you playing hooky from school?" She poured herself a tall cup of black coffee and waited to hear why Jack had not gone to work this fine Friday morning.

"Kind of." He dug through the rumpled newspaper and extracted a map folded with western Oklahoma on the outside. "How would you feel about a road trip?"

"Where to?"

"Down by Anadarko. I have to scope out the surface property on a new mineral lease."

Savoring a big gulp of coffee, Phoebe nodded in understanding. "Land rights."

"Yep," he piped back in a crisp voice.

Phoebe knew one thing that did not come with a mineral lease was automatic access to the surface. Road rights and land leases had to be obtained before a site could be surveyed and any drilling could begin. Otherwise, it was plain old trespassing in some shotgun-wielding farmer's pasture. This was where she had always been useful. Born and raised in rural Oklahoma, she knew the rhetoric and was familiar with the lifestyle. Farmers liked doing business with people they understood. Sometimes Jack came off a little too *urban* for the overalls and flannel shirt set.

Taking another sip of coffee, Phoebe backed against the sink cabinet. "What happens at Northwest Properties isn't any of my business. Not anymore. I don't care if it makes money or not."

"Ah, c'mon, Phebes." For some undisclosed reason, Jack looked a little desperate. "It's just a short drive in the country."

"To help you swindle some farmer out of his land rights." Phoebe sipped cooling coffee. "No thanks. You're going to have to do better than that."

"Okay. I'll bite. What do you want?"

"Clear deed to the property?" The suggestion was so ludicrous, she laughed at it herself.

Jack chuckled and looked almost human. "Besides that."

"Well, let me think. What could I get for having to spend the day with you?" It was obvious that Jack was enjoying this poker game, so she pondered an appropriate ante. Several things came to mind. *No more drinking. No more slapping. No more threats.* She figured Jack would agree to anything now and break his promise later. No, what she needed was something tangible. Something to make a point. Something in her hand before they walked out that door. "I've got it. Give me the money for my half of this year's property taxes."

Jack's eyes narrowed to evil gray slits. "You're an expensive date."

"It must be an important piece of land," she countered. "Otherwise you wouldn't be asking for *my* help."

"Will you take a check?"

"Why not," Phoebe piped back with triumph. That was one less bill she would have to pay for the year. It was curious, though, how Jack caved in without hesitation. "You write the check while I change my clothes. We can deposit it on the way. Not that I don't trust you, of course."

"Of course. Then we'll stop by the bakery and pick up an apple pie. Farmers love apple pie."

* * *

AN hour down the interstate, Phoebe squirmed in the car seat and wished Jack's mouth had an *off* button. It felt good to get out of the city, but the sound of his voice was beginning to grate on her nerves.

Jack rattled on and on about how to approach James Severs. He wanted to make it look like a small oil operation on a shoestring budget. Instead of his burgundy sedan, they drove Phoebe's less expensive compact. Instead of slacks and a tie, Jack wore jeans. Instead of snakeskin boots, he had stepped into comfortable sneakers. Appearance was everything, or so he claimed.

Phoebe was not sure why she had played that little negotiation game with him earlier. Maybe it was to see if, just once, she could make the master poker player blink. Whatever the reason, it ended up serving her purposes well. The odd thing about Oklahoma property taxes was that a person could pay three years of back taxes on a piece of land and automatically be awarded the deed to it by the county in question. Phoebe really did not need the money for the taxes. She just wanted Jack to be aware that he would not take the land away from her over something so simple as back taxes. And having the check in the bank did not hurt anything, either.

Just before reaching the Weatherford exit, Jack turned off Interstate-40 and headed south toward Anadarko. After about twenty miles, he pulled onto a dirt road and drove up to a two-story white farmhouse with a long silvery tin barn looming behind it.

"The show's on," Jack warned. After cutting off the engine, he piled out and stretched his long legs. Then he circled the car and opened Phoebe's door.

She grabbed the pie and the coffee thermos. A little display of gallantry might fool the farmer, but it would not fool her. She got out and braced against a blast of unpredictable Oklahoma wind. Her auburn ponytail whipped back and forth in protest.

Sitting in a folding chair on the back porch was Jack's presumed prey. Dressed in blue overalls and a faded flannel shirt, the fifty-something farmer had his fingers interlaced on top of a round midsection. A baseball cap, bearing the insignia of a local feed store, covered his balding head. Crystal blue eyes stared out from a round face that sported a couple days growth of graying beard.

Jack walked up to the porch and offered a hand in greeting. "Mr. James Severs? Jack Henderson of Northwest Properties."

With his gaze fixed on the bruises under Jack's eyes, Severs kept his fingers entwined across the expanse of his stomach and left Jack's hand hanging in the air. "Northwest of what?"

"Northwest Oklahoma City, Mr. Severs. And this is Phoebe."

"Good afternoon, Mr. Severs," she said with a good old Okie accent and then nodded in typical rural greeting. Something told her this farmer was not going to be as easy as Jack thought. Maybe this would be fun, after all.

Severs' icy blue eyes gave Phoebe a thorough look up and down. "Pie and coffee and a pretty woman. Henderson, why don't you just tell me what you're here for and save the bullshit?"

Biting back a smile, Phoebe looked off across the prairie for a few seconds. *How did that old saying go? Never judge a book by its cover?*

Jack gave a savvy grin and dropped a sneaker on the second porch step. Every move forward got him closer to the back door. "You got an old pumpjack rusting on the northeast corner?"

"Yep. You want it?"

"Not exactly." Jack stepped onto the concrete porch. "I just bought the minerals under that pumpjack."

A coarse laugh wrinkled Severs' weathered face. He readjusted the cap on his head and rocked the metal chair back on two legs. "You're fifty years too late. There ain't no more oil under there, boy."

"That's not entirely true." Jack's body language indicated caution but did not appear predatory. Everybody knew old farmers always had a shotgun or a rifle or two tucked just inside their back doors. "This is the Anadarko Basin. There's plenty of oil. We just have to go deeper."

"Yeah." Severs' chair dropped back on its front legs and his voice lost some of that deceptive accent. "But it's not economical. Deep drilling is too damned expensive, and Mid-East oil is too damned cheap."

"Times change," Jack countered, raising a finger and flashing those gray eyes. "We've got better equipment and new drilling materials. In its day that well was a good producer."

"True." Severs took another look at Phoebe and the pie. "But you have the minerals, not me. Why should I let you in there to cut up my pasture and put mud pits near my cows?"

A greedy smile broadened Jack's face. He rubbed his thumb and first two fingers together in a well-known gesture for money. "Because I'm going to pay you very well for the land rights. Can we talk over coffee and pie?"

Severs pushed the cap back on his head, revealing a tanned forehead. "Is it apple?"

"Yes, Sir," Phoebe answered on cue and stepped up on the porch.

"You bake it, honey?"

"Nope. But I could have."

Severs began to take interest—in Phoebe, at least. He groaned, pulling his stout body out of the rusty chair. "Where're you from, sweetheart?"

"Lincoln County."

"Lots of oil in Lincoln County once upon a time."

Phoebe nodded. "And cotton before the dust bowl. But we still have the best pecans in the world."

"You know how to make pecan pie?"

"Yes, sir."

Severs opened the back door for Phoebe. "Henderson, this woman's too good for a slick-talking oil man like you."

Noting the insult on Jack's face, Phoebe grinned and walked into the kitchen.

* * *

SEVERS' green sixty-something Chevy pickup provided transportation to the northeast corner of the farm. Phoebe sat in the middle.

Each time the old farmer moved the column shift, he rubbed her breasts with a flannel-covered elbow. Throwing her arm over the seat, Phoebe stared through the cracked windshield and tried not to think about it. Given half a chance this old farmer would tackle her in the grass in broad daylight. Jack had yet to offer her as part of the contract, but she would not put any limits on his greed. All she could do for the time being was hold her tongue and hope the afternoon passed without further incident.

The dirt road through the pasture was full of ruts and weeds. In a few minutes they topped a hill and rolled down toward a rusting pumpjack. Severs dropped into low gear and killed the noisy engine. "There she is," he announced and took one more opportunity to slide a hand where it should not be.

To Phoebe's surprise, Jack looked a little mad. He kicked open the door, wrapped an arm around her waist, and pulled her out on his side. Fingers snapped and pointed her away from the well. Then, like magic, that cool expression returned to his clean-shaven face. Following Severs toward the rusting hulk, Jack blithered on about new technologies, fluctuating oil prices, and government taxes.

Chewing a stalk of sweet prairie grass, Phoebe wandered into the shadow cast on the east side of the rusting pumpjack. Weeds had grown up around the concrete pad. Green and copper grasshoppers buzzed at the base, like thousands of tiny offspring hovering nearby for parental protection. The old rig reminded her of some prehistoric insect, fossilizing above the ground instead of pulling fossil fuel from below it.

A gust of wind forced her to face northeast to avoid getting dust in her eyes. Halfway across the field she spied the ghostly form of a man clad in black. Phoebe waded through thick prairie grass and stopped within ten feet of the apparition. With the sun to her back, she tried to get a better look at muted features. The wind changed direction, bringing with it the scent of *Musk Rain*. It was Master Lin, reaching out through the ethers.

A question rang clearly in her mind: *Are you all right?*

She was careful not to let Jack or Severs catch her talking to herself or, heaven forbid, spirits. Her response was a cautious whisper. "I'm fine."

Warm gold eyes blinked, and the head nodded in slow motion. Then Master Lin's astral image dissolved, fading to nothing on the stuttering breeze. An immediate sense of longing tugged at Phoebe's heart.

Jack's hoarse voice called across the field. "Phoebe! Let's saddle up!"

A little shaken, she turned and shaded her eyes from the harsh sun. An astral thread had been spun. All she had to do was follow it back to Oklahoma City.

* * *

JACK drove into the office parking lot and pulled up behind his burgundy sedan. "Wake up, Phebes."

"I'm awake. Where are we?"

"The office building."

Yawning, she remembered that was where they had left his car this morning. "What time is it?"

"Seven-thirty. I want this contract ready to file Monday morning. Don't wait up for me." With the car still running, he maneuvered his tall frame out of the bucket seat and grabbed a legal-sized folder from the back floorboard. Without saying good-bye, he slammed the door and walked toward the darkened high-rise.

Phoebe stretched tired shoulders and slid long legs over the gearshift. With a little squirming, she settled into the driver's seat. The radio display confirmed the time. It was too late for her to make it to martial arts class. Her stomach growled, giving her a better idea: the mall coffee shop and those huge soft pretzels covered with cinnamon and sugar.

* * *

THE mall sat on what used to be a big prairie field on the northwest corner of Oklahoma City. Now it was upscale residences, schools, churches, and gas stations all wrapped around an enormous, sprawling mall.

With a pretzel in one hand and a cup of coffee in the other, Phoebe looked through a broad expanse of glass from inside the lower level of the mall. Through the windows, an enormous orange sculpture rose from a bed of shrubs and gravel. Years ago, Rachel had said it was supposed to be an abstract quail, but Phoebe had yet to find a bird in those twisted metal beams. Half of the malls and housing editions in this corner of the city carried names with quail in them, even some of the churches. Names viewed trendy by the ultra-rich seemed just plain silly to her. Blue quail. Red quail. Orange quail. As far as she knew, the birds Grandma called "bob whites" only came in speckled-brown. She took the last bite of the cinnamon-and-sugar-coated pretzel and sneered for her own amusement.

Jack could have gone to the office tomorrow to get those documents ready to file. It did not have to be done tonight, unless there was something in it he did not want anyone to see. Probably, he had another rendezvous with the "tart" and did not want people to know he was screwing an Indian on a regular basis. Either way, Jack being gone gave Phoebe a few hours of peace.

She noticed the crowd thinning throughout the mall. Since no watch of any kind would ever run on her wrist, she leaned over the railing and addressed an elderly couple sitting at a nearby table.

"Excuse me," Phoebe said. "Do you have the time?"

The woman checked her wristwatch. "Sure, honey. It's eight-forty-one."

"Thanks," Phoebe replied with a polite nod. The mall closed at nine o'clock, which meant she had better make her way toward the car. Tossing her empty coffee cup in a trash bin, she took the stairs up to the ground level, two at a time.

Around the corner, she found a rather nasty snarl of teenage boys at the north exit. Even in an upscale mall like this, trouble happened. It was not that she was afraid of all teenagers in this day and age, but intuition told her this particular situation carried danger. If she went out another exit, it would be a long walk to the car, which could be just as dangerous as running that gauntlet.

Before she could reach a decision, a familiar smell filled the air around her and a deep voice tickled her ear.

"Phoebe, I'll walk you to your car." Stepping in front of her, Master Lin slipped his right hand into her left one.

Thus far, she had not seen the man wear anything except black. Tonight was no exception. Black jeans made his legs look even longer, and a black silk shirt shimmered with every movement. The air around him remained electrified, and her fingers tingled where they wrapped around his.

She was thankful for the rescue, but puzzled. "Don't you have class tonight?"

"Friday night, he explained with a shrug. "It was just me and Sara, so we quit early."

The explanation seemed logical enough. She wondered if he consciously knew she had seen him only a few hours earlier in a southwestern Oklahoma prairie field. Spirit-walking was not a subject she dared discuss with the average person. Of course, nothing about this man seemed average. She just did not know him well enough, however, to make casual conversation about spirit medicine, especially not in the middle of the mall.

"I'm sorry I missed class," Phoebe offered. "I had to go out of town."

"Business?"

"Yes. Well, sort of. I helped my brother-in-law check out an oil lease in western Oklahoma. It was a long drive."

Master Lin's fingers wrapped through hers brought unexpected comfort. Men, even as aloof as this one, did not hide their desires very well. Women just seemed to know when they were wanted. No doubt about it. Master Lin wanted to do more than teach Phoebe stances and kicks and punches.

"Stay close," he whispered, leading her toward the doors. Strong fingers twitched around hers, as intense golden eyes stared at the wad of teenage boys blocking the north exit.

As anticipated, the boys were looking for trouble. Master Lin led Phoebe through two sets of glass doors and past a round of rude remarks and wolf whistles. Once outside he kept a steady pace toward her car. The parking lot was almost empty and, as fate always had it, there was no security guard.

Vulgar remarks and infantile laughter crept closer. Then one voice echoed on the night air. "Hey, José! Bring her back. We'll be real nice to her. We promise."

Near the car, Master Lin pushed Phoebe behind him. "Don't move. Let me handle this."

Phoebe had no intention of letting him out of her sight. With the driver's side of the car behind her and Master Lin making a stand in front of her, she was as safe as she could be in a situation of this type.

If the teenagers had understood the nature of the person with whom they were trying to pick a fight, there was no doubt they would have run like hell. But it was too late for admonitions, too late for negotiations. The obvious leader of the pack, a muscular kid who looked eighteen or nineteen at the most, stepped up and made a terrible mistake. He curled both fists and swung. The first fist found nothing but humid air. The second one came to an abrupt stop with Master Lin's long fingers wrapped completely around it. By the time surprise registered on his face, the boy was on the ground.

A trace of oriental accent warped Master Lin's usually crisp words. "Leave now, or I *will* hurt you."

Humiliated but otherwise no worse for wear, the kid got to his feet and retreated toward the others. Halfway across the parking lot, they collected around two old cars. Obscenities and rude gestures flew. They sounded brave from a distance, but did not approach again.

"Phoebe, get in the car," Master Lin ordered point-blank.

She did not argue. Shaky fingers dug through her jeans pocket to produce a small ring with only three keys on it. Two for the car and one for the house. She opened the door and slid into the driver's seat.

A four-hour car ride with Jack, dealing with that horny farmer, dreams of Master Lin, and now teenage thugs. It was too much at once. Emotional exhaustion pulled at her last thread of composure and caused a few hot tears to trickle down her cheeks.

"Don't cry, Dragonfly." Master Lin sat on the edge of the car frame. Long fingers wiped salty tears from her cheek. "You're safe. Please, don't cry."

With a shoulder tucked under his arm, Phoebe looked into those mesmerizing gold eyes. Her heart beat faster and harder to match his. His touch changed from nurturer to lover. Fingers slid around her neck with polished purpose. In slow motion he dropped his mouth over hers and pushed the tip of his tongue between her teeth.

This time it was not a dream, but it mimicked past dreams to perfection. This was the same man Phoebe had held beside that astral lily pond. These were the same lips she kissed the night she *dreamed* he came to her bed.

He pulled his mouth from hers and offered a drunken gaze. "You make me crazy," came a strained whisper. Nimble fingers buckled the safety belt. Then he slammed the door and stepped away from the car.

The day had already been eventful enough without adding a tryst in the mall parking lot. Phoebe would have liked nothing better than to follow him to his apartment, but he did not ask. And she certainly was not ready to bring him to the farm, not with Jack causing trouble at every turn.

After a short, uncomfortable silence, Phoebe accepted the fact that she would be going home alone. She started the engine and pulled forward through empty parking spaces. The car bucked when she shifted into second gear. Tires squealed and threw up oily dust.

She watched the rearview mirror until Master Lin's reflection shrank to just a ghost in the evening fog.

*****

CHAPTER 9

Fox in the Hen House

SATURDAY morning came with a fiery sunrise and the roar of Jack's sedan pulling into the spacious garage. He shut off the engine and clicked the remote. The double garage door creaked and made a steady descent, leaving Jack in a moment of relative darkness.

He turned on the inside car light and pulled down the visor mirror. The face that greeted him was not a pretty one. Bruises under his eyes and over his nose gave him a pitiful hound-dog look. A full day's growth of beard stuck out like brown fuzz on a peach. His sweat-stained shirt was wrinkled. And no one should wear the same pair of socks two days in a row and not expect them to itch a little. Such was the price of philandering. Yet, the memory of Erin Hayes' perfect body writhing beneath him was still vivid. A few hours in yesterday's clothing was a small price to pay for what he had scored last night.

Whistling a phrase from an old country song, Jack climbed out of the sedan. Halfway across the garage he realized there was an empty slot to the right of Danny's red pickup. The little black car was gone. Jack's sneakers slid to a stop on bare concrete, making that old trick knee crackle a little in protest. He had known Phoebe for eleven years, had lived with her for six months now. She was a confirmed night owl. Only emergencies got Phoebe up at this time of the morning. For a long moment Jack stood there, staring at the empty parking slot. Maybe that little bit of calculated kindness yesterday had worked. Maybe Phoebe had finally given up, packed her bags, and left.

"Naw," Jack intoned and shook his head. Not likely. That girl's veins ran full of stubbornness.

Phoebe was no quitter. Maybe that was why she fascinated him. In Oklahoma pretty girls were a dime a dozen, but resolute ones were rare in any corner of the world. Jack would never admit it out loud, but he admired Phoebe's tenacity. Like a soldier staring down the barrel of an enemy gun, she stood her ground just on principle. It was the sexiest game Jack had ever played. He got a hard-on just thinking about having an argument with that girl. If she moved out, he would miss the thrill of conflict. But he would win the war.

Jack wheeled around, his sneakers squeaking on the dusty concrete, and headed out of the garage. Long strides took him across the narrow breezeway. Cursing under his breath, he fumbled with the lock on the kitchen door. The deadbolt slid back with a distinctive click and the door swung inward. A little cautious, Jack stepped inside the kitchen.

"Phoebe? Phoebe!" His voice echoed through the big, silent house. When no one answered, he checked the telephone. No messages.

After dropping his car keys on the snack bar, Jack headed up the back stairs. The door to the master bedroom had been left wide open. The bed was made and the room clean. One look in the walk-in closet told him Phoebe had not gone far. Her old brown moccasins were still in the middle of the closet floor.

The crunch of tires on gravel could be heard even in that upstairs closet. Jack pivoted and hurried downstairs. He slid into the kitchen just in time to see Phoebe walk in the door.

She shook a sack and pointed toward the insulated carafe sitting toward the back of the snack bar. "Coffee and donuts?"

"Where have you been?"

Phoebe's voice struck a sarcastic chord. "At the donut shop, perhaps? Duh."

A crooked grin eased onto Jack's unshaven face. "I was worried. I thought you'd left me."

"Sorry to disappoint you, Jack."

"I'll get over it."

"I'm sure you will." She grabbed a chocolate-covered donut. With a cup of coffee in one hand and the donut in the other, she paused just inside the hallway. "Jack?"

"What?"

"Take a shower. You smell like a whorehouse." With a cocky stride she crossed the hallway and disappeared into the den.

Jack shoved half a donut in his mouth and washed it down with lukewarm coffee. The war still waged, and Phoebe's stiff-backed, nose-in-air defiance still aroused him.

* * *

DESPITE the fact it was Labor Day, Jack went to the office Monday morning and was happy to have the building all to himself.

Light drifted through the corner windows and blended with the glow of a desk lamp. Rocking back in his chair, he dropped expensive cowboy boots on the credenza and laid a file folder across the lap of his fitted jeans. Long fingers thumbed through a geologist's report and a list of old oil wells.

This new contract had to be handled with extreme privacy. Neither Sam nor Genny knew about the files in the green cabinet. Before he had lost himself in Erin's charms last Friday night, he copied the old farmer's lease and other pertinent materials. Saturday morning on his way home he put the package in the same-day-delivery bin and sent it to the "buyer" in California.

On schedule, the telephone rang. Jack scooped the receiver off the base. "Northwest Properties. This is Henderson."

Jack? Fred Kaufman, here. I got the package."

"What do you think?" Jack asked, tucking the receiver under his chin.

"It looks perfect. Just like you said. Lots of lost circulation zones, and the location is rural. Damn near remote by the looks of the map."

Jack rocked back and forth in the chair, filling the office with a rhythmic creak. "I drove that road myself. Your trucks won't have any problem getting in and out. You'll have to lay gravel on about a quarter mile of pasture road, but that's easy enough."

"Great. Let me finish looking over the reports. We'll talk it over on this end tomorrow and work up a proposal. How does that sound?"

"No problem. But I have to tell you I have a couple of local buyers waiting in the wings."

"No need to up the ante, Jack. You'll get your money's worth on this one. I'll call you at home tomorrow evening."

"That'll be fine, Fred. Tomorrow night then."

The line went dead and Jack dropped the receiver back on its slim base. He was going to make a lot of money on this deal. No doubt about it.

A quick double-ring emanated from the side of the telephone. This call was also right on time. He punched the button to activate the intercom. "Jack, here."

A sexy voice flowed out of the speaker. "Buzz me in, Honey-Jack."

"You got it, sweet thing." Big boots hit the carpet with a muffled thud. Whistling a country tune, he crossed the private office. An electronic security panel hung on the far wall. He pressed the button marked Back Entrance. When the panel chimed in response, Jack knew Erin was on her way up. So was his arousal. Still whistling, he pulled off his boots, unbuttoned his shirt, and shed his belt.

The hallway elevator chimed and in a moment Erin strode into his office. As always, just to please him, she wore a low-cut sweater and a high-cut skirt.

Locking the door behind her, she held up a small brown bag. "I brought lunch. I figured you haven't eaten anything but corn chips and candy bars."

Preoccupied with those long, tan, bare legs, Jack unzipped his jeans. "Not now."

Erin's soft brown eyes narrowed in sultry delight and she set the lunch bag on the desk. She kicked off her shoes and hiked up her mini-skirt, revealing hard thighs and a bare bottom.

"Come here," Jack whispered.

Lifting her off the ground, he wrapped her legs around his hips and immediately shoved himself deep inside her. Half-dressed, tight jeans tugging at his crotch, he took her standing. One hand grabbed her thick hair and pulled back her beautiful face. He wanted to see the tears in her eyes. It was not love. It was hard-driving animal sex. All Jack cared about was how it made him feel.

* * * * *

CHAPTER 10
Tea Time

JUST after Jack left Monday morning, Phoebe flopped down in one of the expensive wingback chairs in the den and turned on the television.

A quick search found the early news. She sipped coffee and waited for the weather report. Jack had looked like hell last Saturday and smelled even worse. What a treat it had been to see him rumpled and speechless for a change.

On the way home from the mall Friday night, Phoebe had found a drive-in, ordered a burger and fries, and ate dinner in the car. She rolled down the windows and cranked up the stereo. Twice she almost turned the car around and headed back toward Red Cedars Corner. Each time temptation knocked, she managed to talk herself out of it. What was she going to do? Bang on the front door and ask the mysterious master to finish what he had started?

At first, she had been hurt that Master Lin had saved her from a potentially dangerous situation, stolen a kiss, and then simply vanished into the night. Later she was glad the situation had gone no further. Anything else would have moved too fast with a man about which she really knew next to nothing.

Two weeks ago she was almost ready to give up on her promise to Grandma, her stubbornness to hang on to this house and land. Then Master Lin came along. He strengthened her resolve somehow. There was no doubt in her mind the *panther* thought of her as more than a student. That passionate kiss in the parking lot had been no accident, and those dreams were more than subconscious fantasy.

Before things got too messy, Phoebe needed some good advice. Despite Jack's admonitions, she decided to speak with the wisest person she knew, Twyla Jones.

***

AROUND mid-morning the next day Phoebe eased her car into a slot in front of the Twylight Bookstore. On the way through the strip mall, she noticed a *Closed* sign in Master Lin's window. *Good.* She would rather speak to Twyla first.

Getting out of the car, Phoebe braced against a gust of wind and recalled the morning's weather forecast. Cooler and wetter. It did not take a meteorologist to predict that. All one had to do was look at the calendar. The Oklahoma State Fair would open soon, which always meant rain.

The tinny little bell over the bookstore's door sounded as Phoebe hurried inside to get out of the wind.

A familiar voice echoed from the back room. "Put up the *Closed* sign and turn the lock. I hope you like sub-sandwiches."

Smiling, Phoebe did as requested and made her way down the center aisle. She stepped into the large back room that served as office, kitchen, and storage area. Dropping her purse on a stack of boxes marked *Romance*, she took a seat at the small metal table. An unguarded sandwich and a can of soda quickly found their way into her possession. "What, no corn chips?"

Twyla plucked a new bag of chips off the work counter. "Here. But don't eat them all."

"Indians have to have their corn." Phoebe's voice echoed across metal furniture and haphazardly stacked boxes. The plastic bag opened with an uneven rip, spilling a few corn chips on the table. "Thanks for making some time for me."

"I always have time for you, Dragonfly. So, what have you gotten yourself into now?"

"I think I have a problem with Master Lin."

Twyla's eyes narrowed to slivers of gold. "Tell me."

Between sandwich bites and corn chip crunches, Phoebe managed to relate her dilemma. She left out the juicier details from the dreams, but told most of what happened in the mall parking lot. "Twyla, an honest interest is one thing, but Master Lin is everywhere I turn. Even in my dreams. In one way he's like some gorgeous guardian angel. In another way it feels like he's the predator and I'm the prey."

"You do run to the dramatic, don't you, child?" After finishing her sandwich, Twyla got out coffee mugs and a thermos. "If you want my opinion, and you're going to get it whether you like it or not, it seems to me that Jack is the predator and Master Lin is the protector."

Phoebe took a mug of coffee and sniffed the aromatic steam. "But I'm still the prey."

"You're only a victim if you allow it. You can solve that riddle if you want to and resolve this mess with Jack. The only thing stopping you is you."

That really was not what Phoebe wanted to hear. Nobody liked to be told some of their problems are of their own making. Way down deep inside she knew Twyla was telling the truth. "If Jack would just be reasonable. All I want is the house and a few acres."

Twyla offered a pinched chuckle. "Don't count on Jack ever being reasonable."

"You've never told me how you know Jack."

"No. I guess I haven't."

"Well?"

"A well is a deep dark subject."

"Riddles," Phoebe muttered. "All I ever get from you and Grandma are riddles. For once I'd like a straight answer."

"Now what fun would that be?" Twyla remarked over the top of her coffee cup.

Exasperated, Phoebe leaned the metal chair back on two legs and studied the rigid expression on her friend's face. "Master Lin showed up just at the right time, didn't he? Almost like somebody sent for him."

Twyla allowed a reserved smile. "The Great Spirit works in mysterious ways."

* * *

AFTER Phoebe's car pulled out of the parking lot and disappeared down the crowded street, Twyla re-locked the front door and turned out the main lights.

Carrying a fat wad of keys on a thick brass ring, she went out the back of the bookstore and headed down the wide alley. In a moment, she stood before the back door of the Lin Martial Arts. She thumbed through jingling keys, and then inserted the correct one into the lock.

The door opened with a telltale creak.

"It's just me," she announced, stepping inside and closing the door behind her. "Where are you?"

A deep voice boomed down the stairwell to Twyla's immediate left. "Up here."

Rattling the keys out of nervous habit and for the joy of the tinkling sound they made, Twyla climbed steep steps and entered the renovated studio apartment.

There were few furnishings. A red silk partition separated the kitchen from the living area. To the right, just inside the doorway, sat a couple of flat-top trunks. Plastic milk crates and an unvarnished board made a shelf for a small television and a boom-box stereo. A very old sword in an exquisite turquoise-studded scabbard hung on one wall. Below that, an inexpensive futon served as both bed and couch. At the far end of the room, a wooden table stood in the center of a spacious dormer. On that table, a brass pot supported three burning incense sticks. Gray smoke carried the tantalizing scent of *Musk Rain* and coated the single window with an oily film.

Toward the center of the room, Master Lin was curled in a papasan chair. Wearing no shirt or shoes, he yawned and smoothed back thick, black hair.

Twyla sat on the edge of a nearby trunk. "Wouldn't want you to over-exert yourself."

The handsome master offered a devastating smile.

"Save the charm for the little girls," Twyla droned.

"What's wrong, Aunt Tea?"

Old memories came to the forefront and gave Twyla a bit of a shiver. "It's been a long time since I've heard that."

There was obvious affection in the way Alex looked at her. "Almost thirty years."

"Thirty years." Twyla She remembered a beautiful, black-haired little boy with big gold eyes and an accent so thick the best his tongue could make of Auntie Twyla was Aunt Tea.

"I just talked to Phoebe," Twyla informed.

He nodded. "I saw her drive out."

"Uh-huh," Twyla droned. "She's scared."

"She should be. Jack is dangerous. So am I."

"And so is this silver-haired old medicine woman. Don't forget that, Alex Lin Jones." Getting off the trunk, Twyla walked into the small kitchen, put two tea bags in the kettle, and adjusted the flame on the old gas stove.

Long ebony hair framed Alex's face and sharply contrasted those brilliant golden eyes. His voice seemed to soften when he spoke of Phoebe. "Why don't you let me tell her the truth? I know we can trust her."

"No. It's too risky."

"You mean because of Jack."

"Yeah, Jack," Twyla groaned. "As long as Phoebe's alone with him in that house, the truth is just too dangerous. If she accidentally says the wrong thing, it might set him off. I don't want her getting hurt because of us."

"You were right about her," Alex informed. "She has great sight. A lot of spirit power. She just needs to learn to use it, to trust it."

Twyla stepped out of the kitchen, hands on her hips. She knew people had to make their own decisions, for good or bad. However, nothing said she could not offer a little advice. "You want trust? Make friends with her before you screw her brains out, boy. Not after."

"She's just so damned irresistible. I don't know what I'd do if Jack hurt her. I really don't know."

"It was you, wasn't it?" Twyla knew the answer before the words left her lips. "You busted poor Jack's nose."

"Poor Jack," Alex snarled and stared at the oriental screen that partitioned off the kitchen. On a canvas of red silk, seven golden leopards stalked each other around a tear-shaped lily pond. "Dead Jack, if he isn't careful."

* * *

WITH the most expressionless face she could manufacture, Phoebe entered Master Lin's class just a few minutes before seven o'clock that evening. There were several new students. *Good.* She wanted his business to do well. After stashing her gym bag beneath one of the benches, she picked a path into the practice area and found a spot to do her usual warm-up stretches.

An unusual amount of incense clogged the air. Actually, it was downright smoky. She did not see Master Lin, but felt him nearby. It was comforting to know, as long as she was in this class, the outside world could not touch her. One odd thing, however, had bothered her all day. Phoebe might be naïve on occasion, but she was not stupid. Twyla harbored a secret. Secrets were like puzzles that nagged at Phoebe until she figured them out. And this one begged for a solution.

"I'm glad you came," a deep voice whispered in her ear.

Startled, Phoebe looked over her shoulder and found Master Lin standing close behind her. As always, his unique scent captured her attention, and his mere presence seemed to electrify the air. "Of course, I came. Why wouldn't I?"

He hesitated and looked a little uncomfortable. "I was afraid you might be angry."

Phoebe found his embarrassment charming. "Because you're human like the rest of us? Actually, it's nice to know you're a little fallible."

Gold eyes sparkled in obvious flirtation. "Fallible?"

"Absolutely." She raised her thumb and forefinger, leaving only a tiny space between them. "But just a little."

"Just a little," he echoed and returned the gesture. One eyebrow raised in mischief. "I have to warn you. We're going to work hard tonight. So no whining."

"I never whine," she retorted with as much nasal quality as she could manufacture.

"It's going to be a long night." He walked to the front of the class and raised his voice. "Line up!"

* * *

WHEN Master Lin had said he was going to work the class hard, he had not been kidding. An hour later, sweat-soaked, tired bodies mumbled and grumbled and wandered out into the street in search of cars to carry them home to nice soft beds.

Before she realized it, Phoebe was again left alone with her flirtatious teacher. Dropping to the floor right where she had stopped, she stared at the ceiling and tried to catch her breath. One kick was interesting, but twenty or thirty repetitions were murder on lazy Americans. What did he call all those horrible kicks? Godmother's kick, invisible, side, tiger, leopard, rooster. Was he teaching a class or training an army? The last time she had this much sweat on her body was fifteen years ago stacking hay in a neighbor's barn in the middle of July. She never thought she would find anything harder than putting up hay in the Oklahoma heat, but this was worse. Much worse.

Master Lin sat on the floor beside her and nudged her leg with the toe of his suede boot. He pulled the elastic tie off his braided hair and shook out wet, black strands. Even he had broken a good sweat tonight. "See? I told you we'd work hard. You did very well. But don't push yourself. I don't expect you to keep up with the college boys."

Phoebe raised a skeptical eyebrow.

"Okay," he admitted with a shrug. "I can't keep up with them, either. Strength and stamina alternate as we age. They can run longer, but I'm stronger. It's a different kind of endurance. You learn to use chi to your advantage."

"How?" Intrigued, Phoebe tried to remember everything she had read on the concept of *chi* and personal energy fields, or *auras* as some people called them.

In a lighthearted gesture, Master Lin poked a finger in her ear. "Slow down. You'll burn up your mind. You're very smart, but you waste chi. Chi is energy. You must learn to focus it. Use it. Pull it from your environment. We're very powerful creatures. Spiritual beings with great knowledge. But most of us have forgotten." He tapped her forehead with the tip of his finger. “You must remember.”

Phoebe closed her eyes and took slow, deep breaths. What she remembered was making love beside that astral lily pond.

“Stop that, or I may be fallible tonight,” he warned. “Don’t tempt me, Phoebe.”

Her eyes opened and a chilly rebuke rolled from soft lips. “Stay out of my head and you won’t be tempted.”

“Use your chi, and I won’t be able to get in your head.”

Phoebe knitted her brows and issued a quiet, feline growl.

As if in response, one panel of overhead fluorescent lights popped and went dark.

“Now stop that.” Master Lin sounded like a father scolding a child. He got to his feet and frowned at the ceiling lights. “Those tubes are expensive.”

“I’m sorry.” Phoebe stood and brushed the dust from her damp uniform. “Light bulbs hate me. And batteries are worse. You know, the little AA’s and AAA’s that go in clocks? If I so much as look at them, they don’t work.”

“Too much electromagnetism.”

“What?”

He shrugged. “Chi.”

“Oh, darn. And here I thought it was magic.” Phoebe was flirting. She knew it, and she knew that he knew it.

“Magic?” Wearing an evil grin, he moved close enough to press his firm abdomen against the points of her breasts. “Like the lily pond?”

Phoebe stepped back and rethought her newfound boldness. “I’m going to go. You look a little too fallible.”

“More than you know.” With a hard focus in his eyes, Master Lin moved toward her.

His expression caused Phoebe to retreat. With every step she took backward, Master Lin took an even longer one forward. It was an intense dance that did not stop until Phoebe felt a cold wall at her back. Her heart raced as she realized he had maneuvered her out of the practice area and into the office.

Glancing to her left, she noted the stairwell that led to what undoubtedly was an upstairs apartment. Maybe flirting had not been such a good idea after all. “It’s late, Master Lin. I really should be going.”

His voice washed across her face like a mesmerizing mist. “I won’t hurt you, Phoebe. You’re in no danger with me. And, please, call me Alex.” He put one palm on the wall beside her head and wrapped the other hand around her waist. His hot body pressed against hers, wet silk gliding against wet silk. The difference in height put her face under his chin and wedged his stiff arousal against her stomach.

This time it was no dream, no astral walk, no semi-conscious state. Instead of feeling trapped against the wall, she found safety in this little niche he had provided.

What Phoebe did next surprised her most of all. She slipped her hands down his back and spread her fingers across his firm derrière. That marvelous butt had tempted her since that first day in the bookstore. Sure enough. It felt as good as she imagined.

"I don't know what to do about you," she admitted, still breathless and sweaty from class.

"Do whatever you want. Or tell me what you want. Let me please you."

For a fleeting moment Phoebe found true psychic clarity, sensing his honesty, seeing his hope, hearing his trepidation, and swimming in his lust. She wanted him but thought about the consequences of unprotected sex. "Are you prepared to take this further?"

"I had hoped." He laid a wet kiss on her forehead and rolled his hips in one undulating move that raked his groin across hers. "Yes. I have what you mean upstairs. Do you want to go upstairs with me?"

Phoebe looked up at his handsome face framed by all that rich black hair. Her hands moved around his chest and flopped over his thick neck. The tip of her tongue traced the curve of his ear, and her breathing almost sounded like a cat's purr.

"I take that as a yes," Alex whispered. Pulling her off the ground, he wrapped her knees around his waist.

He took one step toward the stairs. Then the shade on the front door rattled.

* * *

"HELLO! Anybody home?" a male voice called.

Alex stepped into the practice area and stared at the sandy-haired man standing just inside the front door.

Wearing a polished social smile, the man approached and offered his hand. "Sam Tillman. Saw the lights and figured you were still open."

Alex knew perfectly well that Sam Tillman was Jack's office manager. To keep Sam from seeing Phoebe, Alex hurried across the room. He accepted the outstretched hand and clamped down just to make a point.

"Easy there, buddy." Sam winced and pulled free. "It's a greeting, not a challenge. Are you the master?"

"Yes."

Cocking his head to one side, Sam gave a cold stare. "Have we met before?"

"All martial artists look alike."

"That's a good one." Sam's tone changed from sarcastic to demanding. "I was looking for Phoebe Henderson."

"Class is over."

Sam glanced around the empty room. "I can see that, but her car is still in the parking lot. Did she leave with someone? Go eat or something?"

Gold eyes darkened to a menacing reddish-brown. In an aggressive move, Alex stepped inside that two-foot circle most Americans consider their personal space. "I don't know why you're looking for Phoebe, but I'd be very upset if anything happened to one of my students."

"Calm down, buddy." Sam backed toward the door and pulled a business card out of his shirt pocket. He laid the card on one of the wooden benches. Something made him pause. When he straightened, he wore a peculiar smirk. A nudge from his elbow pushed open the door. "Phoebe's a friend of mine. I have every right to make sure she's okay. If she needs any help, have her call my cell-phone. The number's on the card. And by the way, buddy, you get more business with a smile."

Wearing a flat expression, Sam spun around the door and let it slam shut behind him.

"Same to you, buddy," Alex growled and picked up the business card. Then he realized what had made Sam hesitate. Phoebe's monogrammed gym bag and old moccasins were stuffed under the bench.

Tapping the card against his thigh, Alex turned the door sign to Closed and switched off the lights. From relative darkness, he watched Sam climb into the shiny sports car. The engine roared to life, and the lights came on. Through the glare of headlights, Alex saw Sam using a mobile telephone. In a couple of minutes the red car backed out of the parking space. Tires squealing, it rocketed out onto the busy street.

* * *

SHIVERING more from fright than cold, Phoebe sat halfway up the darkened stairs. She knew Sam Tillman was nothing more than Jack's faithful lackey.

Soft footsteps approached. Alex's broad form blocked the light bleeding in from the office below. "He's gone."

Pulling her knees to her chin, Phoebe offered a brief explanation. "Jack probably sent Sam to check up on me. It's a long story. I have to get out of here."

Alex climbed the stairs and dropped one knee on the step beside her. "Sam saw your gym bag and shoes under the bench."

"Great. He'll tell Jack for sure."

"I think he already did. He used the car phone before he pulled out."

"Then I'm toast." Hot tears found their way down Phoebe's pink cheeks. Nobody could look at Alex and not know he was Native American. Sam would tell Jack, and Jack would blow his lid. Again. "You don't understand. It's a complicated situation."

Long fingers brushed stray hairs out of her face. Alex's voice flowed like a soothing balm. "Phoebe, listen to me. Leave the bag and the moccasins. If Jack asks, tell him you forgot them. Do you have another pair of shoes with you?"

"I keep an old pair of sneakers in the trunk for emergencies. But Sam saw my car. How do I explain that?"

"There's a cafe across the street. Just say you went to eat after class."

Phoebe took a few deep breaths and realized she had finally stopped shivering. "It sounds logical. The CIA could use you."

Gold eyes sparkled and a smile warmed his face. "Probably in more ways than one. Come on. I'll make you some tea, and you can tell me your life's story."

"I really should go."

Alex's jaw was set in implied stubbornness, and his voice remained firm. "Come upstairs and talk to me. Trust me. It'll be okay. Come on."

There was nowhere for Phoebe to go but up the stairs and into his apartment. A few minutes before, this modest abode had held the promise of ecstasy; now all she could think of was hiding from Jack and Sam.

A single light shone from the kitchen, illuminating the red silk partition. She scanned the modestly decorated room and noted incense burning in the dormer at the opposite end. Grabbing a quilt from the futon, Phoebe curled up in the chair, while Alex rattled around in the kitchen. Through the red partition, he looked like some netherworld alter ego moving gracefully behind kindred golden leopards.

Soon the tea kettle sang its high-pitched song. After a moment, Alex walked into the main room and set a tray on the carpeted floor in front of the chair. Phoebe watched a curious process. First Alex washed the tiny teacups with hot water. Then he steeped tea in a small iron kettle. In a moment he poured each of them a cup and handed one to Phoebe.

She took the cup, noting the delicate bamboo pattern painted on fine bone china. Raising the cup to her lips, she looked over the rim and waited for him to drink first.

The sparkle in those gold eyes proved Alex was pleased. "We drink together."

Phoebe followed his lead and took a sip. The tea was warm and aromatic, filling her nostrils with soothing steam.

Setting the teacup in front of him, Alex stretched out on one side and propped up on an elbow. "Tell me about Jack."

Startled, Phoebe sputtered as a little tea rushed up her nose, making her eyes water and her ears hot with embarrassment. Alex's panther persona became more vivid as he reclined on the floor, wearing sweat-stained black-silks and looking up with glowing golden eyes.

"What about Jack?" she replied evasively.

"I want to understand the situation. I tried to ask you about it the other day, but all you said was Jack is your brother-in-law and your husband died six months ago. Tell me what's going on, Phoebe. Maybe I can help."

Phoebe took another sip of tea, this time in a more dignified manner, not choking or sputtering like an idiot. "Well, as I told you, my husband, Danny, was Jack's younger brother. They were very close, and not just because they were only a few years apart. They did everything together. Well, actually, it was a threesome. Jack, Danny, and Jack's army buddy, Sam Tillman. Danny was a partner in the family business, Northwest Properties. It's a real estate firm mostly, but Jack dabbles in oil leases and political contracts. If there's a way to make money, Jack can find it. Danny was really just along for the ride."

"You loved your husband," Alex observed, propping his head on his hand.

"Yes, I did. Maybe not as much as I should have. But, in my own way, I did love him. Danny was a good man and, for the most part, he was good to me. We enjoyed each other. He had his faults, but don't we all?"

"What about children?"

Cradling the teacup in her hand, Phoebe offered a momentary frown. "We wanted children, but Danny was sterile. Measles in college. It happens. Anyway, when he talked about adopting, Jack volunteered his 'services' so the child would be a true Henderson. Bloodlines are very important to Jack." Phoebe gave a visible shudder. "But the thought of having any part of Jack inside me, I don't care if it is just a gift in a cup, was more than I could handle. I declined Jack's offer and that was the end of that."

"You don't like Jack very much, do you?"

"Never have," Phoebe spat in a forceful voice and downed the last sip of tea. "Don't suppose I ever will."

"So why is he living with you?"

"Because he's a jackass." Phoebe set the teacup on the carpet. Settling into the big round papasan chair, she bundled the blanket around her and regretted the harsh tone of her voice. There was no reason to snap at Alex. "Sorry."

"No need to apologize, but I would like an answer."

"After Danny died I found out Jack co-owned the land the house was built on. I don't know how property laws work in other states, but in Oklahoma that means Jack also co-owns the house. Always did, I guess, but Danny never told me. I found out at the reading of his will."

"That must have been quite a shock."

Phoebe nodded. "But not as much as seeing Jack walk through the kitchen with his luggage. I had just gotten home from the lawyer's office when Jack started moving in. He plopped a contract on the snack bar and told me to sign and get out of *his* house."

"What kind of contract?"

"A buyout on my half of the property. My house."

Alex stretched his legs and readjusted his propped-up arm. "I understand it's your home, but is it worth all this misery? Why not take the money and start new somewhere else?"

"It's not that simple. There's a reason I can't leave, not yet anyway." Phoebe felt those gold eyes boring a hole to her soul.

"And the reason?" he persisted, like a man determined to solve a puzzle.

Phoebe hated to leave him hanging, but she was not yet ready to talk ghosts and riddles and promises with a man she hardly knew. A few minutes ago she had been ready to share his bed, yet she was not willing to share her pain. It was ironic and, she supposed, a little sad.

Sidestepping his question, Phoebe changed the subject. "Why a lily pond?"

"Leopards at the lily pond," he explained and pointed over his shoulder.

Looking past him, she spied the red silk partition with its golden lily pond and dancing leopards. "Oh, I see."

"Do you enjoy the lily pond?" Alex asked in a sensual purr.

Well, Phoebe had done it again, flirted when silence would have served better. Now she had to face the consequences. She could have tried to wiggle out of an awkward moment by changing the subject again. Instead, she gave an honest answer. "I used to have nightmares. Now I have the lily pond."

Agile as the dancing leopards on that red silk screen, Alex got to his knees and grabbed the sides of the chair, trapping Phoebe where she sat. His voice found a hypnotic note. "There's more to the dream. A stream feeds the pond and a small waterfall feeds the stream. For years, I've dreamed of a beautiful woman in a red silk dress. That woman is you, Phoebe."

She could not break away from his intense gaze. "I don't understand."

"You will." He washed her face with breath that smelled of jasmine tea. Leaning forward, he pressed his lips to hers. The kiss began as a sweet exchange, but passion quickly replaced tenderness. Alex's hands moved from the chair and tugged at the folds of the blanket.

Overwhelmed by the depth of her own passionate response and a little frightened of his, Phoebe pulled out of the kiss. Regret put a rasp in her voice. "It's late. I really have to go."

* * *

TWENTY minutes later Phoebe tiptoed across the breezeway and inserted her key in the kitchen door.

The deadbolt popped back with a distinctive click, and the knob turned easily in her hand. She opened the door and slipped into the lighted kitchen. The door closed without a squeak. She dropped a bag of donuts on the snack bar and headed toward the sink. The kitchen clock read 9:15 p.m. Jack's sedan was in the garage, and Sam's sport car was parked out front. She knew they were waiting for her.

Muted conversation filtered down the main hallway, and she saw lights on in the office next to the den. A tall figure appeared in the dim hallway and walked toward her. In a couple of seconds Sam's face moved into the light. Still wearing the day's business suit, he slid onto one of the barstools and dropped his elbows on the snack bar.

Phoebe quivered inside, but her outer composure remained intact. "Where's Jack?"

"On the phone with California." Sam offered an evil smirk and kept his voice low. "I dropped by your class about an hour ago."

"Really? I must've just missed you. I walked over to that little cafe across the street." The lie rolled easily off her tongue. Too easily. She nodded toward the bag of donuts and her voice carried believable nonchalance. "How about a pot of coffee to go with those?"

"Sure. Coffee would be great."

It took Phoebe only a minute to load the coffeemaker. When she turned, she found Sam staring at her old sneakers.

Scowling, he pulled a plain cake donut from the sack and caught the crumbs on a napkin. To say Sam was compulsively neat would be an understatement. "That master of yours is a hard-nosed son-of-a-bitch," he commented, his blue eyes narrowed for effect.

It takes one to know one, echoed in Phoebe's mind.

The coffeemaker grumbled and threw steam.

"Coffee's ready," Sam announced with a mouthful of donut.

Phoebe took three mugs from the cabinet and noticed a box of tea bags on the second shelf. Jasmine tea. It was a reminder of how close she had come to consummating her relationship with Alex. If Sam had not interrupted, Alex would have carried her up those stairs and she would have made love to him.

There had been no reason to lie. She was a widow and had every right to see any man she chose. She had lied because she was afraid of Jack. Afraid he might fly off in a fit of anger and find some legal loophole to throw her out of her home. She could not keep her promise to Grandma if that happened. In the back of her mind she whispered a tiny plea for help.

What am I doing wrong, Grandma? Please, talk to me. Tell me what I'm supposed to do.

It was going to be a very long night. Exhausted both mentally and physically, she poured the coffee and wished it were tea.

* * * * *

CHAPTER 11
Partnerships

"WAKE up, Phebes!" echoed across the master bedroom.

Groggy, Phoebe threw back warm covers. She shaded her eyes from the ceiling light and rubbed life into her sleep-numbed face. Annoyance added an additional coat of hoarseness to her voice. "What time is it?"

Jack straightened his tie. "Five-o-four."

"In the morning?" Phoebe complained amid a deep yawn.

"Yes, in the morning. Get up. I need you to take me to the airport."

Phoebe rubbed her eyes and sat up in the bed. "How about Cape Kennedy? You can catch the next moon shuttle."

"Cute. Just get your clothes on. You know I hate to leave my car out there."

"Yeah, I know. Just give me a few minutes to brush my teeth and find some coffee." Last night Phoebe had visited with Sam as long as it seemed necessary, then she went to bed. A moment ago, Jack's clear voice jerked her away from the astral lily pond and her favorite two-legged panther. Hearing the word *airport*, however, was worth the interruption. "You were on the phone with California a long time last night. Problems?"

"Nothing I can't handle," Jack answered with a flip of his wrist. "I have to fly to Los Angeles. I may be gone a couple of weeks."

Something one of Phoebe's cousins used to say in lieu of Amen at family reunions rang in the back of her mind: *Hallelujah! And pass the salt!* Before drifting off to sleep last night, she had wished for a little time alone. The first thing she learned this morning was that Jack was leaving town.

Sometimes wishes do come true.

Her eyes took on a glassy satisfaction that camouflaged for sleepiness. "Is Sam going with you?"

"No, it's just me. If you have an emergency, call him. He'll know how to contact me. I might wind up in San Francisco before it's all said and done."

"If you do, bring me some chop sticks from Chinatown."

A rare thing happened. Jack offered a genuine smile. "You're a cheap tourist, girl. I can handle chopsticks. Let's call it a truce for a couple of weeks. What do you say?"

"It's a deal." She did not like Sam being left to spy on her, but two weeks without Jack was two weeks of heaven.

***

JUST after seven a.m., Phoebe pulled the car under the loading zone awning of Will Rogers Airport on the southwest corner of Oklahoma City.

She took the car out of gear, depressed the emergency brake, and looked over at her well-dressed, clean-shaven brother-in-law. Despite years of drinking and carousing, Jack still fell into the *handsome* category. All Phoebe could see, however, was the greedy beast trying to steal her home.

Before they left the house, he had fussed about her blue jeans and flannel shirt, but Phoebe refused to change. She saw no reason why she had to dress up just to drive him to the airport. A yawn added a rosy glow to her tired face. She knew Jack well. He was so organized, so methodical, so calculating. It would be hilarious if he actually forgot something.

"You have everything?" Phoebe asked in a mocking voice. "Tickets? Credit cards? Cash? ID? Notebook? Files? Did you check your list?"

Unruffled, Jack pulled a small notepad from his inside jacket pocket and gave it a quick scan. "Everything is checked off." He hesitated and glanced over at Phoebe. There was something odd in his expression. Something lurked in the back of those cold gray eyes, and a hint of menace rode the wave of his voice. "Nothing has changed. This is just a temporary truce. Don't forget that."

As cool and crisp as the September air, Jack opened the door and got out of the car. He dragged the luggage cart out of the back seat and wheeled it onto the curb. Looking nervous for some undisclosed reason, he glanced toward the terminal's tinted glass front.

Curious, Phoebe leaned across the passenger seat and stared out the open door. Through the expansive glass on the north side of the airport, she saw a leggy dark-haired woman in tight blue dress. It was Jack's *tart* from the restaurant. Dressed like a knit-wrapped morning snack, she had a fur coat slung over one arm and two suitcases at her feet. So, Jack was not traveling alone, after all.

"Jack?" Phoebe called with an evil lilt.

He poked his head back into the car. "What?"

"Have a good time."

For a moment, Jack offered a look that could best be described as perplexed. Then in a smooth coordinated movement, he straightened and shut the door.

Phoebe considered waiting in the loading zone, just to see what he did inside the terminal.

A horn honked from behind and an airport employee glared through the passenger window.

She put the car in gear, released the emergency brake, and inched forward. The lane curved just enough to let her see the terminal through her rearview mirror. Jack entered the airport and in polished nonchalance pulled the cart past the tart, which promptly grabbed her suitcases and followed him toward the ticket counter.

Another honking horn reminded Phoebe to watch the road and forget about Jack, at least for the next two weeks.

* * *

SITTING at a table in one corner of the bookstore, Twyla looked up from a stack of used paperbacks. "You're grinning like a 'possum. Oh, my God. You killed him, didn't you?"

Phoebe put a finger to her lips and pointed to the customers browsing at the other end of the store. "Keep your voice down, silly. No, I didn't kill him. I did the next best thing."

Twyla tried to whisper, but her laser-sharp voice was so clear it would almost slice glass at twenty yards. "Which is?"

"I put the bastard on a plane to California."

A wicked smile spread across Twyla's face. "How long do you have?"

"Two whole weeks." Phoebe held up two fingers in triumph. "But I have to watch out for Sam. Jack told him to check up on me. Poor Sam. He'll never be anything but Jack's lackey. It's a shame. Basically, Sam has a good heart. He's like this big kid running around without parental guidance. Why he listens to Jack, I'll never understand."

Twyla's long fingernails drummed out a good war song on the back of an old book. For a moment she looked lost in thought. Then her face glowed with mischief. "Well, if he gives us any trouble there's always Muskogee."

"Sometimes I don't know whether you're kidding or not." Phoebe quickly changed the subject. She sat on the corner of the desk and lowered her voice. "I have a plan. It's risky, but it might work."

"Tell me."

"I learned something very curious after Danny died. It seems that old Martin Henderson willed a fourth of the business to a man named A. L. Jones. I tried to get some information out of Genny, Jack's secretary, but the woman just plain hates me. Always has. Anyway, she did tell me the paperwork for this other partner is sent back and forth from an office in Sedona, Arizona."

A strange expression tugged at the lines of Twyla's finely sculpted face. "How can this partner help you?"

Leverage."

Twyla leaned her elbows on the high stack of worn paperbacks. "How so?"

"The way I figure it, Jack might be more willing to negotiate if he thinks I have an ally. Sam likes me, but he won't go against Jack. If Jack gets mad enough, he'll fire Sam. I know it and Sam knows it. I don't care if they have been friends for twenty years. Sam won't stick his neck out for me, but maybe this A. L. Jones is somebody I can deal with. Of course, it isn't going to be easy tracking down someone named Jones, especially in the Southwest." Phoebe paused, remembering that was also Twyla's surname. "No offense, but it's as bad as looking for Smith or Johnson."

"How are you going to find this man?"

"I'm having lunch with Rachel. She's going to let me use her computer at work. I don't want Jack backtracking any email records from the house computer. You know how he is. Anyway, I have a list of businesses to query in the Sedona area. I'm going to get on the Internet and see what I can find."

"Just be careful," Twyla warned.

A pained expression drew lines on Phoebe's lovely face. Her hands twisted the long handle of her small purse. Making sure no one else could hear, she whispered across the stack of dusty books. "Last night I almost did something a little careless."

"With whom?"

"Alex—uh, Master Lin."

Twyla leaned back in her chair, eyes wide in undisguised surprise. "And how did that *almost* happen?"

Blushing, Phoebe felt like a teenager caught necking in the back seat of a car for the first time. The truth carried delicious wickedness that was hard to regret. "It just did. After class, we were alone. He was flirting. I was flirting. It got a little dicey for a few minutes."

Twyla folded her arms across her ample bosom and pursed her lips. "Well, that was fast."

"I don't know anything about him, except he's gorgeous and he smells good. He could be an ax murderer for all I know."

"Phoebe, what does your heart say?"

"My heart says slow down and get better acquainted. My body says trip

Alex and beat him to the ground. What I should do is probably somewhere in between." After a long pause, Phoebe slid off the table and gave Twyla a pat on the back. "Got to run. Rachel's waiting."

* * *

PHOEBE figured she had a couple of days before Sam started to interfere, so everything she did not want Jack to know about had better be done today. Since she was already at the shopping center, she might as well see Alex while the sun shined and her resolve remained intact.

Leaving the bookstore and its tinny doorbell, Phoebe walked toward Lin Martial Arts. The closer she got, the faster her heart raced. By the time her fingers wrapped around the silver door handle, she panted as though she had run a mile. Determined, she stepped inside and let the door rattle shut behind her.

The scene that greeted her stole what was left of her breath.

Clad only in an old pair of red sweatpants, Alex ran through one of the weapons forms. She had learned that the lance in his hand was called a kwan-dao. Seven feet long from steel tip to wooden shaft, Alex wielded the sixty-pound weapon as easily as Phoebe carried her purse. In a moment he reached the end of the form, gave the traditional bow, and replaced the kwan-dao in its niche on the weapons rack.

Alex turned and wiped sweat from his eyes. "What's wrong?"

Phoebe remained outside the practice area. "Nothing. I was down here running errands, so I thought it was a good time."

He walked over and sat on the sturdy waist-high railing. Sweat glistened across his rippled chest. That single braid of black hair was pasted to his neck. His expression suggested tenacity. His rich voice carried a rough edge. "If you're going to say good-bye, I don't want to hear it."

Phoebe reminded herself that only those golden shades and one pane of clear glass separated them from anyone who might be watching from the parking lot. She was tempted to brush stray hairs out of his eyes, but kept her fingers locked around the small purse. Her gaze followed beads of perspiration that trickled down the center of Alex's chest and pooled on the waistband of his sweat pants. Sweat-soaked red material clung in places that were hard to ignore, especially now that she had a pretty good idea what he kept under there.

After a long pause, Phoebe took a cautious step forward. "Jack caught a plane for L.A. this morning," Phoebe informed him with composed delight. "He'll be gone a couple of weeks."

Alex tilted his head and stared down one flirtatious eye. "Then all you have to worry about is me."

The implication was received and understood. Phoebe raised an eyebrow. "I would be more comfortable if we slowed down a bit. Last night was a little reckless, if you know what I mean."

A smile softened his masculine features. He rolled one shoulder and shook the braid loose from his back. Standing, he leaned his fists on the railing and looked her straight in the eyes. "Okay. We'll slow down, but I won't give up the lily pond."

Nose-to-nose with what she sensed was one of the most dangerous things walking on two feet, Phoebe felt a shiver run up her spine. Alex would keep his hands to himself, but the dream-walks would continue. "It's a deal."

Grinning, he straightened and took a short step back. "Class tonight. Seven o'clock. Don't be late."

"I'll be here."

* * *

PHOEBE took a sip of cold coffee and winced.

She had not realized she had been sitting in front of the computer that long. The corner of Rachel's private office was cozy although a little stuffy. Notes and pens and candy bar wrappers fought for space to the left of the computer keyboard.

"What time is it?" Phoebe asked, scowling at the mess she had made.

From across the room Rachel looked up from her paperwork. "Almost two."

"Two o'clock?" In response, Phoebe hastily gathered her notes. "Why didn't you say something?"

"Don't worry about it. You're not in the way. Did you find anything?"

"A little," Phoebe replied. A quick shuffle created a neat pile of handwritten notes and printed pages. "I have a few leads. I sent out a couple of email queries. If I get any responses, they'll come back here. I hope that's okay. I'm afraid to have them come to the house."

"No problem. Maybe this Jones fellow will be the answer to your problems."

"I hope so," Phoebe replied with a hint of mental fatigue. "I'm ready to get on with my life."

Rachel rocked back in the chair, showing a generous proportion of shapely legs. "I've been thinking. When you get this mess with Jack straightened out, maybe you should invest in a business of some kind. Why don't you talk to your friend Twyla? Perhaps you could open a bookstore like hers."

Phoebe stared at Rachel's reflection on the computer monitor. "How much seed money would a venture like that take?"

"I don't know. Twyla's the one you need to talk to." Rachel tapped the desktop. "You haven't told me the latest about the panther."

"Alex," Phoebe said in a breathy voice. "He's like something out of a dream I can't completely remember."

"Alex? Since when are we on a first name basis?"

Phoebe felt the heat of a tell-tale blush. "Since last night."

"You're not telling me everything, are you?"

"Nope." Phoebe stuffed the stack of notes into a manila folder and got to her feet. Her old blue jeans and flannel shirt looked out of place next to Rachel's navy pinstripe skirt and jacket. "I better get out of here before your boss shows up."

"What about the fair? How about next Wednesday?"

Phoebe had always loved the Oklahoma State Fair, one of the biggest in the country. Just the thought of cotton candy, fresh corn dogs, and the mandatory double Ferris Wheel brought a big smile. "It's a date."

* * *

STEAM filled the small shower stall.

Alex put his hands on either side of the faucet and leaned into the stream. Hot water pounded his thick chest, washing suds down his hard body and past a throbbing erection. He took a deep breath and focused on the water. Years of training had nurtured a tremendous cache of kundalini, that primal energy flowing from the root chakra at the base of the spine. The same energy that empowered his kung fu, however, also enhanced his sex drive. Sometimes knowledge was a double-edged sword.

With a groan he dropped his forehead on the wall beneath the faucet and let cool water cascade down his muscled back. Last night replayed in his mind. He could almost taste Phoebe's sweet tongue in his mouth. He could still feel her silk-covered breasts rubbing against his chest. He shivered, recalling how her breath caressed his neck. They had been so close to what they both wanted, with her long legs wrapped around his back and her arms draped over his neck. Then Sam rattled the front door. Afterwards, if Phoebe had understood the depth of Alex's desire, she might not have gone upstairs with him. She might have been afraid and probably should have been.

Huge hands balled into granite fists, but Alex resisted the temptation to pound the wall. He could punch right through smooth tile and thin sheet rock as easily as ripping through paper. The situation would be less difficult if he gave up those sensuous dream-walks by the lily pond, but he just could not bring himself to abandon such perfect private moments.

When Phoebe left his apartment last night, he wondered if she would have the courage to return. Seeing her walk into the building morning had been a great relief. It proved she still trusted him. But would she trust him when she learned the truth?

A familiar voice swam through the roar of the water, vaulting his mind back to the here and now. He turned off the faucet, opened the plastic shower door, and wrapped an old towel around his waist. Dripping water with every step, he walked out of the tiny bathroom and stopped in the middle of the apartment.

"Hello, Aunt Tea."

The epitome of cool stoicism, Twyla placed a small telephone on top of the television. She looked at the towel wrapped around him. "Anything you'd like to tell me?"

"Not really."

"Did I see Phoebe duck in here a little while ago?"

"I don't know? Did you?" Mindful of the towel, Alex curled up carefully in the papasan chair.

"You're not going to tell me, are you?"

"Nope."

"I think you have a problem." Twyla's tone of voice was as serious as the expression on her face.

"I assume you mean more than the obvious."

"Don't get rude with me, boy." Twyla folded her arms over a thick bosom. One moccasin tapped the floor in obvious agitation. "Phoebe has decided to locate A. L. Jones and use him to make Jack negotiate on the house."

Alex laughed softly. "She's a smart woman, isn't she? And a little devious. Intelligence is so damned sexy."

"Think of something besides sex for a minute," Twyla scolded. "What are you going to do about this?"

"Nothing. The paper trail on A. L. Jones is not that easy to find. But I'll be careful just in case." Alex nodded toward the small telephone sitting on the top of the television. "I assume that means you called the phone company."

"They'll be here Friday, so you can stop using my phone." An odd expression settled onto Twyla's face. "I never wanted to lie to that girl, but it just couldn't be helped. When this is all over, I hope Phoebe understands.

Yell if you need me."

Without the formality of good-byes, she turned and padded softly down the steep stairs.

"I hope she understands, too," Alex muttered after his aunt was out of hearing range. His gaze settled on one of the old trunks sitting near the stairwell.

Climbing out of the chair, he walked over and unbuckled heavy leather straps. The lid lifted with a distinctive creak. Inside there was a jumble of things, from clothing and books to sashes and silks. He took out a ragged shoebox held together mostly by gray tape. The trunk closed, snapping like the jaws of a cranky crocodile.

Alex curled up in the chair again and stared at the box in his lap. After a moment, he peeled back just enough tape to remove the worn-out lid. The scent of cedar filled his nostrils. He pushed aside a dried cedar sprig and dug through a stack of old letters. Bold script printed at the top of the stationery spelled out Twylight Bookstore.

He pulled one letter off the top of the stack, carefully unfolded it, and read in silence: "Greetings from Oklahoma. Thanks for sending the snapshot. You have grown up to be such a handsome man. You look just like your grandfather. It's so good to hear from you. I never get in front of a loaded camera myself, so instead I've enclosed a picture of a nice Cherokee girl I know. Her name is Phoebe. She's not only lovely, but a dear as well. She takes care of her great-grandmother, Gray Owl, was an old teacher of mine. A medicine woman of some repute. She's very old and won't live much longer. I'm learning what I can from her and encouraging Phoebe to do the same. When you come back to Oklahoma, I'll introduce you to Phoebe. But don't wait too long, or someone else will come along and pick this pretty peach. Stay in touch. Peace and much mischief, Aunt Twyla."

Alex flipped over the letter and looked at the faded snapshot taped to the back. With a mane of auburn hair flying out in the wind, a beautiful nineteen-year-old girl stood at the base of a Ferris Wheel. He had received that letter eleven years ago. The desire and enchantment he felt the first time he looked at that picture remained just as strong today. This sweet spirit dancing in the Oklahoma breeze continued to live in his dreams, appearing as a vision of passion wrapped in a red silk dress.

Eyes clouded with unshed tears and strained to focus on the next letter in the stack. He did not need to read it again. The words remain seared in his aching heart. "You waited too long. Danny Henderson just picked your peach. Phoebe married Danny. I tried to talk her out of it, but I know why she did it. Danny has money, and Grandma has been very sick."

Danny has money, and Grandma has been very sick....

Alex growled to drown out the echo in his mind and stuffed the letter back into the shoebox.

It was a persistent ten-year-old pain. No amount of meditation or hard work or even plain old whoring had ever been able to numb the instant love he felt for Phoebe. Last night he had wanted her so much. Just to lay with her, to be joined with her in a way that transcended mere physical contact, consumed him now that they were in the same city.

Alex had planned to come to Oklahoma City, hoping to forge a relationship with the recently widowed Phoebe. There was, however, another reason. Inside sources had hinted that Jack was into questionable, if not illegal, business deals. Alex had to find out what Jack was up to without putting Phoebe in additional danger.

The thought of that son-of-a-bitch Jack Henderson living in the same house with *his* Phoebe brought a burst of fury. It would have been so easy to kill Jack the other night. Alex could have shoved that nose up into the bastard's scheming brain. Maybe next time he would.

*****

CHAPTER 12
Cats & Dogs

BY the time Alex dismissed class Friday night, Phoebe was drenched with sweat. Even the college boys moaned and groaned in exhaustion.

The last three days had been wonderful in one sense, uneasy in another. Yesterday, she and Twyla had discussed Phoebe either opening her own bookstore or investing in an existing one. Twyla's exact words had been, "Why in the world didn't I think of that?"

It was a shame neither of them had thought of it years before. Phoebe could have been financially established by now. Another one of Grandma's old sayings sprang up in the back of her mind: *Everything arrives in its own time.* The idea came when it was time for it to come. No sooner. No later. There was no use fretting over what might have been.

Phoebe leaned against a bare spot of wall and glanced at Master Lin, at Alex. Like the notion of the bookstore, he also had shown up right when she needed him. Despite the fact she had been alone in that big house since Wednesday with no one to watch her coming and going, he remained a perfect gentleman, not even asking for an invitation. A couple of times in class he had put a hand where it did not belong, but no one else seemed to notice. Then every night, as soon as her head hit the pillow and her eyes closed, he met her at the lily pond. To each delicious astral encounter, he brought something new and different. It was like having a private sexual candy store.

She was so focused on how the wet black silk clung to Alex's sensuous long legs that she failed to notice Sam Tillman standing just inside the door.

"Hi, Phebes!" rang through the building.

Startled, Phoebe pushed from the wall. She knew Sam would be checking on her but hoped he would not come back to her class. Over her shoulder, she observed Alex's normally stoic expression change into something dark and menacing. Something had to be done before those two bulls initiated some inane head-butting ritual.

Stepping into Alex's line of sight, Phoebe turned and bowed. Nonchalantly, she walked out of the practice area and located her gym bag. Somehow her voice found a perfect carefree pitch. "Hello, Sam. Haven't seen you all week. Anything wrong?"

Sam's gaze remained fixed on the grim-looking master, who now sat on the waist-high railing within easy reach of Phoebe. "No. Just thought you might like a little company for dinner."

"All I have is jeans and a sweatshirt. I guess we could do pizza, if that's okay?"

Sam fondled her long braid of wet auburn hair, a gesture that inferred intimacy. "Pizza is fine. I thought you might need a little company."

"And you need a life," she blurted without thinking first. There was no way out of this and Phoebe knew it. It was part of the game and she had to play it carefully. Exhaustion camouflaged her half-hearted attempt at a smile. Pulling out her car keys, she threw the strap of the gym bag over her shoulder and gestured toward Alex. "Sam, this is Master Lin."

Anger pinched the nerves in Sam's taut jaw line. His terse response was nowhere near friendly. "We've met."

"Oh, yeah, that's right," she intoned in an absent lilt and immediately wished she had kept her mouth shut. When all else failed, she usually deferred to the airhead bimbo mode. That always worked with men. "Goodnight, Master Lin. I'll see you Tuesday. Have a good weekend."

Alex's resonant voice filled the room. "Be careful driving home."

On her way out the door with Sam at her heels, Phoebe glanced back. Gold eyes literally glowed red. Any jealous man could be dangerous, but an out-of-control martial artist could be downright frightening.

* * *

WEARING old jeans and an oversized sweatshirt, Phoebe pulled one foot up onto the padded seat and tried to look comfortable. Sam had insisted on this shadowed booth in the back corner of the pizzeria. She was not sure what he had in mind, but the amount of beer he had drunk did not bode well.

Sam pushed the pizza tray toward her. "Finish it off. You're too thin, girl. We need to put some meat on your bones."

"Yeah, right," Phoebe muttered, but she did take the last fat slice of pizza. Class always left her starving and thirsty.

"Phoebe, there's something I want to talk about. And I'd like it to remain between us."

"Okay."

Sliding closer to her in the booth, Sam offered a serious, albeit slightly drunken expression. "I know Jack's been a little rough on you lately."

Phoebe stared at Sam's partially shadowed face and wished she could read his mind like Alex could read hers. She doubted Sam knew how *rough* things really had gotten. "Well, you know Jack."

"Too well, unfortunately." Looking a little nervous, Sam ran his finger around the edge of his beer glass. "Don't sell him the house, Phoebe. Not yet, anyway. Give me a little time first."

"Time for what?"

Sam's tone of voice carried a hint of anger. "He shouldn't have moved in with you like that. It wasn't right. I know the land belonged to his family, but Danny built that house for you. Let me talk to Jack. Maybe I can convince him to move out. If he'd just clear the title on a few surrounding acres, that might be enough to keep peace."

"Do you really think Jack wants peace?"

"I'm not sure what Jack wants." Sam poured himself another beer. "He has control of the business now. That should be enough."

Phoebe took a risk. "What about Jones?"

"What about him?"

"That's what I'm asking you. I didn't even know he existed until after Danny died. Does he ever come to the office? What's he like?"

Taking another gulp of beer, Sam shook his head. "Never met the man. A. L. Jones is one subject Jack won't talk about."

"How does he do business with a partner he's never met?"

Sam shrugged. "Everything is done through the mail. A paper trail is all we have on this guy. That and an address in Sedona, Arizona."

"Why doesn't Jack buy him out?"

"Jones won't sell. He gets a nice cushy profit-share and all he has to do is sign a few papers now and again. It's a sweet deal."

Phoebe agreed. It was a sweet deal. It was the same deal she and Danny used to have. "Jack likes to be in control, doesn't he?"

"Jack has a nose for business, and that's good for my bank account. I just don't want him to put you out on the street. It isn't fair. It isn't right."

"I appreciate that," Phoebe offered with pinched sincerity. For a second she thought she could hear an echo in the back of Sam's mind, a non-verbalized addendum to his last statement: *It isn't right...but I'm not going to say that to Jack.* It was obvious even Sam was afraid of Jack Henderson.

* * *

PHOEBE walked out of the restaurant.

Her stomach grumbled in undetermined protest. Either she had eaten too much pizza too soon after exercising or Sam's company just did not agree with her. At least the weather was nice. Stars shined in a velvet sky, while a soft breeze stirred cooling air into a pleasant evening soup.

When they reached Phoebe's car, Sam circled like a coyote on the prowl. Before she could open the door, he put a hand on the glass and used his body to trap her against the side of the car. "Are you sure you're safe out there alone in that big house?"

Phoebe's voice was as stiff as her body. She winced at the alcohol on his breath. "Obviously, safer than in this parking lot."

"Am I interrupting?" rang a deep voice. Clad in his usual black jeans and shirt, Alex sat on the hood of Sam's red sports car and folded muscled arms across his chest. It was an aggressive posture.

Stepping back into an empty parking space, Sam looked like the proverbial fox caught with a mouth full of chicken feathers. "No. Just saying goodnight. What're you doing here?"

"The same thing you are." The reply was as enigmatic as the expression on Alex's face.

Sam's mouth twitched. "And what might that be?"

"I'm hungry. I am allowed to eat, aren't I?"

"That depends on what you're hungry for," Sam countered, each word sounding a little nastier than the one before it. "And that car is worth more than most houses. So I'd appreciate it if you wouldn't park your ass on it."

Wearing a menacing smile, Alex got up and walked toward the car. He stopped within easy reach of Phoebe and backed against the rear fender.

Sam curled his fists at his sides. "Listen, you irritating bastard. I've had just about enough of you."

One finger raised in warning, and Alex's eyes flashed in the odd half-light. "Don't."

Phoebe had not moved. She had been relieved when Alex appeared, but now she was worried for Sam's safety. A little drunk, a little reckless, and too egotistical for his own good, Sam could get himself killed in this parking lot if he did not find the good sense to back down.

Before Phoebe could think of something clever to break the tension, Sam did the most stupid thing he could. Rocking back in a fighting stance, he curled both fists and threw an ax-kick. His right foot moved straight up and sliced down at a sharp angle. All he connected with, however, was the cool night air. By the time Sam saw he had missed his target, he was staring nose-to-nose with a polished martial artist who had merely stepped out of the way of a well-executed kick.

"I warned you not to do that," Alex said in a forced hush. "If you can drive, get in that red sardine can and go home. If you're too drunk, I'll drive you. Either way, you're going to leave Phoebe alone. Now, back up."

To his credit, this time Sam made the wise choice. He uncurled his fists and performed a careful retreat. Backing around the car, he mumbled a few curses but made no other aggressive moves. After a moment to straighten his clothes and realign classic composure, he offered a deceptive smile. "I'm worried about you, Phebes. I don't know this bastard and I don't trust him."

Looking over the top of her car, Phoebe came to Alex's defense. "Well, I do trust him, Sam. It's okay. Really. He isn't going to hurt me. Are you all right?"

"Yeah. I guess I had a little too much to drink. I didn't mean to startle you. I'm fine. I'll call you tomorrow." Sam pulled his keys from his pocket, unlocked his car, and slid into the leather bucket seat. Without further conversation, he started the engine, dropped into first gear, and gunned it. The little red rocket threw dust and gravel, as it pulled forward across the parking lot and bounced onto the four-lane street.

As soon as Sam's car was out of sight, Alex handed her a small piece of paper. "Here's the phone number at the building. They just turned it on this afternoon. You left before I could give it to you."

"You could've given it to me over the phone."

"But I can't give you this over the phone." Alex leaned down and planted a firm, wet kiss on her lips, holding the connection just long enough to wrap his tongue around hers. In a moment he straightened, licking his lips and offering a devilish grin. "I'm still hungry. I guess pizza will have to do. Call me if Sam gives you any trouble."

Phoebe hesitated. Her eyes drifted down Alex's solid frame and paused on the swell at his crotch. For a second, temptation tugged. Sam was, no doubt, halfway across Oklahoma City by now. He would not bother her again tonight. That big house was just sitting empty out there on the prairie. She could take Alex home with her and no one would know.

In her typical honesty, Phoebe spoke when silence would have served better. "It's gets harder and harder to say goodnight to you."

Gold eyes twinkled, and a closed smile gave the illusion of youth. Alex stepped back. "Goodnight, Phoebe. Drive carefully."

* * *

AROUND two a.m. and under the light of a quarter moon, Alex parked Twyla's dark blue four-wheel drive within walking distance of Phoebe's locked front gate.

After getting out, he put a finger in each corner of his mouth and gave a shrill whistle. With surprising grace, two Rottweilers piled out of the back and hit the ground. Huge feet made little sound on rough gravel.

Alex walked up to the long gate with the huge brass "H" soldered to its center. He grabbed the top rail and easily vaulted over it. Old sneakers hit the ground with just the fraction of a skid.

He snapped his fingers. "Kiki! Elsa! Up!"

In unison, both dogs backed up and then sprang, clearing the gate in one nice leap and sliding to a controlled stop.

"Good girls," he whispered and gave each dog a reassuring pat. His fingers snapped again and he slapped his leg. On cue both dogs filed to his left and followed him up the long, winding driveway.

He had brought the dogs with him from Sedona, partly because he thought they would prove useful but mainly because he just could not stand to leave them behind. Since the kwoon was too small for these furry behemoths, he had stashed Kiki and Elsa at Twyla's house.

The cool country air smelled good. The close, waxing moon gave adequate light. Red cedars grew in clumps between looming pecan trees. Short, tenacious blackjack oaks jutted from the prickly underbrush. Somewhere in the distance, a whippoorwill offered a lonesome serenade, and crickets added to the song like thousands of tiny back-up singers. The land felt warm and alive through his old sneakers.

At the last turn in the long private road, the huge house came into view. Small lights outlined the manicured shrubs lining the driveway. Gray rock enwrapped the bottom level of the rambling ranch-style home. Dark shutters framed the second-story windows. To Alex the house looked like a huge spotted dragon asleep on the rolling prairie, a dragon he was about to invade.

After one tour around the outside of the house to make certain everything was in order, he stepped into the breezeway. Snapping his fingers again, he pointed to the center of clean flagstone. "Stay."

Kiki and Elsa ambled across the breezeway, circled each other once, and then lay down. Big brown eyes watched as their master took Twyla's duplicate key from his pocket, opened the kitchen door, and entered the darkened house. In a minute he returned with a plastic bowl of cold water.

"Good girls," Alex whispered before stepping back inside and easing the door closed.

An amber nightlight near the kitchen sink strained to add useful illumination. Old sneakers lightly kissed plush carpet as Alex made one methodical security check of the lower level. More amber lights created a dim golden haze through the formal dining room, down the long hallway, around the enormous main living area, and through the deserted den.

Satisfied that all was in order, Alex made his way up the back stairs. At the top he halted, his large sneakers sinking into the carpet.

A silvery-mist took shape in front of the master bedroom. In a few seconds, the figure of an old woman leaned against the closed door. Arms folded across a calico-covered bosom, and diamond eyes seemed to bore a hole through space and time.

Alex offered his palms in gestured peace. *I'm not here to hurt her, Grandmother. May I pass?*

The old ghost gave a good impression of a sigh before fading out of view.

Alex reached for the door. It was closed, but not locked. The brass knob turned with a quiet click. He eased the door inward and stepped into the bedroom.

Moonlight filtered through the thin curtains that veiled glass balcony doors. Soft breathing emanated from the enormous bed. Smiling, he took comfort in the soft breathing. Somewhere in that tangle of covers and fat pillows lay Phoebe. Long hair painted an auburn stain across a pale pillowcase, and the smell of *Musk Rain* oil filled the warm room.

Alex squatted beside the bed and ran a hand along Phoebe's sleeping form. A contented moan rose from the covers. He leaned over and located an ear.

"Shh," he coaxed, stroking her shoulder, measuring a trim waist, massaging a firm hip. The moment for him was so intense, he switched from English to Mandarin and then back again in a random mess that nobody could have deciphered. "I am here, my pretty. Follow the stream. Come to the waterfall…."

He backed up and sat in the center of the room, long legs folded in front of him lotus fashion. Closing his eyes, he threw back his head, took a few deep breaths, and then ventured into the astral realm.

* * *

PHOEBE moaned. Vague awareness of her body on the bed evaporated as the lily pond came into sharp focus. Barefoot and wearing nothing but that same red silk oriental dress, she approached the edge of the lily-covered pond and waited for the panther to spring out of the water.

Instead, a deep voice called in the distance. "I am here, my pretty. Follow the stream. Come to the waterfall."

She looked across the small pond and for the first time noticed the narrow stream that fed it. A warm breeze filtered through looming trees, their leaves shimmering overheard like millions of emerald stars. Water trickled inch-deep over a bed of pebbles and sand.

And follow the stream she did. Her bare feet sank into the sponge-like grassy bank as she moved deeper and deeper into the dense forest. The voice beckoned once more, so she pulled up the dress and stepped into the stream. Sand and smooth pebbles squished between her toes. Cool water rushed over her ankles. She forged on, following that sensual, familiar voice.

Low branches closed in, forcing her to duck beneath them. When she straightened, she found herself standing in the shallow end of a jade-colored pool. At the other end, water cascaded in a broad blue sheet from a rock ledge nearly twenty feet above the pool. Mist rose and hung in the air, trapped in place by the thick forest canopy. Everything was bathed in a greenish glow.

A man stepped through the waterfall. Standing naked in waist-high water, he smoothed back long black hair and wiped water from bright gold eyes. Moisture clung to muscled shoulders and glistened on thick arms. He gave a hungry smile, and motioned her forward.

Without fear she waded into deep water. The silk dress clung to her and felt heavier with each step. Finally, she met her lover in front of the waterfall. He pulled her close, pressing silk-covered breasts against his bare chest, burying his hands in her long hair. Their lips found a perfect fit and his hot tongue coated her mouth with sweet jasmine. His musky aroma blended with the swirling mist. Just below the water line, she felt his arousal pushing against the dress. His hands moved across her breasts, hesitating for a moment. Then long fingers unfastened the frog loops, one by one, until the dress slipped off of her and floated across the water like a red stain.

Her arms dropped over his neck, and her knees wrapped around his waist. Their eyes met in unblinking drunken lust as he pushed his arousal deep inside her. For a moment, both shuddered at the joining. The sound of the waterfall added natural rhythm, fueling their collective passion. At first, his hips rolled in long, slow strokes. Then his rhythm and intensity increased. Water lapped up around them, keeping perfect syncopation. Techniques alternated, and animal urges escalated for what seemed like hours. In simultaneous climax, her fingers buried in his hair as his hands gripped her hips. One final thrust brought their flesh as close as possible. He held her in a rigid embrace, emptying body and soul inside her....

* * *

BREATHLESS, Phoebe rolled over in the bed and threw off the covers.

Her eyes opened to narrow slits.

The room was a darkened blur. She thought she saw Alex sitting on the edge of the bed, but believed his image was just more of the same dream. She felt long fingers stroke her face, while that hypnotic voice wooed her back to sleep.

* * *

WITH a long yawn and outstretched arms, Phoebe awakened to a strange noise. Deep-throated howls pierced the morning calm. She stumbled out of bed, untangled her cotton nightshirt, and walked to the balcony doors. The western horizon was alive with brilliant mauves and blues. She was on the wrong side of the house to see the sunrise, but imagined it was just as spectacular. Again, a canine chorus echoed from somewhere below her room.

After wiping sleep from her eyes, Phoebe climbed into last night's jeans and sweatshirt, slipped on her sneakers sans socks, and headed for the bedroom door. The knob refused to turn. She did not remember locking it last night. After unlocking it, she opened the door and headed down the back stairs.

The persistent howling was loudest in the kitchen. Without hesitation, Phoebe opened the breezeway door.

"What the—" The rest of the sentence dissolved in her mouth, as she stared down into two sets of huge brown eyes. Whining replaced howls, and bobbed tails wagged.

"Well, hello there." Immediately, Phoebe was met by cold noses and wet tongues. The huge dogs pushed and shoved until they managed to get into the kitchen. "Oh, for Pete's sake. Don't drown me."

She grabbed cloth collars and tried to herd the enormous dogs back toward the door. They refused to leave the house. No doubt, each outweighed her by at least thirty pounds. She figured the only way she was going to get them outside was to go with them.

"Come on! Come on!" Phoebe cajoled, stepping into the breezeway. To her surprise, the dogs just sat on the kitchen carpet and considered her with huge eyes. "Now, really. This is ridiculous."

Frowning, Phoebe went back into the kitchen and inspected the dogs woven collars. Someone had written their names in bold letters. The heavier dog was Elsa. The leaner one was Kiki. "Well, Elsa, Kiki, you girls look a little lost."

Brown eyes blinked and bobbed tails thumped the carpet.

"How about I find some coffee and make a few phone calls? Let's see where you girls belong. In the meantime, maybe I can find you something to eat."

Phoebe nudged the door closed and prayed those behemoths were housebroken.

* * *

PHOEBE spent all morning and most of the afternoon trying to find out to whom these beautiful dogs belonged. She called every neighbor she knew, but nobody had lost any Rottweilers.

Finally, she loaded the dogs in the back of Danny's old truck and drove to the feed store a couple of miles away on the county line road, where she posted a handwritten "lost dogs" notice in the front window.

While the hefty clerk wedged a 100-pound sack of dog food into the passenger's side of the pickup, the store's owner admired the Rottweilers sitting politely at Phoebe's feet on the fine gravel. "If nobody claims them, I'd be happy to take them off your hands. They'd make good watchdogs for the store."

"We'll see. Thanks." Phoebe realized she was already becoming attached to her new companions. She slapped the tailgate. "Kiki, Elsa, up!"

On command both dogs leaped into the back of the truck, long claws scraping red-painted metal.

The feed store owner tipped back his ball cap. "On second thought, maybe you need them worse than I do."

Phoebe shut the tailgate and waited for the metal echo to subside. "What do you mean?"

"I worry about you out there in that big house. I hope nobody comes looking for those dogs. They'll keep you safe. Besides, you'll be needing a lot of dog chow, and that's good for my business. Take it easy, Phoebe." With a wave, he walked back into the store.

Once again, fate had provided for her. Phoebe pondered the coincidence, wondering why those dogs had chosen to land on her breezeway the same night after she had trouble with Sam. Grandma would have called it an omen and told her to be careful. Thinking that was probably good advice, she decided to do just that, be careful.

After making sure the dogs were camped contentedly in the back of the truck, Phoebe climbed into the driver's seat, ignored the strong smell of dog food, and started the engine.

* * *

IT was a short drive back to the house, three or four miles of two-lane blacktop at the most. When Phoebe reached the gate, she found it already open.

A chill ran down her back. It could be Jack home early enough to witness the dogs scratching up the back of Danny's truck. Or worse, it could be trespassers. There was only one way to find out. She eased through the open gate and drove up to the house.

The mystery was solved by the sight of Sam Tillman's red sports car.

Relieved, Phoebe stopped near the garage and killed the engine. As she got out, she spied Sam's sandy-haired head bobbing out of the breezeway.

"Hi, Phebes," he began with a sing-song voice and walked toward the pickup. "Is something wrong with your car? Why are you out in this old thing?"

Without warning two enormous dog heads popped over the side of the truck bed.

Sam's mouth fell open and his blue eyes widened. "Holy shit. Where the hell did they come from?"

"They just showed up on the porch this morning." Interpreting the look in Sam's eyes, Phoebe offered a word of warning. "You know, dogs can smell fear. I really don't think you should—"

Too late. Before Phoebe could finish the sentence, Sam made a run for the little red sports car with Kiki and Elsa in swift pursuit. Sam managed to open the door and slam it just in time.

Elsa pressed her wide nose to the driver's-side window, showed long fangs, and growled from the depths of hell. Each deep breath fogged the glass. Kiki circled, rearing up on her hind legs every once in a while and showing off a nice set of teeth. It was a good thing the little car was a hardtop and not a convertible, or Sam might have been dog chow.

"Call them off!" he yelled through the glass.

After Phoebe collected her wits, she sprang into action. "Kiki! Elsa! Sit!"

Smooth as silk, both dogs dropped their hindquarters to the gravel. Growls continued to emanate from thick throats and fangs glimmered in the sunlight, but the dogs stayed put.

Phoebe walked to Sam's car and was careful not to get too close. She was not quite sure how to handle trained attack dogs. *Sit*, *come*, *stay*, and *up* were the extent of her expertise. If she said or did the wrong thing, they might decide to open that little car and dismember its ashen occupant.

"Gee, Sam, I'm sorry," Phoebe apologized, scratching her head. "I fed them, now they're kind of protective."

"Kind of?"

Elsa emitted another long growl in response.

"Yeah, right back at you, bitch," Sam muttered under his breath. He raised his voice toward Phoebe but did not take his eyes off Elsa's ivory fangs. "I wanted to apologize for last night. I guess I got a little drunk. Sorry about that. I was just worried about you."

"About me?"

"Yes, you. I don't trust that son-of-a-bitch martial artist of yours. I was afraid he might follow you home or something."

Phoebe looked properly surprised. "Master Lin? That's silly. He's just protective. You know, like the dogs."

"Well, he doesn't need to protect you from me."

Obviously, he does. Phoebe shoved her hands in her back pockets and offered a shrug. "Was there anything else you needed?"

"No. Are you sure these monsters are safe?"

"The dogs? Oh, yeah. They love me."

"All right. Well, call if you need anything." Frowning, Sam started the car, revved the engine to back up the dogs, and then drove toward the gate.

Phoebe heard Sam's tires squeal on the oily blacktop country road and waited until the gate offered a distant, distinctive clang, indicating it was closed and locked.

She looked down at the dogs. "Good girls. That'll take care of Jack's little spy."

*****

CHAPTER 13
Fair Weather

THE next Tuesday in the corner of a quaint sidewalk cafe, Jack took in the sights and sounds and smells of San Francisco's Chinatown. The last time he was in California, he sat at this very table. Then it had been Phoebe's face looking across at him, not Erin's. That day, almost three years ago, Danny had gone deep sea fishing while Jack and Phoebe had done the tourist thing.

His thoughts slipping back to the present, Jack sipped cooling coffee and grinned as Erin attempted to eat fried rice with blunt chopsticks. She was making a terrible mess but enjoying the effort. Phoebe, on the other hand, wielded chopsticks like a professional. Jack reached inside his blazer and readjusted the long slender package hidden in a deep pocket. As requested, he had bought Phoebe chopsticks with a Chinatown logo stamped on them. The package and ribbon cost more than the gift, but it was what she had requested. Erin, however, was still collecting jewelry, clothing, shoes, and trinkets of every description. He had already determined Erin's "stuff" would have to be shipped back to Oklahoma rather than toted on the airplane.

It was a beautiful afternoon. Jack loved the odd smell of the fall coastal air. In truth, this trip to San Francisco was pure pleasure. He had finished his business yesterday morning in Los Angeles. Then he and Erin caught a quick flight north to celebrate. If Phoebe were here, she would have wanted to snoop through the used bookstores in Berkeley. But Erin was content to sip wine in the hotel, have sex all night, and shop until she dropped.

Erin's sweet, sultry voice broke the easy mood. "Let's get married."

"Say what?" Jack had not expected this so soon.

"You heard me." Big brown eyes narrowed. "We're good together, Jack. I have a degree in business with a minor in computers. I like socializing. I'm only twenty-three, so we could spend a lot of time alone before worrying about kids."

"Kids?" Jack dumped lukewarm coffee into his mouth and swallowed hard. His mind whirled like an Oklahoma tornado, throwing dust and debris in its frenzied path. "Don't you think that's moving a little fast?"

"Well, what did you have in mind?"

"I had in mind to take things a little slower. My brother just died six months ago, and I've got to work out things with Phoebe."

"What things, Jack?"

"The land. The house."

"Just buy out the bitch," Erin said with a flip of her wrist.

Annoyance shifted into full-scale defensive anger. Jack did not like to be questioned. "It's my business, and I will deal with it."

Pouting at the rebuke, Erin pushed aside her plate. "I'm not hungry anymore."

Jack knew it was time for a little damage control. He reached across the table, taking Erin's small brown hand in his large tan one. There was a slight hiss to his voice, as if the cobra intended to charm the flute. "Come on. Let's take a walk."

* * *

SEVERAL hours later, back at the hotel, the telephone rang at a most inopportune time. Jack muttered a particularly foul curse, rolled off Erin's exquisite naked body, and grabbed the trim receiver.

Impatience gave his voice a sandpaper rasp. "Henderson, here."

"Did I interrupt anything?" Sam's voice barely pierced a bad telephone connection that crackled and popped like grease in a hot skillet.

"Yes, but nothing I can't finish." Jack sat on the edge of the bed and pressed the receiver to his ear. "What's up?"

Sam coughed up a coarse laugh. "Now that's a setup if I ever heard one. Everything go okay in L.A.?"

"Smooth as silk," Jack moaned, running a hand over Erin's luxurious bare thigh. "Everything all right back home?"

"The office is fine, but—"

"But what?"

"Well, I'm a little worried about Phoebe."

Jack did not like the sound of that. "How so?"

"For one thing, she picked up a couple of stray dogs. Rottweilers. The nasty little bitches nearly chewed my ass off. I thought I should warn you."

Jack dipped his fingers between Erin's thighs. He wanted her to concentrate on him, not the telephone conversation. "Noted. And the other thing?"

"I took Phoebe to supper last Friday. Picked her up after her martial arts class. You haven't met her teacher, have you?"

It was not Sam's words but the tone of his voice that piqued Jack's interest. "No. Why?"

"Well, let's put it this way. He isn't some nice eighty-year-old grandfather. This is a big buck in the prime of life. He's Native American. Maybe a little oriental, too."

"What are you saying?"

"It looks like Phoebe is pretty enamored with this guy. He's good-looking and a class-A ass-kicker. I'm worried about her, Jack. She's a pretty young widow with a big house and the appearance of money, if you know what I mean."

"Yeah. I have a pretty good idea. Keep an eye on things."

"My pleasure. I don't want to see anyone hurt that girl," Sam half-yelled over the bad telephone connection.

Without offering a response, Jack slammed the receiver onto its base. He grabbed a short, fat glass and emptied fiery whiskey into his mouth. If anyone was going to take advantage of Phoebe, it was going to be him, not some half-breed interloper.

Erin's hot hand snaked around his waist and dipped to his crotch. "Something wrong, Honey-Jack?"

Lying back on the rumpled bed, Jack stared at Erin's reflection in the mirrored ceiling. Tan legs contrasted white satin sheets and firm breasts undulated with every breath. After a long pause, he transformed nervous energy into cold lust. "Nothing for you to worry about. It's just business. Climb aboard, kitten. I want my dessert now."

* * *

THE next morning just before nine a.m. Sam raised his head from a mound of paperwork and focused on a voice filtering through the open office door.

He stepped into the main bay and found a familiar face. "Phebes! This is a pleasant surprise."

Phoebe handed a stack of mail to Genny, Jack's executive secretary.

"Thanks," Genny mouthed with cool disinterest.

Sam, however, was very interested. His eyes drifted down Phoebe's sweatshirt and tight jeans. Casual attire on a body that was anything but casual. "How about lunch?"

"Thanks, but I can't. I have to meet Rachel in a few minutes. Actually, I'm running a little late." Phoebe headed toward the elevator and pushed the Down button.

Sam followed. "Wait. Where are you off to in such a rush?"

Shiny silver doors parted and Phoebe stepped inside the empty cubicle. "The Fair."

The doors closed, leaving Sam with a response wilting on his tongue. He considered trying to catch her but thought better of it.

"Damn," he muttered, and gave the elevator a shallow kick. Spinning on the heels of expensive loafers, he bellowed across the office. "Genny! What's my last meeting today?"

Unruffled by the outburst, Genny thumbed through the appointment book. "Dinner with Harold from the Chamber of Commerce at six-thirty."

"Cancel it."

* * *

AT the north gate of the enormous state fairgrounds, Phoebe asked the attendant for the time: 10:28 a.m.

The day was overcast and a little cooler than normal, but the air was alive with excitement for anyone who wished to sample the energy. Phoebe loved the Oklahoma State Fair.

Near the north side of the space needle, Rachel sat on a concrete retaining wall, sucking down hot coffee and getting more cinnamon roll on her than in her. She watched the observation ring slowly turn, rise, and fall the full length of the structure, giving its occupants a panoramic view of the expansive fairgrounds.

"Where's mine?" Phoebe called over the roar of the crowd and the mish-mash of music.

"Right here, and you're right on time." Rachel pointed to a lidded foam cup and a cinnamon roll the size of a saucer.

Smiling, Phoebe sat beside Rachel and joined the feast. "This blows my diet for the entire week."

"Does that mean you don't want a corn dog later?"

Phoebe brushed cinnamon and sugar from the front of her sweatshirt. "Don't be silly. Where to first?"

"International building," Rachel announced, getting to her feet.

Phoebe made short order of the pastry and finished the coffee. Then she followed Rachel around an outcropping of red-striped tents and past a set of fountains that had not worked for at least ten years.

Just ahead, the oval inflatable dome-shaped roof of the international building undulated high above them. With Phoebe in tow, Rachel pushed her way through the crowd and into a long, narrow foyer. As usual, there weren't enough revolving doors to accommodate the people, but a little persistence got them inside.

The interior of the International Building seemed so much more spacious with that domed roof. Vendor stalls filled both sides of six long aisles. It was a buyer's feast, providing everything from Oriental incense to Native American jewelry. Great fun to browse through, it was a catchall of unusual items with a good dose of cheap.

Down the third aisle, Phoebe lingered at a stall selling colorful blankets. She ran her fingers across woven llama's wool and could not help but smile at what she psychically perceived.

"Be careful," a familiar voice warned.

Startled, Phoebe pulled back her hand and looked over her shoulder. It was Alex. The air around her was filled with his intoxicating scent. He was clad in black, from shirt to jeans to dusty canvas sneakers. Those gold eyes beckoned. Memories of lovemaking under that astral waterfall skipped through her mind like hummingbirds flitting from flower to flower, lingering only long enough to drink of sweet nectar.

He snaked an arm around her waist and slid close enough to look over her shoulder. "Lots of energy on that blanket. An old woman sitting at a loom with the sun at her back."

"That's what I saw. Why did you tell me to be careful?"

His face lowered to her ear, and his deep voice tumbled inside her head. "This seller can see what you're doing. Be a little more discreet in here."

"Oh. I hadn't thought of that." Phoebe understood his caution. Most of the vendors in this building were not typical Anglo-Americans, who eschew the extra senses like bad smells on a calm day. No, these people came from the Orient, from South and Central America, India, and Indonesia. They hailed from cultures that openly discussed spirits and reincarnation and the energies of nature. They noticed the spiritual nuances western culture simply ignored.

Phoebe caught herself staring at Alex. He had such a handsome profile. She shivered at the warm energy passing between them. It was a private moment hiding in a public place.

"I think you're horning in on my date." Rachel's big brown eyes danced with mischief. She put her hands on her trim hips and stuck out her jaw.

In response, Alex wrapped his other arm around Rachel. "Actually, I thought the two of you were *my* dates."

Rachel stared back in cool consideration. "Think you can handle both of us?"

"If not, I will die a happy man." Alex offered a feral smile.

"What do you say, Phoebe?" Rachel asked. "Shall we let him tag along?"

Weaving her fingers through the long warm ones tugging at her waist, Phoebe leaned into his muscled warmth. "I say we keep him. Anyway, we'll be safe for sure."

"For sure," Rachel echoed and let her expression turn serious. "And won't people talk."

Alex planted a soft kiss on Rachel's forehead. "Where shall we go first?"

* * *

THEY did all the buildings. The last one they came to was the Modern Living Building or, as Phoebe had called it as a kid, the *signing-up building*, because it was filled with merchants hawking their latest products through contests and prizes.

It was one long switchback aisle. Once inside, there was no way out but forward or backward. This was where the corporate sellers congregated, hawking their latest wares and inventions, offering raffles and free chances on everything from sewing machines to encyclopedias.

Phoebe watched Alex handle the crowd. Smooth and quiet, he proceeded like a gentle plow moving snow out of its path. His long black hair hung loose about his shoulders. It drew evil glares from ruddy-faced farmers and admiring drools from their well-fed wives. All Alex had to do was grin and every woman within twenty feet turned bubble-gum pink. Sometimes he looked to be the tallest person in the crowd. Other times he was hard to distinguish. Like a chameleon, he blended with his surroundings. More than once, he had to peel a lost child off his leg and hand it through the air to some distraught mother. His magnetism and easy charm spilled on everything and everyone in his wake, including Phoebe.

She knew full well Alex did not have a clumsy bone in his body. Yet every time she paused to inspect a display, he tripped into her, his hips sliding against hers, his quick hands touching her in private places. If Phoebe drifted too far ahead in the thick crowd, a long finger dipped into one of her jeans pockets and jerked her to a stop. It was a delicious game.

Just as they reached the center of the immense building, thunder cracked and the lights flickered. Phoebe backed against Alex and got a good hold on his denim shirt. A storm front had teased them all day. Now somewhere in Oklahoma City lightning drained the life from electrical lines. Another round of thunder rumbled. Then all the lights in the building, from ceiling panels to blinking displays, shuddered once and died. Rain pounded at the metal roof.

A large hand tilted up her face. In the relative darkness, all she could see was Alex. Black hair framed the exquisite contours of his face as he leaned down. She welcomed his hot tongue in her mouth, but kept her ears trained on the crowd.

A child cried, and a mother's voice worked its tender balm.

Two men discussed the particulars of power transformers.

Someone sneezed and received a quiet, "God bless you."

A clear female voice whispered, "Will you look at that?"

Another woman responded, "Look at what?"

"Shh! I'll tell you later. Come on."

Alarmed, Phoebe pulled out of the kiss just as the lights flickered to life. She scanned the cheering crowd, but did not find a familiar face.

"Someone you know?" Alex whispered in her ear.

"I'm not sure. She was probably just jealous."

For the first time Phoebe realized Alex was just a trifle shy. Her comment brought a flush to his cheeks. An involuntary smile splattered across his face.

"Oh, he's cute when he blushes," Rachel teased.

Alex flipped back thick hair and gave a fierce frown. "I never blush."

"You don't lie either." Rachel raised an eyebrow, as if daring him to object.

One gold eye narrowed in menace, and his head cocked in mock warning.

Rachel waved her hand in arrogant dismissal. "Oh, please. You'll have to do better than that to scare me."

His expression softened. "Really? Like what?"

"My grandfather is a medicine man. You want a good scare? Go with him into the sweat lodge. That'll give you more than a few gray hairs."

Phoebe allowed a subtle grin. "Rachel, I think you shocked him."

"Just putting things into perspective," Rachel offered over her shoulder and moved on through the crowd.

Admiration was evident in Alex's expression. "She's really something, isn't she?"

Phoebe nodded. "Rachel's the best. Sometimes I wish I were half that brave."

"How so?"

"She is what she is. Blunt and honest. Right now she doesn't even have a boyfriend."

"Maybe she should look for men instead of boys."

Phoebe wondered for a second if he was kidding, but decided

otherwise. A twinge of jealousy sharpened her words. "Did you have anyone in mind?"

"No," he answered quickly and put a hand on her shoulder. "I just meant that she's very mature. She might get along better with someone a little older and wiser."

The conversation dug at her conscience. Rachel never put aside the teachings of her ancestors just to please the entrenched society, but Phoebe had. Perhaps that was why Grandma's pipe called out to her, even now in this busy place.

Alex brushed a hand through her long ponytail and massaged the back of her neck. "You hide twice as much power as Rachel will ever have."

"I know," came a quiet admission. "But—"

He saved her from having to say it. "But your husband forbade you to practice your medicine. Now Jack is applying the same pressure."

"And you're encouraging me," she said

There was more than just a difference in color between Jack's eyes and Alex's. Jack's gray eyes reminded her of a frozen lake, harsh and demanding and unsympathetic. Alex's eyes resembled faceted amber, old and wise and born of Mother Nature's bounty.

Grinning, Alex dropped his arm over her shoulder and blinked in bold flirtation. Before either of them could think of something clever to break the tension, Rachel's sharp voice pierced the crowd.

"Come on you two! The rain's stopped, and I want to see the midway."

* * *

EVENING came much too soon.

Rachel paused in front of a local television station's booth and noted the time. "Well, guys, it's been fun, but I've got to pick up the kids. Their grandmother is probably pulling out her hair by now."

Phoebe looked at Alex then back at Rachel. The only thing better than an afternoon at the fair was a night at the fair. But if she stayed alone with Alex and someone saw her, Jack was bound to find out and start another fight. She, however, did not want this perfect day to end.

Before Phoebe could speak, Alex made the decision for her. "We'll stay. Rachel, do you want me to walk you to your car?"

"No, I'm parked just outside the north gate. Right on the front row." Rachel gave a tentative smile and hesitated. "Phoebe, are you sure about this?"

Phoebe noted the unspoken plea radiating from Alex's warm eyes. "You know how I love the Ferris Wheel at night."

"I hope you know what you're doing." Rachel turned her attention from Phoebe to Alex. "It's been a pleasure. Take good care of her."

He winked in reassurance. "Be careful going home."

"Well, you two have fun and try to stay out of trouble." Rachel hesitated, checked her watch again, and then headed toward the north gate.

Alex slipped a huge paw around Phoebe's waist. "Shall we?"

A tickle of panic fluttered in Phoebe's stomach as Rachel's slender dark-haired form disappeared in the thick crowd. "Where to?"

"The Ferris Wheel, of course."

* * *

THE midway bristled with hucksters and buzzers and cotton candy and blinking lights. Parents kept close watch on their children, big and small. There were lots of baby strollers crowding the aisles and toddlers with leashes buckled to their tiny wrists. Gaming booths sported all kinds of paraphernalia, from jewelry to stuffed animals.

Above dozens of striped tent awnings, Phoebe saw the Ferris Wheel adding color to the cloudy night sky. Then she focused on something much closer. To her immediate right, a huge stuffed black panther with bulbous gold eyes swung on a booth hook.

Wearing a closed smile, Alex stepped up to the booth and pointed at the panther.

The game attendant opened his mouth to begin his usual ritual, but appeared to think better of it. He clamped his jaws shut and took a more reserved posture with this particular customer. Holding up five fingers, he pointed to the basket target at the back of the deep booth.

Most of the games were set-up to make winning almost impossible. Almost. Phoebe figured if anyone could outsmart a spring-loaded basket it would be Alex. Intrigued, she leaned against the awning post and watched the master work.

Alex bought chances for five and only five baseballs. He stared at the basket and tossed one baseball in his hand. Offering a wink in Phoebe's direction, he threw the ball. It dropped in the basket, spun around several times and did not pop out. One down. He gave the attendant a stern look. It was an unspoken warning not to mess with that basket or remove the ball. Then he threw again. Two, three, four, five, in rapid succession. The balls tumbled around each other like popcorn in a cooker. One ball sneaked up the side but lost momentum and fell back in submission.

"What's the lady's pleasure?" the attendant asked with a deflated shrug.

Grinning, Phoebe lifted the stuffed panther off the hook, wrapped her arms around soft black fabric, and looked up at her handsome champion. "Thank you."

"You are welcome, Dragonfly." Alex smoothed back that unruly auburn ponytail and bent down, poised for a kiss.

Phoebe's eyes opened wide, and she pulled back just before their lips connected. It was risky enough kissing in the dark in the Modern Living Building, but pawing each other on the midway was a recipe for social suicide as long as Jack remained in the equation.

Disappointment pinched Alex's response. "Right."

Breathing a deep sigh, Phoebe hugged the stuffed panther. "Ferris Wheel?"

"Yes." Something spicy lurked in the corners of Alex's smile. He wrapped an arm around her waist and dipped one mischievous finger into her front pocket. With just a tug, he pulled her into the flow of people.

Navigating the crowded midway was more difficult with that enormous stuffed panther in her arms, but Phoebe did not mind. It was her trophy. Meanwhile, the real panther kept close contact. One long finger remained in her front pocket and stroked a little too close for public comfort. The other hand roamed from her hair to her neck. His hips slid across her bottom with a familiar swoosh of denim against denim. It was the best sex she never had.

The narrow aisle soon spilled into a huge concrete expanse covered with carnival rides. Near the center stood the double Ferris Wheel, two lighted circles rotating on a long central axis. By far, it was the largest ride on the midway.

In a moment, Alex had the tickets in hand and they stood at the front of the line. Even the sour face of the ride-keeper did not dampen the mood. The wheel stopped, and the safety gate opened on a bright red basket. Phoebe sat on the left and put the stuffed panther on the seat between them. The metal door clicked shut, and the wheel moved upward in uneven increments as others got off and on below them.

At the very top, their bucket stopped, rocking back and forth with a telltale creak. A surreal view greeted them. The lights of Oklahoma City filled the horizon in uneven clumps. A little here, a little there, spreading over nearly nine-hundred plus square miles with less than half a million inhabitants. Patches of trees and prairie grass isolated islands of offices and residential areas. To the east, the high-rise buildings of downtown cut a jagged outline. Like a procession of glowing ants, headlights filled the crisscrossing interstate highways to the southeast. From below, music and conversation rose on steamy cotton-candy air.

Phoebe noticed Alex staring at her. His hand closed around her shoulder, crushing the stuffed animal between them. "Did you arrange for the car to stop up here?"

"Maybe." Alex's free hand slipped around her neck, tilting her face to meet his. Only the stuffed panther, the stars, and that huge moon witnessed their passionate kiss.

The taste of sweet jasmine tea had been lost in corn dogs and nachos and coffee, but that did not dull the sensation of Alex's tongue wrapped around hers. A huge hand caressed her neck. One dusty sneaker slipped between her feet and a knee eased over hers. A moan rumbled up his throat and tickled the inside of her mouth. Holding the stuffed animal with one arm, Phoebe's free hand slipped off the safety rail and made a brave slide across Alex's knee. Her palm stroked a muscled leg, moving toward that forbidden inner thigh.

The Ferris Wheel jerked, and the car eased downward. Phoebe pulled out of the kiss and licked her lips. "I guess the ride is over."

"For the moment," he amended. "Only for the moment."

* * *

A couple of hours later Alex walked Phoebe to her car. A varied and colorful assortment of vehicles crowded the dirt parking lot. Voices pierced the night air. Children squealed, and teenagers laughed. Adults raised their eyebrows at both.

Phoebe opened the car door and placed the stuffed panther in the passenger's seat. Without warning, Alex wrapped both arms around her and bent down, poised for another sloppy kiss.

"Wait," Phoebe warned. "There are too many people."

"I don't care." He kissed her, long and deep, his tongue probing the length of her mouth in lustful inference.

Pinned against the frame of the car, Phoebe managed to moan a vague objection. The scent of musk and rain traveled up her sinuses and acted like a narcotic to enhance her senses. Alex's body pressed against her, wedging an iron erection against her stomach. His tongue glided inside her mouth, back and forth, up and down, tickling the back of her teeth, testing, teasing. Public display be damned. This was just too good to refuse. Phoebe slid one hand up into dark hair and the other one down a muscled thigh.

* * *

SAM clenched his fists and peered around the back of a van. Chewing a foul curse, he watched Phoebe wrap herself around her martial arts teacher.

For hours Sam had wandered through the crowded fair before remembering how much Phoebe loved the Ferris Wheel. With a bag of popcorn and a draft of beer, he had camped on a park bench in front of that enormous, spinning contraption. It had not taken long. About halfway through the popcorn, he spotted them. A man clad all in black with his arm around an auburn-haired woman carrying a big stuffed panther. He had watched them get on the Ferris Wheel, witnessed their indiscreet behavior at the top, and then followed them after they had gotten off the ride.

Stalking a wary martial artist through the fair at night had reminded Sam a little bit of army maneuvers. At first it was exhilarating, but soon turned maddening. Several times he thought about approaching, but reconsidered it. In the crush of people, a good martial artist could have put Sam on his ass and walked away without anyone seeing who delivered the blow. Crowds could be funny that way. Instead, he had followed from a discreet distance.

Now in the parking lot, Sam choked on the urge to take action. Right there in front of God and everybody, Phoebe swapped spit with that arrogant, gold-digging mongrel and had her hands all over his body.

Soon the scandalous embrace ended, and Sam wished he was close enough to overhear the words whispered between two careless lovers. In a moment, Phoebe slipped into her car. The engine roared to life and the headlights ignited. In a tornado of dust and gravel, the little black car blasted out of the parking slot and was lost in a sea of red taillights.

Sam closed his eyes to let a cloud of dust roll past him. When he looked again, the air had cleared. The parking space was empty, and Phoebe's dubious "date" had vanished.

Stepping out from behind the van, Sam scratched his head. "Now where the hell did he go?"

"Where did who go?" a rich voice inquired.

He turned to find Alex leaning against the side of the van. Sam had been caught spying. "You scared the hell out of me."

"Did you enjoy the show?"

"Not really," Sam grumbled.

"You've been following us since the Ferris Wheel."

"Following? That's a little paranoid, don't you think? It's a big fair and a free country."

"Following." Alex stepped forward, closing the distance between them until they were nose-to-nose.

Sam felt heat rise up his neck and spread across his cheeks. Then a clever tactic popped into his brain. He figured a few clever, albeit misleading remarks might do the trick. "Didn't Phoebe tell you? She and Jack have an…understanding."

Cocking his head, Alex sighted down one glowing eye. "What do you mean?"

"Oh, come on. You're a grown man. You know what I mean. Phoebe's the gorgeous young widow. Jack's the handsome brother-in-law coming to her rescue. It's a perfect match. These things happen. Why don't you back off and let them work things out?

"Them?"

"Jack and Phoebe. If he knew about this, he'd be mad as hell. All I have to do is make one phone call and Jack'll be on next plane home. Think about it."

Alex's hands came out of nowhere. He locked one set of fingers around Sam's neck and the other onto Sam's right wrist, preventing a fist from forming. "All I have to do is squeeze and snap your head right off. Think about *that.* If anything happens to Phoebe, I'll hold you responsible. Understand?"

This was precisely the kind of confrontation Sam had hoped to avoid. "Yeah. I get it. Tell Jack and lose my head."

"You got it, buddy." Alex opened both hands and backed behind the van.

Rubbing his throat, Sam looked at the handprint on his right wrist and knew he was lucky to be in one piece. He glanced around the side of the van, but found no one. Alex had vanished. Again.

A little shaken, Sam made his way to his car, deactivated the alarm, and slid into the tight driver's seat. For a moment, he stared at the car phone in the center console. He considered calling Jack anyway, just to prove he had the balls to do it. Then he came up with a better plan.

Smiling to himself, he started the car and raced out of the crowded parking lot.

*****

CHAPTER 14
Harvest Moon

AROUND midnight, Phoebe sat in the kitchen breakfast nook. With a cup of coffee in one hand, she stared at the huge stuffed panther posing on the table in front of her. Beneath the table, Elsa and Kiki curled around each other in a hot, furry mound. The big house seemed to snooze in regular moans and creaks, contented with its little niche on the cedar-speckled prairie.

When had Phoebe's day at the Fair turned into a date at the Fair? What started out as nothing more than an adventure between two old friends somehow turned into a lovers' rendezvous. She had been careless and knew it. She had the right to be with any man she chose, but this business with the house and Jack was restrictive at best. As much as Jack would probably like to see her remarry in hopes she would move away, she doubted he would tolerate having Alex around very long. Jack hated Native Americans, and nobody could look at Alex and take him for anything but. In one way Alex could be her savior, in another way her downfall.

Phoebe had tried to maintain a low social profile these last few months to keep Jack reasonably sane while their battle raged. After today's performance at the fair, however, there were bound to be rumors.

Whose voice had that been in the Modern Living Building? Did anybody see the kiss on the Ferris Wheel? Were there any witnesses in the parking lot? How would Jack react to the news that she was dating an *Indian*?

Being with Alex today had been as perfect as anything she could have imagined. Had she fallen in love with him so soon? Did she even know the difference between being safe and being loved? She stroked one of the stuffed panther's perky ears. Alex had *cheated* just a little to win it for her.

A knock at the kitchen door startled Phoebe; she almost tipped over the coffee cup.

With claws clicking on clean tile, Elsa and Kiki dug out from under the table and whined for attention.

A comforting voice vibrated through the door. "Phoebe, it's Alex."

Phoebe took a deep breath, slid out of the corner bench, and unlocked the kitchen door. There in the breezeway stood Alex, a duffel bag in one hand and a grocery sack in the other.

"What are you doing here?" she asked.

"Finishing what we started." He pushed his way into the kitchen and set the brown paper sack on the snack bar.

Instead of trying to tear him limb from limb, Elsa and Kiki circled in excitement, noses in the air, big brown eyes glued to the sack. With a sharp snap of Alex's fingers both dogs sat at attention. It did not surprise Phoebe that the dogs greeted him as a friend. Alex had a way with girls.

Phoebe took a deep breath of musk and rain. Heat rose between her thighs. Her breasts perked up beneath that old sweatshirt, making her nipples stand out like bullets. In the fair parking lot, he had whispered his desire to be warm inside her. It had made her blush then, and it made her blush now.

She cleared her throat to find a strong voice. "How did you get here? I didn't hear a car."

"A friend dropped me off. I walked in from the gate." With the duffel bag still slung over one shoulder, Alex advanced on her. One hot hand snaked up the inside of her shirt and cupped a bare breast. His mouth tasted her temple then her ear. "Where's the bedroom?"

There was no reluctance in Phoebe's heart. Alex had come for a night of ecstasy. Maybe a couple of nights. Maybe more. A little dizzy with old-fashioned desire, Phoebe slipped out of his embrace and headed toward the back stairs. "Come on. I'll show you."

After commanding the dogs to stay in the kitchen, Alex followed Phoebe up the narrow stairs.

She felt his presence behind her, but his sneakers made no sound on carpeted steps. At the landing, she calmly made her way into the master bedroom. Streams of cool moonlight rained through the glass balcony doors and fell over the bed like a cosmic spotlight.

Dropping his duffel bag on the floor, Alex took a long look around the bedroom. Then he ran a hand up Phoebe's inner thigh. His voice dipped to a husky purr, and his breath steamed the back of her neck. "I'll put up the groceries and secure the house. Take a nice, hot bath. I'll be waiting right here when you're ready for me."

* * *

TWENTY minutes later Phoebe looked at her naked reflection in the bathroom mirror, hoping her body and face would not disappoint a man who could snap his fingers and have just about any woman he wanted.

She reminded herself that he had pursued her. Alex was there because he wanted to be. No one had coerced him, like that was possible. The scent of *Musk Rain* oil floated on the steamy fog created by her hot bath.

Her body had ached since Alex had kissed her goodnight in the Fair parking lot. The way his tongue filled her mouth, stroking the length almost to her throat, was just a sample of what she had been missing. Astral walks had a special magic all of their own, but there was no substitution for flesh on flesh.

From the bedroom that rich voice beckoned. "Phoebe?"

Well, there's no backing out now.

She tied a thick towel around her waist, leaving firm breasts bare and moisture soaked. With a deep breath she opened the door and walked into the moonlit bedroom.

Silvery slivers of light outlined Alex's form. He stood in the middle of the room, waiting patiently in a moonlight waterfall. A white towel hugged solid hips, and his sexual arousal was apparent. Wet black hair stuck to his neck. Gold eyes shined with inner fire. He raised his hands and toggled long fingers. "Come here, Dragonfly."

Some day she intended to ask him where he learned her Cherokee name, but not tonight. Phoebe stepped into cool moonbeams and took Alex's outstretched hands.

He pulled her close, pressing her breasts against his chest and washing her face with sweet jasmine breath. Male pheromones ignited with moisture riding the moonlight, electrifying the air with his unique scent. Slowly, he sank to his knees, slipping his mouth down her face and neck until hot lips steamed her bare breasts. Large hands explored the curves of her back, and one jerk on her towel loosened the makeshift knot. Soft cotton slid to the floor, leaving her naked body caressed only by him and the moonlight.

Phoebe's eyes drifted in and out of focus, and her body tingled with neglected desires. Burying her fingers in his hair, she tilted his face to meet hers. "I want you."

A growl rumbled from deep in his throat. Alex got to his feet, losing his towel in the process. His broad, towering form blocked the moonlight. Even in the shadows, those strange eyes seemed to glow. Pressing his hips against hers, he leaned down and slipped his tongue in her mouth.

Sliding a knee up his ribs, Phoebe reveled in the feel of flesh against hot flesh. It had been so long since she had held a man this close. And this man was more perfect than anything she could have imagined. She moaned and arched against him, feeling his arousal crushed against her stomach, sensing his anticipation, drinking from that enormous cache of primal energy.

"Enough foreplay," he whispered right in her mouth. Lifting her from the floor, Alex carried her to the bed.

Phoebe sank into cotton sheets and let Alex's hot body mold on top of her. She heard the familiar rip of foil and knew when he had the condom in place. Like the soft trill of a hummingbird's wings, she breathed a sigh.

Alex rolled his hips and joined his body to hers. He was careful at first, making sure it was not too much too soon. When everything seemed comfortable to both of them, he let his full weight fall.

For a moment they lay still, shuddering as flesh and spirit mingled. Phoebe's hands moved around his waist and settled into the curve of his lower back. He was heavy and solid, muscle coating almost every inch. His chest felt hot and smooth against her breasts. Broad shoulders covered her like a protective shield. Strands of soft hair drifted into her mouth, tickling her tongue.

Then he moved, taking long undulating strokes that rocked her hips back and forth. Over and over. Rhythm by rhythm. Minute by minute. Method by method, until nearly an hour later angle and repetition found that one spot that invoked ecstasy. Phoebe's mouth hung near his ear. Her back arched, and a staccato moan signaled orgasm with full tantric energy.

The backwash from her exploding chi hit Alex like a bolt of lightning. He tensed and groaned through a long-awaited climax.

Sinking into the mattress, Phoebe welcomed his weight. She had read about tantra, but this was her first time to experience it. Every sound, from Alex's steady heartbeat to the hum of distant crickets, was magnified and purified, as if she were hearing for the first time. Objects around the room glowed with fuzzy energy fields, some displaying bright colors, others casting mischievous astral shadows. Moonbeams appeared to dance, as if rejoicing in the moment. Time seemed irrelevant. Distance and form lost their equations. The astral blended with the physical in a delicious duality that left Phoebe dizzy. All spirit senses combined with the senses of the flesh. Making love to Alex was nothing less than physical and emotional rapture.

Phoebe smoothed his dark hair away from that chiseled face. It had been a long day. With her head on his chest, she eased the sheet and blanket over just past her shoulders.

The panther had pursued her and caught her. If she could have sent the moon to stalk the sun in order to delay the morning, she would have.

***

SHE awakened with a start and sat up in the rumpled bed. The curtains were pulled back from the balcony doors, revealing a gray morning. Lightning exploded within a ceiling of dark cotton clouds and thunder echoed. Fat raindrops peppered the glass doors. Mother Nature scrubbed down the land with a noisy vengeance. The inside of the house remained quiet, as if it were somehow acquiescent to the external storm.

Yesterday replayed in Phoebe's mind. A day of fun. An evening of tension. A night of ecstasy. Alex. She pulled up the blanket to cover bare breasts and tried to ignore the throb in her groin. Alex. The rain invoked memories of the lily pond and the waterfall. Last night had been incredible. Physical lovemaking and astral interplay entwined and climaxed in perfect unison. Not once, but three times. The last time she had looked at the clock it read 3:54 a.m. Now it was past ten. She had almost slept through the morning. A closed smile pulled at her face. The big stuffed panther sat on the end of the bed, a visual reminder that last night had been no dream.

The creak of the hallway door broke the silence. A rubbery black nose poked inside the room and sniffed in tentative inquisition.

"Come on, girl." Phoebe patted the bed.

Kiki butted the door, pushing it half-open. At the threshold she sat on her narrow haunches and whined, the bobbed tail thumping the carpet.

With the opening of the door came the strong enticement of coffee. Phoebe took a deep breath and smoothed back tangled hair. A little shy about her daylight nudity, she jumped from the bed, hurried into the closet, and crawled into comfortable sweats. With old moccasins hugging her slender feet, she met Kiki at the door and gave the big dog a good scratch behind the ears.

"Such a good girl," she intoned in that silly, sweet voice people reserved for children and pets. "Let's get some coffee. Lead the way."

Brown eyes widened, and that bobbed tail wagged.

Phoebe followed Kiki down stairs through the laundry room and into the kitchen. Her first stop was the coffee pot.

"Good morning," a deep voice sounded.

Alex. With a tall mug of coffee in hand, Phoebe turned. There he was, curled up on the bench in the corner of the breakfast nook, a coffee mug in one hand and a section of the morning paper in the other. His denim shirt remained unbuttoned, revealing that smooth muscled chest. Faded blue jeans hugged those marvelous legs and thighs.

Phoebe started to approach, but hesitated, suddenly conscious of her disheveled appearance. Hair that needed combing. Teeth that needed brushing. Eyes that needed the sleep washed out of them. Embarrassed by her appearance, she remained behind the snack bar. "Good morning. Did you send Kiki to wake me?"

"No. I think Grandma did."

Worried that this topic had arisen so soon, Phoebe leaned on the snack bar. "Grandma? You've seen Grandma?"

"Haven't you?"

"Well, yes." Phoebe swallowed hard, hoping having a ghost in the house would not frighten him away. "Does that bother you?"

"Your grandmother's ghost? Or the fact you see her?"

"Either one."

Alex grinned. "The dogs accept it. Should I do less?"

"Grandma used to say dogs are smarter than most men," Phoebe replied.

Maneuvering out of the corner, Alex stepped over Elsa's furry mound and approached the snack bar. Long legs wrapped around a barstool. He sat, dropping his elbows on the cool tile countertop. A strange hunger lurked in those glistening gold eyes. His voice rumbled like a sensual purr. "Did she say anything about cats?"

Phoebe felt her cheeks grow hot. She took a deep drink from the mug and swallowed strong coffee. "Grandma said cats can find their way in the dark because they see so many things. She also said the same claws that protect can also kill. Cats are the most beautiful creatures on Earth and the most dangerous."

For several moments, a strange silence filled the kitchen. Outside, the rain augmented from drizzle to downpour. Alex responded in a quiet, unfettered manner. "Your grandmother was wise. Very wise. I am dangerous, but I could never harm you. However, I make no promises about Jack. If he's smart, he'll stay out of my way."

Phoebe looked at Alex's strong fingers intertwined on the tile counter. She had seen those hands in action, knew how powerful they were and how tender they could be. "I'm afraid Jack is more arrogant than smart. I don't know what he'll do when he sees you here. You're not exactly in his game plan. He wants me out of this house."

Rising from the barstool, Alex leaned across the snack bar and donned a sober expression. "He won't hurt you as long as I'm here."

Phoebe realized why Alex had brought both a sack of groceries and his duffel bag. "You're staying, aren't you?"

"If you're staying in this house with Jack, then I'm staying, too. I'm not stupid, Phoebe. I know you're afraid of him."

"Is that the only reason you're here? To protect me from Jack?"

"I'm not *that* selfless." Alex leaned a little closer, those golden eyes sizzling with emotion. "Run away with me, Phoebe. I'll protect you with my life and love you forever. I swear it on the graves of my ancestors."

The offer was tempting, but Phoebe remained bound to a promise and a riddle. "I want to go with you. I really do. I've never felt this way before. You make me crazy, Alex Lin. You work a wicked magic on my soul. But I can't leave. Not yet. There are things you don't know about this house."

Characteristic stoicism returned. Looking patient yet undaunted, Alex leaned a hip against the snack bar. "Tell me."

Phoebe cleared her throat and carefully chose her words. "How good are you at riddles?"

He shrugged. "Let's hear it."

"*Take care of the land and the land will take care of you.* That's what Grandma said the night before she died. That was almost seven years ago. She made me promise not to leave this property until I understood the riddle. The night Jack moved in about six months ago, Grandma showed up. Since then, she's looked in on me and scared the hell out of Jack a few times. I'm afraid she's a bit of a mischievous ghost. Jack always hated her. Still does. Grandma was a medicine woman. Everything she did and said had a reason. I know she's here to make sure I solve that riddle."

A scowl drew lines on Alex's tawny face. "This is why you stay and fight Jack? To honor the promise to your grandmother?"

"Is that silly?"

"No, just rare. A medicine man once told me there is only one thing you are born with that no one can take from you. Your honor. It's the only thing the world cannot touch. Only you can give it away. And once it is gone, it is gone for the rest of that life. If your honor demands that you make a stand on this land, then I'll stay and help you."

"Jack hates Indians, despite the fact that he's part Cherokee," Phoebe informed with calm candor. "If he finds you here, he's going to explode."

"I understand what you're saying, but I can't leave you out here alone with him. We'll deal with Jack together. I can be a stubborn Cherokee, too."

Dropping her elbows on the snack bar, Phoebe kept her gaze trained on Alex's vivid eyes. "I'm afraid of Jack. I admit that. But I'm not sure how I feel about someone else fighting my battles. I don't think I could deal with you or anyone else getting hurt on account of me."

"Phoebe, I'm not going to let Jack hurt you. And like I've already told you, Jack isn't big enough to hurt me. We'll get through this. You'll see.

Now, shall I buy you breakfast or lunch?"

So many things tumbled in Phoebe's mind. She wanted to tell him how much she enjoyed last night, but *thank you* seemed inappropriate for some of the services rendered. "Breakfast. I'll go get cleaned up."

He planted a warm kiss on her forehead and slid his face down her cheek. The tip of his tongue slipped inside one corner of her mouth. It was an erotic, unaligned kiss. In a moment, he retrieved his tongue. "Take a nice hot bath while I'll make another pot of coffee."

"Uh-huh. Okay," Phoebe moaned in response. She left the coffee mug on the snack bar, turned, and stumbled up the stairs.

* * *

AFTER brushing her teeth and pinning that ton of hair on top of her head, Phoebe slipped into a hot bath. Her eyelids grew heavy, and her shoulders molded against the back of the tub. *Musk Rain* oil rode the steam and coated the bathroom with its exotic scent. Memories of last night's lovemaking brought a moan to her throat.

The door creaked and the main light switched off, leaving only the frosted bulbs over the mirror to pierce the fog. A hand cupped around the back of her neck, pulling her forward just enough to let Alex's tall body slither into the huge tub behind her.

Long, tan legs entwined with hers. She relaxed against Alex's chest, feeling the heat of his groin and the evidence of his arousal. Sensual hands moved across her, smearing water and oil up her stomach and over the peaks of sensitive breasts. His hot tongue mopped moisture from her neck and face, like a cat lapping up milk. With a growl, he turned Phoebe's wet body to face him, pulling her knees around his hips, and positioning himself for easy, anticipated entry.

"Wait," Phoebe admonished. Her fingers spread through that lustrous black hair. "We have to be careful. We already have enough problems."

"I'll be careful." He wrapped his hands around her hips. Then with one long thrust slipped inside her.

"What about breakfast?" she reminded in a whisper, tickling his face with her breath, reveling in the sloppy lust contorting his face.

"This is breakfast," came a raspy whisper. His hips rolled and he began to thrust. The uneven rhythm splashed water out of the tub, soaking the throw rug and the short-pile carpet.

Phoebe wrapped her hands around the back of his head, threading her fingers through wet, thick hair. She closed her eyes, feeling so many sensations at once. His tongue pulling at her breast. His hard arousal probing at just the right angle. The water sloshing over her bottom and up her back.

A picture solidified in her mind. At the same time she knew she was in the bathtub with Alex, she was also making love to him beneath the astral waterfall. Two concurrent events. Physical pairing and astral joining rushed toward the same blazing conclusion. Minutes passed. Phoebe's fingers buried in Alex's hair, and she shivered as though she had been struck by lightning. After a long moment, the energy waves subsided and her fingers slid out of his hair. Only then did Alex withdraw and allow his own physical release.

Sexually sated, they lay still in the warm water and listened to rain dancing on the roof.

* * *

IT was the first time Alex had been able to check out the house during daylight and under legitimate circumstances.

While Phoebe cleaned the kitchen after breakfast, something she had insisted on doing alone, he ambled through the living room. It was beautiful and spacious, tastefully decorated. Halfway up, the unique staircase opened to a fan-shaped landing. Then it turned sharply to the left and narrowed the rest of the way.

The storm had moved on for the day, leaving the afternoon cloudy and humid. Alex slid open one of the glass patio doors along the west wall of the living room and walked into the manicured backyard. Unlike most large residences in the area, this one did not sport a backyard pool or hot tub. Instead, gray flagstone, matching the rock on the house, cut curving pathways through thick Bermuda grass and around oval shrubbery beds. In the northwest corner of the yard proper, flagstone circled a seven-sided gazebo.

Following the stone path, Alex made his way to what he sensed was Phoebe's favorite retreat. Inside the gazebo, he sat in the center a wooden swing that appropriately faced west. The chains creaked as they adjusted to his weight. With one foot on the concrete, he moved the swing back and forth in gentle rhythm.

An odd gust of wind whipped his loose black hair. Instead of smelling cedar and prairie grass, the mixed aroma of coffee and gingersnaps bombarded his sinuses. Then the ghost materialized inside the gazebo, right in front of him.

Putting both his sneakers firmly on the concrete, he brought the swing to an abrupt halt.

"Ah ho, Grandmother," he greeted in a cheerful but respectful voice.

The translucent figure mentally communicated a derisive *hmmmph.*

Surprised by the reaction, Alex leaned forward, resting his elbows on his knees. "What's wrong, Grandmother? Phoebe is safe from Jack, and you must know I care for her."

Shimmering eyebrows arched in silent argument and crystalline eyes flashed disapproval. *Is that so?*

"I believe it is so," he replied, confused by the ghost's cold demeanor. "Have you come to explain the riddle to me?"

Laughter bounced through the gazebo and echoed across the yard. The ghost shook her transparent head and dissipated like glitter on the wind.

"I suppose not," Alex intoned, frowning. "Well, fine then. Plan B. We'll figure it out ourselves."

"Who are you talking to?" Phoebe asked, stepping into the gazebo.

"Myself, apparently."

Nodding, she sat beside him in the swing. "Were you trying to get the riddle out of Grandma?"

Alex shrugged, feeling a bit foolish. He had to try, of course, but should have known it would not be easy. "Maybe."

"Good luck," Phoebe said with a chuckle and started the swing moving. "Smell that? Fresh cut hay."

Alex noted the huge round hay bales dotting the rolling pasture on the next farm to the north. "Won't it rot out there in the rain?"

"Naw. The outside gets a little soggy, but there's really very little damage. That's why everyone went to the big bales. As soon as the ground dries enough for the tractor, they'll spear them with that forklift thing and haul them off." Phoebe paused to drink in a deep breath of Mother Nature. "I've always loved fall."

Alex tucked her tightly under his arm and pulled her head against his chest. Thick auburn hair tickled his nose, while the warmth of her tickled his soul.

Then the thought of Jack made his blood boil. Phoebe had Grandma's riddle, but Alex had a riddle of his own to solve. What kind of shady business was Jack into? A gut feeling said Jack went gone to California to broker something unsavory. Alex did not know what it was, and he could not confide in Phoebe. Not yet.

"We're going to have trouble when Jack gets back, aren't we?" he asked, not really expecting an answer.

"With fall comes the harvest, as Grandma used to say. I guess, in this case, that makes Jack the reaper." Phoebe threw back her head and laughed. "Get it? Jack the Reaper?"

Alex gently kissed Phoebe's forehead. He got the joke, but found it too close to the truth to be funny.

* * * * *

CHAPTER 15

Temper Tantrums

THAT afternoon rain streaked the outside of thick office windows, and quickly dropping temperatures made the office a bit chilly.

Jack's executive secretary, Genny, wrapped a sweater over her legs and took a sip of hot coffee. She glanced at the digital clock on the far wall: 2:15 p.m. It had been a slow, sleepy day. Maybe things would liven up before quitting time.

Sam padded out of his office and dropped a short stack of notes on Genny's desk. "I'll be gone the rest of the day. If Jack calls, tell him I need to speak with him ASAP. Be sure he has my cell phone and pager number, okay?"

"I understand." Genny noticed Sam snapping his fingers in nervous agitation. Both of her bosses often took lengthy *recreational* lunches. Sam's mannerisms, however, were wrong for a midday tryst. Something was afoot. Something she might find interesting. "Is there anything else?"

"No. If you need me, leave a message on my pager."

"Okay." Genny scribbled a note on her desk pad and watched him stalk into the corridor. "Sam?" she called in afterthought.

He pressed the elevator button and glanced over his shoulder. "Yeah, Gen?"

"Take it easy in Little Red today. The roads are wet."

An easy smile complimented Sam's freckled face. "Will do. See you tomorrow." The elevator doors parted, and Sam impatiently stepped inside the plush cubicle.

As the silvery doors closed, one word echoed in Genny's mind: *curious.* The pace in the office generally remained steady to the point of tedium. Today, however, she sensed a storm brewing in the office to coincide with the one being pitched outside by good old Mother Nature.

The main line rang. Genny picked up the receiver. "Northwest Properties."

"Genny, this is Jack."

Long, mauve-painted fingernails clicked on the desktop. She knew something, but was not sure how to tell it. "Good afternoon. How is San

Francisco?"

"Wet. It's been raining for two days. How's everything there?"

"The same. It never fails. The Fair comes to town and brings the rain." Genny's fingernails continued the tinny tapping.

"Is the office okay?"

"All's quiet." Genny clicked her tongue on the roof of her mouth and let the conversation lapse into noticeable silence.

"All right, Gen. What's wrong?"

Genny leaned forward in her chair and lowered her voice. "Well, I hate to spread rumors, but there's something you ought to know. I went to the Fair yesterday and guess who I saw?"

"Spill it."

"Phoebe. I saw Phoebe at the Fair. With a man." The line remained quiet for several seconds. "Jack? Did you hear what I said?"

"What man?" came an angry demand.

"I don't know," Genny answered. "He was about six feet tall. Black hair. Tan complexion. A real looker. And Rachel Gray was with them."

"Are you sure he wasn't Rachel's date?"

Genny huffed. "He had his tongue down Phoebe's throat in the Modern Living Building. Right in front of God and everybody." Again, there was silence on the other end. "Jack? Jack? Are you still there?"

"Yeah, I'm still here."

"Look, I'm sorry to have to tell you this. It's just that, well, Danny's only been gone a few months. It just didn't seem right to me. I thought you should know. Is there anything I can do?"

"Have you told anybody else?" Jack's tone was curt and his words clipped.

"No."

"Good. Don't. Let me handle this. Is Sam there?"

Pleased with herself, Genny rocked back in her chair. Mauve fingernails worked to uncoil the long telephone cord. "He's gone for the rest of the day. He wants you call him, but he didn't say why. Do you have his cell phone and pager number?"

"I have them. If I don't catch him this afternoon, tell him I'll be back in a couple of days."

Genny opened her mouth to say good-bye, but the line clicked. Smiling, she hung up the receiver and considered herself a loyal employee.

* * *

JACK slammed down the telephone and gritted his teeth. Sitting naked on the side of the bed, he felt anger rise up the back of his neck to create a thunderous pounding in his ears.

Indian was the one word Genny had not used to describe Phoebe's supposed boyfriend, but it was the obvious conclusion. Jack had used isolation to keep Phoebe afraid and off balance, believing it would eventually cause her to leave the house. He had tried his best to keep her away from the likes of Rachel Gray and Twyla Jones, and not because they were native. It was much more than that. Rachel and Twyla were both strong personalities, women of backbone and character, qualities that might rub off on his kindhearted sister-in-law. Jack needed to get Phoebe off the property and away from that meddling ghost. This was not a good sign.

"What's the matter?" Erin asked, lying naked on top of white silk sheets.

"Indians," Jack seethed through clenched teeth. "I'm so damned tired of Indians."

"Jack—"

"Shut up! Just shut up and get dressed. The fantasy's over, Pocahontas. Pack your trinkets. We're leaving."

Horrified, Erin curled up in a ball, wrapping the sheets around her. Heartfelt sobs echoed through the hotel suite, and tears stained expensive silk.

Oblivious to the injury he had just inflicted, Jack stomped into the other room, grabbed a telephone, and began punching numbers.

* * *

SAM hated waiting rooms, especially this one. Fake ferns in the corners. Chairs that must have been reupholstered at least twice. Seventies-style gold shag carpet. A receptionist popping chewing gum bubbles with vacant disregard, while nimble fingers clicked away at a computer keyboard.

He shifted his feet and looked at his wristwatch for the fourth time: 3:15 p.m. One Italian loafer started tapping a muffled protest on the matted carpet.

The inner office door swung open and a mountain of a man filled the frame. Short-cut brown hair stood up in an obedient crew-cut. An off-the-rack suit strained at his rounded middle and across meaty shoulders.

Clear blue eyes stared out fixedly, as if his wire-frame glasses gave him X-ray vision. "Mr. Tillman? I'm Harold Swearingen."

The professional greeting surprised Sam. He blinked and quickly collected his wits. Getting to his feet, he took the man's huge outstretched hand. "Thanks for working me in on such short notice."

"No problem. Come on in."

Sam retrieved his hand and wiggled his fingers to restore circulation. Following Swearingen into the private office, he sat in a standard padded chair and looked across a messy desk. The sign at the front of the clutter read: *Harold Swearingen, Private Investigator.*

"Let's get to the point," Sam said. "You came highly recommended. I hear you're thorough and discreet. You do international reports, right?"

"International?" Swearingen rocked back in his desk chair and balanced a yellow notepad on his knee. "Maybe you'd better tell me exactly what you're looking for."

A little nervous, Sam again took to tapping one foot. "Information on Lin Martial Arts. It's a kung fu school on the northwest side in Red Cedars Corner. I want a background check on the teacher."

Swearingen looked over the top of his glasses. "A kung fu master?"

"Yes," Sam piped back. "His name is Lin. L-I-N."

Fat fingers dwarfed a small pen and scribbled large letters on the yellow notepad. Without looking up, Swearingen offered a quick assessment of the situation. "Let me see if I can guess. We have a good-looking, relatively young teacher who's stolen somebody's wife or girlfriend. That about right?"

Surprised, Sam sat forward in the chair. "Something like that. How'd you know?"

Swearingen offered a guttural laugh. "Martial artists. They're all alike, even the old geezers. They have lots of energy and reek of mystique. Most women don't really want to learn to fight. They just want someone to protect them. They tell their troubles to the teacher. Cry in his arms a few times, and here we go." Swearingen set the yellow notepad on top of a pile of folders. "Is he Asian?"

"He has a trace of accent. Looks a little oriental mixed with Indian."

"American Indian?" When Sam nodded, Swearingen continued. "Kung fu, you said? Hmm. The Chinese government shut down those temples before you and I were even born. Most people don't know that. There are a few temples in other Asian countries. There are even a couple in the States. But if he's mixed-blood and has some accent, I'll bet he came out of a Hong Kong school. Maybe Macau. If the business is in his name, there'll be a paper trail. Either way, I'll find something. It would help if I knew which fighting system he favors. That would narrow the search on the schools."

"I can get that for you. Anything else?"

Swearingen glanced over the rim of his glasses. "Do we need to discuss money?"

"No. I'll find out which fighting system he uses. You start the computer check. We'll go from there."

"Great. I'll get started immediately." Pulling his solid six-and-a-half-foot frame out of the chair, Swearingen offered a hand over the desk. "It's a pleasure, Mr. Tillman."

Sam took the offered hand and squeezed hard in self-defense. From what he had seen so far, he believed Swearingen was the right man for this job.

* * *

BY late evening, the rain had stopped in northwest Oklahoma City, but a heavy blanket of clouds obscured the stars and veiled that enormous harvest moon.

Near the end of kung fu class, Phoebe put down her head and fought to catch her breath. The air was cool but humid, leaving everyone drenched with sweat, even the master. Phoebe thought going back to class might be uncomfortable after consummating her relationship with Alex, but she had had no problem.

In the kwoon, he was Master Lin. At home, he was Alex. It was the way he wanted it. All through class Alex was full of nervous energy and smiling with little provocation. It pleased Phoebe to know she was the reason for his buoyant attitude.

At eight o'clock Alex dismissed the rest of the class but snapped his fingers at Phoebe. "Come over here. I want to start you on something new."

Frowning, Phoebe dragged her tired body toward the back of the practice area.

At the front door, Sara wrapped a shawl around her shoulders and paused. She was the last of the other students to leave. "You two be good."

Offering a respectful bow, Alex grinned. "Yes, Mother. I assure you. We are very good."

A blush put even more rose in Sara's cheeks. "Well, I walked into that one, didn't I? Goodnight all." She opened the door with her trim derrière and pivoted out into the foggy night.

Phoebe wiped sweat from her neck. "You don't have to keep me after class, you know. We can just go home."

"I want to show you something, and you'll need some room to practice it."

What Alex taught her was the first section of a primary 54-step practice form. To her amazement, she managed the moves and the stances reasonably well, but remembering it step-by-step was a challenge. Bow, block and punch, turn and kick, over and over in different forms and combinations that, when done properly, made a steady, strong advancement across the practice floor. Phoebe got lost a couple of times and had to back up and start over, but her concentration never wavered.

"Good," Alex praised. "Go through it a few times, but go slow. Understand the moves. I hate to admit it, but you're my best student. Too bad you're not a boy."

A mischievous reply teetered on the tip of Phoebe's tongue.

Alex gave her long auburn braid a friendly tug. "Be nice. I'll make sure the back door's locked. Keep practicing."

After Alex disappeared up the back stairs, Phoebe went over the new steps. Block and punch. Long horse stance and upper cut. Horn and sweep. Overhand and whip.

"Hello there, lethal weapon."

Startled by a familiar voice, Phoebe lost her place and spun around to find Sam standing just inside the door.

"Is something wrong?" she asked, a little breathless. "Or did you come for pizza again?"

This time Sam wore sweats and old sneakers. His expression veered toward dark and menacing. With a swagger in his step, he entered the practice area without the traditional bow. "I came to check out the class."

"Why?"

"To see if I want to join."

"Join this class?" Phoebe heard the squeak in her voice and was annoyed that she had allowed him to unnerve her.

Sam performed a few simple stretches and then threw a couple of practice kicks. "Why not? I've had some training. I learn pretty fast."

"We'll see," a deep voice challenged. Alex strode into the room, still clad in wet black silk. He sauntered to the front, dropped a denim duffel bag on one of the benches. Then returned to the center of the practice area.

Sam continued to take an aggressive posture. "So, what forms do you teach?"

"Hung gar. Wing chun. Tai chi chuan. A little taikwondo, if you like those forms. But I specialize in black tiger."

"Southern Shaolin," Sam noted.

"Mostly. Are you interested?"

Sam backed up and threw a few punches in the air. "Maybe. Show me some moves. Let me see your style."

Shaking his head, Alex stretched long fingers, as if forcing them not to form into lethal fists. "I don't spar with students. If you want to join the class, come back tomorrow night at seven."

"What's wrong with now?"

"It's late. Class is over. Come back tomorrow."

Alex's expression showed dangerous annoyance. He ushered Phoebe out of the practice area, both offering quick bows. Then herded her toward the front door.

Alone in the practice area, Sam spread his arms and looked perplexed. "Are we leaving?"

Phoebe's uneasiness increased. She grabbed her gym bag and held open the door. "Yes, Sam. We're leaving. Come on. We're going for a hamburger."

There was an odd scowl on Sam's freckled face. Pale fingers raked through short sandy hair, and one foot tapped in frustration. He exited the practice area and gave Phoebe a strange look on his way out of the building.

In a moment, all three stood on the sidewalk.

Alex hastily locked the door and accidentally brushed too close to Sam. The sparks flew before Phoebe could protest.

Sam reached out, intending to lock a hand around Alex's muscled forearm. Instead of finding silk-covered flesh, Sam got nothing but a fistful of foggy air.

Backing up, Alex raised a finger in warning. "Enough. You're not drunk this time, so no excuses. Go home."

An audacious sneer proved Sam was either too stubborn for his own good or certifiably insane. "I came to see if you're as good as you think you are. Come on. Show me your stuff, tough guy." Without taking his eyes off Alex, Sam tossed snide remarks over his shoulder. "Wise up, Phebes. He's only looking for a good screw. He's just using you."

Phoebe saw something frightening, something oddly familiar in Alex's expression. She had seen it before in both Jack and Danny. It was a feral, dilated stare that too often heralded unchecked reaction.

"Alex, don't," she implored. "Whatever it is, just don't."

With an unblinking gaze fixed on his prey, Alex seemed oblivious to her pleas. Long fingers twitched at his sides and his knees bent just a little, like a cat getting ready to spring.

Although she could not see the look on Sam's face, Phoebe witnessed actions that bespoke stupidity born of male ego.

Sam struck in precise left-right sequence. Tight-fisted, polished punches would have broken bones, if they had connected with anything solid. But they did not. Instead, the bottom of a large sneaker found the flat of Sam's stomach, lifting him several inches off the damp sidewalk. The instant his feet hit the pavement Sam's knees buckled. He went down on his palms and promptly colored the sidewalk with the remnants of his last meal.

Sickened, Phoebe opened the car, dove into the driver's seat, and closed the door to shut out as much vile sound as possible.

Alex just stood there, watching his opponent retch. "You wanted to see my stuff. Now I've seen yours. I'm not impressed."

Old sneakers squeaked on the sidewalk as Alex turned. He climbed into the passenger's side of the car and slammed the door.

Phoebe gripped the steering wheel with one hand and turned the key with the other. The engine sputtered to life and headlights flipped on, illuminating Sam's pathetic form. Phoebe had seen Alex anxious, jealous, protective, drunk with animal passion, and now enraged.

She was reminded of the fact that, in truth, she knew very little about Alex Lin. Questions raced through her mind, each one planting a tiny seed of doubt.

"We can't just leave him here." Her voice faltered a little.

"Yes, we can," came a deep-throated reply. Alex slid lower in the bucket seat, pushing his knees up against the dashboard. "Drive—before something worse happens."

She was not afraid of Alex. She was afraid for Alex.

Dropping the car in reverse, she backed around Sam's red car and headed for home.

* * *

PHOEBE paused with her hand on the bathroom doorknob. Alex had been silent during the ride home. Then he had stormed into the house, ignored the dogs, and thundered upstairs. That had been thirty minutes ago. It was time to check on him.

She took a deep breath and opened the bathroom door. Steam rushed past her, escaping into the bedroom like a genie released from the bottle. Hot water fogged the corner shower stall, its textured glass revealing a tall, blurry form.

Phoebe walked up to the shower and tried to sound brave. "If you don't come out right now, I'm coming in."

A deep voice rattled the glass door. "Go away."

That old stubborn streak stiffened the back of Phoebe's neck. "You've got two seconds, mister. Then I'm coming in after you."

"If you come in here, you'd better be prepared to do more than talk."

Shedding her sneakers and silks, Phoebe stood naked in front of the shower. She tapped the glass with one knuckle. "I'm not afraid of you, Alex."

"You should be."

"Well, maybe. But I'm not. Now open the door."

For a moment, a distorted face considered her through rough-textured glass. Then the inside lock clicked, and the door swung partially open. A huge hand wrapped around her waist and pulled her inside the stall.

Phoebe found solid footing on slick tile and tried to get her bearings in the thick steam. Warm water gave a soothing massage, while Alex's huge hands played through her hair. She did not fight him. She just allowed Alex to do what he wanted, to take what he needed.

Alex's shaking hands skimmed over Phoebe's wet body, crushing firm breasts, measuring a trim waist, daring to probe between her legs. His tongue left a hot trail down her neck.

"I shouldn't have hit him," he admitted. "I lost control."

"I know." Phoebe relaxed against him. It reminded her a little of that wonderful astral waterfall conjured from his vivid imagination.

"I'm still not in control."

"I know."

He stared her straight in the eyes. "You're not afraid, are you?"

"No."

His gaze drifted down her wet body and his breathing became deep and erratic. "I can't be gentle right now."

"Just always be honest." Phoebe smoothed wet dark hair away from his face. The look in his eyes startled her. "Alex? What's wrong?"

Water matted thick, black lashes. "Nothing. Just kiss me."

*****

CHAPTER 16
Culture Clash

AT seven o'clock the next morning, Phoebe stood in line at the local 24-hour supermarket, her grocery basket full to the brim.

She had awakened about five o'clock, untangled herself from Alex's jealous embrace, and whispered for him to go back to sleep. Figuring a big homemade breakfast and fresh flowers on the table would bring back that handsome smile, she had left a scribbled note on the snack bar and sneaked out of the house.

Phoebe liked "odd hour" shopping, but usually did it at midnight, not early in the morning. She was the typical night owl who would prowl all night given the chance, crash in bed at sunrise, and wake up at the crack of noon. But since society did not run by that schedule, she had spent her life trying to adjust to daylight hours.

Needless to say, seven a.m. was not her preferred time of day. Phoebe yawned while the clerk weighed plastic bags of fresh vegetables and fruits, and passed boxed and canned goods over the bar code reader. She was on a mission: surprise Alex with a grand breakfast and then a romantic dinner.

With the groceries sacked and paid for, Phoebe headed to the car, a dutiful clerk trailing along with a cart full of groceries. She opened the trunk and yawned again, while the clerk packed the car for her.

Elsa's wide rubbery nose pressed to the inside of the back window. Despite Phoebe's coaxing and tugging, the dog had refused to get out of the back seat. Therefore, Elsa had made the trip to the grocery store, filling the small of the car like a big bear in a little cave.

The clerk shut the trunk and jumped when he noticed the huge Rottweiler in the back seat. He offered a routine, "Have a nice day," and hurried back to the store.

Smiling, Phoebe tapped on the back window and cooed at the huge dog. "Elsa, you're a booger. Yes, you are. And such a pretty booger."

Suddenly, all of the hair stood up on Elsa's broad neck. She showed huge fangs and growled from the pit of hell.

Before Phoebe could react, someone turned her around and slammed her against the side of the car. Her eyes quickly focused on a familiar face.

"Shut up, bitch!" Jack thundered at the snarling dog. "I'll deal with you later."

A hundred things rushed through Phoebe's mind, but the top of the list was regret. She had not figured on Jack coming back early. But a 165-pound angry Rottweiler would back him off, if she could only reach the door latch.

She had witnessed Jack's fury before, but was not sure she had ever seen him like this. Those gray eyes glistened in the morning sunlight. His six-foot-two frame loomed over her. Dark brown hair was disheveled, curling in at the collar of his cotton shirt. Long sleeves were rolled up to his elbows, showing the veins in his tanned forearms.

Elsa switched from snarling to howling. The small car vibrated from her deep-throated calls.

Jack grabbed Phoebe by her arms and again rammed her against the side of the car. "I'm not gone two weeks and I hear you're screwing some damned Indian!"

"You can't tell me what to do," Phoebe said through gritted teeth. "Let go!"

He pulled back one hand and slapped her across the cheek. "Don't ever raise your voice to me."

Phoebe was too mad to be afraid. She clenched her teeth clenched and narrowed her eyes. "Let go of me."

An evil smile spread on Jack's face, revealing straight white teeth. "And what if I don't?"

"If you don't," a deep voice warned, "I'll rip your heart out with my bare hands."

Still holding Phoebe against the car, Jack glanced over his right shoulder.

Not ten feet away, Alex stood in front of Danny's old pickup. The engine was running and exhaust fumes billowed from the tailpipe. In the front seat sat another Rottweiler. All fangs and growls, this dog was leaner and younger and looked ready to do battle. The same could be said of the driver.

Jack clicked his tongue on the roof of his mouth. He was trapped and appeared to have the good sense to know it. Slowly, he opened his fingers and backed away from Phoebe. Facing his male opponent, he rolled one shoulder and cracked his knuckles.

"Well, well," Jack said. "This must be the infamous kung fu master. And driving Danny's pickup. And screwing his wife, no doubt."

A siren echoed in the distance. Tires squealed on oily pavement as a black and white police car rolled into the parking lot. The car stopped and two burly officers got out.

"What's the problem, folks?" the brown-haired officer asked, one hand tapping his holstered pistol.

Jack's demeanor changed 180-degrees. Appearing calm and deceptively sane, he walked up to the policemen with palms raised. "No problem, Officers. It's just a mis-understanding."

The officer in charge glanced back and forth from Phoebe to Alex, taking note of the Rottweilers snarling behind each. "Explain it to me."

"This is my sister-in-law," Jack explained. "I've been taking care of her since my brother died a few months back. I saw this man driving my brother's truck and thought it had been stolen."

"The deceased brother's truck," the officer said in a slow monotonous tone and gave a patient nod.

"Apparently," Jack continued in a steady voice, "she hired this man to help her while I was out of town. Like I said, Officer, it was just a misunderstanding. I apologize if we frightened anyone. I assure you, it won't happen again."

The officer squinted one eye and appeared skeptical. He looked hard at Phoebe. "Are you all right, Ma'am?"

Phoebe nodded. "Yes, sir. I'm fine."

"The 911 call said someone hit you. Do you wish to press charges?"

Phoebe considered the consequences of filing assault and battery charges on Jack. He would go to jail for a couple of hours, make bail, and come home swinging mad. No, filing charges would only make things worse. She glanced at Alex, who sat smugly on the truck's front bumper, arms folded across his chest.

"Ma'am?" the officer repeated and took a strategic step forward.

"No, Officer," Phoebe answered. "The caller was mistaken. May I go home now? I have a whole trunk full of groceries."

The officer hesitated. "You can leave. But not them."

Phoebe fumbled with the key in the lock. Mindful to not let Elsa out of the back seat, she climbed into the car and slammed the door so hard it rattled the glass.

She hated to leave without knowing the outcome, but the best thing for her to do was start the car and head for home. That was exactly what she did. On the way out of the parking lot, she glanced in the rearview mirror and saw the officer in charge shaking his finger at both Jack and Alex.

* * *

HALF an hour later, just as Phoebe put the last of the groceries in the refrigerator, the breezeway door flew open and Jack thundered into the kitchen.

Elsa made a stand in front of Phoebe, stiff black hair rising on her broad back, yellowed fangs bared, and a menacing growl tumbling around in her massive throat.

Certain that Elsa could hold Jack at bay, if necessary, Phoebe stood her ground. "Jack, if you had him arrested, I'll get a gun and kill you myself. I swear to God I will."

A sneer distorted Jack's expression. "Oh, I'm scared."

"Jack—" Phoebe warned, pointing a stiff finger.

"Phoebe!" rang a third voice. Alex entered the kitchen and snapped his fingers at Kiki, who obediently scurried over to join Elsa's surly vigil. "I'm all right. The officer just talked to us. Made us promise to be good little boys. Then let us go."

Jack backed against the cabinets and glared at Alex. "Don't you work?"

Grinning, Alex sat on one of the stools in front of the snack bar. "I work here. That's what you told the cops. Remember?"

"Then take the day off and go home."

"I am home." Alex offered a territorial smile.

"What?" Jack looked at Phoebe. "He lives here? No, he doesn't. This is my house, dammit! I say who lives in it!"

Phoebe stomped across the kitchen and stopped at the hallway threshold. "No, this is not your house, dammit. As much as I hate to admit it, for now you and I share this house. I can do anything I want with my half. And I say that Alex stays. If you don't like it, you can go right down the River Styx. I'll be happy to provide the boat and the paddle!"

She snapped her fingers at the dogs. "Come on, girls. We're going for a walk."

Long claws dug into expensive carpet as Elsa and Kiki scrambled to catch up with Phoebe. Like unshakable shadows, they followed her down the hallway, through the huge living room, and out the back patio doors.

* * *

"SHE got you told," Alex said with a snicker.

"Screw you," Jack snarled and headed toward the hallway.

"Leave her alone, Jack."

Jack's cowboy boots skidded to a stop on the hallway's dark carpet. Wheeling around, he dropped his hands on his hips and gave Alex a long hard stare. He just could not believe Phoebe was bedding down some gold-digger, despite what Genny had said on the telephone. "I hear you did a number on Sam last night."

Alex shook his head. "It was an accident. He swung. I reacted. He only lost his supper. And a little pride."

That was not the way Sam had explained it at the airport this morning, but Jack found Alex's version more believable. "So, you run your own martial arts school? Kung fu forms, I understand."

Shrugging in response, Alex went to the refrigerator. Quick hands retrieved two canned drinks and all the makings for a couple of sandwiches.

Jack leaned a shoulder against the hallway wall and remained where he could see Alex's face. "Do the students in the kwoon call you Sifu or Master?"

"Master. Do they call you Master or Sensei in the dojo?"

"Master. I prefer English," Jack piped back.

Alex finished slapping together two fat sandwiches and shoved them in a small paper bag. With two cans of soda in one hand and the lunch bag in the other, he sauntered down the hall and right past Jack. "Then I will be careful, *Master.*"

"You condescending kung fu bastard," Jack muttered. "You think you're untouchable, don't you? Well, I'm not afraid of you. And I don't believe you can rip my heart out with your bare hands."

Pausing, Alex looked over one shoulder. Gold eyes darkened to a rusty orange. "Believe it, Jack. I advise you to believe it."

As the echoes of his words died, Alex continued the length of the hallway and turned into the enormous living room. Jack soon heard the familiar swoosh of the patio doors.

"There's more than one way to cut out a heart, you cocky son-of-a-bitch."

With that threat delivered to empty air, Jack stormed into his office and locked the door behind him.

* * *

PHOEBE sat in the middle of the sun-warmed pond dock and watched the dogs circle the pond. With youthful curiosity, they sniffed, tasted, waded, barked, and generally had a great day of it. The sun dominated the cloudless sky. About halfway across the pasture her temper cooled enough to allow a frightening realization. She had left Jack and Alex alone in the house.

Why did I have to go and do a stupid thing like that? What if Alex kills Jack and goes to the electric chair for it?

Of course, by her way of thinking, killing Jack should earn someone knighthood, not punishment.

"No one is dead, and no one is going to die." The old dock shook under Alex's weight, but his footsteps remained silent.

Phoebe slid around to face him. He had that granny-square afghan from the living room couch thrown over one shoulder, a brown paper bag in one hand, and two cans of soda in the other. "Are we having a picnic?"

He dipped a shoulder, prompting her to catch the blanket. "You were going to make breakfast, remember? This will at least keep us from starving."

"Sorry about this." Phoebe spread out the crocheted blanket, making a nice pallet. "I just wanted to surprise you. I had no idea Jack was back in town."

"I know." Alex crossed his legs and settled onto the blanket beside her.

"What am I going to do about him?"

"We will deal with him. In peace, if possible. If there's bloodshed, it'll be of his doing, not ours." Alex took a deep breath. "About last night, I'm really sorry. It won't happen again."

Phoebe waved a hand in dismissal. "Forget it. Sam got what he deserved. I hate that it upset you."

"It's a beautiful place," Alex observed, looking across the water. "So peaceful. It reminds me of our lily pond."

Phoebe saw no resemblance between this mud hole and their lovely astral lily pond. "In what way?"

"Water and frogs and dragonflies. And us."

His intentions became clear. Phoebe felt her cheeks flush. She scanned the rolling horizon. The nearest farmhouse was half a mile away, but it was broad daylight. "Here? You're serious, aren't you? What if Jack shows up?"

"He'll get an education." Alex shed his shirt, slipped off dusty sneakers, and then unzipped his jeans.

Phoebe's eyebrows raised, not in objection but surprise. "I see now why you brought the blanket."

* * *

THEY returned to the house around mid-afternoon.

Disheveled and hungry, Phoebe read a scribbled note tacked to the refrigerator. "Jack's gone to the office. He'll be back for dinner. His lordship commands me to be here and you to be gone. Oh, I don't think so."

Huffing at Jack's endless arrogance, Phoebe wadded up the note and tossed it in the garbage. She had no intention of being left alone with Jack for now, never if she could help it. The crack of that slap in the grocery store parking lot again rang in her ears, and she could feel the sharp sting of his palm against her cheek.

Alex settled onto one of the barstools and raked back wind-blown hair. "I have some things to take care of this afternoon. Will you be all right by yourself?"

Rummaging through the refrigerator, Phoebe called over her shoulder. "Sure. I saw a stack of paperwork on Jack's desk Wednesday. It'll take him all day to work through that pile. He won't be home until seven or eight. I'll be fine. Go run your errands, and take Danny's truck."

"Are you sure? I used it this morning because it was necessary. Jack's mad enough as it is."

Phoebe had already thrown caution to the wind. It was too late now to worry about upsetting Jack. "Take the truck. It needs to be driven."

"I'll only be gone a couple of hours at the most."

"Don't worry. I'll be fine." One item at a time, Phoebe set the makings for a hearty lunch on the tile counter. She enjoyed creating something delicious out of fresh ingredients. It was a kind of magic she understood. And, at that moment, she was feeling particularly magical. "How about some stir-fried veggies and rice for lunch? Then a fat juicy steak for dinner? Chilled wine and all."

"Sounds great."

After shutting the refrigerator, Phoebe moved everything toward the stove. "Is there anything I can help you with this afternoon?"

"No. I'm going to call a friend and ask him to teach the class for a while. At least, until we get things settled with Jack."

Phoebe's heart pounded with anticipation at the thought of having Alex around day and night, but she did not want him to jeopardize his business because of her. "Are you sure you can afford that?"

"It's not a problem. Really." He chuckled and raised his eyebrows. "Did you think I was broke?"

"Well, I wasn't sure. It does look that way. You don't have a car, and you have very few possessions that I've seen. I kind of figured you for a wandering medicine man of some kind."

Alex offered a handsome grin. "That's not a title I've earned yet, but I have studied with a couple of medicine men."

"I think you're too modest." Phoebe put an old cast-iron skillet on the electric stove and turned on the burner. "Tell me more. You're not exactly from around here."

"Not exactly. My mother was Chinese-Portuguese. My father was Cherokee. He was in the air force. He died when I was ten. After that, my mother took me to China. That's where I learned kung fu. Actually, my training is rather eclectic. I studied several styles and forms. A little of this discipline. A little of that. Mother died while I was in college back here in the States. Her family made the funeral arrangements without me. I got there in time to dust off the headstone. Anyway, I returned to college and never went back to China."

Hot oil sizzled in the skillet, reminding Phoebe to pay attention to the food. She dumped vegetables and rice and seasoning into the skillet and stirred carefully. "I was right. You *are* a wandering medicine man."

"Well, I guess so. In a way."

A sinking feeling filled the pit of Phoebe's stomach. "Does that mean you're just passing through? Or do you plan to stay a while?"

Getting off the stool, Alex walked to the stove and inspected the contents of the skillet. He wrapped a strong arm around Phoebe's waist and buried his face in her thick hair. "Do I act like a man just passing through?"

"You tell me."

"All right. I will. You are my dream, Phoebe. The empress from the lily pond. The temptress from the waterfall. The only way you'll ever get rid of me is to demand I leave. Does that answer your question?"

"Poetic but convincing." Struggling against his iron hold, she managed to slide the skillet to a cold burner. "Fix the drinks. I'll get the bowls. And you can quote some more poetry, unless you're afraid of spoiling me."

Alex stepped back, sliding his hands down her backside. "I've only begun to spoil you, Dragonfly."

* * *

JACK was so mad when he arrived at the office, that he gave everyone the rest of the day off—with pay.

There was a mound of paperwork on his desk, but he did not feel like working through the stack. He took care of the new California contract and filed it in the slender green cabinet next to his desk. The locked cabinet to which only he had keys. The one that contained six years of perfectly legal albeit politically unpopular contractual agreements.

He rocked back in his chair and stared out the corner windows. Another storm front rolled in from the north, crowding the early afternoon sun and cooling the air. But Jack's temperature remained at the boiling point.

Indians! I'm so damned tired of Indians!

Abandoning his grandfather's land to Phoebe was not an option. He knew the moment he moved out, Phoebe would have Twyla Jones out there waving smoke and feathers and talking to that meddling old ghost. Having that arrogant Alex on the place was bad enough, but he would not tolerate Twyla Jones anywhere near the house. Jack had sworn on Martin's grave twelve years before that he would rather commit murder than let Twyla Jones set foot on the Henderson property again.

Jack thought he had had everything under control. He truly believed a strong hand and a good bluff was all he needed to maneuver Phoebe out of her half of the property. It appeared, however, Phoebe was ready and willing to up the ante. What Jack needed was a good ace in the hole.

A knock on the open door echoed through the office. Jack's focus shifted from the jagged skyline of Oklahoma City to the familiar reflection on the inside of the glass. "It's about damned time you got here."

Sam's eyebrows raised. "Rough day?"

Getting out of the chair, Jack began to pace in front of the window. "I told you to watch Phoebe. Do you know what she's done?"

"From what I saw the other night, I'd say she's shacking up with Master Lin."

Jack spun around and slammed his fists on the desktop. "In my house! She's screwing that bastard in my house!"

"She's a grown woman, Jack. It's her house, too."

"Whose side are you on?"

"I'm just telling you the truth." Sam looked relatively unruffled. "Now calm down and sit."

Jack flopped into the chair's padded seat. Something in Sam's demeanor indicated all was not lost. "You know something."

"Not yet, but I will. I hired Harold Swearingen to do a background check on Master Lin."

"You didn't tell me that this morning."

"You didn't give me a chance." Sam shoved his hands deep into his trousers pockets. "That's the reason I got the shit kicked out of me last night. Swearingen wanted to know what fighting form Lin specializes in. He's going to run a search on schools, here and overseas."

Jack rocked back in the chair. "My apologies."

"Accepted."

"Besides getting the shit kicked out of you, did you learn anything last night?"

A wry smile drew a crooked line across Sam's freckled face. "Leopard and black tiger. Southern Shaolin. Swearingen put out a search on the Hong Kong and Macau schools."

"He could've learned to fight in the States."

Sam shook his head. "I don't think so. I've seen this guy work. He's too smooth. It's instinct, like he's been doing it since he was a kid. I think we'll find training on both sides of the ocean." Pausing, Sam dug the toe of one shoe into the carpet. "I'm all for Phoebe finding another man, but this Lin fellow scares the hell out of me. Martial artists tend to run in a pretty rough crowd. Too rough for Phoebe."

"I like the way you think."

"Why, thank you." Sam batted his eyes in flirtatious mockery. "So where's Erin?"

Jack rocked the chair in agitated, uneven movements. He had enough trouble right now without catching any fallout from his brief relationship with Erin. He chose his words carefully. "Things didn't work out."

"Is it over?"

"As far as I'm concerned." Jack entwined his fingers across his stomach and continued rocking. "I've already told Genny not to forward any of her calls to me."

"That's a shame. She was a pretty girl."

"That's the problem, Sam. We're getting too old for young girls." Jack pondered his and Sam's collective marital misadventures. Jack had an ex-wife in Dallas he never wanted to see again, and a seventeen-year-old son headed for college who did not want to see his father. Sam had fared a little better with two amiable ex-wives in the city and a teenage daughter who adored him. "The young ones are looking for husbands and children. We've already been there and done that."

Sam gave a quiet chuckle. "Well, maybe Erin wasn't such a good idea."

"She served her purpose." Jack had gotten both a mineral lease and a few good tumbles. Now he had to work things out with Phoebe. "Sam, what're you doing for dinner tonight?"

*****

CHAPTER 17
Ways of the World

INCENSE burned on the little table sitting in the dormer of the tiny studio apartment above the kung fu kwoon. Alex stretched the telephone cord over to the round papasan chair, set a notepad and a pen in his lap, and punched in a long-distance number.

After two rings a woman answered. "Jones Realty. This is Karen."

"Karen, it's Alex."

"Hey, good-looking. You're not calling from Twyla's."

Alex pulled his feet into the chair. "That's what I get for buying you a fancy phone. Do me a favor. Don't write down this number. If there's an emergency, call Twyla."

"You're the boss. I just got another packet from Oklahoma City. You want me to forward it?"

"Yeah, I guess you'd better. Send it to Twyla's house and include anything else you need my signature on. Overnight it, okay?"

"Got it."

Alex scribbled a note on the corner of the yellow pad. "Everything all right in Sedona?"

"No problems. It's been real quiet. Except for a couple of strange emails from a computer firm in Oklahoma City."

"Emails?" It did not take Alex long to figure out who had sent those Internet inquiries: Phoebe. He danced lightly around the truth. "Did you answer them?"

"No. I just printed them off and put them on your desk. You said not to give out any information."

"Good girl." Alex paused. He knew Karen was not going to like his next request. "Would you mind if Bobby came to Oklahoma City for a bit?"

"To do what?" Karen asked with a suspicious tone.

"I want him to teach some classes for a few weeks."

"Classes I don't mind, but no war games," Karen warned. "I want my husband back in one piece, Alex Lin Jones."

"Can Bobby come to Oklahoma and play?" Alex whined in a child's voice. "I promise we'll be good boys. We'll eat our veggies and wash behind our ears and go to bed on time. Pretty please?"

"You're impossible." Karen sounded a bit miffed. "It's okay with me, if it's okay with Bobby."

"Great. I'll leave the information with Twyla. He can call her at home tonight. If he can come, I'd like for him to be here by Monday. Tell him I'm sorry about the short notice. I'll explain when he gets here."

The sound of a pen scratching across paper sifted through the telephone receiver. "Have Bobby call Twyla for directions," Karen droned. "Okay. What else?"

Alex stared at the golden leopards on the red silk partition. "Let me know ASAP if you get anymore strange calls or inquiries. Okay?"

"Can do. Sounds like you're going to be gone awhile."

"Maybe."

A familiar click-clack of long fingers on plastic echoed across the line. Karen hummed a couple of flat notes. "She must be very interesting."

"Who?"

"The reason you're staying in Oklahoma so long."

"Good-bye, Karen." Alex climbed out of the chair and let the telephone cord spring back to a tight coil. Smiling, he dropped the receiver on the base. The red silk screen stood in front of him. His gaze focused on the delicate lily pond and those mesmerizing dancing leopards.

A crisp "hello" echoed up from the first level. Alex cocked his head and paused. He had not expected to hear that voice in this building.

* * *

ALEX exited the office and stepped into the kwoon.

"Those spines are sharp," he warned.

The look on Jack's face could be best described as arrogant amusement. He plucked the red silk fan from its hooks on the wall and paused to admire the colorful luck dragon painted across its scalloped surface. One finger tested the chiseled edge of a sharp spine. "What an elegant weapon. I can see the lovely courtesan now. Stealing up to her victim. Blinking coyly over the silk dragon. Then striking." Jack waved the fan in a feminine fashion and made a quick horizontal slice at throat level. An evil grin plastered across his face, and gray eyes glistened with malice. "Of course, if the lady doesn't move quickly, she gets drenched in her victim's blood. But such is the plight of an assassin. Yes?"

"I wouldn't know." Alex kept a safe distance. As much as he would enjoy beating the arrogance out of Jack, the patience was the wiser course of action. "I thought you were buried in work."

"Buried? Interesting choice of words. Naw. I have all weekend to catch up on paperwork." Jack sank into a defensive posture and wielded the fan like a shell-shaped sword. After a minute of private play, he straightened and put the fan back onto its display hooks. "You have some nice weapons. I assume you know how to use them."

Alex gave a shallow shrug and leaned against the back wall. "What do you want, Jack?"

"You saw my house. I thought it was only fair for me to see yours." Jack flashed a plastic grin. "Are you enjoying my city?"

"Your city?"

"Oh, yeah. My city. My playground. My wonderful money machine. A lot of people look at Oklahoma City and only see prairie grass and rusty oil wells."

Alex played along. "What do you see?"

"Opportunity. It's a young state. A young city. There's plenty of land. New faces. Fresh ideas. A smart man could build an empire. A stupid man could die here."

"I suppose that's meant to give me a choice." Alex pushed away from the wall but was careful not to get within reach. Again, he reminded himself it was neither the time nor the place for a test of fighting skills. "Don't be coy, Jack. Speak your mind."

"I want you out of my house and away from Phoebe." Jack walked toward the front and sat on the waist-high railing. "Listen, I don't blame you for being interested. It shows you have good taste. Phoebe's the best. Really, I don't have anything against the girl, except for an occasional lapse in judgment."

"Meaning?"

"This idiotic fascination she has with Indians."

Unruffled, Alex glanced at the mandala and ceremonial pipe on the east wall. "You mean, Native Americans?"

"I mean, social suicide," Jack spat. "You can't climb the social ladder in moccasins."

"Why climb it at all?"

"Money," came a hard, direct response. Jack gazed at the painted mandala for a second, and then focused on the weapons displayed on the opposite wall. "And power. They both mean survival in this world. Not everybody knows this, but I have some Cherokee blood. Like most people in Oklahoma, one-hundred-and-fifty years ago I had ancestors on both sides of the Indian wars. My Cherokee kin started out on the trail of tears, but escaped into Arkansas and Missouri. They didn't let the army put them on a reservation. They refused to be locked away from the rest of society. They cut their hair. Polished their English. Changed their clothes. Found jobs. Educated their children. Built businesses."

"They pretended to be white," Alex interjected.

"That's right. They did. So what? My people had these." Jack pointed at his glistening gray eyes. "Lots of Cherokees had them, but the government didn't know that. They thought all Indians had black eyes. My ancestors found an opportunity and took it. Hell, my great-great-grandparents even made the 1889 Land Run."

People, both friends and strangers, were always telling Alex their troubles and often private stories. It was a mysterious part of his *medicine* that had always defied explanation. He had not expected that particular energy, however, to work on someone as cold and controlling as Jack Henderson. Yet, Jack talked freely about, what was obviously for him, a disturbing ancestry. It was easier to despise a man when you saw him as two-dimensional, when you did not know what motivated him. Ten minutes before, Alex could have engaged in physical battle with Jack and not cared about the outcome. Now he started to understand Jack. Began to feel sorry for him. Once sympathy came into play, it made blind hatred almost impossible. Almost.

Alex wanted to hear more. He was tempted to be as honest with Jack as Jack had been with him, but he swallowed that urge because of Phoebe. He must not endanger her. "That's where the one-hundred-and-sixty acres came from. The property must mean a lot to you."

"You have no idea." The veins in Jack's temples bulged. "You look like an intelligent man. Make Phoebe understand this isn't a game. I want that land. Not part of it. All of it. When she agrees to that, I'll give her a nice settlement. Enough to take care of her for many years."

"And if she doesn't agree?"

Getting to his feet, Jack exited the practice area and paused with his elbow on the front door handle. "Then we're going to be living together a very long time. Tempers flare. Accidents happen."

For a long moment the two men shared a cold silence.

They were at crossed purposes. In some ways, they were a lot alike, sharing common interests and talents and more. Under better circumstances, they might have been friends. The way of the world, however, was to find balance between light and dark, good and bad, yin and yang. A delicate dance of equal and opposite held the universe together.

Jack finally broke the tension. Wearing a stern expression, he slipped out into the steamy afternoon and let the door slam behind him.

Standing in the middle of the practice area, Alex watched as the shade bounced against the glass door. He winced at its discordance rattling.

What Jack had just delivered was a threat, pure and simple. Phoebe was not safe, not anymore. Alex could send her to Sedona for a while, but that would break her promise to her grandmother. Phoebe was fighting to define her spiritual identity as well as her temporal role. As much as he wanted to keep her safe, he could not ask her to give up her honor.

For the moment, Alex would just have to hold Jack at bay. One predator backing down another.

* * *

MOTHER Nature's late summer bath was not over yet. Cold rain fell from gray cotton clouds, and a northwesterly wind whistled a taunting tune. *Gloomy* best described that Friday afternoon.

Soaked to the skin, Alex sloshed into the Twylight Bookstore. This time the off-key bell announced his presence. Fluorescent light panels winced, protesting his unusually negative energy. Outside thunder cracked and rattled the plate glass windows.

Twyla padded to the front, her arms full of heavy hardbound books. Gold eyes looked over the rim of half-size reading glasses. "Why do I get the feeling I'm going to need something stronger than coffee?"

"Because you're a wise woman." Alex headed straight to the storage room. Wet sneakers squeaked on the wood floor and a trail of water marked his path. Fortunately, there were no customers in the store.

"Oh, Lord," Twyla muttered, setting the books on the counter. Mindful not to slip on the wet floor, she followed Alex to the back and eased the door half-closed. "All right. How bad is it?"

Alex flopped into a metal folding chair and unbuttoned his wet shirt. "There are a couple of things you need to know."

Pouring each of them a cup of hot coffee, Twyla appeared calm and collected. "Item one."

"At the moment, I'm living with Phoebe. Jack is, of course, not happy about it. But she's not safe out there with him anymore. There just wasn't any other way."

Twyla handed him a coffee cup. "So much for trust before sex. Item two."

"Jack was just in the kwoon. We had an interesting conversation. I'm a mystery to him. A thorn in his side. He'll probably have me investigated.

I've already called the Sedona office and warned them not to answer any questions. I want you to be prepared for the same."

Twyla took a long drink from the coffee cup. She shook her head, making long beaded earrings rattle. "I'm so sorry I got you involved in this mess."

"I'm not. If you hadn't yelled for help, I wouldn't have met Phoebe. I just hate lying to her."

Twyla backed against a row of storage cabinets. "I know, but you see what I mean about Jack."

This mess began to test what little patience Alex possessed. "Why don't you just talk to Jack?"

"Me? Last time I tried to talk to that boy, he slapped the—" Twyla's jaws snapped shut, and she hastily gulped down the rest of the sentence.

Alex felt the muscles in his neck tighten. "He hit you. Jack hit you, didn't he?" A string of foul curses spilled off his tongue, first in English then in a convoluted blend of Portuguese and Cantonese. "Is there no honor in this man? What did Martin do to him?"

"I don't know," Twyla replied in whispered defeat.

Alex drew a deep breath and let it out in short exasperated puffs. "Do you know why Danny's share of the business reverted to Jack instead of going to Phoebe?"

"I don't know how Jack managed to pull that off, either. I have an attorney looking into it, but I wouldn't get my hopes up. Jack is smart. I doubt he left any loopholes."

Staring unfocused across the storage room, Alex thought about Phoebe. "Poor little Dragonfly. Caught up in someone else's storm."

"Are you sure about that?"

Startled, Alex blinked until his eyes found a hard focus. "What do you mean? She didn't cause this mess. Martin Henderson sent this ugly snowball rolling downhill over thirty years ago."

"Uh-huh," Twyla intoned. "And maybe Phoebe is just the ray of sunlight this family needs to melt that ball of ice. Maybe it's her destiny."

"Why, Aunt Tea, I didn't know you were a poet."

"There are many things you don't know about me. In time, every secret sees the light of day."

"What does that mean?"

"It means that sooner or later Phoebe will find out who A. L. Jones really is."

Alex rocked the chair back on two legs. His reply was as cold as it was honest. "Sometimes I don't even know who A. L. Jones really is."

"Then I suggest you figure it out before Jack does."

* * *

THAT night at the Henderson house, Alex rinsed the last china plate, carefully placed it in the dishwasher, and closed the door. It was not his favorite way to spend a Friday evening, but for Phoebe's sake he had been on his best behavior.

All he could say about dinner was the wine was good and the steaks were rare. The conversation, however, had been stilted and tedious at best with this less-than-ideal foursome. Phoebe sat close to Alex, but kept her eyes on Jack through the whole meal. Sam rattled on and on about the latest trials of his teenage daughter, while Jack clinked his silverware, picked at his steak, and drank more than his usual share of the wine. All the time, Alex prayed for a quick end to the whole ordeal.

Now he was stuck in the kitchen with "babbling" Sam, while Phoebe headed down the hallway to have a heart-to-heart with Jack.

These Oklahomans were about to discuss Alex to death. He was a man of action, not words. Right now he would have preferred to work the punching bag, run a sword form, go through a tai-chi set, anything but talk.

Then Sam said something that caught him completely off-guard. Alex turned around so fast his braided hair whipped around his neck. "Who?"

"Rachel," Sam repeated. Sitting at the snack bar, he poured himself another glass of wine, emptying the amber bottle. "What do you think of her?"

Alex shook his head to make sure he had heard that right. "Rachel Gray?"

"You know, Phoebe's friend. The Apache goddess. Have you met her?"

"Yeah. She spent the day with us at the Fair. Actually, it was their day at the Fair. I crashed the party." It took Alex a few seconds to put two and two together. "You're interested in Rachel?"

Sam offered a broad shrug, looking both drunk and uncomfortable. "Silly, isn't it? Every time I see her she calls me *white-bread* and tells me to go away and die. I guess I'm just a glutton for rejection."

"Well, there are worse things." Alex took a peek down the hallway. All seemed reasonably quiet for the moment, so he concentrated on Sam. "Why don't you just ask her out?"

"I really want to impress her. You know? I thought maybe you could give me some advice. Native girls are different."

That remark really hit home. Alex gave a staccato nod. "You got that right. They don't like games. They demand honesty and intelligence. And they know the difference between love and sex. Approach Rachel with an open heart. Talk to her like a friend. See what develops. If you play games with her, she's liable to cut your balls off and use them for hood ornaments."

Sam dropped his head to the cool countertop and offered a long moan.

Smiling, Alex patted his newfound friend on the back. "It'll be all right. Just sober up before you talk to Rachel." He took another look down the hallway and wished he had not promised to stay in the kitchen.

Where's that ghost when you really need her?

* * *

THE room Jack had claimed for his office used to be Phoebe's sewing niche, but no one would guess that now.

Heavy furniture, upholstered with burgundy leather, looked trapped by a forest of looming brass lamps. Gone were the ruffled curtains. Dark green shades covered two tall and narrow windows. An enormous wood desk filled the center of the room like a modern throne.

Jack eased into his desk chair. The leather squeaked against his soft blue jeans, and the springs sighed in mild protest. Rocking back and forth, he folded his hands across his chest and focused on his sister-in-law. "If you needed a good screw, you should've asked me."

"Why? So you could buy me a man? No thank you. I found one all by myself." Phoebe offered the most hateful grin she could manufacture and sat in one of the wingback chairs. She felt brave tonight and wanted to give Jack a good dose of his own bitter medication.

Jack's expression darkened. "I know what you're doing."

"Oh, really? What I am doing, Jack?"

"You think you can intimidate me with that kung fu clown. I'll give you credit. It's not a bad move, but I still don't have to like it. Go ahead. Enjoy your weekend. Wad the sheets. Ream out the plumbing. Get it out of your system. Monday morning I want this house back the way it was before I went to California. You understand? I want Alex out of here, Phoebe."

She leaned back, letting the huge chair engulf her. "Or what?"

"Or he may find out how tough it is to start a new business in Oklahoma City. But then, we don't have to fight about this." Jack reached into the long, narrow central drawer and pulled out a contract selling her share of the whole 160 acres plus the house. "The offer still stands. Sign it and you'll get your first payment at the end of the month. Take the money and go make babies with your Indian Brave. Just be out of here by Monday morning. You hear me?"

For a moment, Phoebe wondered if a body could walk around without a spirit inside it. Jack was the coldest, most soulless person she had ever met. With her resolve intact, Phoebe got out of the huge chair and reached over the desk. She ripped the contract in half and tossed the pieces in the air. "I hear you, Jack. I just can't help you."

Looking unruffled, Jack pulled another copy of the contract from the drawer. That was the fourth one Phoebe had torn this month. By now, it was a routine scene. "I have a whole desk full of these. The offer remains the same. You'd better sign this soon, or we're going to war."

Phoebe walked to the doorway and paused, looking over her shoulder. "Isn't that about what Custer said to Sitting Bull?"

A muscle in Jack's jaw twitched. "The Sioux Nation lost that war."

"But they won at the Little Bighorn and took out Custer in the process. Now, I'm going upstairs with my *Indian Brave* and make as much noise as possible for as long as possible. Sweet dreams, Jack."

* * *

NEAR midnight, Phoebe stomped out of the steamy bathroom and stopped in the center of the starlit bedroom.

One towel was wrapped turban fashion around her wet hair and another was knotted at her waist. Modesty was the last thing on her mind. She was furious with Jack, possibly madder than she had ever been.

Alex sat cross-legged in the middle of the floor, wearing nothing but tawny skin. Dreamy eyes opened as he pulled out of a long meditation. "My little dragonfly went into the cocoon and came out a full-grown dragon."

The sound of his voice worked like a healing balm. Phoebe's stance softened, and the fire in her eyes settled down to a simmer. "I know. I let Jack upset me."

"As sexy as this is, I have to warn you. It's not very good for your blood pressure."

"Probably not," she conceded. "Just a minute. I want to show you something."

Going into the closet, she retrieved a small leather bundle from a niche behind stacked shoes. The leather bundle rested unattended in the crook of her arm, seemingly intent with her touch and presence. Phoebe gave it a loving pat, like a mother reassuring a sleeping child. "The first time you spoke to me you asked if I knew anything about pipes. Well, here's what I know."

"That's your grandmother's pipe?"

"I had to hide it all these years from Danny. He didn't approve of such things. Now that he's gone, I should be able to do what I feel is best. But Jack hates our ways even more than Danny did, and he's always underfoot. It's just so frustrating!"

Alex cocked his head to one side and offered that masterly tone of voice. "You can't open that bundle with any anger or fear in your heart."

Looking down, Phoebe remembered watching her grandmother bead the ends of the two leather ties that held together the bundle. "That's why I've never used it."

"Never?"

Shame shivered through Phoebe and settled in the base of her stomach like a bad meal. "Grandma will be dead seven years come November 8th. I didn't intend to show you the pipe. You don't get out a pipe, unless you're going to use it. I know that much, at least. I just wanted you to know where it was and what the bundle looked like. I wanted to share."

"Thank you. I feel honored."

"Honored was how I felt when Grandma gave me this pipe. She trusted me care for it. I have, but probably not the way she intended." Frowning, Phoebe returned the leather bundle to its hiding place.

When she straightened, the towel slipped a little at her hips. She knew that once she got within Alex's long reach the discussion would be over and the lovemaking would begin. Since there was something else she wanted to discuss, she kept her distance.

"Despite everything that's happened the last few weeks, I have noticed being more in control."

Alex offered a reserved smile. "It's the kung fu. The stances and exercises increase your energy. They're sneaky that way. You don't realize they're working until something happens and you get a real head-rush."

"That's what I felt tonight with Jack. I wasn't a bit afraid of him. Sure, I admit it's easier to stand up to him with you in the house. But, to be honest, I wasn't thinking about you. I was focused on Jack. I really stood up to him." Errant thoughts rolled in like dusty tumbleweeds, and her bravery began to wane. "But I'll probably have to pay for it later."

"Don't let yourself be sideswiped by old fears. Focus on the now."

"The now?"

Alex's gold eyes glowed with primal hunger. "Come here, Dragonfly."

CHAPTER 18

War Games

WITH the sunrise came a shift in the direction of the wind and the promise of a sunny day. Phoebe rubbed her eyes and tried to untangle from wadded sheets and blankets.

Elsa's furry mound snored at the end of the bed, while Kiki stood in the middle of the room and sniffed the morning.

Fully clothed, Alex sat on top of the covers, his long legs crossed at the ankles and the telephone receiver tucked under his chin. "Yeah, I'll explain it when I get there. Give me about an hour. I really appreciate this. Uh-huh. Well, I don't know. I'll ask her. See you in a little bit. Bye." He eased the receiver back onto its slim base and cast a knowing smile toward Phoebe. "Good morning. Want to go into town with me?"

She yawned and ran her fingers through unruly auburn strands. Letting that long hair dry without combing it out first had been a mistake, but there had other things on her mind last night. "Town? Who was that on the phone?"

"A friend of mine. Bobby Three Stars. He's going to teach my class for a while. At least until we get this mess settled with Jack."

Sitting up, Phoebe realized she was not wearing a nightgown. Naked to the night was one thing. Naked to the day was another. She pulled the blanket up just high enough to cover the peaks of her breasts.

Alex laughed and planted a kiss on her forehead. "Don't be so modest, girl. I've seen what's under those covers. And believe me, the dogs don't care."

"Ooooh." Her complaint was quickly forgotten as a new question raised in her mind. "I guess Bobby is another ass-kicking, wandering medicine man."

"Colorful but accurate, I suppose. What do you say? You want to go with me? Find a big breakfast and get Bobby settled in?"

"Yeah. Give me ten minutes." Phoebe kicked off the blankets just to spite modesty. Grinning, she rolled over Alex and hit the floor with both feet.

* * *

ALEX waited for Phoebe in the corner of the breakfast nook, coffee cup in one hand and a section of the paper in the other.

From beneath the table, Kiki offered a low growl.

He comforted the dog with the toe of his sneaker and grinned at the accuracy of this old-fashioned early warning system.

Within seconds Jack stumbled down the back stairs and slid into the kitchen. He opened the breezeway door and paused on the threshold, giving Alex a massive go-to-hell stare. "Are you still here?"

"I was about to ask you the same thing." Alex smirked and gave the dog a comforting nudge to keep her calm.

"I live here. You just screw here."

Amused by the agitation he had caused his ill-tempered opponent, Alex manufactured a broad grin. "And how is Jack going to spend his Saturday? Working or playing?"

"None of your damned business. If a fight is what you're looking for, you're about to find it, buddy." Jack bounded out the door, letting it slam behind him.

A stiff breeze rose from nowhere and blew the papers out of Alex's hand.

Grandma's misty form coalesced in the archway that led to the central hallway. Her small hands rested on her hips, and fire blazed in her astral eyes. *Isn't there enough bad blood here already? Must you make more? You not only look like Martin Henderson, but you have the same bad temper.*

Alex blinked, shocked by both the reprimand and the reference. "I look like Martin? Twyla said I was the image of my grandfather, but I thought she meant Granddad Jones."

Well, that's what you get for thinking. Behave or Grandma's gonna cut your hair, boy. With her nose raised in gestured contempt, the old ghost turned and walked down the hallway, leaving behind a trail of silvery mist and tiny moccasin footprints in the carpet.

"Yes, Grandma," he intoned. There were some things with which Alex would argue and some things he would not. The cranky ghost of an old medicine woman definitely fell into the *not* category.

Just as the response rolled off Alex's tongue, Phoebe bounced into the kitchen. "Who are you talking to?"

Alex slid out of the breakfast nook. "Never mind. You ready?"

* * *

HAROLD Swearingen went to Red Cedars Corner shopping mall to get a few pictures of Lin Martial Arts and to check out the surroundings. He had not expected to have company.

From the anonymity of his dull gray sedan with the tinted windows, he raised a professional camera and clicked away, getting as many shots as possible of two Native American men and one auburn-haired woman he immediately recognized as Phoebe Henderson.

The man with long braided hair fussed with the front door lock, while Phoebe chatted with the short-haired man. As soon as the door opened, all three slipped inside and out of view. In the light of day, it was impossible to see through those golden window shades.

"Well, well, there's Miss Phoebe. But which one of you two bulls is the lover?" Harold set the camera on the seat next to him. Fat fingers abused the small pencil in his hand, scribbling out the license numbers of the two cars parked in front of the kwoon. Years of surveillance work had left Harold with one odd habit. He talked to himself. It was his way of working through the possibilities, as well as providing peculiar entertainment. "Bachelor number one had the key. Bachelor number two seemed a little short for our auburn Amazon. Besides, bachelor number two came in an airport rental. Looks like bachelor number one gets the kisses and bachelor number two is the apprentice. God, I love easy money."

Grinning to himself, he started the car and pulled forward through empty parking spaces. First stop, the photography shop. Second stop, the airport.

* * *

MONDAY morning Jack shuffled out of the office elevator at precisely 8:31 a.m. and headed right past Genny's empty desk.

"Mr. Henderson?" a deep voice called from the corner of the office.

Startled, Jack dropped his briefcase on the floor and wheeled around, striking a classic defensive pose.

A huge man pulled himself out of a typical lobby chair and raised his hands in gestured peace. "Easy there, fellow. The name's Harold Swearingen."

Jack put both feet solidly on the carpet and straightened his jacket, mentally scolding himself for being so jumpy. With his nerves repaired and his composure back to its usual polished stone, he offered his hand in greeting. "You're the P.I. Sam hired, right?"

"That's right." Swearingen took Jack's hand, gave it one strong shake, and then pulled a manila folder from under his other arm. "I have something I think you should see."

"You found something already?"

"Well, I'm a little confused, Mr. Henderson. Can we talk in private?"

"Sure. Follow me."

Jack led the way into his private office and shut the door behind them. He maneuvered behind his desk, got comfortable in the swiveling chair, and folded his hands over his flat stomach. "So, what confuses you?"

"This." Swearingen spread several photographs on the desk and then rifled through a manila folder. "The one with the braid is the man you know as Alex Lin, correct?"

"Correct." Jack leaned over the desk, his interest piqued. "Who's the other guy?"

"Bobby Three Stars. He arrived Saturday morning on a flight from Phoenix. That got me to thinking, so I made some phone calls. Now here's where I'm confused."

"About what?"

Swearingen dropped huge palms on the desk. "The way I figure it, either you're playing games with Mr. Tillman, or I found the skeleton in your family closet."

Jack felt the color drain from his face. "Family?"

"Family." Swearingen pulled a picture out of the pile and laid it across the bottom of the report. "You see, the first thing I do when I take a new case is investigate the people who hired me. I don't like surprises. It was the guy from Phoenix who tipped me off. You have a business partner in Sedona, Arizona. A. L. Jones. Now, *A. L.* kept tickling my ear." Swearingen tapped a photograph of the front of Lin Martial Arts. In the corner of the picture was an out-of-focus sign that read Red Cedars Corner. "Pay attention, Jack. The key here is Twyla Jones. She owns Red Cedars Realty, this strip mall and two others in the city."

"I don't need you to tell me who Twyla Jones is," Jack snarled, feeling uncomfortable with the turn of this conversation. Skeletons indeed. "You were hired to investigate Alex Lin."

"I was hired to find out who owned Lin Martial Arts. And the answer is Twyla Jones." Swearingen adjusted the wire-rimmed glasses on his nose. "When your grandfather, Martin Henderson, died twelve years ago, he left one quarter of Northwest Properties to A. L. Jones. This piqued my interest, so I did a little digging and found some interesting birth records. It seems Martin Henderson had illegitimate twins by a woman named Felicia Jones. A girl named Anna and a boy named William. William had a son named Alex Lin. Get it? A. L.? Alex Lin. Alex Lin Jones. And, of course, you know who Anna was. So my question is why are you having me investigate your business partner? Your own cousin?"

Jack rummaged stiffly through the photocopies of several birth records. There it was. The one thing he did not want anyone ever to discover sat right in the middle of his desk, glaring at him like a haughty neon light.

He tapped the document in question. "Have you shown this to anyone else?"

"No," said Swearingen. "I thought I should talk to you first, considering what I found."

Nodding, Jack reached into his desk and pulled out his checkbook. "I'll double what Sam quoted, if you don't show him what you found."

"It's a deal."

* * *

AFTER Swearingen left, Jack sat facing the window, watching the traffic, and tapping his fingers on the arms of the chair. If he had not been so shocked, he might have found humor in the situation.

What was that old saying? Hide in plain sight?

The truth was right in front of him. Alex was the mysterious business partner, A. L. Jones. But why had Alex come to Oklahoma City? And why had he insinuated himself into Phoebe's life?

Jack believed this was Twyla's doing. That it was her revenge on Martin Henderson for refusing to acknowledge William and Anna as his heirs all those years ago. And it would have stayed that way if Martin had not left that quarter share of Northwest Properties to a grandson he had never met. Jack still had not forgiven Martin for that.

Phoebe's motives for refusing to sign over the land and house were still not completely clear, but Jack at least had a few clues. Surely, that rich old witch Twyla Jones and her mongrel nephew Alex had suckered Phoebe into a conspiracy.

The door to his private office squeaked, and Sam's voice echoed with that usual carefree lilt. "Genny said you wanted to see me."

Jack's focused hard on Sam's reflection. "Close the door."

"Okay." Losing that upbeat tone of voice, Sam did as requested. Shoving his hands in his pockets, he walked to the window and leaned a shoulder against the cool glass. "What's wrong, Jack?"

"Swearingen was waiting in the office when I got here this morning."

"Wow. That was fast. What did he find?"

Rocking back and forth in the chair, Jack considered the turn of events. "The nail for Phoebe's coffin."

Sam looked uncomfortable. "What does that mean? What'd he tell you?"

"I paid off Swearingen," Jack said, evading the question. "I'm keeping the report and I want you to forget about it. That's an order."

"We've been friends for twenty years. That's the first time you've given me a direct order outside of the Army."

"This has nothing to do with friendship. This is family. Stay out of it."

* * *

THE evening was warm. Jack rolled down the car windows and cranked up the stereo. Wind and music occupied his ears, while his nostrils filled with that unique smell of the edge of the prairie. Grass, short oaks, and red cedars. With his tactile senses entertained by the physical world, Jack pondered the situation.

First, there was Twyla Jones. Her motives did not need re-evaluation. Had she really brought Alex here? Had she advised Phoebe to hang onto the house and the land? Probably.

Second there was Alex. Was Alex here to back up Twyla? To provide muscle and nothing more? Maybe.

Third there was Phoebe. At present her motives defied explanation. Why fight over land that belonged to Jack's family? Maybe she just could not bear to leave the house where Danny had lived. Perhaps.

Then a new thought popped into Jack's head. Could Phoebe be the architect of this whole mess? She was a smart girl. Perhaps Phoebe had known about Twyla and Alex for years. Perhaps she intended to leave Danny years ago. Imaginary conspiracies popped up like chickweeds, crowding the yard that was Jack's mind.

He swallowed his questions and his personal outrage for the moment, reminding himself that patience must preside. The reasons he would give Phoebe, the words Alex would surely overhear, must be solid and unquestionable. His behavior had to be conciliatory yet true to form. He needed to make the offer without emotion. Then the trap would be set.

* * *

JUST as the sunset faded into the west, Phoebe heard Jack's sedan roar into the garage. She hoped an old-fashioned country dinner would make her brother-in-law amenable, if not agreeable.

The kitchen was a mess, but it smelled wonderful. Chicken fried steak sizzled in the electric skillet. Potatoes boiled on the stove. Homemade biscuits browned in the oven. Fresh salad overfilled a bowl like a still life painting. A colander full of fried okra set in the sink, corn oil draining down the garbage disposal. Phoebe could not keep from sampling a few crispy nuggets and moaning approval at her own culinary expertise.

Jack kicked open the breezeway door. His voice carried an unusually friendly lilt. "Do I smell biscuits?"

Surprised, Phoebe turned around. "Indeed you do. I was worried you were going to miss this. It'll be ready in about fifteen minutes."

The door opened again. Like clockwork, Alex slipped into the house and took his sentry position in the breakfast nook. Pitiful whines emanated from the breezeway as the dogs bemoaned their exclusion.

Setting his briefcase beneath the snack bar, Jack shed his suit coat and kept one eye on Alex. "Phoebe, I have a proposition for you. How about a temporary truce?"

Alex put one foot onto the bench seat and propped his arm on an elevated knee. Those gold eyes darkened with obvious suspicion, but he remained the silent observer.

Backing against the sink, Phoebe wiped her hands on an old tea towel. "I'm listening."

Jack's voice rang firm and clear. "As much fun as all this bickering is, I really need to take care of business."

"The election party," Phoebe surmised.

"Right. It's going to be a big election this year and I want to throw a party to match. If you'll help me, I'll agree to behave myself until then."

"And after the party?" she asked.

Jack loosened his silk tie and leaned against the refrigerator. "I'm not going to lie to you, Phoebe. I haven't changed my mind about the land. I thought we could let it simmer for a while. Give everybody time to think. Come November, we'll throw one hell of a party. After that, we'll talk. I'm offering you a few quiet weeks in exchange for doing this party for me. I'm lousy at party plans. You know that. And you've always done such a good job." Moving to the sink, Jack stole a couple of pieces of okra. "So what do you say? Is it a deal?"

After checking the steaks and the biscuits, Phoebe turned toward Jack. The offer sounded cold and selfish enough to be genuinely his, but something had been left unsaid, something that made the back of her neck prickle in psychic alarm. Yet how could she turn down his offer? A few easy weeks would be heaven after all she had been through. She glanced at Alex and saw suspicion in his eyes. Clearly, he did not trust Jack, either. But what would it hurt for her to host one last party?

Finally, Phoebe wiped the flour from her hand and thrust it in Jack's direction. "It's a deal."

* * *

WITH one of Grandma's handmade quilts wrapped around her shoulders, Phoebe crossed the back patio and stepped inside the gazebo.

Alex sat in the swing, rocking methodically back and forth, his head laid back, his eyes seemingly focused on nothing.

The huge dogs romped and played like puppies, turning the outside of the gazebo into a private racetrack.

"May I join you?" Phoebe asked. The swing stopped just long enough for her to sit down. Then it moved again in brisk increments. "What's wrong? You didn't like dinner?"

"Dinner was great. It was the company I didn't like," Alex muttered.

Phoebe tucked her feet beneath her and snuggled against him. "You don't trust Jack."

"And neither should you. He's up to something, but I can't see what it is."

"And that bothers you, not being able to see what's in his head?"

The swing stopped and Alex planted his feet firmly on the concrete pad. "He has a lock-down in progress. No emotions. No thoughts. The perfect poker face. The perfect poker player."

Phoebe allowed a reflective smile. "I told you Jack wasn't easy to deal with. What's the old saying? Walk a mile in my moccasins? I've tried reasoning with that man. Yelling at him. Pleading with him. I've done the stubborn thing. I've threatened the legal thing. Don't feel bad because you can't snap your fingers and make him acquiesce. Jack's a tough nut to crack."

Those gold eyes made a menacing shift in her direction, and an evil smile turned up one side of Alex's sensual mouth.

"Don't even think about it," Phoebe scolded and pushed the swing with her moccasin-covered feet. "I have no doubt that you can crack Jack's skull. But we're not going there. We'll find another way."

"What if there is no other way?"

"You don't really believe that, do you?"

Alex slipped lower in the seat and rested his head on the back. "I thought I could reason with Jack, but he has a lot of hatred in his heart. Hatred is not reasonable. He's up to no good, Phoebe. No good at all. And I can't see what he's planning. That's what worries me the most. I didn't expect him to have that much—energy."

"Let's not worry about it tonight, okay?" The question was rhetorical.

She really did not expect an answer.

Phoebe curled up her legs and laid her head in Alex's lap. The swing moved in easy arcs, back and forth, its metal chains creaking. Kiki nipped playfully at Elsa's thicker haunches and the race continued. High clouds drifted over the face of that enormous harvest moon and gave it a murky hue.

A cool breeze buffeted the folds of the blanket and brought the scent of cedar. A silvery, transparent figure paced an agitated line between the gazebo and the house. Grandma.

Phoebe silently agreed with Alex.

Difficulty lay somewhere over the horizon.

Trouble was coming, and there was nothing they could do to stop it.

*****

CHAPTER 19

Eye of the Storm

ON the first Monday morning of November, Phoebe pointed to an empty storefront in Willow Creek shopping center. "It's that one. Pull in over there."

Easing the car into a parking space, Alex killed the engine and read the address out loud. "2121 Willow Creek. It has a nice ring, and it faces east. That's good."

"That's what I thought." Phoebe jumped out, nudging the car door closed with her hip. She fumbled with a huge ring of keys and located the one marked with a small strip of tape. "Come on. I want you to see this."

She inserted the key in the huge old-fashioned lock. It would not budge. Determined, she gave the door a shake and tried again. This time the deadbolt clicked, and the release moved easily under her thumb. With a lot of dust and a little creaking, the door eased inward, taking Phoebe with it.

"Well, what do you think?" she asked.

Morning light poured through the opening, warming stale air. Just inside to the left was a long dusty counter. Floor to ceiling shelves covered three walls. Free-standing bookshelves created a clever maze through the interior. Sunlight glinted off the brass tips of sleeping overhead fans, pointing the way to a second-story mezzanine and more silent bookshelves.

With his hands in his pockets and a strange expression on his usually stoic face, Alex stepped through the door and gazed around. "Not bad. It's about the right size. And the location's good."

"I think it's perfect," Phoebe declared, walking down a shadowed aisle.

Perfect just about described the last few weeks. The truce with Jack would officially end after the party tomorrow night. September and October had passed so quickly, so uneventfully compared to the six months before it. Jack kept his promise and was reasonably behaved. A few snide remarks escaped through clenched teeth, and if looks could kill he would have burned Alex to a cinder by now. Yet, to everyone's surprise, Jack had upheld his part of the bargain.

As for Alex, he could not have been more loving or attentive. He had managed to spoil Phoebe completely rotten and she knew it. No one had ever been so understanding of her space and headspace. When she needed to walk the pasture alone, he just smiled and said, "Put on your moccasins and make tracks." When she needed time with Rachel, he shook a finger and warned, "Don't talk bad about me." It was exactly the relationship of which she had always dreamed. The easy, breezy, trusting kind of give-and-take that should carry a couple through life's journey. This was the man with whom Phoebe hoped to spend the rest of her life.

From the relative darkness of the middle of the empty building, she imagined a brightly lit and bustling bookstore. Dreamcatchers for sale hung in the windows. In one corner glass gondolas held candles and figurines and perfume oils and knickknacks of all kinds in keeping with a New Age-Native American flavor. New books filled the center aisles and looked toward tomorrow. Old books held up the walls with the wisdom of yesterday. A computer purred on the polished tile counter, keeping track of inventory and sales, profits and taxes. A brass bell with a dragonfly etching hung over the door. Unlike Twyla's doorbell, this one rang with a clear voice.

"You're at the crossroads," Alex commented and leaned an elbow on the dusty counter.

Phoebe turned. The sunlight pouring through the door covered Alex with a fuzzy golden halo, forcing her to squint to find the features of his face. "Crossroads?"

"Facing a choice. Do you go this way or that? Left or right? Up or back? This is a big decision, Dragonfly."

"How so?"

"A business is a huge commitment. You'll be spending your days and nights here for quite a while. If it does well, after a while you can hire people and have a little more freedom. Are you sure you want to tie yourself up like that?"

Intrigued, Phoebe sauntered to the counter and batted feathery lashes. "Did you have something else in mind?"

Alex's cheeks sported an uncharacteristic rosy glow. "I kind of hoped we might plan the future together."

"That would be nice." She gestured toward the center of the store. "With a little hard work this place could provide a nice income. Between the bookstore and the school, we could do quite well. And in a year or so, maybe—"

"Maybe what?" Alex gave a wry smile.

This time Phoebe blushed. She had been thinking about children, wondering if that was possible with Alex. "First, we have to settle this stupidity with Jack. If I get to keep the house, that'll make things a lot easier. No mortgage. No rent. So do you really like this place? Does the energy feel right?"

Alex offered a smile that was adoration come to life. "It's a nice fit."

"I think so, too," Phoebe said. "There's a phone booth around the corner. I'll call Twyla and tell her I'm interested. We're interested. I'll be right back."

* * *

FROM the doorway of the empty building, Alex watched Phoebe walk down the sidewalk and up to a wall-mounted public telephone.

After scanning the immediate area to make sure she was safe, he looked back inside the abandoned bookstore. Phoebe's vision of crowded bookshelves and knick-knack displays came to life in his mind's eye. It was the other part of the dream that haunted him. Children. Phoebe had envisioned beautiful, black-haired golden-eyed imps sitting behind the counter with coloring books and stuffed animals.

His heart skipped a beat. Would Phoebe still want him after she learned he had lied to her all these weeks? Would he ever be able to explain why he kept his identity a secret?

The warm, colorful vision of a happy bookstore and contented children withered before his eyes, like cotton candy dissolving in a hot rain. In its place came the stark reality of someone else's broken dream. Lonely shelves. Frozen ceiling fans. Shaded windows. Rusted locks. Creaking doors.

Alex closed his eyes, forcing the lily pond to focus in the back of his mind. He must not lose the dream. He must not lose Phoebe.

A voice broke through his mental fog. "Alex? Are you ready to go?"

He spun around, squinting at the sunlight. "Ready?"

"Twyla wants her keys back and I'm starved. How about some lunch?"

"Sounds good." Shading his eyes, he stepped outside and closed the door.

The fat ring of keys rattled against the brass plate and the deadbolt fell into place with an eerie finality.

* * *

THAT afternoon Jack sat at his desk, pondering the situation he had set into motion.

With a stack of papers under one arm, Sam knocked on the frame of the open office door. "You want to see these copies?"

Jack remained distant. "No. Just make a list. I can pull them later if I need to. Did you find a date for the party?"

"Not yet. We've been so busy around here, I'm afraid I haven't done much socializing." Until last month Sam had loved coming to work, but not anymore. Jack had been sullen and strange, reclusive and secretive. Sam was out of the information loop and knew it. "But I'll find a date. Don't worry. The party's going to be fine."

"Fine indeed," Jack hissed in reply and offered a wicked grin. He rocked back in his chair and propped his shoes on top of the messy desk. "It should be quite a show. Do you think popcorn goes with champagne?"

"No, not really." Sam stepped up to the desk. "What are you up to, Jack? And don't tell me nothing. What's the matter with you? For the last month you've treated me like a stranger. You know you can trust me."

"When the party's over, you'll understand. That's all the explanation you're going to get."

"I guess it'll have to do." Looking defeated, Sam headed toward the door.

* * *

JUST before six o'clock, Sam leaned forward in his chair and tapped his finger on the corner of the telephone. Everyone had gone home for the night and a relative calm had overtaken the floor. The building's circulation system thumped out of rhythm with the hum of fluorescent lights. Only a modicum of city noise filtered in from the outside. With the pulse of the building and the grind of traffic in the back of his ears, Sam contemplated a little treason.

A faded note hung on the side of the telephone. Using that number might risk what was left of his friendship with Jack and could even cost him his job. Yet, Sam's concern for Phoebe grew by the hour. What horrific surprise did Jack have planned for the poor girl? Did it have anything to do with what the private investigator found? If so, that would make Sam partially responsible. He was not generally predisposed to premonition, but he had a bad feeling about tomorrow night's party.

Sam had seen Phoebe a few times this month. She had looked so happy, sounded so calm and hopeful. One evening after she had cooked a sumptuous dinner for three hungry men, Sam stayed in the kitchen to help her put up the dishes. Phoebe's words from that night come back to haunt him. *Everything will be all right after the party. Jack just needed some time to calm down, to sort things out. He won't take my house. You'll see. In the end, Jack will do the right thing.*

The right thing. Sam shook his head, pushing aside the mental echo of her voice. "Jack, I'm sorry," he said to himself. "I can't let you torture that girl any longer." Determined to do the right thing for once in his life, Sam picked up the telephone receiver and punched in the number written on the faded note.

After only one ring, a crisp voice answered. "Hello?"

"Rachel? This is Sam Tillman."

Rachel's voice faltered. "Is something wrong? Is Phoebe all right?"

"For now."

"For now? What does that mean?"

Sam cleared his throat and lowered his voice. The office was empty, but caution was always wise. "The election party is tomorrow night."

"I know. Phoebe's been busy planning Jack's little foray."

Rachel's comment made the back of Sam's neck prickle. "Listen, Rachel. This party worries me."

"Me, too, Sam."

"So come with me."

"To Jack's party?"

"Yes," Sam confirmed in a strong voice. "Don't worry about Jack. His head is in the ozone right now. I'd really like you to be there. I think Phoebe needs you. And I'd be honored to be your escort."

There was a moment of silence on the other end of the line. Then Rachel's clear voice filled the speaker. "Pick me up at six-thirty tomorrow night. I'll give you the directions. Got something to write with?"

Sam grabbed a pen. "Ready."

* * *

AROUND seven-thirty that evening, Alex paused in the doorway between the office and the practice area. Bobby had done such a good job with the class, especially with Phoebe. Right now the substitute teacher had his students paired off with boxing gloves and mouthpieces, and was ready to start a simple sparring exercise.

Satisfied the class was in good hands, he slipped unnoticed through the office and out the back. The night air felt good against wet silks. He jogged up the alley and knocked on a gray metal door.

After a couple of minutes, the lock clicked and the door swung inward.

"What took you so long?" Alex complained, stepping into the back room of the Twylight Bookstore.

Twyla closed the door and frowned. "Ever heard of customers?"

He sat on the corner of a sturdy table and offered a grim expression. "If I don't do something fast, I'm going to lose her, Aunt Tea."

"Perhaps you should stop worrying about it and just let it happen."

"What kind of advice is that?"

"The best advice I know." Twyla put strong hands on her nephew's silk-covered knees. "Just because you lose her doesn't mean you aren't destined to find her again."

"It doesn't mean I am, either."

"Maybe. But you can't second-guess destiny. It's going to happen the way it's going to happen. There's nothing you can do about it. Just sit back and enjoy the journey. Take the good with the bad."

"Go down without a fight?" Alex shook his head. "No way. I'm going to tell her who I am. She's going to be mad for a while, but I can't keep this a secret any longer. She deserves the truth. The hell with the house and the land. I don't care if it did belong to our family. Let Jack deal with the old ghost. Believe me, he won't stay there very long by himself."

Twyla's eyebrows raised. "So, you've met Grandma."

"Several times." Alex could see his face reflected in the glistening golden orbs that were his aunt's eyes. The mirror effect sent chills up his spine. "I've tried to get her to give me the answer to that damned riddle, but all she does is shake a finger at me."

"That ghost was once a powerful medicine woman. She loves that girl as much as you do. She wouldn't risk Phoebe's happiness or welfare unless there was something important at stake."

With an impatient snort, Alex brushed Twyla's hands off his knees and got to his feet. "Tomorrow night after the party, I'm going to tell Phoebe who I am and why I'm here. Then ask her to marry me. If everything goes as planned, we should be on a plane bound for Arizona by Wednesday afternoon."

"And the riddle?"

"If we can solve it in the next thirty-six hours, fine. If not, we'll just have to work on it from a distance. A safe distance from Jack."

Without a "thanks" or a "goodnight," Alex slipped out the back door, slamming it behind him.

*****

CHAPTER 20
Social Dues & Don'ts

ALEX had both anticipated and dreaded the arrival of the election party. Something evil was afoot. All he could do was keep his senses on alert and stay close to Phoebe.

Most of Jack's guests had arrived at the house, milling through the huge living room and the formal dining area. The men looked like clones in their unimaginative tuxedos, while the women made a charming bouquet in assorted sequins and lace. Alex had never seen so many social climbers in one place and hoped he never would again. The tone and timbre of this party already threatened to curdle his supper.

He had bowed to pressure from both Jack and Phoebe and agreed to wear one of those damnable, restraining tuxedos. Except for the conspicuous braid of black hair, he quietly conformed to dress code. The crowd did not seem to know what to make of him. He received a few pinched but polite *hellos* and lots of stares, which was fine with him.

Across the living room, he noticed Jack's nod. Alex understood. It was time for Phoebe to greet her guests.

Climbing the elegant staircase two steps at a time, Alex left the roar of the party. He made his way down the upstairs hallway and knocked on the door of the master bedroom.

"It's me," he announced, opening the door. The sight that greeted him brought a moan of approval to his lips. "Wow. You look good enough to eat."

Phoebe put the finishing touches on her ensemble by slipping into beaded high heel shoes. Her exquisite figure had been poured into a black tea-length beaded dress that split up one side and showed her thigh when she walked. Auburn hair was piled on her head in a fashionable twist and sported iridescent sprigs of something meant to resemble floral baby's breath. For the first time Alex saw her wearing makeup, eyeliner, blush, red lipstick and all. The transformation was startling.

"Stay right where you are," Phoebe warned and shoved a stiff finger in his direction. "Don't you dare muss me up after all this hard work."

Alex put his hands behind his back. "Yes, ma'am. You are

breathtaking, my dear. I hate to share this vision, but duty calls."

"Yeah, I guess it's time. Is everything okay with the caterers?"

"Everything's running smoothly. We're just waiting for you."

"Right," Phoebe intoned and walked toward the open door. High heels forced a provocative sway to those hips and caused that dress to reveal a lot of silk-clad thigh. "Let's get this over with."

* * *

WITH Alex at her side, Phoebe made her grand appearance down the front stairs. This was the last one of these parties she intended to host. She wanted to make it a good one. The house was full of tuxedos and party dresses, or as Phoebe called them, penguins and petunias. There were so few formal affairs in this city, people made these rare events as showy as possible, like children playing dress-up. Phoebe found one surprising face in the crowd—Rachel Gray hanging on Sam Tillman's arm. Perhaps the evening would be interesting after all.

"You ready?" she whispered to the handsome man at her side.

"As ready as I'll ever be. Just don't get too far from me tonight, okay?"

"Don't be such a worrywart," she fussed. "It's just a party. What can happen?"

"Are you really asking?"

"No," Phoebe piped back under her breath. "Let's get it over with."

The stairs were a little tricky in those high heels and that long dress, but Alex lent Phoebe a strong arm. At the bottom, she glanced at Rachel and her unlikely date. "Would somebody like to explain this?"

Taking advantage of the opportunity, Sam gave his date an affectionate kiss on the cheek. "No, I think we'll just leave you to wonder."

"Behave," Rachel scolded and pointed toward the bar. "Why don't you two studs make yourselves useful. Get us some champagne."

Sam gave a mocking huff. "Well! I know when I'm not wanted. Come on, Alex. We're interfering with the girl talk."

Wearing a lopsided frown, Alex followed Sam across the room.

"Jack's going to be furious having all these Indians at his hoity-toity party," Phoebe whispered. "And I'm not too pleased, myself."

"Why?"

"I can't be the prettiest girl in the room with you here. This is my party. I should be the belle of the ball."

"Don't blame that on me. Look over there." Rachel nodded toward the patio doors and offered a staged hiss.

A sneer pulled at one side of Phoebe's face. Jack's *tart* from the restaurant hung on the arm of a tall, blonde-haired man and flirted shamelessly with a potbellied senator. "Well, well. Shall we make the rounds and introduce ourselves?"

Rachel offered a feline grin that showed off perfect teeth. "Absolutely."

* * *

LIKE a dog working a flock of sheep, Jack kept the crowd contained and contented.

By nine o'clock the election results had been announced and absorbed, cheered and grieved as appropriate for this political group. The only kinks thus far in the evening had been Sam's shocking choice of a date and Erin's appearance on the arm of a rival businessman. Jack figured Erin staged it just to make him mad, but her little schoolgirl antics would not dampen his mood. Not with what he had planned.

Jack noticed Alex looking uncomfortable in that fitted tuxedo and out of place with this stiff crowd. *If you think you're uneasy now, cousin, just wait. It's about to get worse.*

Stepping up to the middle landing of the elegant staircase, Jack let his sharp voice echo through the house. "Everyone! Attention please! Bartender, make sure everyone's glass is full."

Phoebe wheeled around, almost spilling her drink on Alex's rented tuxedo.

The crowd gathered at the base of the stairs.

"As you know, we lost my brother, Danny, this year," Jack began. "You've all been very kind and supportive during this time. I have a few special people I would like to thank. To Sam, my friend of twenty years and my office manager. You've always been there for me." Jack took a sip from his glass.

The crowd offered a resounding, "Salute."

Looking appropriately humble, Sam gave a gracious bow.

Jack's gaze shifted. "And to my sister-in-law, Phoebe, our lovely and gracious hostess. I want the world to know how brave you have been through all of this. I cannot thank you enough." Again, Jack raised his glass and the crowd followed.

Undaunted by Phoebe's stiff nod and cold smile, Jack turned his attention to the man at her side. He had been waiting for this moment for weeks. He did not want to hurry it or spoil it in any way. It had to be perfect. "And finally, to someone none of you have met before. A man who has been a hard-working silent partner in the business all these years.

Just a name at the bottom of so many contracts. I take great pleasure in putting a face to that name. Ladies and gentlemen, may I introduce my cousin, Alex Lin Jones."

Alex looked frozen in place as the eyes of the crowd followed the direction of Jack's raised glass.

Shocked, Phoebe hung onto her wineglass, but just barely. Her gaze shifted from Alex to Jack, and then back to Alex.

Eyes narrowed, Alex raised his glass and accepted the salute. "The pleasure will be mine, cousin."

* * *

JACK had outmaneuvered him. Alex knew it, but did not know what to do about it.

"Dragonfly, wait," Alex implored, reaching out a hand. "Let me explain."

"Leave me alone," Phoebe seethed through clenched teeth and slapped away his hand. Her eyes were gray-green fire. Her breathing was rapid and erratic. She waded through the crowd, stormed out the patio doors, and headed straight for the gazebo.

When Alex started to follow, Rachel put the sharp edge of a hand to his chest. "Just leave her alone."

"I know she's upset, but there is an explanation. This isn't what it seems. I need to explain it to her."

"I don't doubt your sincerity," Rachel replied in a calm voice. "I like you, Alex, and I think you've been great for Phoebe. But it looks like Jack outsmarted you tonight. Back off for now. I'll take care of Phoebe."

His senses were scrambled. All Alex could do was look at Rachel and try to interpret her body language. After a moment, he nodded, acquiescing to her argument. Then he watched Rachel exit the house and head for the moonlit gazebo in the center of the manicured back yard.

Voices echoed around him, men and women trying to make his acquaintance. Instead, he offered polite excuses and found his way to the small sitting area beneath the staircase. Balance remained elusive. He took several strategic deep breaths and tried to find that calm place deep inside his soul. It did not work.

He should have told Phoebe who he was at the bookstore yesterday. She would have been shocked and confused, but at least he would have had a whole day to explain it to her. It might be too late now. Jack had pulled off the perfect coup. There was nothing Alex could do about it except sweep up the mess and try to make the best of things.

"Did you enjoy my little show, cousin?" Jack asked.

Alex emptied the contents of his champagne glass into his mouth and swallowed hard. "How long have you known?"

"Long enough. The look on Phoebe's face made it worth the wait. By morning she'll be ready to sell her share of the land." Jack held up two fingers. "That's two birds. Phoebe and the house. Now for the third."

"What do you want, Jack?"

"I want your share of the business. Don't worry. I'll make you a fair deal."

Anger brought the faintest trace of oriental accent to Alex's rich voice. "Yeah, right. And I have some nice lunar property that might interest you."

Jack's gray eyes sparkled like bubbles rising in the champagne. "It's over. By the end of the night I'll have the land. By the end of the week I plan to be sole owner of Northwest Properties."

"Did it ever occur to you that our grandfather wanted us to get along? Maybe that was why he made me a partner."

"Martin was a fool," Jack snarled. "He got sentimental in his old age, but he wasn't always like that."

Alex remembered something Twyla had said. "Look at me, Jack. What do you see? Who do you see? Does this face look familiar?"

Triumph faded from Jack's expression, and a dark menace replaced it. "No. It doesn't. I don't know what you're talking about."

"Yes, you do. I look like Martin. Oh, he was older and grayer when you knew him, but this is his face. Martin couldn't hide what he was. He was Cherokee, and so are you. Why is that so bad?"

"Give me what I want, cousin, or it's war. All out war."

One corner of Alex's mouth turned up, creating an evil, crooked smile. "We've been at war for months, cousin. Haven't you figured that out? By the way, Jack, does the nose still hurt?"

Jack's face went slack. "You broke into my house and busted my nose. That was you."

A regal nod was the only response Alex allowed.

Jack looked like someone had just put something sour in his drink. "Anything else you'd like to confess while you're on a roll, cousin?"

"No, but keep in mind you're not the only one who inherited Martin's temper. I've learned a little control, but don't push your luck."

"Oh, I don't know. I've been pretty lucky tonight. My candidates won, and Phoebe thinks you're a no-account, low-down liar. Jackpot." Gray eyes sparkled with mockery, as Jack backed out of the alcove and rejoined his party guests.

Alex had no doubt that Jack was ready, willing, and able to wage a formidable personal war. Tonight's little toast was just a sample of his nasty tactics. This had to stop before something more than just pride and feelings got hurt. Setting the empty wineglass on a decorative ledge, Alex started to leave the darkened alcove.

A dark-haired woman with long legs and a short sequined dress blocked his exit. "Mr. Jones? Do you have a moment?"

"I'm sorry. I really have to find someone."

"This is very important. Please? It'll take only a minute."

Alex paused and tried to be patient. "Okay. One minute."

She smiled, showing off a beautiful face and a flawless smile. "Are you really a partner in Northwest Properties?"

"Yes."

"Great. My name is Erin Hayes. Jack conned me into signing a mineral lease a few months back. I wonder if you could help me get it canceled?"

Mineral lease. Land contracts. Grandma's riddle. A possible connection between those three things began to emerge in Alex's mind.

"I'm sorry," Alex stammered. "What did you say your name was?"

* * *

THE air was cold but Phoebe's blood ran hot. She shivered in the sleeveless party dress and continued pacing the inside of the gazebo. If she stopped, she might start crying. She did not want to give either Alex or Jack the satisfaction of seeing tears. No, she would rather keep moving and stay mad.

Alex. Yesterday she had all but proposed to him. Now her lovely dream of the future looked as abandoned as that musty bookstore. In the past two and half months she had given herself, body and soul, to this mysterious panther. Had hope and love been built on a stack of lies? The more Phoebe paced the farther away the lily pond slipped and the emptier her soul felt.

Sitting in the swing, Rachel rocked back and forth in rhythmic patience. "You need to calm down, Dragonfly. Let's go back inside where it's warm. It will be all right. Trust me. This will pass. I know you're shocked. We all are. But there is an explanation. I know there is."

Phoebe grabbed the side of the swing and jerked it to a stop. "I let that man in my house. In my bed. I trusted him. And he lied to me."

"There's more going on here. You need to give Alex a chance to explain."

"I gave Alex a chance," Phoebe seethed. Why had he kept the truth from her? Had he just used her to get to Jack and the business? Had she been nothing more than a tasty ticket onto the family land?

Alex appeared at the entrance of the gazebo. "Phoebe, honey, you're letting your imagination run wild. No one has been used. I never needed you to get to Jack. I could've walked up to this house and knocked on the door anytime."

"You lied to me."

"Yes. I lied. But—"

"No buts, Alex. How long were you going to play this charade?" When Alex opened his mouth, Phoebe raised a hand. "No. Let me finish. You've had since the third week of August to tell me the truth. All I am to you is a way onto this property and into Jack's life."

"You need to calm down."

"Don't tell me what I need, Alex Lin Jones. I'm through being your student and your stooge. I thought you loved me. I really did."

"Phoebe, I do love you. Let me explain."

"I don't want to hear it. Just get out. Take your lily pond and your lies and get out. I'll bet there's somebody here who can offer you a ride into town. I want you gone by the time I get back to the house. Is that understood?"

Alex just stood there, fists curled at his sides, breath rolling in and out of flared nostrils. After a long moment he gave a curt nod and backed out of the gazebo.

For the first time Phoebe could hear his footsteps all the way back to the house.

* * *

THIRTY minutes later Jack opened the kitchen door and waited. A self-pleased grin contorted his face. He had been waiting for this moment for weeks.

Wearing jeans and an old sweatshirt, Alex walked down the back stairs and into the kitchen. His left hand gripped a fat suitcase, and a duffel bag was slung over his right shoulder.

Jack took a quick glance down the hallway and focused on Alex. "Well, cousin, I think this is where you get off. Did you enjoy the ride?"

Three long strides took Alex across the kitchen. He stopped on the breezeway threshold, one foot on warm carpet, the other on cold concrete. "If anything happens to Phoebe, I'll rip your heart out and feed it to the dogs."

"Maybe one of these days we'll see if you're as tough as you think you are, but not tonight. I have a party to finish."

"It isn't over, Jack." With one angry roll of his shoulder, Alex stepped into the breezeway.

Hands in his trousers pockets, Jack leaned out the door and savored his moment of victory. He watched Alex stalk across the front yard and move along the line of expensive cars filling the driveway. Far down the twisting pavement, a four-wheel drive waited. Alex climbed into the passenger side and the vehicle immediately lurched forward. Jack got a clean view of taillights roaring toward the gate.

When he was certain Alex had left the property, Jack slammed the door. Last month's confrontation in the grocery store parking lot replayed in the back of his mind. He remembered the lie he had concocted to keep them from being hauled off to jail, telling the officer Alex was just the hired hand.

"Good help is so hard to find," Jack said with a chuckle.

* * *

PHOEBE sat alone on the middle landing of the elegant front staircase and looked across the empty living room.

It was somewhere past midnight. The caterers had packed up the last of the food and vacated. Alex was gone and she did not care how. Rachel had reluctantly left with Sam. The dogs were still chained up out back. At least they had not betrayed her.

Her head swam. She kicked off high heels and let the dress drape to one side, revealing long legs and silky hose. With both hands she cradled a glass of champagne and tried to divine the future in those energetic bubbles.

Still wearing his tuxedo, Jack sat near the base of the staircase. "I'm sorry to have shocked you like that, Phebes, but I couldn't risk tipping off Alex."

"Cut the crap, Jack. You planned this little show just for me." When Jack started to comment, Phoebe cut him off. "I don't want to hear your side of it, either. I don't care what you and Alex do. I don't care about that damned business. I don't care if you two kill each other. I don't understand this family feud, and I don't want to. I don't want to be part of it anymore. I just want to get on with my life."

Maybe it was the wine, maybe it was fatigue, but Jack almost showed a hint of decent regret. "We'll talk about it in the morning."

"No, we won't, Jack, because you won't be here in the morning," Phoebe informed with icy resolve. "I want you out. Right now. Pack what you need to get you through the week, and leave. I don't want to play anymore."

"You don't have the right—"

"Don't get legal with me, Jack. I'm not in the mood. You've spent your last night under this roof with me. You want to take me to court? Fine. Go round up your lawyers, because I'm not letting you back in here without a court order. Now, I'm going to change my clothes and unchain the dogs. I want you packed and out of here by the time I'm ready for bed."

Getting to his feet, Jack rolled his fists in his trousers pockets. "Or what?"

Phoebe stood, letting her voice convey the fire in her mind. "Or I scream the paint off the walls and you can explain it to the police."

"You can't be serious. Nobody will believe you."

"Really?" Phoebe threw the wineglass, making Jack duck. The expensive crystal goblet cleared the sofa and crashed against the wet bar. "You never drink? Never fight? Never get upset? I don't know, Jack. I don't think you have such a good reputation."

His eyes narrowed. One foot moved up to the next step.

Phoebe raised a finger in warning. "Remember the 911 call at the grocery store? I don't think that cop quite bought your story."

"Bitch," Jack seethed. "I show you the truth about Alex and this is how you repay me?"

"What did you expect? Oh, I get it. You thought I'd be so upset I'd finally sign that contract. Well, forget it, Jack. This is my house and I'm never leaving it. Never. Get out."

*****

CHAPTER 21

Ghost of a Chance

BOBBY Three Stars waited in the shadows near the back of Jack's bedroom. He had heard the argument. Now he listened closely to heavy footsteps ascending the front staircase.

Over the last month Bobby had grown fond of Phoebe, and not just because she was Alex's girl. Any man who would hurt a good woman like that needed his head examined and his teeth rearranged. Bobby hoped for a chance at the latter.

Jack pushed open the bedroom door and stepped inside. Light from the hallway spilled across the threshold, casting stringy shadows onto the carpet.

"That little bitch," Jack seethed. "Who does she think she is, giving me orders?"

A warm breeze, ripe with coffee and gingersnaps, drifted into the room as a shimmering figure coalesced in the hallway.

Jack turned toward the ghost. "Go away, old woman. I got rid of Alex, and Phoebe's next. If I have to burn this house to the ground, I'll get rid of you, too. Try and haunt a pile of ashes."

"I don't think so," Bobby interjected from the shadows.

Spinning around, Jack drew his fists.

Bobby stepped into the half-light. His tight T-shirt and sweat pants gave him the advantage of mobility over Jack's constraining tuxedo.

"What are you doing here?" Jack demanded.

"I don't care how good you think you are, Jack. You don't want me. Now, the lady asked you to leave and that's exactly what you're going to do."

"Oh, really? Well, I don't think you want me, either."

Shaking his head, Bobby inched forward. "Jack, Jack. Are you always this cocky?"

Jack swung, but his fist found nothing but air.

Then Bobby kicked. Clean and sure, the bottom of a large sneaker grazed the side of Jack's face. One perfect blow and that was it. Jack fell in a heap, blood trickling from his mouth to stain that expensive tuxedo.

After offering a reverent bow to the ghost in the hallway, Bobby closed the door and looked down at his sleeping victim. "Come on, Jack. Let's get you packed and out of here."

* * *

"GET in the left lane," Rachel demanded.

Sam down-shifted the red sports car, as the first set of city stoplights came into view. He figured he had already cooked himself with Jack. It was bad enough to have to look for a new job at forty-something, but now Rachel wanted to go see Alex. "I don't care if you promise to have my children. There's no way I'm going over there tonight."

Long fingers draped over Sam's right knee, and a warm voice purred in his ear. "Alex is the only one who can fix this mess. We have to talk to him. Now make a left."

"Woman, if you think playing with my knee is going to make me turn left—" Sam paused and gave a soulful sigh. "Damn."

The left turn signal blinked, as he maneuvered the car through the intersection. After a couple of more lights and a right turn, they rocketed into the empty parking lot of Red Cedars Corner. Sam eased the car up beside a navy-colored four-wheel-drive and shut off the engine. The lights were on inside Lin Martial Arts and a single silhouetted figure could be seen through the shaded windows.

Sam looked at his beautiful, albeit manipulative date. "Would you sleep with me now so I can die a happy man?"

"Don't be silly," Rachel scolded and planted a wet kiss on Sam's shocked lips. "I'll protect you from the big bad kung fu man. Come on."

"Promises, promises," Sam muttered, getting out of the car.

* * *

ONLY a few candles added amber light to the kwoon. Alex paced back and forth in the middle of the practice area, eyes focused on the darkness, fists swinging stiffly at his sides, dusty sneakers gliding silently over the padded floor.

Since meeting Phoebe this summer, Alex had been an emotional mess. If being in love was like this for everyone else, he wondered how humanity had survived this long. He had lost all sense of personal control the instant that cautious dragonfly flitted into his life and made a home in his heart.

The front door swung open with the usual rattling of its shade, and two elegantly dressed guests entered. Rachel's glittering tea-length dress shimmered in the candlelight, while Sam's tuxedo appeared a bit rumpled.

Sneakers squeaking to a stop on short-pile carpet, Alex leveled a smoldering gaze on Sam. "You'd better tell me you didn't know what Jack was up to."

Sam raised his hands in surrender. "I swear to God. I've been trying to get the truth out of Jack for weeks. He hasn't spoken to me since...."

"Since what?" Alex stalked toward the front and dropped his knuckles on the waist-high railing.

"Since I hired that private investigator."

"You what?" Rachel and Alex blurted in unison.

Sam sat on a narrow red bench and gave a deflated sigh. "I hired a private investigator after I saw you guys at the Fair. Jack ordered me to watch Phoebe while he was in California. It was part of my job." His voice found a stronger chord. "I've always liked Phoebe. I didn't want anybody to hurt her."

"What about the private investigator?" Alex asked with grating impatience.

"I hired him the next day, after the episode at the fair," Sam explained. "I had no idea Swearingen was going to work so fast. By the time I got to the office on Monday, Jack had already intercepted the report and wouldn't let me see it. Now Phoebe's alone out there with him. Things are worse than ever."

"Phoebe's not alone," Alex informed him, absorbing Sam's tale and trying to make sense of the information. "Bobby's there. Phoebe doesn't know it, and Jack won't know it unless he tries something stupid."

"That makes me feel a little better," Sam stated in a tired voice. "So what do we do next, boss?"

Alex's eyebrows shot upward. "Boss?"

"Technically, you are my boss. Remember?"

"Yeah. I guess I am." Alex sat on the railing and folded his arms across his chest. He remembered the gorgeous girl from the party who had asked for his assistance. "In that case, I need you to show me the mineral lease for Erin Hayes."

* * *

A few minutes after Rachel and Sam left, Alex stood in the alley behind Lin Martial Arts and looked into the back seat of Jack's burgundy sedan.

"This is too easy," Alex said with a snicker.

Bobby leaned against the side of the car. "Now that we have him, what do we do with him?"

Drumming his fingers on the top of the car, Alex thought for a moment. "Pack your things. You're going home. But first I need you to drop off a little package for me." He glanced at the bloodied and disheveled tuxedo-clad unconscious figure filling the sedan's back seat. "Well, Jack, are we having fun, yet?"

* * *

SUNLIGHT rained through the car windshield and shattered into a million brilliant colors.

Moaning, Jack cupped a hand around his stiff neck and leaned forward. His forehead dropped on the center of the steering wheel, and the horn offered a deafening off-key blare.

"What the—"

Jerking back his head, Jack tried to get a fix on his surroundings. His ears rang with the thunder of a jet airplane.

"Where the hell am I?"

He recognized the sedan as his own, but had no idea where he was. Looking through the prismatic windshield, he noticed a passenger plane straining to make altitude.

Then he focused on the sprawling metropolitan skyline in the distance. He knew that horizon, and he knew the parking lot. He was at the Dallas airport.

"How the hell did I get to Texas?"

A face solidified in the back of Jack's muddled mind and last night's events fell into patchy order.

The party. Alex. Phoebe. Phoebe tossed both of them out. He went upstairs and someone was in his room. The ghost. Then someone else. Alex's kung fu buddy.

Jack reviewed every movement until he got to the last thing he saw, the bottom of a worn sneaker. He rubbed his jaw and gingerly moved it back and forth, just to make sure everything still worked.

Damn that Alex! No wonder he left without a fight. He had been ready for trouble with a man posted upstairs.

Stiff from sleeping in the car, Jack strained to reach into his trouser pocket. To his relief, his wallet and credit cards were still there. He looked around the car and found everything in reasonable order. Even the doors were locked for his safety. He checked the car phone in the center console, but someone had removed the batteries.

Alex, being a true Henderson down to his Cherokee bones, had played an old-fashioned practical joke on Jack. A little mischief to go with the madness.

He had a long drive ahead of him, which meant he had better find a way out of this parking lot maze, get some chow, and head toward Oklahoma City. If he hurried, he could reach the office by early afternoon.

Looking at his sad reflection in the rearview mirror, Jack shook his head.

Pitiful. A good joke, but pitiful nonetheless.

He wiped dried blood from his face, cursed the ruined tuxedo, and started the car.

* * *

ALL afternoon, the secretaries at Northwest Properties tripped over each other to wait on the mysterious and handsome A. L. Jones.

"They never bring me any coffee," Sam complained with a sour expression.

Grinning, Alex rocked back in the leather chair and sipped hot coffee. Sam's private door remained open to avoid causing him anymore trouble with Jack. Outside in the lobby, secretaries whispered and giggled and shuffled from desk to desk. Alex overheard bits and pieces of gossip, including speculations regarding Jack's speech at last night's party.

He had never known a secretary who did not have the eyes of an eagle and the ears of a fox. When he spoke, Alex did so with care and in a quiet tone. "The Hayes girl said Jack filed that mineral lease. It has to be here somewhere."

"I'm telling you it isn't. The only place I haven't looked is—" Sam snapped his jaws shut.

"In Jack's office?" Alex finished the sentence.

Sam took a strategic glance out his open office door, making sure there were no prying eyes or trained ears. "This is as much as I can do for you. I'm still Jack's employee."

"And his friend."

"Maybe his only real friend."

Alex twirled the ceramic mug in his huge hands. He had Erin Hayes' Tulsa telephone number. He could get the land description and location from her. If Jack had left a paper trail, it could be found with a little persistence. There was no need to put Sam's job or friendship in further jeopardy.

When Alex had arrived in Oklahoma, he and Sam had found each other at crossed purposes. At first he thought Sam was personally interested in Phoebe, but eventually came to believe it was genuine friendship. He began to understand the man sitting across the desk from him. Perhaps Sam was a little cavalier about life but, all in all, he was a good-hearted individual with tolerable rough edges.

"You're a decent man, Sam Tillman. Why have you hung around Cousin Jack all these years?"

"There are a lot of things you don't know about Jack," Sam said, rocking back in his chair.

"I know he was slapping Phoebe around before I intervened." Alex did not try to hide the anger in his voice.

Sam looked uncomfortable. "Jack's been under a lot of strain since Danny died. They were very close."

"That's no excuse."

"No, but it's an explanation." After a brief pause Sam continued. "Jack's a complicated man. As far as business goes, he stays within the law. Well, okay. Maybe he hangs on the edge of it sometimes, but he's not a criminal. He likes to make money, but he rarely spends any of it. He just likes making it. It's a game to him. And he loves beautiful women. He tried the marriage thing years ago, but he just couldn't give up the other women. It's a shame, too. He married the most beautiful girl you've ever seen. And they have a great kid, Marty. He's about ready for college now. Jack doesn't get to Texas very often to see him."

Alex fought back a smile, and then nodded toward the pictures hanging on the wall. "Is that your daughter?"

"Maggie? Yeah. That's my princess. Her mom and I had a rough split, but we're friends now. I get to see her as much as any father gets to see a teenager. How about you? Any kids?"

"No, I have never met the right girl."

"Until now," came a knowing reply.

"Until now." For the second time in as many days, that old psychic chill ran up the back of Alex's neck. He knew trouble was about two steps away. "Thanks for making me feel welcome."

Sam tossed his palms in the air. "You're a partner. I'm just an employee."

"I won't betray you," Alex vowed, lowering his voice. "What was said in confidence last night stays in confidence."

"Happy to set things straight," Sam said.

After nodding in response, Alex heard the elevator doors part. He sat up straight and looked over his shoulder.

Jack had arrived. Wearing clean clothes but looking a little haggard, he thundered through the lobby. His cowboy boots slid to a stop in front of Sam's office. Gray eyes riveted on Alex. "Where's your buddy?"

"What buddy?" Alex asked, as innocently as he could manage.

"The one you sent to rearrange my jaw and drive me to Dallas?"

Alex merely shrugged. "So that's where you went. Bring back any souvenirs? How about one of those postcards with a man riding a two-thousand-pound jackrabbit?"

"Get the hell out of my office," Jack ordered.

"Technically, it's my office, too, Jack."

"Technically, I don't give a flying rat's ass!" Jack's gaze shifted to Sam. "I want to talk to you."

Red-faced with anger, Jack stormed into his private office and slammed the door so hard the glass partitions rattled in the lobby.

Sam tossed a questioning look in Alex's direction. "Dallas?"

Getting out of the chair, Alex nodded. "Walk me to the elevator and I'll explain."

* * *

JACK sat with his chair facing the windows and his fingers laced over his taut waistline. His focus shifted from the warm November afternoon outside to Sam's reflection on the inside of the glass.

He began in a carefully controlled voice. "Is he gone?"

Sam sat on the corner of the desk and nodded. "Yeah."

"Do you know what that son-of-a-bitch did to me last night?" Jack seethed.

"He just told me. I swear, Jack, I had no idea. He said he was worried about Phoebe being out there with you alone. She was confused, and you were mad. It was a bad combination."

"That land belonged to my grandfather. I won't give it up."

"Who said you have to? Just back off a little." Sam was obviously trying to sound like the proverbial voice of reason. "Why don't you move in with me for a few days? Give everyone time to cool down. What will it hurt?"

"My pride." Jack turned the chair and dropped his arms on the cluttered desk. Fatigue scored rough spots in his throat. "You want to explain this business with Rachel Gray?"

"What's to explain? She's beautiful and intelligent. I needed a date, and I knew she wanted to check on Phoebe. It isn't exactly rocket science."

"I was beginning to think you'd gone over to the enemy."

Sam shook his head. "This isn't war, Jack. I'm your best friend and always will be. I look out for you. You know that. But I do need some straight answers on a couple of things."

"Like what?"

"Did you ever hit Phoebe? Yes or no. Tell me the truth."

The truth brought a twinge of shame in the bright light of this unusually warm November afternoon. Jack felt sweat running beneath his cotton shirt. "We had a couple of arguments this summer. I got mad and slapped her. That's all. I didn't hurt her. I swear."

"Okay, Jack. I believe you, but you have to promise me that kind of thing won't happen again."

"Scout's honor."

A knot formed in the pit of Jack's stomach, because he knew it was a promise he had no intention of keeping. Last night Phoebe said she was ready to fight him for the land. He would do anything to keep her from winning that fight. Anything to get that medicine woman's nosy ghost away from Phoebe and off his grandfather's property.

*****

CHAPTER 22

On the Path

PHOEBE had forgotten how big her house really was.

A day and a half ago it had hummed with conversation and warm bodies. Now in the pre-dawn hours of Thursday morning, its only occupants were one woman, two dogs, and a disquieted spirit.

To her surprise, Jack left as requested Tuesday night, packing a few items and disappearing out the back way while she was downstairs cleaning up the living room. She figured he would be gone only a couple of days at the most or however long it took him to conjure up some legal loophole allowing him back in the house. He could return any minute ready to throw fists or lawyers or both at her. The fight was not over. In fact, the worst had probably not yet begun.

Wearing only a damp towel cinched around her waist, Phoebe lay on the bed and stared up at the ceiling. In just a few weeks, she had grown accustomed to having Alex's weight and warmth on the other side of the mattress and his clothes hanging in the closet beside hers. Now her heart felt as empty as both the closet and the bed. A few minutes ago she used the last drops of Musk Rain oil in her bath water and, at this juncture, did not plan to buy more.

Since Tuesday night, she had paced empty rooms and hallways, staying one step ahead of sleep yet one step behind understanding. The dogs skulked around the house, ears drooped and eyes watchful. Grandma had been conspicuously absent, despite Phoebe stamping her feet and demanding an explanation.

In the dark and cold hours before dawn, Mother Earth quietly exhaled that last breath of night and prepared to inhale the dawn. A strange west wind buffeted the glass balcony doors. It pecked at the window like a forlorn lover begging to arrange a rendezvous.

Phoebe rolled over, put her back to the doors, and ignored the sound as best she could. Patting the empty side of the bed, the side Alex used to occupy, Phoebe clicked her tongue and offered an invitation to Elsa. The big dog did not disappoint.

Elsa stepped onto the bed, long nails sinking into the blankets. With a contented sigh, she stretched out and dropped a rubbery nose over huge front paws. After one more elongated breath, the dog drifted off to sleep. The bed shook again, as Kiki claimed the foot of the mattress, lying on her side, long legs hanging over the cushioned end.

Let Jack run this gauntlet!

Phoebe's smile faded as sleep finally caught her. Reality's coin flipped, shifting her conscious mind from the realm of the flesh to the world of the spirit….

* * *

THE mattress transformed into a bed of soft, green grass. Phoebe rolled onto her back and opened astral eyes. The ceiling became a dome of diamond-like stars that displayed a pantheon of familiar constellations.

Draco protected Ursa Minor, the Little Bear whose tail was Polaris, the northern star.

Pleiades' seven sisters watched from nearby.

Orion, the hunter, stood poised for battle.

Arcturus guarded the west with a bright amber light.

The blue swan of Cygnus dipped her wings into the Milky Way, forever fleeing Aquila, the Eagle.

The lily pond stirred and a familiar fragrance filled Phoebe's nostrils. A man, naked to the night, bare to the soul, stood over her. Water dripped from his long black hair. Amber eyes smoldered with pain and desire. Tawny skin glistened in ample starlight.

"Go away," Phoebe ordered, her clear voice shooting to the heavens like an astral arrow and nicking one of Aquila's stardust wings.

"Never," her lover vowed.

"I don't want you."

"I don't believe you," he answered and lay in the grass beside her. A strong arm fell across her waist, while a hand stroked her neck and cheek. "Rest, Dragonfly. Just rest. Everything will be all right. Trust me."

"You lied to me," she whispered but neither pushed him away nor accepted his embrace. Hot tears fell from the corners of her eyes, little iridescent pearls of pain tumbling to the grass.

Her lover's long fingers drifted up and covered her eyes. "Sleep, Little Dragonfly. No bad dreams will intrude. No one will disturb you. Rest."

Although her spirit still ached from earthly misfortune, Phoebe trusted her lily pond lover enough to sleep in his astral arms while the stars harmonized overhead.

* * *

BRAVING the chill in the air, Phoebe stood on the bedroom balcony and watched the western sky brighten minute by minute. Behind her, the yellow sun rose in the East. Clad in an old red sweatshirt and faded blue jeans, she held a large cup of hot coffee and marveled at the color of the fall sky.

When she had awakened after a couple of hours of badly needed sleep, her face was streaked with fresh tears. She remembered dreaming about the stars and the lily pond and Alex lying naked in the grass beside her. Even now in the open air, the aroma of *Musk Rain* enveloped her. That stubborn erotic scent seemed imbedded in her skin. She had found the emotional power to throw Alex out of the house, but could not toss him out of the astral realm.

You lied to me.

The echo of that silent cry blew back in her face, chilling her ears and numbing her cheeks. Their relationship could not go forward without trust. Alex tried to explain things at the party, implored her to listen, but Phoebe had been too mad, too shocked to listen. Jack got more meaningful conversation out of her that night than Alex, which proved she had not been thinking straight.

You know better than to let your emotions rule!

Phoebe's fingers closed around the cold, damp railing, and she focused on undulating golden prairie grass. Over the rise and beyond a hidden meadow lay that peaceful tear-shaped pond. In her mind's eye she could see the cattails waving hello from around the muddy shoreline. On the dock a silver-haired figure, wearing beaded moccasins and a two-piece calico dress, waited in silence. *Grandma.* In the old woman's outstretched translucent hands lay the tobacco pipe, a trickle of gray smoke dancing upward.

No more excuses. Phoebe knew what must be done. She would begin a three-day fast. Then Saturday morning at dawn she would face her past, her future, and herself.

* * *

DESPITE the rumble in her stomach, Phoebe dropped the last box of Jack's clothes in the middle of the downstairs office.

A puff of dust circled the room. Stifling a sneeze, she stood straight and admired the morning's work. This was the best way she knew to make her point. She had been serious Tuesday night. She wanted Jack gone. All of his things, from clothing to pictures to toiletries, filled the office floor in boxes and trash bags and a few pieces of expensive luggage.

"There!" Phoebe brushed dust from her sweatshirt and off the knees of faded blue jeans. She glanced down as Elsa's warm frame leaned against her leg. "What do you think, old girl? Will this make Jack mad or what? And do we care? No! Not a twig's worth."

Elsa wandered the maze of boxes, sniffing at her mistress' handiwork and growling occasionally at the scent of Jack.

Kiki, however, remained stretched out in the cool hallway, flat on her side and snoring in canine contentment.

The polished wooden surface of Jack's desk caught Phoebe's eye. How brave did she feel this morning? She looked over her shoulder and listened to the sounds of the house. After making certain she was still alone, she climbed over bags and boxes and got behind the huge desk.

Swallowing her last remnant of hesitance, Phoebe grabbed the front center drawer and pulled. It was locked. That should have been expected. Fortunately, a few months ago, during a mad cleaning binge, she had found where Jack hid his extra key. Without hesitation she walked to the bookcase and dipped one finger inside a brass pumpjack figurine. The small key slid out without resistance.

"Gotcha!"

Phoebe moved back to the desk and unlocked it. In the top center drawer, she found a folder with at least a dozen of those unsigned contracts that granted Jack sole ownership of the house and land. Snorting in defiance, she ripped the contracts in half and dropped them in a nearby trash can. Next she grabbed a felt pen and wrote on the inside of the folder: *Sitting Bull was here.* Giggling, she shoved the folder back into the long center drawer and continued to snoop.

The bottom left drawer yielded an interesting manila pocket folder. Phoebe pulled it out and untied the strings. Inside she found pictures and newspaper clippings, things she had never seen in all of her years with Danny. She spread the contents across the polished desktop and sat rather clumsily in the chair.

"Well, I'll be," she muttered.

One set of old photographs showed several angles of a large house. With the exception of the breezeway and garage, it looked about the same as her home. There were no shutters and the ground level was brick instead of rock, but the resemblance was eerie. A little shaky, she rifled through newspaper clippings and found a headline that read: *Henderson Estate Burns. One Dies in Fire.*

She had always wondered why this land remained empty for so long. According to the article, Martin Henderson's wife had died in the house fire. A chill ran up her spine.

Phoebe studied the photographs of the other house, checking the surrounding trees and horizon. The location became clear. Her house had been built on the same spot as the one that burned over thirty-five years ago.

Secrets. So many secrets.

"Danny, why didn't you tell me?"

She concentrated on the faces in the pictures. The two small boys were undoubtedly Jack and Danny, and the stately man beside them was Martin Henderson. Except for the gray eyes and silvered hair, Martin and Alex could have been twins. So, Alex really was Jack's first cousin. The proof lay in the genetics.

Leaning back in the chair, Phoebe wove her fingers across her lap. One sneaker tapped a silent code into the plush carpet. Why had Alex kept his family tree a secret? His relationship to Jack would have been all he needed to open a conversation with her last summer. There had been no reason for deception, at least none of which she was currently aware.

Alex's reasoning remained elusive, but Jack's behavior was just downright baffling. Subtlety had never been Jack Henderson's strong suit. The stakes must really have been high for Jack to proceed with such careful civility in those weeks before the election party. One possibility popped into Phoebe's head. Perhaps Jack had not known who Alex was, at least not at first. It was possible that Jack still did not know much about Alex, maybe even less than she did.

After bundling the newspaper clippings and photographs back into the folder, Phoebe dropped it into the desk and shut the drawer with her knee.

The right center drawer rattled as she pulled it open. Tightly packed hanging files sat sideways in a drop-in metal frame. Clicking her tongue in mindless rhythm, she thumbed through the labels until one cryptic tag grabbed her attention: *PI.*

Pulling the contents from the PI folder, she laid them out in front of her. What she found was even more surprising than the photographs and newspaper clippings. Several pages of classic gray paper bore the letterhead: *Harold Swearingen, Private Investigator.* A colorful peacock feather eye adorned the top right of each page.

The symbolism was cute. Yet Phoebe found nothing humorous in a report dated back in September. The surname Jones glared at her like a neon light and a shady Henderson family tree began to grow in Phoebe's mind. Clipped to the back of the report were pictures of her and Alex and Bobby standing in front of Lin Martial Arts. It was the written report, however, that left her hands shaking.

According to the private investigator, a teenager named Felicia Jones gave birth to illegitimate twins, William and Anna. Their father was Martin Henderson, a prominent Oklahoma City businessman married to a woman named Margaret. Years later Felicia died giving birth to a girl named Twyla, whose father was not listed on the birth certificate. This left all three siblings to be raised by their maternal grandparents, the Joneses.

William Jones joined the Air Force right out of high school and completed one tour of duty in the Orient. He brought back a wife, Maria Lin. Shortly thereafter, she gave birth to their only child, Alex. After William died, Maria took their son back to Hong Kong.

Phoebe recognized this part of the story from some of the things that Alex had told her. It was Twyla's connection with the Henderson family, however, that provided the biggest shock. Twyla Jones was Alex's aunt.

"What a mess!" Phoebe exclaimed.

Twyla had lied to her. Perhaps not in the traditional sense. Not point-blank in verbal conversation, but strategically by omitting certain facts. Lies hurt, but Phoebe had the good sense not to dwell too long on a few bruised feelings. There was more to this sordid family tale. Much more. Those old newspaper clippings were like the lily floating on the water with the bulk of the plant submerged beneath. Thirty-five years ago something terrible had happened between the Hendersons and the Joneses. Phoebe was certain the key to unraveling this mess lay in the events surrounding that house fire.

A shimmering mist coalesced to one side of the desk. Grandma's translucent form leaned against the bookcase and offered the trace of an enigmatic smile.

Phoebe studied the old ghost, noting the tilt of her head, the gleam in her crystalline eyes, the silent tapping of one beaded moccasin.

"I'm close to the truth, aren't I, Grandma?"

The ghost nodded and then dissolved like sugar in the rain.

* * *

FROM her favorite perch, the bedroom balcony, Phoebe enjoyed an unusually warm afternoon. A few wispy clouds wandered across a pale blue canvas, giving just a hint of how deep and wide the sky really was. The temperature headed toward the seventies, and the wind had stilled.

Phoebe's stomach grumbled in protest after only a few hours of fasting. She was determined to properly prepare herself, however, drinking only small amounts of fruit juice and plenty of water. Despite what most people thought, fasts were not ritual punishment. They helped rid both the body and the mind of toxins. Phoebe reminded herself she only had to hang on until Saturday. Everything would come to light then. All questions would be answered. Of this, she was convinced.

In the back yard below, Kiki and Elsa stopped playing and raised their noses to the air.

"What's the matter girls?" Phoebe called.

With big feet churning up sod and grass, both dogs headed around the house.

The first thought in Phoebe's head was that Jack had returned. She went back into the bedroom, slipped on her sneakers, and grabbed Danny's old .22 from inside the closet. One-by-one she shoved hollow-point shells into the top of the rifle and hoped they weren't too old to fire. Last, she dropped a shell into the chamber and headed out of the bedroom.

Not worrying about silence or stealth, she hurried down the back stairs and crossed the kitchen. The back door opened with a creak. She exited the house and stopped in the middle of the breezeway, listening for the dogs and taking her own psychic sniff in the air.

Distant barking offered the first clue.

Phoebe crossed the front yard, the rifle clutched tightly in one strong hand and a finger poised on the trigger. She stepped onto the pavement and paused, craning her neck. Down the twisted driveway, the dogs danced around a shiny black pickup. In a moment, she spied a familiar head of black hair, bobbing just inside the open gate. Alex.

Relieved, Phoebe lowered the nose of the rifle and walked down the driveway.

Wearing tight blue jeans, dusty sneakers, and a mischievous grin, Alex looked over a bare shoulder. "Good morning, Dragonfly."

Phoebe tossed a frown at the dogs prancing about in the bushes, their tongues hanging out and their eyes sparkling. "Some guards you two turned out to be."

"Looks like you have the situation under control," Alex said, as he pulled the housing off the security gate's electric box. "Do I get a chance to explain before you shoot me?"

"I haven't decided." Fighting back a smile, Phoebe leaned the gun against the pickup's back bumper and walked over to inspect the work on the gate. "Mind telling me what you're doing?"

"I'm putting a new code in the remote and installing an intercom. I hear you threw out Jack. This will make it harder for him to get in." With the back of his hand, he wiped a trail of sweat from his face and continued to work. "I also have new locks for all the doors and the garage. So unless you're going to shoot me, I'll be up to the house in a few minutes."

Just when Phoebe thought she could stay mad at this man for more than an hour, he once again came riding to her rescue. And why did he always have to look so damned good doing it? Bare-chested and sweat-soaked. That single braid of black hair pasted down his back. Faded blue jeans hugging long legs and that tempting, heavy crotch.

Phoebe looked up to find gold eyes watching her watching him. She shoved her hands in her jeans pockets and walked a nervous circle in the path of the open gate. She could not allow herself to forget that she was mad at him, that he had lied to her, and that he owed her an explanation.

I'm mad at you, Alex Lin Jones. You're not going to charm your way back into my heart that easily.

"I thought you didn't want an explanation," he remarked as he popped the cover back on the metal box.

Sliding to a stop on oily pavement, Phoebe shoved up the sleeves of her old sweatshirt and tried to look angry. "Stay out of my head, Alex Lin Jones."

"Use your chi and I won't be able to get in your head."

"Oh, no. I'm not falling into that trap again." Before her resolve evaporated in the sunlight, Phoebe made a quick subject change. "I'm ready to hear that explanation now."

A sexy smile broadened Alex's face. He raised one of the new garage remotes and clicked the center button.

Phoebe squeaked in surprise and jumped toward the pickup to avoid the rolling iron gate. An electronic click followed a metal clang, announcing the driveway was sealed and once again secure. Unless she decided to scale the gate, she was locked on the property with the lover she had thrown out of her house only two days ago.

"You wouldn't really go over the fence, would you?" Alex slid his toolbox into the bed of the pickup. Before Phoebe could tailor a smart remark, he patted the metal tailgate. "Come here. Sit down and let me explain. With all this family has put you through, I think you deserve to hear the truth. Or at least as much of it as I know."

A little contrite, she circled the truck and climbed onto the tailgate. At the party, she had been too confused to sort out the details, but in the warmth of this beautiful fall afternoon she wanted to hear the other side of the story. Needed to hear it.

Alex sat beside her, his sneakers skidding on the pavement. Sunlight glistened off that jet-black hair and played in the shadows of his muscled back. The burr in his rich voice smacked of regret. "Twyla Jones is my aunt."

"I know," Phoebe reported in a no-nonsense tone. "This morning I found a private investigator's report in Jack's desk. It seems Martin Henderson and Felicia Jones had illegitimate twins named William and Anna. Felicia died a few years later giving birth to another child, Twyla, father unknown. Did I get it about right?"

"Close enough. What else did you find in that report?"

Phoebe kicked her feet and wrapped her fingers around the sun-warmed edge of the tailgate. "There were some newspaper articles about a house fire. Apparently, my house is built on the foundation of the old Henderson house. Danny never told me that. I guess there were a lot of things Danny didn't tell me."

"More than you know."

"Enlighten me," Phoebe said in a flat voice.

Alex frowned and looked decidedly uncomfortable. "Around the first of March, Twyla called and said Jack had moved in with you and was making your life hell. She called again about the middle of August and told me to get to Oklahoma City on the next plane. She thought maybe Jack had started to get violent. She loves you very much. I hope you realize that."

Exasperation spilled off Phoebe's tongue. "Why didn't you just tell me this in the first place? Why did you lie?"

Alex ducked his head and breathed a deep sigh. "I wanted to tell you the truth right from beginning, but—but Twyla made me promise not to."

"Twyla asked you to lie? Why?"

"Jack. She was afraid if you knew too much, you might let it slip. It wasn't that she didn't trust you, honey. She was afraid for you."

Phoebe mentally reviewed the private investigator's report. Martin Henderson's affair with Felicia Jones had produced twins. There was nothing in the report, however, about Martin and his wife, Margaret, having any children of their own. So who was Danny and Jack's mother? Phoebe knew Martin had raised the boys and that their mother had been Martin's daughter. According to Danny's version of the story, his parents died when he was very young. Phoebe had never even learned their names.

Martin's daughter rang in Phoebe's ears like the report of a .22-caliber rifle.

"Oh, my God," she blurted. "Anna Jones was Jack and Danny's mother. Which means Twyla is their aunt, as well as yours."

Alex gave a reluctant nod. "Martin took the kids away from Anna about the time I was born. When I was ten, Martin tried to take me, too. That's why my mother moved back to Hong Kong after Dad died. Now they're all dead with their secrets. Dad, Mother, Martin, Felicia, Margaret, and Anna."

"And Danny." Phoebe felt a few tears welled up in her eyes. "Did Danny know Twyla was his aunt? Did he know who his real mother was?"

"Twyla was never sure how much Danny was told, but Jack has always known. He was old enough to remember what happened."

"Why does Jack think having Twyla for an aunt is so bad? That's the problem, isn't it? Jack doesn't want any of his friends to find out that crazy Cherokee medicine woman is his aunt."

"I'd say that's about right. What was it Jack told me a few weeks ago? Oh, yeah. *You can't climb the social ladder in moccasins.*"

"Typical." Phoebe leaned forward, resting her arms on her knees. "If you think about it, there is a resemblance, between Jack and Danny and Twyla. I always thought it was just common Cherokee genetics. I never suspected they were actually family. Do you know what happened to Anna?"

"Well, yes, but—"

"But I'll have to wrestle that out of Twyla." Phoebe looked back at the peaceful prairie. Dry leaves clung stubbornly to scrubby blackjacks and rustled like sandpaper in the scant breeze. Most of what she had known about her husband and his family turned out to be little more than half-truths mixed with bold-faced lies. Phoebe began to understand why Twyla and Alex had played their little charade, but she still did not have to like it. "Jack's going to lose what's left of his itty-bitty mind when he finds out I know this. He hates Twyla."

"Which is why it would be best if you didn't say anything to him. Not yet, anyway."

"You wouldn't believe the elaborate stories Jack tells about his dead parents. I always wondered why Danny just frowned and left the room when Jack started in about this wonderful mother and father who had mysteriously died in Europe. What nonsense!" Phoebe stared at the handsome man sitting on the pickup tailgate beside her. "Are all you Hendersons crazy? Or did I just get tangled up with the nutty ones?"

Alex offered a modest smile and a casual shrug. "That's something you'll have to decide for yourself."

"I feel like a pawn on a prairie grass chessboard. And I don't like it one bit." Phoebe stared up at the seamless blue sky. "I know more now than I did when I got up this morning, but it still doesn't solve Grandma's riddle.

There's something else going on here, something Grandma wanted me to discover or uncover. I don't know which. There's more to this puzzle. More to this feud between Twyla and Jack."

Sliding off the tailgate, Alex dropped hot palms on Phoebe's denim-clad knees. His expression darkened and his words turned crisp. "Marry me, Phoebe. Right now. I have a big empty house in Sedona just waiting for you to brighten it up. Forget the land. Forget Jack. Forget that damned riddle." Alex leaned in, tickling her lips with the tip of his tongue. "Let me love you and take care of you. I didn't come here for Twyla or the land or the business. I came for you."

Phoebe pulled back just enough to see the smoldering gaze in his eyes. Her stomach protested the fast with noisy growls, and her knees were weak from more than Alex's electrifying touch. "I need a little time to think. Talk to me again after Saturday."

"What's happening Saturday?"

"Something that should've happened a long time ago. This time you'll have to trust me."

Alex got that familiar glassy look in his eyes. One side of his mouth twitched with the tickle of a smile. "Okay, if you'll make love to me right now."

"Here?"

"Right here. Right now," he insisted, trailing the tip of his tongue down her neck while expert fingers unfastened the top button of her jeans.

"We can't," Phoebe protested, pushing back his hand.

"Nobody can see us. There're enough trees in the way. If a car comes, we'll duck out of sight. Come on. You know how I love the sunlight."

"You love the sunlight, the moonlight, the darkness, the wind, the water, the table, the chair. Alex, you just love making love. Anywhere and everywhere."

"So?"

"I'm mad at you, remember?" Phoebe sputtered. Only a fence, a wrought iron gate, and a sliver of stubby blackjack oaks separated them from the narrow two-lane road.

"Be mad at me later," Alex said in a husky tone. "Make love to me now."

"No. I need time to think." Phoebe slid off the tailgate and picked up the rifle, letting the barrel hang casually toward the pavement. It was not a threatening move, just her way of showing she was ready to leave.

Alex closed the tailgate and offered a scowl with more than a hint of disappointment. "At least we're on speaking terms. Right?"

"I'm not mad anymore, if that's what you're asking. I just need some time to sort things out."

"Understood." Alex gave a lazy, sun-induced yawn and patted his flat stomach. "Get in. Let's run down to the drive-in for a burger and fries. I'm starved and I know you are. I can hear your stomach growling."

Giving a shallow shrug, Phoebe tried to ignore the grumbling in her belly. "I'm on a fast."

Alex's eyes widened in surprise and then narrowed in understanding. "The pipe. You're doing the ceremony on Saturday."

Phoebe nodded. "It's about time, don't you think?"

"I feel like an ass. Here you are trying to get focused on your path, and all I can think about is sex and food."

"Which just proves you're male."

"That's my girl," Alex replied with a twinkle in his eye. "Steady and sensible. Get in. I'll drive you to the house and change the rest of those locks."

Sidling up to the side of the pickup bed, Phoebe extended her free hand. "Give them to me. I need to work."

"And it will get me out of your hair, right?"

"Something like that," she answered and offered a closed smile. "Don't worry. I know what I'm doing. Changing door locks is a piece of cake. All you need is a screwdriver and a little patience."

Alex grabbed a paper sack from the bed of the pickup and gave it a good shake. "I'll go on one condition. You call me Saturday, okay? Don't leave me hanging. I want to know if the ceremony goes well."

Taking the sack, Phoebe nodded. "I'll talk to you Saturday afternoon. I promise."

The scowl on Alex's face suggested reluctance, so did the way he dragged his feet over the dusty pavement. The driver's side door opened with a squeak. He climbed inside the truck and looked strangely uncomfortable behind the wheel.

Phoebe felt tension on the invisible thread that bound the two of them together. Dropping the sack on the pavement while the rifle remained clutched in her other hand, she draped an arm through the open passenger's side window and studied Alex's forlorn gaze. Then she spied a ragged shoebox that looked to be more tape than cardboard.

"What's that?" she asked, pointing to the sad-looking carton.

"Oh, yeah. I almost forgot." He slid the box across the seat and gestured for her to take it.

Intrigued, Phoebe coaxed the limp box into her free hand. "What's in here?"

A forced smile turned up one corner of his mouth. "My heart. Please be kind. I'll see you Saturday, Dragonfly. Open the gate for me, will you? And watch the dogs."

* * *

PHOEBE stood inside the closed iron gate and listened until the roar of Alex's pickup moved out of hearing range.

With the dogs nipping at her heels she walked back to the house, carrying the shoe box stuffed into the heavy sack in one hand and the rifle in the crook of her other arm. Leaving the dogs outside, she entered through the kitchen and went straight upstairs to the master bedroom.

After standing the rifle in a corner of the closet, she sat on the bed and pulled the box out of the heavy sack. Without hesitation Phoebe dumped the contents of the shoebox across the bed.

It was just a few letters and a dried cedar sprig.

She rummaged through handwritten correspondence. Taped to the back of one letter was an old picture that showed a younger Phoebe standing in front of the Ferris Wheel at the State Fair. Clipped to another letter was a snapshot of Grandma sitting on the pond dock. Phoebe had forgotten how much the area had changed over the last few years. When that picture was taken, willows lined the west shore and trailed northwest up the hill, following a trickling spring that fed the pond. For some undisclosed reason, Danny had cut down the willows and allowed cattails to overtake the pond's small shoreline.

Phoebe dropped the snapshot and thought about Alex. "That's where he got the idea for the lily pond."

It took her only a little more than an hour to read eleven years of letters written by Twyla to Alex. A pattern emerged. Although Phoebe could not see what Alex had written back, she could interpolate by following the sequence of questions and answers. Eleven years ago Twyla told Alex about Phoebe and sent that snapshot from the State Fair. Later Alex learned about Phoebe's marriage to Danny. The tone of the letters changed after Grandma's death.

In one letter, Twyla plotted a little family treason: *"...Danny has taken up Jack's bad habits. It seems they've been living it up on business trips lately. I heard Danny has a mistress in Dallas. What does he need with a mistress? He can't take care of his wife! I should tell Phoebe, but how? Poor girl. I saw her a few days ago. She looked so sad with her grandmother gone. Phoebe and Danny don't belong together. Never did. You're the one she was supposed to marry. Maybe it's not too late. Why don't you move to Oklahoma City and get all these family skeletons out of the closet, once and for all? Go to Northwest Properties and tell Jack and Danny who you are. Then steal Danny's wife right out from under his nose. ~ Aunt Twyla."*

The contents of that letter glued a lump in Phoebe's throat. She had not known about Danny keeping a mistress. How many other things had she not known? Getting angry now seemed a waste of energy, but she could not help it.

Phoebe rifled through the mess of letters and found the most recent one: *"July 29th. Alex: I tried to get you at the office, but your secretary said you were out in the desert on another vision quest. Please call as soon as you get back. I feel that Phoebe is in great danger. I've thought about going to Jack's office and having it out with him, but that will only make him crazier than he already is. I'm the last person he wants to talk to. I can't help Phoebe, but I think you can. I have an idea. Come to Oklahoma City and open a kwoon. There's an empty slot in Red Cedars just down from the bookstore. As soon as possible I'll introduce you to Phoebe. I know she'll have the good sense to love you and trust you as much as I always have. I just don't know what else to do. Phoebe won't leave that house and Jack won't leave an Indian in it. I'm at my wits end. Please help. ~ Aunt Twyla."*

Phoebe tossed the letter onto the pile. Shame washed over her in foamy waves. Everyone had been trying to help her, yet what had she done to help herself? A few hot, salty tears trailed down her cheeks. Saturday morning she would honor her duty to her grandmother by conducting her first solo pipe ceremony. If all went well, she should receive the answer to the riddle and be back in Alex's arms by Saturday evening.

*****

CHAPTER 23
Smoke & Mirrors

WHISTLING a favorite old tune, Alex parked the truck behind Lin Martial Arts and went in the back door.

The morning had worked out better than expected. Not only had Phoebe listened with patience and understanding but she told him to come back Saturday night. He could not have been more pleased to see her finally picking up on her grandmother's work. Of course, it meant he would have to respect her space occasionally, but he could never be jealous of the medicine work. That newfound commitment to her heritage only made him love and respect her more.

Just as he started up the stairs, he heard a rap on the front door and the muffled echo of a woman's voice. Turning around, he ducked into the practice area and strained to see the face on other side of the door's golden shade. It was Erin Hayes.

"Hello?" she called again and rattled the locked door.

"Just a minute!" Alex gave a quick bow in and out of the practice area and then opened the door.

Dramatically, Erin entered the kwoon. An off-the-shoulder knit sweater revealed deep cleavage, and tight knit pants showcased incredibly long legs. She sauntered into the practice area and waved a fat manila envelope. "You're a hard man to find, Mr. Jones. I think I have something that might interest you."

After giving another obligatory bow, something that was just second nature to him, Alex re-entered the practice area. "I'm listening."

Erin's attention shifted to the weapons on the walls. "My, my. Do you really know how to use all these swords and things?"

He offered a modest shrug and wished she would get to the point of her little surprise visit.

"Wow," Erin intoned, her body language becoming more and more sultry. "You must be something pretty dangerous."

"What's in the envelope?" Alex asked, trying to side-step her practiced flirtations.

Erin used the envelope for a makeshift fan and batted feathery lashes.

"The contract I was telling you about at Jack's party. What are you willing to give me for it?"

A nervous laugh sputtered from Alex's lips. He could see where this was leading. Erin appeared adept at using what she had to get what she wanted. He had better be careful. "If you let me see the contract, I'll make sure it gets canceled. That's what you want, isn't it?"

"It was what I wanted when I came in, but that was before I knew you were such a warrior." Erin batted her eyes and rolled her hips in a well-orchestrated, stationary sashay.

Clasping his hands behind his back, Alex moved just within reach and sited down one eye. "I'm a spoken-for warrior."

Big brown eyes narrowed for effect. "How spoken for?"

"You want my help or not, Erin?" Alex warned.

"I'm the one with the envelope," she reminded, waving it in his face.

He resisted the urge to snatch the document. Instead, he extended a large hand and waited. "Yes, you are. And I'm the one with the power to make Jack pay for what he did to you. Wouldn't you like to see Jack pay?"

"He used me," she admitted with a quivering voice.

"He uses lots of people."

Fat tears welled up in Erin's eyes. She slapped the envelope into Alex's large palm. "Make him pay for what he did to me."

"I will."

"Make sure you do," Erin said. Then she rushed out the front door and let it slam behind her.

"Whew!" he breathed after she was gone. He opened the envelope and sifted through a stack of photocopied documents. What he saw did not please him. "Jack, you lowdown son-of-a-bitch. What are you up to?"

* * *

THAT night the lights of Oklahoma City reflected off the mirrored sides of the octagonal office building that housed Northwest Properties. At two a.m. there was not a car in the parking lot, not even one belonging to the dark-clad figure punching in the computer code on the back door's electronic security panel.

Gloved fingers flew over the tiny keypad. In a few seconds the panel chimed in recognition and double locks released with a muffled clang. The door opened easily but with a slight creak. Inside the stairwell, the hooded man manually re-locked the back door and then climbed the stairs three steps at a time.

At the tenth floor, he paused to recover his breath. He noted the security cameras hung in the corner of the stairwell and smiled knowingly beneath the hood. Again, long gloved fingers danced on a computer wall panel and in moments the emergency exit opened.

The dark-clad man stepped onto the tenth floor near the public rest rooms. Amber footlights gave sparse illumination to the curving inner corridor, and overhead air vents offered a rhythmic purr. With elegant agility, the man navigated through the shadows, skimming around benches and potted plants and an occasional credenza. In a moment, silvery elevator doors glistened before him.

Suede boots rounded the corner into Northwest Properties' main lobby and came to a smooth stop in front of the door to Jack Henderson's private office. Pulling a sliver of crooked metal from his pocket, he let the device do what it did best, pick the lock. In a few seconds, there was a shy click. Then the door handle turned in his gloved hand. He slipped into Jack's inner sanctum, closed the door, and yanked off the hot silk hood.

Alex took a deep breath and shook out loose hair. It had been a long time since he had crept around in the dark like this, and then it had been practice exercises designed by his masters for war, not burglary. He rationalized that, since he owned part of this building, his actions were not illegal. Even if he were caught, which he seriously doubted, he could not be prosecuted for going into his own building late at night. Unless looking like a stunt-man reject from a bad martial arts movie was a misdemeanor.

A bright moon bathed Jack's office with cool silvery light. Alex twirled the lock-pick between gloved fingers and clicked his tongue on the roof of his mouth. "Now if I were a questionable contract, where would I hide?"

His gaze circled the room, passing bookshelves and coffee tables before stopping at a short wooden hanging-file cabinet.

"Naw, too obvious."

He considered the desk for a moment. Then his attention shifted to a slender green file cabinet wedged into the corner near the windows.

"Bingo," he announced in a husky whisper.

With the pick-lock in hand, he went to work on the top right corner of the cabinet. In a few seconds the lock popped out with a quiet metallic *thunk* and the top drawer rolled easily, revealing tightly packed documents. He located the folder assigned to Erin Hayes' mineral lease and rifled through the stack of papers. It did not take long to ascertain the true nature of the lease.

"Damn you, Jack. How many of these have you done?"

Hindered by the thin gloves, Alex fumbled around on Jack's desk before locating a notepad and pen. Quickly, he wrote down the legal land description of every folder in the top drawer of that file cabinet and completely removed Erin's contract.

Just as Alex closed the drawer and reached for the next one down, he heard the elevator chime. Footsteps echoed in the curving corridor and one drunken voice was unmistakable: Jack. With the notepad and Erin's contract folder tucked tightly under his arm, Alex shifted into the shadowy corner near the swinging office door and waited.

A woman's high-pitched western accent mingled with Jack's slightly slurred speech. Laughter and giggles proceeded through the lobby. In a moment, the private office door swung inward, stopping within an inch of Alex's nose. Seemingly oblivious to the presence behind the door, Jack and a leggy blonde in a short bouncy shirt literally stumbled inside the room.

"Wow, Jack, you really are an executive," the blonde cooed, using the arm of a nearby couch to steady her balance.

"Of course, honey. Give me just a second here. Then we can get down to business." Jack leaned over his desk and fumbled in the top right drawer.

That was just the break Alex needed. While the blonde watched Jack dig around in the desk, Alex slipped from behind the door and made a silent retreat through the lobby and into the central octagonal corridor.

* * *

THE next morning Alex sat on the floor of his tiny studio apartment. With a telephone pasted to one ear, he scribbled furiously on a yellow legal pad and wished his fingers moved as fast as his brain.

"Thank you, Mr. Severs," Alex spoke. "Lock your pasture gate and let me take care of things on this end… Uh-huh... Well, I'm sure he will, but he's my problem, not yours. I'm sorry for any inconvenience… No, you keep it. Consider it compensation for all the trouble we've caused you… Yes, I'm authorized to say that. I'll be in touch with you. Call the 800 number in Sedona if there are any problems... Uh-huh. You bet. And thank you, again."

The telephone receiver bounced twice before settling onto its slim base. Behind him, the tea kettle whistled.

Dropping the notepad and pencil on the carpet, Alex rose smoothly to his feet and circled behind the red silk screen. In a moment, tea was poured into the tall ceramic mug that Phoebe had bought for him. Shiny black inside and out, the only contrast was two enormous gold feline eyes staring out from one side.

He took a sip of jasmine tea and then moved around the red silk screen. Tomorrow was Saturday. If everything went right in the pipe ceremony,

Phoebe would find the answer to the old ghost's riddle. By next week, he should be making marriage plans. Alex had no intention of letting that little dragonfly drift out of his sight again.

His gaze fell on the documents spread across the living room floor. He had suspected something shady about the last few leases that had passed across his desk in Sedona, but he would have never had thought of this.

Damn you, Jack! How many of these waste-dumping contracts have you done since Martin died?

Decades ago, some corporate engineer got the bright idea that non-producing oil wells could be used for waste chemical disposal. Since the sixties, manufacturing companies had found it more difficult and more costly to dispose of chemical by-products in ways that satisfied government regulations for environmental safety. Pumping dangerous solutions deep inside the earth via old oil wells seemed the perfect solution, and it was legal.

Alex cringed. His signature was at the bottom of Erin Hayes mineral lease. He had signed it without question. How many other such contracts had been resold to chemical companies by Jack?

Folding long legs beneath him, Alex sat on the floor and put aside the mug of tea. He grabbed the telephone receiver and punched in the long-distance number scribbled at the bottom of the yellow notepad.

After the third ring, a woman's chipper voice answered. "Kaufman Enterprises. How may I direct your call?"

Alex smiled, knowing this was going to send poor Jack right over the edge. "Fred Kaufman, please."

"Who may I say is calling?"

"A. L. Jones from Northwest Properties. Tell him it's urgent."

* * *

SATURDAY morning, Twyla unlocked the bookstore a few minutes before ten o'clock.

Outside it was a beautiful fall day, warm and sunny and full of promise. This was the day Phoebe would step onto a new path, the day she would finally take up her grandmother's pipe and begin carrying forward the traditions for the next generation. Whistling a happy tune, Twyla shuffled to the back room to make the morning's first pot of coffee.

She could not have been more pleased if she tried. Pleased that Phoebe was finally finding her native path. Pleased that Phoebe had agreed to see Alex again. Twyla always believed those two were destined to be together. The medicine path could be a lonely trail, something she knew all too well.

It was both rare and wonderful for a man and woman to be able to share such a journey. Twyla had walked her trail alone in this lifetime, but hoped with all her heart that Phoebe and Alex would get to share theirs.

The brass bell over the front door rang its tinny little tune.

"Be right with you!" Twyla called. After plugging in the coffeepot, she hurried back into the store.

Halfway down the center aisle her moccasins slid to an unsteady halt on the polished wood floor. Her mouth fell open. Standing in front of her was Jack Henderson. Perhaps she should watch the news more often. Nobody told her that hell had just frozen over.

She cleared the shock out of her throat and forced some control into her voice. "It's been a long time."

Cold anger glistened in Jack's stark gray eyes. The muscles in his jaws twitched, and the veins in his temples bulged. "Where is it?"

"I've missed you, too."

Wrapping long fingers around his estranged aunt's upper arms, Jack gave her a good shake. "Where is it?"

"Back off, boy," Twyla ordered with cold warning just as a strange wind whistled down the aisle.

Jack's fingers opened on command. He stumbled backward a couple of steps, as if someone or something had just pushed him.

"Damned old witch," he seethed through clenched teeth. "Martin always said you and Anna weren't fit to raise kids."

"Like you are, boy?" Twyla dropped her fists on her hips. "Drinking. Fighting. Carousing. Yeah, Martin did a good job with you. At least Danny had some sense. Not much, but some."

Jack's hand came out of nowhere. With a sharp crack, he slapped Twyla across the mouth. "Don't you ever speak about Danny. Ever! He didn't remember you or Anna, and I didn't remind him. This is between you and me, *Auntie*." He leaned on that last word as if it stuck to his tongue.

"I see." Twyla rubbed the corner of her mouth. If she wanted to, she could hold her own with Jack, despite the size differential. There were powers at her disposal of which Jack would be afraid to dream. But fighting served no purpose and answered no questions. "What do you want, Jack?"

"What do you want, old woman? And don't pretend you're not encouraging Phoebe to fight for the land. I'm not stupid."

"No, Jack, you're not stupid, just self-serving." She let the echo of her words die. "I'd like to see Phoebe keep the land. She's the only one who really loves it. And it loves her."

"The land loves her," Jack snarled cynically. "Land doesn't love, old woman. It doesn't feel. It doesn't watch. It doesn't grieve. It if did, it would cry buckets over what you did out there thirty-five years ago."

"How many times have I told you? I had nothing to do with that fire."

Jack stepped closer, those cold gray eyes glaring with undisguised hatred. "I heard you arguing with Martin that night. I remember what you said. You came to take me and Danny back to Anna, but Martin wouldn't let you."

Breathing a staccato sigh, Twyla backed up a couple of steps and leaned a shoulder against a sagging bookshelf. "I didn't know you heard that. I was fighting to get back my sister's children. I was angry and frightened. I said a lot things. But I'm not an arsonist. I'm not a murderer. It was an electrical short. The police said the fire started in the attic. Rats or mice must have chewed through some wires. It was tragic, but it was an accident. You must believe that."

"Believe? I'll tell you what I believe," Jack said, his voice ripe with menacing accusation. "I believe you have the power to make accidents happen. I remember seeing you talk to animals and birds and snakes. I wasn't very old, but I remember. I heard you tell a gopher to get out of your garden. The little furry bastard popped right out of his hole and ran into the woods. So don't tell me you couldn't tell rats to go into the attic and chew on a bundle of wires!"

Twyla was stunned, first by the accusation, second by Jack's understanding of her relationship with the natural world. It had never occurred to her that a small child would remember something as innocuous as telling a gopher to get out of the garden. It was clear now. All of these years, almost four decades worth, Jack had believed Twyla used *medicine* to start the fire that killed his step-grandmother and destroyed his grandfather's house. What could she say? Yes, she could have chatted with the rats. She could have caused the disaster, but she had not.

It was no wonder Jack hated her.

"I'm so sorry, Jack. I didn't know what was going on inside that thick skull of yours. I know you don't want to hear it, but in many ways you're very much like Alex. You would've made a good medicine man."

Jack poked a long, stiff finger in Twyla's face. "Don't ever say that again, old woman. Do you hear me?"

"I hear you. What do you want?"

"I want that contract back right now! I know Alex took it. I banged on his door, but he didn't answer. You've really made a mess of things this time, old woman. Kaufman is ready to back out of the deal. Do you have any idea how long it took me to put together that contract? Or how much it's worth?"

Twyla pushed away from the bookshelf. "I have no idea what you're talking about. Honest."

Those gray eyes squinted in unchecked menace. "Fine. Play stupid. I'm onto your game now. If Alex isn't here, then I know where he is."

Without an apology or a good-bye, Jack wheeled around and thundered out the front door.

For a moment Twyla just stood there, stunned and confused. Then she marshaled enough psychic energy to extract a disturbing picture from Jack's crowded mind.

A reverberating "No!" leapt off her tongue.

* * *

STARTLED, Alex stepped back from the small gas stove in his apartment and pulled a sharp knife from inside his suede boot.

Heavy footsteps ascended the stairs and Twyla's voice rose like a warning klaxon. "Alex! Alex!"

In a moment she burst into the apartment, breathless and visibly panicked.

Alex stood in the kitchen, the knife still clutched in his hand. "What's wrong?"

"Jack," she wheezed. "He was just in the bookstore. Looking for you."

"I just got back from the grocery store," Alex explained, slipping the knife back into its sheath inside his boot. "Take a deep breath and tell me exactly what happened."

"He thinks you took some kind of contract out of his office and he wants it back. He's on his way out to the farm right now. Do you know what he's looking for?"

Alex plucked a fat manila folder from the top of one of the black trunks. "This."

"What is it?"

"The answer to Grandma's riddle," Alex declared. Then a chill crept up his back, as the rest of Twyla's words finally registered: *Jack's on his way to the farm.*

Springing into action, Alex tucked the folder under his arm and raced down the stairs.

Behind him, Twyla screamed, "Wait for me!"

CHAPTER 24
Web of Life

PHOEBE did what she should have done seven years before. On the seventh anniversary of her great-grandmother's death, she spread a blanket in the center of the pond dock and prepared for her first solo pipe ceremony.

Mother Nature provided a beautiful Saturday morning. The wind remained tame and warm. Only a few wispy clouds dotted the blue sky, like so many stray notes on a sheet of music.

Phoebe sat on the woven blanket. Around her she arranged simple items, including an eagle feather, an abalone shell, a cedar sprig, a braid of sweetgrass, a leather tobacco pouch, and the pipe bundle. First she put cedar and sweetgrass in the abalone shell and lit it. Using the eagle feather, a family heirloom, she smoked off the area and then herself.

Finally, she opened the pipe bundle for the first time in seven years. With great respect, she put the pipe together, attaching the cedar stem to the green stone bowl and then loading it with seven precise pinches of tobacco. It lit easily, which was a good sign.

Drawing her first draft of smoke, she closed her eyes and addressed the first of seven directions.

***

EAST, the land of tomorrow.

Phoebe saw the outline of a man standing in the golden glow of the sunrise. He stepped forward and his face came into sharp focus. It was Alex. Kneeling before her, he offered his palms. His deep voice echoed across the spiritual realm. "Come see the future with me."

Phoebe refused to take his hands. "You lied to me."

"I came to protect you, to love you. Listen to your heart, Dragonfly. Listen to your heart…."

Phoebe opened her eyes, disturbed to realize that she did not trust Alex the way she had before Jack's party. She thought she had forgiven him. She thought she understood. Apparently, there were a still few doubts hiding in her heart. Things she would have to resolve before continuing their relationship.

She drew another puff of smoke and released it.

* * *

SOUTH, the source of warm wind and growth.

Phoebe's eyes closed.

She was a small child again, chasing an old yellow tomcat through a cornfield, darting in and out of tight rows before colliding with her great-grandmother's calico skirt.

"Slow down, Dragonfly," Grandma scolded and thrust a woven basket into her arms. "Here. Make yourself useful. Hold this while I pick the corn. And don't drop it."

"Yes, Grandma."

The ornery old cat, nicknamed Popcorn because of his bulbous golden eyes, hid beneath Grandma's floor-length skirt, leaving only his tail wagging outside to churn reddish dirt.

"Silly old Popcorn," Phoebe said with a giggle, watching the cat struggle to stay inside the skirt as the old woman shuffled down the cornrow.

Phoebe opened tear-filled eyes and wiped her nose. She had forgotten that foolish old tomcat, who used to torment her and compete for a place in Grandma's lap.

The corn. How Phoebe had loved to pick corn with Grandma. The sounds and smells of the garden remained vivid in her memory. The rustling of that calico skirt dragging over musty clumps of red clay and catching on scratchy cornstalks. Grandma's patient voice giving instructions on planting and nurturing and harvesting the corn. One generation passing knowledge to the next.

Message received, Grandma.

Moving on, Phoebe closed her eyes. She took another draw on the pipe and addressed the next direction.

* * *

WEST, land of the setting sun, realm of the ancestors.

A figure emerged from the shadows. A tall, lanky man with crystal gray eyes and a gentle smile sauntered out of thick fog. "Hello, Phebes. I missed you."

"Danny. Not you. I'm so sorry. So very sorry."

"About what?"

Phoebe melted at the sight of that familiar, easy smile. "Danny, I'm so sorry. I didn't marry you because I loved you. I married you because of Grandma."

"I knew that. Honey, I didn't love you either. Not at first. I wanted you. And I wanted to help you. But I learned to love you. And I think you learned to love me, although I did a lot of stupid things. Do you forgive me?"

"Forgive you? I've felt so bad since—"

"Since I died?" he finished for her. "Why feel bad? I was always happy with you. I miss you, Phebes."

"I've missed you, too," she said.

Danny began to fade out of reach. His voice dimmed, echoing like soft wind through a wooden flute. "Be well, my sweet, and be happy."

"Danny," Phoebe whispered, opening her eyes and choking on cascading emotions.

For the first time, she realized that she and Danny had shared something of which she could feel proud. But their time together had run its course. It was over.

Phoebe's hands shook on the pipe, and she could not help but marvel at the fact that it was still lit. The next direction brought a hint of trepidation. Her eyes clamped shut and her mouth closed around the pipe.

* * *

NORTH, the place of trials, the source of wisdom.

Phoebe shuddered at the onslaught of images.

Scattered scenes from the last few months replayed in rapid progression. Little bits of intimidation delivered by Jack. Confrontations intensifying. Arguments escalating. Phoebe's resolve slipping, day by day. She watched herself run into the Twylight Bookstore on a stormy August afternoon, rain-soaked and discouraged. The man she would later come to know as Alex brushed by her in a narrow aisle. Her blind pursuit of Alex provided just enough distraction to keep her from crumbling beneath the weight of Jack's tyrannical reign. The scene changed to her argument with Jack at the house a few weeks before. It had been the first time she had really stood up to him, exchanging stinging remarks over his desk and refusing to cower beneath his threats.

Startled out of the vision, Phoebe blinked in surprise and stared across the muddy, tear-shaped pond. Alex had not saved her from Jack. She had done it herself.

Jack had unwittingly provided the adversity she needed to forge her inner strength into a powerful spiritual sword. Heating it and hammering it and thrusting it time and again into cold water until, at last, the metal was unbreakable and able to hold a fine edge.

Moving on, Phoebe let her eyelids flutter shut. She drew heavily on the pipe and blew the smoke downward.

* * *

MOTHER EARTH, the pulse of creative energy.

A strange image solidified in Phoebe's mind.

She walked through dry prairie grass and stopped in front of a rusted old pumpjack. It was the oil well from the back of Mr. Severs' property. The land lease she had helped Jack acquire a couple of months back. The pumpjack groaned to life. Great counterbalances rowed like the paddles of a steamboat. Its tapered head bobbed up and down. To one side, she saw a diesel truck with a huge skull and crossbones painted in red on its silvery cylindrical tank. A clear plastic tube ran from the tank to the pumpjack. Liquid flowed out of the truck and into the ground. Mother Earth cried, thunderstorms rocking the land with lightning and hail and pounding rain. *Take care of the land and the land will take care of you...take care of the land and the land will take care of you.*

Her eyes opened. She had been around oil men long enough to know what that particular vision meant. Someone was using land leases for oil field waste-dumping. Was that someone Jack? Or was she supposed to enlist Jack's help? She did not know. The vision had been too vague.

Shutting her eyes, she took the sixth draw from the pipe and blew it upward.

* * *

ABOVE, the realm of the spirit.

The night sky unfolded, like a cosmic map.

She saw a panoramic view of space. Cool planets with their circling moons. Swirling galaxies and their blazing stars. Tiny strands of light raced from one end of the universe to the other, bouncing back and forth, weaving a pattern of energy that connected all these grand heavenly bodies, sewing them together in a strange and wondrous tapestry of possibilities.

All things connected. All things were one. All things came from spirit. Sound and color and warmth were just different aspects of the same energy. Every strand of the cosmic web was just as important as the one after and the one before. The weaker strands made the stronger strands pull harder to keep that perfect circle, yet no strand was discarded.

A little dizzy, she opened her eyes and focused on the grassy field beyond the pond. It seemed so small in comparison to the infinite view she had just been shown. Every strand of the cosmic web was important, even Jack. The message was undeniable. Don't give up on anyone. Understand the whole.

The last part of the ceremony had always been the most difficult for Phoebe. This time she did not close her eyes, but took a deep draw from the pipe and let the smoke ease out of her mouth and wrap back around her body and face.

* * *

CENTER, the Self.

It was the last vision and the most obscure. Phoebe glanced down at the still water of the pond and saw her own reflection. Grandma's voice rang in her ears: "Look at the dragonfly in the mirror and find your destiny at twilight."

* * * * *

CHAPTER 25

Prairie Pawns

A stream of colorful and highly improbable curses flowed through Jack's gritted teeth. He pointed the remote at the entrance gate and clicked it for the third time. Nothing happened. Obviously, someone had changed the code.

He considered just stepping on the gas and crashing through, but figured it would probably do more damage to his sedan than to that heavy iron gate.

Blocking the entrance to the driveway, Jack put the car in Park and shut off the engine. He did not want to leave the sedan at the road, but it could not be helped. All he could think about was getting back that contract and smoothing things with Fred Kaufman before the whole damned deal was blown.

He climbed out of the sedan and slammed the door. The echo flowed through the trees, scaring up a flock of crows that made a temporary dark smear overhead. Without hesitation he vaulted over the gate and landed on his feet with an ominous thud. Long strides took him up the winding driveway.

In a couple of minutes he stood in front of the house. Even if Alex was not here, those dogs probably were. Making his way into the breezeway, Jack paused at the kitchen door and listened. Muffled growls greeted him.

"There you are, you mouthy little bitches," he muttered.

Realizing too late that he had left his keys in the car ignition, he took two steps toward the side door of the garage and planted a cowboy boot near the handle. The metal dented and the lock broke. With a subdued creak, the door swung inward. Jack glanced into the garage and found the situation in his favor. The black pickup he had seen Alex driving yesterday was not there. No extra vehicles meant no witnesses. This was going to be between just him and Phoebe.

All he had to do now was get rid of those dogs.

***

PHOEBE sat on the dock. She reflected on the spirits, who had chosen to speak with her, and on the lessons received.

The pipe lay in two pieces on the blanket before her and a few wisps of smoke rose from the offerings in the abalone shell. It had been a good ceremony. A long overdue ceremony. She went into it without fear or anger and allowed the universe to speak to her. It had, and she had listened.

Without warning, the dock shook and an angry voice broke her serenity.

"So this is where you are," Jack snarled.

Startled, Phoebe got up and turned around just in time to be knocked flat on her back. Weak from three days of fasting and drained from the emotional intensity of the pipe ceremony, she fought to remain conscious.

The dock continued to creak as he paced a slow circle around her. Somewhere to her right was her grandmother's pipe and the eagle feather.

"What did you do with it?" Jack demanded.

Phoebe sat up and shaded her eyes. She tried to figure out what *it* was. Had Jack rummaged through his office in the house while she had been in ceremony? Had he found something missing or misplaced?

"Take it easy, Jack," she said in a calming voice. "Just tell me what you're looking for. Maybe I know what box I put it in."

"The contract, you addle-brained bitch! Where's that oil contract?"

"Oil contract?" Phoebe recalled the vision of that rusted pumpjack dumping chemicals into a crying Mother Earth. Grandma's riddle echoed in her mind: *Take care of the land and the land will take care of you.*

Phoebe looked up at Jack, towering over her. Those gray eyes were as wild as his wind-blown hair. His hands hung at his sides, curling in and out of tight fists. She could smell his panic. A cold wind came out of the north. It stirred through dry prairie grass, rippled across the pond, and whistled beneath the dock, warning Phoebe to be careful.

"Jack, what have you done?"

"It's all clear now." His teeth were clenched. The wild look in his eyes suggested questionable sanity.

"What's clear, Jack?"

"Blackmail," he spat. "What do you want? The house? The land? Money? And if I don't agree to your terms, then what? A media blitz? Reporters? Protesters? More threats from that old ghost? I know how this works. I've been here before. Just remember, blackmail works both ways."

Phoebe wrinkled her nose and tried to make some sense of Jack's tirade. Blackmail? Protesters? Oil contracts? "Jack, I swear. I don't know what contract you're talking about."

"That meddling old ghost," Jack's voice shook as much as his knees. "She told you, didn't she?"

"Grandma?" Phoebe thought back to the night before the old woman had died, trying to piece together the events.

She and Danny had gone to dinner that evening. When they returned, they found Grandma in her bed, dying. Phoebe knew death had been stalking the old woman for several months, but it had still been something of a shock. Also, it was not uncommon for medicine people to make peace with the world and just lay down to die. That was what Phoebe always thought happened to her grandmother. But had there been more?

Phoebe did not pause to think through her words, but should have. "Grandma found out you were selling oil leases for chemical waste dumping, didn't she? She threatened to tell Danny and me and alert the media. Am I right, Jack?"

An evil smile showed Jack's perfect Cherokee teeth, and those eyes glistened like poisoned mercury pools. "She didn't like my counter-proposal. I guess she decided curling up her toes and dying was better than what I was going to do to her granddaughter."

"When you moved in last spring, you didn't count on a ghost, did you?" Phoebe regretted the remark as soon as it had left her lips. This was no time to be antagonistic.

Jack shook his head in jerky increments. "Tell me where that contract is or else."

Something instinctive clicked in the back of Phoebe's mind, something Alex had taught her in kung fu class. Lying on her back, she waited for Jack to make the first move.

He did, leaning forward with his hands outstretched.

In smooth, quick reaction, Phoebe locked her fingers around Jack's wrists. Her feet connected with the flat of his stomach. Using all the strength she could muster, she rocked backward and threw him cleanly over her shoulders and off the dock where he landed face first in thick prairie grass.

Despite wobbly knees and blurry vision, Phoebe scrambled to her feet. Jack had moved beyond mad and into sheer madness. She had to get away from the pond. On dry land, she had a fighting chance. But, in the water, she was no match for him.

Adrenaline surged, giving her enough strength to leap from the dock and hit the grass running.

* * *

ALEX slammed on the brakes and sent the pickup sliding sideways. It stopped just inches short of the bumper of Jack's burgundy sedan. The situation was clear. Jack had jumped the gate and walked to the house.

Using the spare remote, Alex opened the gate and climbed out of the truck. One quick look in the sedan proved Jack's haste. He had left the keys in the car and the doors unlocked.

"Twyla!" Alex bellowed. "Bring the truck and leave that gate open."

"Right," she piped back crisply and slid to the driver's side of the pickup.

Without looking back, he hopped into the sedan, started it, and thundered up the driveway. The road curved through the trees and formed a circle in front of the house. He hit the brakes at the top of circle and killed the engine.

Alex climbed out of the car and walked cautiously toward the house. To his horror, the front door hung half-open on broken hinges.

With gears grinding and tires squealing, Twyla slid the truck to a stop behind the sedan and climbed out, her moccasins sinking into dry grass.

"Stay back," he warned.

"Where are the dogs?"

Alex stepped onto the front porch and listened.

Faint whining carried on the cold breeze.

"They're locked in the basement," he informed. "I'm going inside, but you stay here. I mean it, Aunt Tea. Stay here!"

Slow and cautious, Alex slipped through the front door. What he found inside only caused more alarm. It looked like a tornado had ripped through the living room, emptying bookshelves and shattering the glass patio doors.

He resisted the urge to call out for Phoebe, knowing surprise and stealth were his allies. One glance down the darkened hallway told more of the story. The carpet was littered with folders and papers, and there was a hole in the wall just outside the den. Obviously, Jack had been searching for the contract.

The house felt empty. Before Alex could decide what to do next, a shimmering mist coalesced in the center of hallway.

The scent of gingersnaps and coffee was overwhelming. Instead of the usual ghostly figure, an old woman stood there as solid as if she were still alive.

"To the pond, boy!" she ordered in a crystal-clear, audible voice. "To the pond!"

Stunned, Alex stood there, his breath caught in his throat.

"Hurry!" the old woman yelled, pointing to the west.

Startled into movement, Alex turned. In a dead run, he navigated the living room and leaped through the opening where the patio doors had been.

* * *

PHOEBE fought to find the strength to run harder, faster. She could hear Jack behind her, growing closer.

She tried to claw her way up the grassy knoll, but the slick soles of her moccasins skidded over loose rock. Before she could stop the downward slide, strong fingers locked around one of her ankles.

"Gotcha!" Jack said.

Phoebe's fingernails scraped the side of an angled rock as Jack dragged her down the steep hill. She did not know if he intended to kill her, but blind rage seemed to have left him without what little sanity he normally possessed.

Just as she lost her grip, a large blur sailed over the rise.

Alex.

Like a panther springing out of a clear blue sky, Alex flew over her. Using combined weight and momentum, he put one foot in the middle of Jack's chest and ripped him off the side of the hill. Amid thuds and groans, both men tumbled through brittle grass.

Phoebe buried her fingers in red dirt to stop her downward slide. In a moment she had pulled herself to the top of the rise and found Twyla waiting there.

"Are you all right?" Twyla asked, running his hands over Phoebe's arms as if looking for damage.

"I'm fine," Phoebe said and then pointed down the hill. "But how do we stop that?"

"I'm not sure we can," Twyla replied, looking over the edge of the rise.

The first one to find his footing was Alex. He sank into a defensive posture, knees bent, fists curled, and eyes riveted on his opponent.

Spitting out a mouthful of dirt, Jack got to his feet and fought to catch his breath. "Indians," he hissed. "Nothing but a bunch of crazy Indians."

"Including you, Jack?" Alex taunted.

"Including me. Come on, cousin. Let's see what you're made of."

Jack and Alex circled each other in thick, dry prairie grass, eyes locked, muscles twitching. The first to make a move was Jack. He threw combination kicks and fists in rapid succession. To avoid the deadly blows, Alex blocked with his feet and his hands, shuffling out of harm's way with quick efficiency. Executing a smooth spinning leg sweep, Jack attacked, again. Alex jumped to one side, landed firmly on the grass, and slammed a fist into the corner of Jack's hard jaw. Dazed, Jack stumbled backward, but did not fall.

"You're good, cousin, but not good enough," Alex warned. "Give it up."

"We'll see about that," Jack snarled, spitting out a mouthful of blood.

Without warning, dusty wind blasted out of the west, churning and curling until it created an upside-down tornado between Alex and Jack. A solid form burst out of the whirling fog. Grandma stood between the men. Her traditional dress, a matching calico tunic and floor-length gathered skirt, ruffled in the wind, while small beaded moccasins sank into the soft ground. Braided silver hair glistened, and her golden face showed a lifetime of wrinkles. Gray eyes sparkled as a feral smile showed off sharp, crooked teeth.

Raising his hands in gestured peace, Alex made the smart choice and backed out of the way.

Phoebe could hardly believe what she was seeing. Grandma was much more than a smoky vision this time. She looked solid and warm and mad, a presence with which to be reckoned.

And the obvious object of Grandma's wrath was Jack.

"Go away, old woman," Jack sputtered. "You're dead. Your time has passed."

"Time is irrelevant. You never understood that, did you, boy?" Grandma's crystalline voice carried on the cold wind. She began to pace, making a tight circle around Jack. "This world is your mother. Out of her came the dirt for your body. The water for your eyes. The air for your breath. And when you die, it all returns to her."

"You're dead!" Jack declared with a quivering voice. "And I won't listen to any more of your lies."

"Lies, Jack?" Grandma stopped in front of him. "Like the lies Martin told you about your own mother? About your aunt? Your grandmother?"

"Get away from me!" Jack tried to push the old woman. Instead, he stumbled through her semi-solid form and fell in an ungraceful heap on the grass. A look of horror contorted his sweat-streaked, bloodied face.

The ghost's laughter echoed across the prairie. "It's all about power with you, isn't it Jack? Martin told you money was power. But you can't take money to the grave. You said you would kill Phoebe if I told anyone about those contracts. I looked in your heart and knew you would do it."

"You're right. I would have," he admitted with cold anger.

"Death is just a doorway. I knew I could watch over Phoebe. Someday, with a little help, the truth would come out. It was Alex who found the contract, not Phoebe. All she had to do was sit tight. I made her promise to hang onto this land until I said she could leave. And she did. She has a strong spirit, much stronger than you will ever understand."

"I don't know what I understand anymore," Jack muttered. Sitting up on the grass, he dropped his hands over his knees. "I thought I knew Martin. He said Anna hated Danny and me, and that Twyla caused Grandma Margaret's death. I believed him. Why wouldn't I? He was my grandfather. He took care of us through school and sickness and army days and everything else. Martin said there was no such thing as ghosts. He also said there was no power in Indian hocus-pocus."

Grandma smiled and leaned toward him. "Who has the power now, boy?"

"What do you want from me?" he asked in breathless resignation.

The old ghost held up four fingers and pointed to each in succession. "One, give Phoebe the deed to this land. Leave and do not return unless you are invited. Two, cancel the new lease. Alex has the folder you seek. Three, no more waste-dumping contracts. And four, sit down and talk to Twyla. Hear the truth. You don't have to love her or even like her. Just for once, listen to her. If you promise to do these four things, I will leave you alone. Break that promise, and Grandma's gonna cut your hair, boy. Mess with me again and I'll take you back through that doorway with me. You understand?"

Jack sat very still, sucking in hard, short breaths. "Whatever you want, old woman. Just go away."

The ghost offered a slow triumphant nod. Then she dissolved, the wind carrying away her iridescent particles.

At the top of the hill, Phoebe sank to her knees. She glanced at Twyla, who stood stock-still beside her. Then she looked down the hill at Jack and Alex. All four had witnessed Grandma's ghost and had heard her words.

The other day Phoebe said she felt like a pawn on a chessboard. If she was the pawn then that made Alex the knight, Grandma the queen, and Jack the evil king who had just been checkmated.

*****

CHAPTER 26
At the Crossroads

FROM the top of the hill, Phoebe watched Jack make his way back to the house with Twyla trailing behind him like a mismatched shadow. Grandma had scared Jack into behaving, at least for the time being.

Sitting in the grass beside her, Alex offered that familiar warm smile. "Are you all right?"

Phoebe nodded and rubbed the corner of her mouth where Jack had hit her. "Yeah, I'm fine. What about you? Jack didn't hurt you, did he?"

"Jack didn't hurt me." Letting the smile fade, Alex pulled a few blades of stiff prairie grass out of Phoebe's thick ponytail. "I'm sorry things got out of hand. I took that contract out of Jack's office Thursday night. I didn't call you yesterday to tell you what I was doing because I didn't want to disturb you. I had no idea Jack would come here looking for the damned thing."

"What contract are you talking about?"

"Do you remember going with Jack to see a man named Severs?"

"Yeah," she piped back. "A few months ago. We drove down near Anadarko. Jack secured the rights for an old well on the backside of Severs' pasture."

"That's the one. Do you remember a pretty Native American girl at the party?"

"The tart?" Noting the surprise on Alex's face, Phoebe waved her hand in dismissal. "Never mind. Inside joke. She was Jack's mistress for a while."

Alex nodded. "Her name is Erin Hayes. She owns the minerals under that old pumpjack."

Things finally began to make some sense to Phoebe. "Jack slept with the girl and got her to sign a mineral lease. Then he used me to coerce the farmer into giving him access to the land."

"You got it. Then he sold the lease to a chemical company in California. I called Severs yesterday and told him what was going on. Someone came to his farm last week and surveyed the road to see about laying gravel for heavy trucks, but they haven't started on the well yet. And they won't if I have anything to do with it."

"I'm afraid to ask, but what were they going to dump?"

"Benzene," Alex informed in a venomous tone. "God knows what else."

"No wonder Grandma wanted it stopped. She was an environmentalist before the word was popular."

A shadow of dread fell across his tawny face. "Phoebe, there's something else I need to tell you."

"If you're married and have a dozen kids in Arizona, I don't want to hear it." Phoebe faked a smug smile and hoped her remark was way off course.

"No, honey, I've never been married." He leaned back, his elbows sinking into dry prairie grass. "Do you remember the night Jack got that bloody nose?"

Fatigue and hunger made memory retrieval a little difficult, but Phoebe managed to pull a few threads from the past. "That was the night Jack and Sam were so drunk."

"You found them passed out in the den. Then you came upstairs, bathed, and dreamed someone came to your bed."

Phoebe did not like what she was hearing. "How did you know that?"

"Because I was in the house that night," Alex confessed. "I knocked out Jack and Sam so they wouldn't hurt you. I was the one who bloodied Jack's nose."

"I see," she intoned, chewing her bottom lip. "And then you came to my bedroom?"

"I was already up there when you got home. My intent was to keep you safe, but you were just too much temptation. I had to touch you."

"And kiss me and make me believe it was nothing but a dream." Phoebe knew she should be furious. Instead, she threw back her head and laughed.

"That's not the response I expected," he said, looking a little confused. "You're not mad?"

Phoebe stared at the golden-eyed panther of her dreams. "I'm not mad. You know why? I remember thinking it was too real. At some subconscious level, I knew you were there."

"I underestimated you. And you nearly caught me."

"It's the past. All's forgiven. Just don't ever do something like that again. I mean it. No more lies." Phoebe sighted down one eye. "Now I have a question for you. Did Twyla tell you to call me Dragonfly or did you pull it out of the ethers?"

"I pulled it." Alex stood, helping Phoebe to her feet in the process.

"Come on. Let's take you back to the house and get you something to eat."

"Alex, wait. There's something else." Phoebe cleared her throat and searched for the right words. She knew what she had to do, but feared it as well. In her mind she saw herself at the proverbial crossroads. She had been sitting in the middle of that dusty intersection for a long time, seven years to be exact. It was finally time to get up and choose a path.

Before Phoebe could continue, Alex scooped her up into his arms and spoke quietly. "You need time to discover your path. Time to find your place in this world. Time to learn to trust me again. That about cover it?"

"Yeah, just about." For once Phoebe was glad Alex could read her thoughts and her heart. Her arms fit nicely over his shoulders and around his neck. The comforting scent of *Musk Rain* filled her sinuses, reminding her of sweet moments at the astral lily pond and of ecstasy beneath the waterfall. "You really don't have to carry me. I can walk, you know."

"This is more fun," Alex replied, as he walked toward the house. "Since you're going to send me away, I have to get in a few good gropes while I can."

"I'll miss you," Phoebe said with a twinge of regret. "But I need some time alone."

In a voice as firm and steady as his footsteps, Alex added, "I know."

"You were quite a sight flying over that hill," she whispered in his ear.

Mischief sparkled in those wonderful gold eyes. "I just watch too many kung fu movies."

* * *

BY the middle of the afternoon, it was only Phoebe and Twyla, two dogs in the back yard, and two carpenters trying to replace the doors in the living room.

A couple of hours ago Jack had rocketed off the property in his expensive sedan. Then Alex followed in the truck just to make sure Jack landed safely at Sam's house.

Phoebe shook her head at the needless mess in the living room and in the lives of everyone associated with Jack Henderson. She walked into the kitchen and climbed on a barstool. "Twyla, are you still cooking?"

"I'm still hungry. How are the repairs going?"

"The front door's fixed and they're hanging the new patio doors right now. Is that a carrot cake in the oven?"

"Yes. And there's fresh cornbread on the cabinet." Twyla rinsed her hands in the sink and turned around. "Enough small talk, kiddo. Ask your questions."

"All right," Phoebe intoned with a business-like nod. It was a bit sneaky, but she decided not to mention she had read those letters between Twyla and Alex. She figured, however, with all that had happened, she deserved some answers. "Why didn't you tell me you were Jack and Danny's aunt? I would've understood."

Backing against the sink, Twyla offered a motherly expression. "Those boys were lost to my side of the family years ago. I was thrilled when you married Danny, but I have to be honest. I always thought you and Alex were a better match."

Phoebe sensed Twyla was trying to steer the conversation away from the past, but this was the best time to get it all out in the open. "Tell me what happened with Martin and the boys, and I promise I'll never ask again."

"Martin Henderson," Twyla hissed in disgust. "Anna and Billy's father was a greedy hypocrite. He married a wealthy society woman named Margaret Beldon. Then fathered twins by a pretty secretary who worked in his office."

"Your mother, Felicia," Phoebe added for her own clarity.

"Yes. After Martin wouldn't acknowledge the twins, Felicia went on with life. She had an affair with a fancy-dancer she knew on the pow-wow circuit. She died giving birth to me. My grandparents wound up raising all three kids: me, William, and Anna."

"I'm so sorry," Phoebe felt compelled to interject.

"Don't be. We had a great childhood. We were loved and respected. You can't ask for more than that."

"What happened to Anna? And who was Danny and Jack's father?"

"Anna married this good-looking Air Force pilot," Twyla droned with arched eyebrows. "He was killed right after Danny was born. Some kind of top-secret test flight or something. The Air Force was tight-lipped about the whole affair. After that, Anna and the boys moved in with me, and we managed the best we could for a couple of years."

Phoebe realized she was finally getting the whole ugly truth. "How did Martin Henderson wind up with the boys?"

"Anna and I went to Seattle for a visit when Alex was born. We left Danny and Jack with our grandparents because we didn't have enough money to take them with us. Our brother was so proud of that baby, but Maria was scared. She knew something was wrong. She always had great psychic senses."

"What happened?"

Twyla continued in a distant voice. "While we were gone, Martin bribed a county official into filing child abandonment charges on Anna. He and Margaret took custody of the boys. When we returned to Oklahoma, our grandparents were hysterical. I thought I might be able to talk some sense into Martin, so I went to see him that night before the house fire. All I wanted was to get the boys back. You know, this house has the same floor plan as the one before. It looks a little different, but the layout is basically the same. Anyway, I banged on the front door and slugged it out with Martin."

Phoebe envisioned a horrible scenario. "You mean, a fight? You had a fist fight with Jack's grandfather?"

"Oh, yeah," she said with a wave of her hand. "We got into it tooth and toenail right there in the living room. Then he threw me out the front door. The next evening we read in the paper that the house had burned and Margaret was dead. A few days later Martin told Anna if we ever tried to take the boys, he'd accuse me of setting the fire and causing Margaret's death. You have to understand, we were from the poor side of town. Martin had money and politicians eating out of his pocket. There was nothing we could do."

"So Anna gave up?"

"Pretty much. She died a couple of years later. Complications from a bad flu that went around. I left Oklahoma and landed in Sedona. Started a realty business. Had a short-lived marriage. Then I came back to the city. I think that about catches you up."

Phoebe had never been comfortable with tragedies, and this tale certainly seemed to qualify. She was tempted to offer a belated "I'm sorry" but figured Twyla would take umbrage at that. Phoebe would not presume to cast judgments on another person's life. Still, she found the story a sad one.

For a poor little Indian girl, Twyla had amassed quite a financial empire. She owned one realty office in the city, plus all of Red Cedars Corner and ran that quirky little bookstore just for the hell of it. No telling what other assets she had yet to divulge. From the simple way that Twyla lived, no one would ever have guessed she was financially set.

"The Sedona office is the one Alex runs, right?" Phoebe asked.

"Uh-huh. Oh, that reminds me." Twyla disappeared into the dining room. When she returned, she had a single document in hand. "Here's the deed to the Henderson property. All signed and ready to file. Jack won't give you anymore trouble. The land and the house are yours. He also agreed to cancel the Hayes mineral lease. Alex will see that he does. Now, little girl, you're going to need some means of support, since you've sent that gorgeous panther back to Arizona."

Phoebe opened her mouth to protest, but Twyla cut her off.

"I know, Dragonfly. You need time alone to think and find your path. I understand, but it still worries me. If I had a man like Alex who loved me that much, I'd have him sewn to my hip. But, then, that's just me." Twyla dropped the deed on the snack bar. "Here's my offer. Instead of taking a risk on a new business, why don't you run the bookstore for me? Alex will know you're safe, and I'll give you more than enough to live on. What do you say?"

"I don't know what to say," Phoebe said, both surprised and embarrassed by such a generous offer.

"Just say yes, so we can have cake and be done with it."

"Yes," Phoebe said in a firm voice.

* * *

THAT evening, with a flashlight in hand and a blanket wrapped around her shoulders, Phoebe climbed onto the pond dock and watched the hungry western horizon gobble up the sun.

The day's events blurred and overlapped in the back of her mind. Earlier, Twyla had walked here with her to help gather the pipe and other ceremonial items. To no one's surprise, the eagle feather had been waiting patiently on the blanket near the abalone shell. Nothing was damaged or lost, despite the fight and the wind.

For the first time in her life, Phoebe was truly alone. In one way it was liberating. In another, it was empty. Alex had been gone for only a few hours and already her heart ached. Was she doing the right thing, sending him away without making any plans to have him return? Would he find someone else while she was trying to find herself? Maybe Twyla was right. Maybe she should get on that plane and go to Arizona with him.

"Grandma, what should I do?"

The dock creaked and a familiar voice echoed across the pond. "Have faith, child, and enjoy the journey."

Startled, Phoebe turned. Grandma stood beside her, just as bold and as bright as she had been earlier that afternoon.

A single warm tear trespassed Phoebe's cheek. "Grandma, I've missed you so much."

"Such a silly child. I was never missing." With an audible groan, Grandma tucked her feet beneath her and sat near the edge of the dock. She pointed to the sunset reflection on the muddy pond. "The sun sleeps in the West. Then rises again in the East. The circle of life."

Seated beside her great-grandmother again after so long, Phoebe marveled at the miracle of the old woman's presence. The aroma of gingersnaps and coffee was thick. A little uncertain, she touched the sleeve of that familiar calico shirt. It felt real. Then she brushed her fingers across the back of a wrinkled hand and found it amazingly warm.

"Grandma, why didn't you tell me what Jack was up to years ago? You could have whispered it. I would have heard."

The old woman raised her weathered face toward the last rays of murky light. Only a sliver of the sun remained above the western horizon, while stars multiplied in the east. "I could not tell you until the time was right, until the panther came to guard you."

"Alex? You knew Alex would come?"

"Twyla spoke much of her nephew. She thinks of him as a son. And you should know, he will inherit as a son. Marry him and you will want for nothing."

"What I want is to be loved."

Grandma smiled, her crystalline eyes getting lost in the folds of sagging eyelids. "Marry him and you will want for nothing."

"You were so certain he would come. Did you have a vision before you died?"

The old woman puckered her lips and shook her head. "No. Just made sense. Alex is the counterbalance for Jack."

"Counterbalance," Phoebe echoed. She kept her gaze glued on her grandmother, certain that if she so much as blinked too slowly the old woman would disappear forever. "Why didn't you materialize before this?"

"I needed a bridge from my side to yours."

"I don't understand, Grandma. What kind of bridge?"

"The bridge you built with the smoke of the pipe." One gray eyebrow arched, and her crackled voice echoed over the water. "I was beginning to think you were never going to smoke that pipe."

Phoebe just shrugged. She also had wondered if she would find the courage to follow in her grandmother's footsteps, but she had. And now she had been given a unique gift, a wonderful second chance to say farewell. "You're saying good-bye for good this time, aren't you?"

The old woman nodded. "Time to go on to the next."

"Grandma, just one more question. Am I doing the right thing with Alex?"

"Just keep doing, child. It's your journey. You have to figure it out for yourself. I can tell you the panther is proud of you. He thinks you are an honorable soul. That is high praise from him." A little mischief sneaked into the old woman's expression. "Alex is a bit arrogant, you know."

"Yes, a bit." Phoebe felt a shiver of fear. "I don't want to lose him."

Grandma offered a stiff shrug. "If looking for your path causes you to lose him, then you did not need him to begin with. Let it go. Let it be as it will. And listen to Twyla. She will be a good teacher."

"I wish you could stay," Phoebe moaned and lay her head in her grandmother's comforting lap. By standing up to Jack, she had fulfilled her promise to take care of the land, and the land had taken care of her by sending Alex. Now it was time for reflection.

Grandma's thin fingers combed through Phoebe's thick auburn hair. Soft humming flowed over the dock and tickled the pond, sending tiny ripples across muddy water. Over and over, that aged voice whispered: "Find your destiny at twilight...Find your destiny at twilight."

* * *

THE next thing Phoebe saw was a brilliant sunrise in the east. Startled, she sat up and threw off the blanket. Grandma was gone, and Phoebe knew she would not return.

*****

CHAPTER 27
Twylight Destiny

THUNDER rattled the front plate glass windows of the Twylight Bookstore.

Startled, Phoebe dropped a heavy box of books on the polished wood floor. In a moment, fat raindrops pounded the parking lot and pecked at the windows. It was the first good rain the city had seen all August.

The last few months had brought some surprises.

Everyone was shocked when Sam and Rachel ran off to Las Vegas and got married. Who would have expected Rachel to find anything in common with Sam Tillman? It just proved that sometimes opposites really did attract. In any case, Phoebe wished them the best.

Then there was Jack. He had done exactly what Grandma had instructed him to do. No more. No less. He canceled the Hayes lease, but did nothing about similar contracts. At least they had stopped one of those waste-dumping deals and there would be no more brokered through Northwest Properties. Maybe there was a streak of humanity inside Jack, after all. Deep inside. And a very small streak.

As Twyla promised, Phoebe worked hard, making an adequate living by managing the bookstore and getting an education in medicine work along the way. It had been both satisfying and enjoyable. Phoebe made a few changes to the store. Alex's red silk screen blocked off one corner to create a reading area for children, replete with the huge stuffed panther and lots of pillows. She reorganized the bookshelves, making clear separations between fiction and nonfiction genres. A computer had replaced the old cash register, and colorful dreamcatchers for sale crowded the plate glass windows.

Weekends and evenings were for studying, meditating, and performing the occasional ceremony as needed. Through Twyla's patient tutelage, Phoebe's understanding of the harmony of flesh and spirit had increased exponentially. She remembered Alex once saying that knowledge was a two-edged sword. Last night, as she looked up at the bright stars, the depth of that adage finally hit her. As a child, she had seen only glitter hung on the curtain of night. As a teenager, she had understood those lights to be glowing suns. But as an adult, she knew planets circled those far stars while aloof galaxies spun in the velveteen distance. The more she learned, the more she knew there was to learn.

Alex had left Kiki and Elsa with Phoebe to provide both comfort and safety. This afternoon Twyla had taken the dogs to get their yearly vaccinations, so it was just Phoebe alone in the bookstore, watching this strange summer storm and reminiscing. The forecast had been for warm, dry conditions, yet here it was cold and rainy. Oklahoma weather, who could predict it? But a good soaking rain was just what the prairie needed. August had been brutally hot and dry, not at all like last year had been.

Last year echoed in Phoebe's head. That and more thunder.

It was exactly one year to the day since she had first seen Alex at this very spot in the store. In one way the months passed quickly. In another, they had seemed to drag on forever.

There was no loving panther to share her bed, no understanding ghost to offer sage advice. It was just Phoebe and the dogs and the house and the prairie. Privacy had allowed her to get a real sense of herself. Who she was. What she wanted. Where she was going. Yet, the nights had been lonely without Alex.

A few months ago, Alex stopped meeting her at the astral lily pond, and he had not written in weeks. She called his office in Sedona a few days ago, but his secretary said he was out and he had not called back. Phoebe would not blame him if he found someone else, although it would probably break her heart.

The sky erupted with near simultaneous lightning and thunder. Rain fell harder, drawing a heavy curtain across the remaining slivers of sunlight. Fluorescent ceiling panels flickered a couple of times then blinked off, leaving the store dark and clammy.

"Oh, great," Phoebe grumbled.

Feeling her way down the narrow aisle, she stumbled into the storeroom. She located an old-fashioned oil lamp kept for just such an emergency. Before she could get the dusty thing lit, that old bell hanging over the front door gave its tinny announcement.

"Be right there!" Phoebe called, fumbling with a match. Finally, the lamp sparked to life and filled the back room with an amber glow.

With the lamp leading the way, she traipsed up the center aisle.

When Phoebe got to the front of the store, she found a bottle of *Musk Rain* oil beside the computer cash register. Setting the lamp on the end of the counter, she held her breath and glanced down the center aisle.

There he stood, at the precise spot where she had first seen him a year ago. His usual black denim ensemble and old sneakers were dripping wet. His hair hung damp and loose at his shoulders.

Phoebe was not sure what to think or say. "I tried to call you last week, but Karen said you weren't there."

"And you thought I didn't want to see you anymore?"

"It crossed my mind."

"You called and I came," he said in a warm voice, those gold eyes sparkling in the odd lamplight. "Please don't send me away again. I couldn't bear it. I've already made arrangements to move to Oklahoma City. Bobby and Karen have agreed to manage the office in Sedona. Phoebe, let's get married and have kids and grow old and cranky together."

There it was, the answer to her prayer.

With a warm smile, Phoebe gestured toward the door. "Did you arrange for the thunderstorm?"

Alex offered a casual shrug. "Would you believe me if I said I had?"

"I might." Everything about this man caused Phoebe to believe in magic.

Offering a wry smile, he walked up to her and stopped so close that he dripped water onto her clothing. "I missed you, Dragonfly."

"I missed you, too."

Phoebe inhaled his exotic scent and felt wonderfully content.

What Grandma had said that last night on the dock rang in Phoebe's ears: "Find your destiny at twilight." This was the twilight Grandma had meant, the Twylight Bookstore.

Phoebe's destiny was the man who smelled of musk and rain.

The End

*****

About the Author

Terri Branson earned an associate degree in math and science before turning her efforts toward the study of creative writing. In addition to being a graphics artist and an editor, she is an award-winning author who has sold articles on the craft of writing and conducted writing workshops. Awards include the *EPPIE 2004 Best Anthology Trophy* for the science fiction and fantasy anthology COSMIC SCULPTURE and the *EPPIE 2005 Best Children's Book Trophy* for the children's picture book BROTHER DRAGON. Terri lives in Oklahoma with her husband, David. Both are members of the Chickamauga Cherokee Tribe. For more information and a list of current publications visit her website at: www.terribranson.com.

* * * * *

Fiction & Non-Fiction Works

A PSYCHIC LIFE
Non-Fiction / Mind, Body, & Spirit

COSMIC SCULPTURE
Science Fiction & Fantasy Anthology
EPPIE 2004 Trophy Award Winner

DRAGON'S DEN
Science Fiction Novel

GEODOODLES
Adult Coloring Book

MUSK RAIN
Paranormal Romance Novel

PRAIRIE FIRE
Western Paranormal Romance Novel

THE WINDS OF AUMRAU
Musical Composition / Sheet Music

* * * * *

Children's Picture Books

A VERY DRAGON CHRISTMAS

BROTHER DRAGON
EPPIE 2005 Best Children's Book Winner

PETE, THE PEACOCK, GOES TO THE ZOO

PETE, THE PEACOCK, GOES TO TOWN

SCOOTER'S WORLD

TYLER ON THE MOON

WATCH FOR FALLING ROCK

*****

www.ingramcontent.com/pod-product-compliance
Lightning Source LLC
La Vergne TN
LVHW091130080826
845145LV00008B/2107

* 9 7 8 1 9 4 9 1 8 7 0 2 1 *